SHE BEGAN AS SHE MEANT TO GO ON . . .

"We're husband _____ _____ _____ aid. "What could possibly be _____ _____ her on our wedding night?"

"Don't ca _____

He grinned _____ _____ _____ ins hands behind his head. He _____ _____ _____ ely embarrassed. He found it riotously funny _____ light of their predicament. "Call you what? Duchess or wife?"

She glared at him. "You are completely without scruples."

"Completely."

"You have no sense of honor."

"None."

She lifted a pillow in her hand and swung it at him. She grinned smugly when she heard the dull thud of compacted feathers connecting with his head. "And your instincts are horrid. You should have deflected that blow. I don't see how I can expect you to defend me when you . . . OH!"

Duncan had wrenched the pillow from her hands, and swatted her across the legs with it in mid-tirade. He grinned at her. "And you think I have bad instincts."

He grabbed the trailing end of the sheet that clothed her. She pulled once. He didn't yield an inch. She pulled again. To her dismay, Arren felt him tug on the sheet. She gripped it tighter, but it began to slip from her grasp when he yanked in earnest. With her free hand, she reached down slightly, delighted when her hand curled into one of the large pillows. When she struck him forcibly on the chest with the heavy pillow, he slipped off the edge of the bed and crashed to the floor with a loud *thud* and a deep groan.

Arren grinned with satisfaction and leaned back against the pillows. She wiggled comfortably into place and pulled the covers up just as his head appeared above the edge of the bed. She looked over at him with a smug smile. "Bad instincts."

DENISE LITTLE PRESENTS
ROMANCES THAT YOU'LL WANT TO READ
OVER AND OVER AGAIN!

LAWLESS (0017, $4.99)
by Alexandra Thorne
Determined to save her ranch, Caitlan must confront former lover, Comanche Killian. But the minute they lock eyes, she longs for his kiss. Frustrated by her feelings, she exchanges hard-hitting words with the rugged foreman; but underneath the anger lie two hearts in need of love. Beset by crooked Texas bankers, dishonest politicians, and greedy Japanese bankers, they fight for their heritage and each other.

DANGEROUS ILLUSIONS (0018, $4.99)
by Amanda Scott
After the bloody battle of Waterloo, Lord Gideon Deverill visits Lady Daintry Tarrett to break the news of the death of her fiance. His duty to his friend becomes a pleasure when lovely Lady Daintry turns to him for comfort.

TO SPITE THE DEVIL (0030, $4.99)
by Paula Jonas
Patience Hendley is having it rough. Her English nobleman husband has abandoned her after one month of marriage. Her father is a Tory, her brother is a patriot, and her handsome bondservant Tom, an outright rebel! And now she is torn between her loyalist upbringing and the revolution sweeping the American colonies. Her only salvation is the forbidden love that she shares with Tom, which frees her from the shackles of the past!

GLORY (0031, $4.99)
by Anna Hudson
When Faith, a beautiful "country mouse", goes to St. Louis to claim her inheritance, she comes face to face with the Seatons, a wealthy big city family. As Faith tries to turn these stuffed shirts around, the Seatons are trying to change her as well. Young Jason Seaton is sure he can civilize Faith, who is a threat to the family fortune. Then after many hilarious misunderstandings Jason and Faith fall madly in love, and she manages to thaw even the stuffiest Seaton!

Available wherever paperbacks are sold, or order direct from the Publisher. Send cover price plus 50¢ per copy for mailing and handling to Penguin USA, P.O. Box 999, c/o Dept. 17109, Bergenfield, NJ 07621. Residents of New York and Tennessee must include sales tax. DO NOT SEND CASH.

THE PROMISE

MANDALYN KAYE

PINNACLE BOOKS
WINDSOR PUBLISHING CORP.

PINNACLE BOOKS are published by

Windsor Publishing Corp.
850 Third Avenue
New York, NY 10022

Copyright © 1994 by Moneesa L. Hart

All rights reserved. No part of this book may be reproduced
in any form or by any means without the prior written consent
of the Publisher, excepting brief quotes used in reviews.

If you purchased this book without a cover, you should be
aware that this book is stolen property. It was reported as "un-
sold and destroyed" to the Publisher and neither the Author
nor the Publisher has received any payment for this "stripped
book."

The P logo Reg U.S. Pat & TM off. Pinnacle is a trademark
of Windsor Publishing Corp.

First Pinnacle Printing: January, 1995

Printed in the United States of America

To Peggy and Arthur Hart for promises kept.

One

The pain was excruciating.

Arren's lungs screamed for air, but she forced her legs to move. The blades of high, wet grass tugged at her ankles like serpents, slowing her pace. She stumbled once, then fell when her foot twisted in a rabbit hole. Her face hit the muddy ground. Tears stung at her eyes, and she fought for breath against the painful stitch in her side. Behind her, she could hear the pounding of horses' hooves and the yip and howl of hungry dogs. She forced herself to stand, despite a sudden wave of nausea, and continued to run blindly into the night. The hounds were closer. The scent of blood hung heavily in the air, making bile rise in the back of her throat.

The darkness was oppressive, and each step carried her farther on her unknown course. In her exhaustion, she could make out the silhouette of a lone rider coming toward her. She shook her head, tried to ignore the pain it caused, and narrowed her eyes. She couldn't determine if the rider was merely a figment of her fevered imagination or a terrifying reality bearing down on her. At her back, she could hear her pursuers closing on her. The pounding in her head be- came so intense that she could no longer distinguish between the frantic beating of her heart and the heavy thrum of approaching hooves.

Straining her eyes, she struggled to focus on the approaching rider. Just as the thought occurred to her that she would be trampled beneath the hooves of the massive horse, a strong arm shot down and wrapped around her waist, lifting her high in the air. She landed across the saddle with such force that the breath was knocked from her lungs. Her scream lodged in the back of her throat. She gasped for breath as the enormous animal pounded the earth below, guided by her captor.

Her body cried out in pain. She saw dogs below her biting at the ankles of the huge horse. Then unconsciousness erased the burning pain in her body. Arren sank into a deep, exhausted faint.

Duncan pressed his heels into the flanks of his horse and galloped full speed toward the thicket of trees at the edge of the clearing. He heard the howling dogs and pounding hooves coming in his direction. It had taken him a minute to make out the figure running toward him. Instinct told him it was a woman. Only her white shirt sleeves and collar were visible in the darkness. He strained his eyes to focus on her. Every nerve in his body drew suddenly taut. The smell of death hung in the air. He'd smelled it before, and recognized it now.

The fragile creature running toward him reminded him of a fox relentlessly pursued by hunters' hounds. Acting more from instinct than forethought, he abruptly changed his direction and pulled her from the ground, slinging her across his saddle.

Arren's pursuers were bearing down on them, and Duncan raced toward the thicket, intent on finding cover. He was aware the instant she fainted. Her body went limp against him. He anchored her there with his hand, then bent low over the neck of his horse.

Duncan guided the animal through a small stream, swollen by recent rainfall, and plunged into the thicket. The water would temporarily distract the dogs, giving him precious moments to find cover. Carefully, he dismounted, lifting Arren from the saddle and slinging her over his shoulder. He led his horse deeper into the thicket and lowered Arren to the ground at the base of a large tree. Detaching the bags from his saddle, he heaved a sigh of regret and slapped the horse on its rump, sending it galloping into the night.

Crouching down beside Arren, he heard the confused howls of the dogs slicing through the stillness of the night. Her pursuers had reined in their horses on the shore of the river where their dogs had lost the scent. Coarse, frustrated swearing punctuated the heavy air. Duncan grinned in satisfaction. They were none too pleased at having been outfoxed.

He listened intently to their conversation, and when they decided to make camp for the night and resume their search in the morning, he turned his attention to his captive. She was still unconscious, and he lowered himself to the ground next to her. What on earth was he going to do with her? He looked at her but could barely make out her features. He remembered the feel of her on his saddle, though. She was slender, almost fragile, and he wondered what had touched off the episode he'd just interrupted. She seemed incapable of inciting a group of grown men to turn their dogs on her, yet they clearly wanted her badly enough not to abandon their foiled search despite the cold, wet evening.

He considered the possibility that she was a fugitive from

the law. He lifted one of her hands and studied it. He dismissed the thought. Fugitives didn't have well-manicured hands. He saw the glint of gold on her third finger and narrowed his eyes. Rich wives did.

The wager that she was running from her husband was sound. He reached over and ran his hand along her neckline. No jewelry. A quick search of her pockets and clothes yielded the same result. There was nothing hidden in her hem, either. She had no money, and no valuables save the ring. Her flight had clearly been hasty, without thought and without planning.

He did a quick mental survey of the surrounding area. It was mostly rural, but there were several large holdings within a thirty-mile radius. She could have come from any one of them. If that were true, the logical thing for him to do was to turn her over to her husband and be on his way. But he was plagued by a niggling suspicion. There had been desperation in her flight, and cold hatred in the voices of her pursuers. He suspected he might not be rid of her so easily.

He frowned. He didn't have time to tend to her problems—whatever they might be—but something visceral prevented him from simply leaving her defenseless. He grasped her shoulder with his large hand and shook her gently.

She awoke with a startled cry, and he clamped his hand over her mouth. Even in the thickening darkness, he could see the fear in her wide eyes.

His eyes bored down into hers, warning her silently to hold her tongue. She nodded slightly, and he removed his hand. She moved back against the tree, shrinking away from him. "Who are you?" Her voice was barely above a whisper.

She spoke in Gaelic, and he noticed immediately the Highland lilt in her voice. His white teeth glinted. He answered in her native tongue. "At the moment, I should think you're hardly in a position to ask questions. Who are you?"

She studied him. "I have no intention of telling you that."

Duncan raised an eyebrow at her dictatorial tone. "I assumed you'd be pleased with my interference. If I hadn't come along, you'd be torn to bits by now."

She made an exasperated sound in the back of her throat. "Fine. Thank you for your interference, but I haven't time to sit here. Now move and let me pass."

He leaned back and stared at her. It was pitch black now, and he could barely make out her profile. Only the sleeves of her white blouse showed against the darkened backdrop. He would be wise to let her leave. The memory of her frightened, fragile body, taut against his saddle, prevented him. He settled a hand on her shoulder. "You can't leave now."

She stiffened and smacked his hand away. "I'll do as I please. I've thanked you for your trouble, and now I'll thank you to mind your own affairs."

He shook his head. Even her whispered rebuke sounded authoritative. She was clearly used to having her way. It was beginning to irritate him. Against his better judgment, he was trying to help the little shrew. He had a good mind to let her solve her own problems, if she didn't stop treating him like an errant schoolboy. "I don't give a damn what you want to do. As soon as you step from this thicket, their dogs will catch your scent. They'll have their teeth in you before you have time to scream."

She drew a sharp breath, casting an anxious glance over his shoulder. She squared her shoulders and looked back at him. She wasn't ready to back down. "I think not. I don't hear them howling. Surely they're down for the night."

He nearly laughed at her. He didn't think now would be a good time to point out the absurdity of that notion, however. He leaned back, motioning to the clearing. "Then by all means, have a go at it."

She rose to her feet and brushed the dirt from her backside. Without sparing him so much as a second glance, she pushed past him and picked her way through the thick, protective bushes, wincing once or twice when a heavy thorn pierced the thick wool of her skirt. He chewed on his lip for a moment, fighting back his irritation.

Insufferable beast! Arren thought, carefully wending her way through the thorny underbrush. Until he'd proven himself to be so unbearably arrogant, she'd meant to thank him, perhaps even reward him financially for his help. But he was entirely too proud of his efforts. Despite her own precarious predicament, Arren thought she'd managed to put him in his place rather soundly.

Resolute, she turned her attention away from the dark stranger, straining her ears for the sound of Alistar McDonan's dogs. Despite her irritation at his arrogance, Arren knew the stranger's warning was not to be taken lightly. A shift in the wind would easily betray her presence in the thicket, and she very much doubted she would escape a second time. Nevertheless, the stranger could not be trusted. There was too much at stake.

She emerged from the thicket and lifted her thumb to her mouth, sucking gently on the scarlet drop of blood where a thorn had pierced her callused skin. Beyond the trees, she heard Alistar's dogs whimpering in the still night, and she drew a deep breath, then edged her way slowly along the tree line.

Duncan was still crouched in the thicket when he heard the first sounds of the awakening dogs. With a heavy sigh, he reached into the bag he'd removed from his saddle, closing his fingers over a large piece of salted mutton. Under normal circumstances, the mutton should have lasted until he reached his destination. Tonight, however, it would have to serve a greater purpose. He shook his head again and rose to his feet, moving effortlessly through the thicket.

When he reached the small clearing, he waited a minute until his gaze focused on Arren's white shirt sleeves. He gauged the distance and cocked his head to listen intently to the dogs. They had grown extremely restless, and she continued to move away from him, seemingly oblivious to her imminent peril. He could make out the orange glow of a fire several furlongs down the riverbank, and knew Arren's pursuers would soon release their hounds.

The insistent baying had risen to a fevered pitch. He calculated the time it would take the dogs to descend on her, and turned to check the distance again. She had stopped to listen to the frantic snarling. He growled a curse under his breath and took off at a dead run in her direction, the piece of mutton still gripped in his hand.

Arren paused, wondering anxiously what she should do. The dogs had begun to sound more frantic—closer—and she froze in fear. The sound of snapping brush sounded behind her, and she jerked her head around. Before she had time to scream, Duncan's arm wrapped around her waist and lifted her into the air. The breath was completely knocked from her lungs when she landed on her stomach across a heavy tree limb.

Duncan dropped the piece of mutton to the ground below them and tugged himself over the limb, still holding Arren with one hand. Arren bit back an exclamation of fear when the dogs ravenously attacked the piece of mutton just below them. She gripped his arm, allowing him to pull her to a sitting position beside him. To her chagrin, she began to tremble. He reached down and tugged on her chin, forcing her to meet his gaze. Even in the darkness, she could see the gold fire in his eyes. She focused on it, inhaled the warm scent of him. The snarling sound beneath them intensified as the dogs began to bite at each other, groping for a larger piece of the salted meat. Without realizing she'd done so, Arren clenched her fingers into Duncan's forearms. Leaning over, he whispered in her ear, "We have to climb higher. I'm going to test each branch first. Then I'll pull you up."

She nodded. He pried her fingers loose, waiting to see that she was securely balanced on the limb. He pulled himself up one limb, and tested its strength. He seemed to be satisfied, and he extended his hand to Arren. She slipped her fingers tentatively into his warm grasp and he pulled her up next to him. She waited in anxious silence while he repeated the procedure two more times before he pulled her firmly against his side, motioning her to be silent.

Below, the dogs were still busily devouring the hard mutton. The warm glow of a torch signaled the arrival of her pursuers. She strained her eyes, silently counting dogs and men. It had been so late when she'd fled into the night. She had never been sure how many of Alistar's clansmen were in the small band. She counted five men and eight dogs, and she shivered, her fingers clamping convulsively into Duncan's side. He wrapped his arm around her shoulders, holding her solidly against him, and she sagged into his comforting warmth.

The men cursed loudly at the sight of their hounds completely absorbed in the nearly demolished piece of mutton. From the comparative safety of their lofty perch, Duncan and Arren listened to the coarse Gaelic floating up through the trees. She wondered a bit frantically how fluent the stranger's Gaelic was, and prayed fervently that her secret would not be betrayed by their angry words.

"Dammit!" A man she recognized as Alistar's brother said. "She's thrown them off the scent with that mutton."

"Aye. We'll have to begin fresh in the morning," another agreed. "She can't gain much ground on us in this cursed darkness."

Arren let out a deep breath when the men gathered the now-quieted dogs and left the foot of the tree amid a steady stream of muttered expletives. She sagged against Duncan in relief.

Duncan shifted her against him, realizing only then that she'd fainted again. With a heavy sigh, he edged his leg over the branch, and pillowed his back against the massive tree trunk. Lifting Arren against him, he pulled her into the wedge of his legs, wrapping his arms securely around her waist. As she moved against him, her hair tickled his chin. He closed his eyes. He hoped she wouldn't awaken suddenly and knock them both from their high perch in the tree. He still didn't know who this woman was, and he'd be damned if he'd become entangled in her problems. He was stuck with her for the night, but come morning, he'd send her on her way.

Two

The sun pushed its way over the horizon, spreading a quiet blanket of warmth over the earth. Arren fought her way through deep layers of sleep. There was an odd tingling sensation in her feet. She wiggled her toes slightly to ensure they were still there. She finally realized that her feet were asleep. Duncan's arms were wrapped securely around her waist, holding her firmly against the wall of his chest. She remembered the events of the previous night. Arren jerked fully awake, nearly toppling off the tree limb.

As soon as she pulled away from him, Duncan was awake. He reached out a hand to steady her, seconds before she went tumbling to the ground. Her hand came up to grasp his wrist, and her eyes flew to his. His face split in a slow grin. "Good morning."

She stared at him, carefully studying his features. His eyes were hooded, still heavy-lidded with sleep. Their clear green color was flecked with gold, and the fringe of red-gold lashes took her by surprise. She remembered him from the previous night as dark and forbidding. She realized only now that his deep green shirt and breeches, coupled with the blackness of the night, had shrouded him in darkness. In the clear light of day, the rusty whiskers that had settled on his chin during the night, along with the gold hoop earring he wore jauntily in his left ear, gave him a rakish appearance. She belatedly realized her fingers were still clamped on his wrist and jerked her hand away as if she'd been scorched. "Get me down," she ordered.

His grin widened at the proprietary tone in her voice. Her disposition hadn't improved with the coming of morning. "Perhaps I'm not inclined to."

She frowned at him. "You got me here. You can get me down."

"No."

"Then how am I supposed to get out of this bloody tree?"

He shrugged. "That's your problem. You seem to have no difficulty getting into trouble. Let's see how well you get yourself out of it."

Her eyes glittered angrily. "What's that supposed to mean?"

He lifted her left hand and pointed to the ring on her finger. "Perhaps you should ask your husband."

She jerked her hand away from his grasp and reached down to steady herself on the limb. "That's none of your affair."

"Then maybe you'd like to tell me why he was chasing you down in the dead of the night. At least I assume it was your husband's dogs that nearly rent you to shreds."

"That's also none of your affair. I've thanked you for your trouble. What more do you want from me?"

He was struck by a perverse desire to see how far he could goad her. He suspected her deep green eyes could shoot sparks when she was properly riled. Her red hair indicated a fiery temper. He wanted to drive the fear and anxiety from her gaze. Even anger would be preferable.

Arren was watching him intently. There was something darkly powerful about this stranger, and it bothered her. He seemed to look clean through to her soul when he watched her like this, and when a slight smile tugged at the corner of his mouth, she wondered what he was thinking.

As if in answer to her question, Duncan lifted one hand and traced his finger boldly across the top of her breasts. The touch scorched her through the thin material of her blouse. Her eyes widened in shock. He leaned closer to her and smiled wickedly. "Perhaps I want to know why you're worth a midnight chase to our friends with the dogs."

She reached back and swung her arm at him. His fingers closed around her wrist a split second before her palm could connect with his cheek. His grin faded, and she drew back in horrified fascination as the gold flecks in his eyes intensified and bored into her. "I wouldn't try that again if I were you. I probably deserved that, but if you continue to act like a shrew, I'll continue to treat you like one. Do I make myself clear?"

She wouldn't back down under his stare. "I'll do as I please," she snapped.

"Then you're welcome to please yourself down from this tree."

She glared at him. "Fine."

He watched her intently as she turned her attention to the branches below. The sun had risen in the sky now, and the distance that they had climbed during the previous night now appeared to be a great way down.

The ground swam beneath her. She wasn't entirely certain she could manage the descent on her own, but she'd rather die trying than admit it to the insufferable man next to her. Something about him disconcerted her, and although he had shown her unexpected compassion the night before, she very much doubted he was inclined to do so now. Swinging one leg over the branch so her hips balanced on the limb, she searched with her foot for the branch below. She could feel it just below her toes and stretched for it, ignoring the need to cry out when the rough bark scraped across her belly.

Duncan winced silently at the sight. He'd learned the hard way, once, how much that hurt. Her feet landed solidly on the lower branch, and she shot him a triumphant look. He acknowledged it with a slight nod, and she turned her attention back to the task at hand.

Her hands were still clamped on the limb where Duncan sat. Her feet rested on the limb below. She looked from one to the other, frantically gauging the distance between branches. If she let go of the top branch, she knew she couldn't grab hold of the lower limb without falling. She hesitated, looking intently at the lower branch again. Drawing a deep breath, she released her grip, hoping to balance long enough to reach the lower branch.

It took her a second to realize she hadn't fallen—thanks to Duncan's fingers on her wrist. Her gaze flew to his, meeting his glare. He scowled at her. "This is becoming an annoying habit," he growled.

She was amazed at his agility when he swung down beside her, still holding her balanced on the limb. He planted his feet firmly on the limb and drew a deep breath, leaning back against the tree trunk, watching her. "Now, suppose we start this over. You'll only get down from here in one piece if you let me help you. You are clearly loath to do that. Why?"

"I don't have to tell you that."

He removed his hands from her waist and she pitched forward off balance. He closed his hands on her shoulders again, steadying her. "Why?" he insisted.

"I can't tell you."

"Why?"

"Because I can't."

"Why?"

She sighed in exasperation. "Don't you know any other questions?"

"All right. Why not?"

She sighed deeply. His gold-flecked eyes were strangely warm, and she had an almost overwhelming desire to confide in him, despite the odd feeling in the pit of her stomach. At the moment, he seemed considerably more capable of handling her problems than she was. She was all too aware she would never have escaped Alistar McDonan's dogs last night if he hadn't assisted her. She anxiously studied him. It would be nice, she thought, to confide in this stranger. He had kind eyes. She opened her lips to speak, then a sudden memory of Alistar McDonan's face snapped into focus. She fought an uncharacteristic surge of tears. "Please," she said. "I'm grateful for your help, but I can't tell you anything else. Surely you understand after last night that my life could depend upon my keeping my secret. So could yours, for that matter."

He raised his eyebrows at the strange statement and waited for her to continue.

She looked away, unable to meet his gaze. "I beg you. Please help me down from here. Then I'll go my way and leave you to whatever you were doing before I interrupted you."

He studied her for a long minute, and reached up to remove a small leaf lodged in her hair. His fingers nestled in the soft locks of her auburn tresses for several seconds longer than was absolutely necessary. "When I get you down, where will you go?"

"I've already told you all that I will."

"Your adversaries are still looking for you. They are

camped across the river. I suspect they'll be after you soon. You can't simply wander off on your own."

Arren closed her eyes and swayed slightly. Good Lord, she was tired. She knew he was right. She wouldn't be able to outrun Alistar's men on her own, but at the moment, there seemed little else to do. She couldn't keep up the grueling pace any longer, and he had proven to her during the night how woefully ill-equipped she was to face Alistar's men alone.

She thought about the man next to her. Even now, she was unsure why he'd assisted her. She had known too many dishonorable men to simply credit his actions to some misplaced sense of chivalry. Yet, he had expressed no other motive to her. One simple truth remained. She was indeed in a quandary. At the moment, he seemed to be her only hope.

She grimaced inwardly at the notion. Even the thought of asking for his help was insane. He was a complete stranger with several exceedingly odd talents, so far as she could determine. She had met him prowling about in the dead of the night. He was not some young nobleman she could simply petition for an afternoon ride in his curricle. Given the circumstances, he could well be an escaped criminal. And she was traveling about, on foot, unprotected and alone. He could kill her—or worse—and no one would ever even know.

On the other hand, an inner voice persisted in arguing, she'd be killed if she were caught. And at the moment, trusting this stranger with his red-gold hair and clear gold-flecked eyes was certainly preferable to facing Alistar McDonan. The stranger could at least help her out of the tree and get her clear of the thicket—no easy trick, she was sure.

Her eyes had remained closed so long, Duncan thought she'd fainted again. When she opened them, he saw the suspicious emotion deep in their depths. She was on the verge of tears. He hoped to God she wouldn't give in. She drew a breath and stared up at him. "Why did you help me?" Her voice was soft, almost cajoling.

He blinked. Her abrupt change of mood startled him. "I don't particularly enjoy the sight of dogs devouring human flesh."

She shook her head. "No, I mean why did you really help me?" She laid a finger across his lips to cut off his protest. "You may have helped me first out of instinct. But not the second time. Certainly not the third. Why?"

He shrugged. "I didn't think about it then. What difference does it make now?"

She sighed heavily. He wasn't being very cooperative. "When I fled, I didn't consider the consequences. Neither did you consider the consequences last night when you helped me. In a way, we're both out on this limb," she indicated the branch, "for that very reason." She sighed again. "I'm nearly too exhausted to go on. Before I ask your assistance, I want to know what your answer will likely be."

He nearly laughed at her. Arrogance came naturally to her. It gave clear testimony to her obvious noble breeding. She was facing hard times now, but she'd clearly known privilege most of her lifetime. He had taken the opportunity to study her during her initial descent down the tree, and decided his instincts had been right. Her rich auburn hair and emerald green eyes were the perfect match for her fiery temper. He saw something besides fire in those eyes now, though. Her admitted exhaustion struck him as understated. She had surely endured a night of unspeakable terror before he'd assisted her flight, and he had no doubt it had taken its toll on her, emotionally and physically. She'd handled it all rather well for a woman, he thought. A slight smile tugged at the corner of his mouth. "It depends on what your question is."

She was losing her patience. She had been right. The man was insufferable. "Stop playing this game with me. I've already told you I haven't the energy for verbal fencing. Are you going to answer me or not?"

He leaned back against the tree, pulling her against his chest. He decided with something akin to surprise that he liked the feel of her there. "Very well. What would you like to know?"

Arren struggled against him, uncomfortable with the close contact. He wouldn't release her, and she gave up, gracing him with a brief glare. She didn't like the way his warmth seeped through her clothes and made her shiver. "Who are you?" she demanded, her tone a bit more breathless than she intended.

"Just as you have secrets you must keep, so do I."

She looked at him suspiciously. "Are you a criminal?"

"No. Are you?"

She shook her head. "No," she answered. "I didn't think you were a criminal. Not really. But you cannot fault me for asking." He nodded briefly, and Arren continued to study him, fascinated by the strong angle of his chin. "Are you employed?"

"In a manner."

She drew her brows together. "What does that mean?"

"It means I'm not in search of work, but not necessarily adverse to it."

Arren dropped her head against his chest. She was so tired—completely exhausted—she couldn't face the thought of another day like the last. Her fear of trusting him was quickly ebbing away in light of her inability to think clearly through the haze of fatigue. She drew a shaky breath and tipped her head to look into his eyes. She hoped to find some clue to what motivated this man.

She flinched instinctively when his hand came up to catch a stray tear on her face. He narrowed his eyes at the action, and gently wiped the tear with his thumb. Arren had been unaware until then of the sting of tears in her eyes. Her lips trembled slightly. When his thumb moved slowly over the curve of her cheekbone, catching the salty tear, she noticed the callused pad of his thumb. She smiled. Capturing his large hand in her smaller one, she studied the palm for several seconds. The calluses gave her the answer she sought. Whoever he was, this man was no over-indulged nobleman.

It was rather ironic that it took callused palms to convince her of that. Few over-indulged noblemen, and she knew many, could lift a woman off her feet at a dead gallop, evade a pack of hungry dogs with the aid of a tree limb and a hunk of mutton, and evidently spend the night as comfortably in a tree as in a feather bed. She sighed, strangely relieved at this new discovery. When she finally lifted her eyes to his, he was watching her intently.

"Is there something you find fascinating about my hand?" he asked.

She nodded. "Your calluses. They speak well of you."

He lifted an eyebrow, but didn't comment.

She drew a deep breath and met his gaze squarely. "Sir, I am prepared to offer you a bargain."

"Yes?"

"I am traveling to London. After the events of last night, I realize I cannot possibly hope to make the trip on my own. As you have more than amply proven your expertise to me, I am prepared to offer you a substantial sum of money in exchange for your escort."

He had watched her throughout the exchange. She was obviously reluctant to enlist his help, but she was just as obviously incapable of going on by herself. And she knew it. He had no idea what her motivation was for wanting to reach London, and he was sure she wouldn't tell him if he asked.

The coincidence was rather startling. He was already headed to London for reasons of his own. Her offer was suspicious in light of that, but he rejected the notion as long-ingrained cautiousness on his part rather than reality. Considering her offer, he knew if he took her with him, his plans would have to change dramatically. She probably wouldn't be capable of maintaining the grueling pace he'd set for himself. On the other hand, anyone searching for him and asking questions around the countryside would expect him to be traveling alone. Her presence would provide him with an excellent cover.

She had grown agitated during his long reverie, and was anxiously drumming her fingers on his chest. "Do we have a bargain?"

He shook his head. "Not yet. I need more detail."

"You can name your price."

"Not about the money; about the bargain. If I agree, it will only be under certain circumstances."

She barely suppressed a sigh of irritation. "You're bloody arrogant to quibble over details. I am, after all, paying you. That puts you in no position to make demands."

He squeezed her waist, cutting off her angry protest. "I'm not making demands, we're striking a bargain. I won't agree unless you agree to certain stipulations."

Arren watched him suspiciously. "What stipulations?"

"You'll do things my way—no questions asked. When I say we ride, we do. When I say we walk, we do. You'll do as I say, when I say, or we don't have a bargain."

She hesitated only briefly before she nodded her consent. It was not unreasonable, and while she didn't particularly like it, she was all too aware that she had little choice in the matter. "All right," she said quietly.

He blinked. "All right?"

"All right."

He clearly hadn't expected her to acquiesce so easily. "Aren't you going to ask me how high my price is?"

"It's not relevant. I'll pay whatever you ask."

He raised an eyebrow. His earlier guess had been right. She was certainly used to having her way, and he doubted she'd actually bend to his will with the readiness she professed. "Are you running from your husband?" He had no idea why he'd blurted out the question, but he had an overwhelming desire to know the answer.

"No." The answer was blunt, invoking no further questions.

He persisted anyway. "Does he know where you are?"

She looked at him carefully, wondering how many details she should give him. "My husband is dead," she said finally. "Does that satisfy your curiosity?"

He grinned. It satisfied it very well. There was something bewitching about this woman, and he was relieved to find she wasn't married. He nearly convinced himself he had wanted to know for legal reasons. It would be unpardonable to assist a wife in fleeing her husband, whatever the reason, and he had no desire to be embroiled in a legal and social scandal. His excuse didn't quite ring true to him, however. His gaze drifted to her soft mouth. He had clearly gone quite mad, but dismissed that thought in favor of the temptation she offered. "I suppose we should seal this bargain of ours," he whispered.

Before she had time to react, he bent his head, then his lips were on hers. She was startled by the cool feel of his mouth. The kiss was nonthreatening, pressuring her gently until her hands relaxed against his chest. She leaned into him and enjoyed the riotous sensations he awakened in her. She sighed once against his mouth, then the kiss ended as suddenly as it began. She looked at him, a startled expression in her eyes. "Why did you do that?"

"Hell if I know."

She shook her head, surprised. She supposed she should feel insulted by his brutal honesty, but couldn't quite muster the necessary indignation. It had been a rather pleasant kiss, after all. "Well, don't do it again," she snapped, hoping he wouldn't notice the flush in her cheeks.

He grinned insolently, telling her all too clearly that he *had* noticed. "I don't make promises I can't keep." He ignored her startled glance and set her slightly away from him. He looked down below. She had nearly forgotten they still were in their treetop perch. She'd have toppled to the ground if he hadn't steadied her with his hands.

"I'm ready to get down now," she said with barely disguised impatience.

He shook his head. "I'll make that decision. I'll have your name first."

She stared at him, wide-eyed, and then started to laugh. She hadn't realized until that moment that she didn't even know his name. For God's sake, she'd just offered this man an unnamed sum of money to travel across Britain with her and she didn't even know his name. "Arren. My name is Arren."

"Is that your only name?" he asked.

She nodded. "Do I get to know yours?"

"Duncan."

"And where do you call home, sir?"

To give her that answer would be too revealing. He was unwilling to risk that yet. "I call the world my home." Even to him, the answer sounded pompous.

"What sort of answer is that?" Arren asked, watching him suspiciously

"I'm a gypsy. I have homes everywhere." It was partially true. He did own fourteen separate holdings in six countries.

She narrowed her eyes at him. She knew there was more to the story, but decided not to press him. She wasn't inclined to give him any more information about herself. She supposed she didn't have the right to demand any of him in return. "Very well, Gypsy. The lines are drawn. It's clear neither of us trusts the other enough to offer details. Therefore, I suggest we refrain from asking."

"You'll trust me with your life, but not with your name."

She shrugged. "My name is more important than my life at this particular moment."

He decided not to press her on the odd statement, and turned his attention, instead, to getting them down from the tree. Arren's pursuers were still camped on the river, and he was worried about the dogs catching their scent again. When he heard the rumble of distant thunder, he smiled. Good fortune seemed to be running in their favor. A heavy rainstorm would successfully mask their scent. He looked down at Arren and sank to a sitting position, pulling her down with him. "We'll wait until the storm begins," he explained.

"Why?"

He laughed, and his breath fanned across her ear in a warm breeze that made her shiver. "You agreed not to question my decisions. Have you forgotten already?"

She shrugged. "If we aren't going to talk about ourselves, we have to talk about something. It's a long way to London."

He smiled above her head and indulged her. "Your friends on the riverbank will have to make one of two decisions soon. They will either begin looking for you now, hoping to outrun the storm, or they'll wait until the storm passes. If they choose the former, they'll actually get ahead of us. That would be ideal. If they wait, their dogs won't be able to find our scent in the rain. Either way, we're better off to wait."

She nodded and leaned her head back against his shoulder. It felt decidedly good to let him worry in her stead. "Do you mind if I go back to sleep for a while?"

"No. You'll probably benefit from the rest later."

She mumbled something unintelligible and leaned back into his arms, listening to the rumbling thunder overhead. He had the oddest effect on her. She had no doubt there would be more than one storm, literal or figurative, in their future. Her eyes drifted shut as she waited for the rain.

Three

A raindrop woke him up. Duncan was still sitting in the tree, with Arren securely tucked against him. She was deep in sleep, her head lolled back against his shoulder. He studied her as several fat raindrops fought their way through the thick protection of the leaves above them.

She looked so fragile. He could hardly picture her involved in the events of the previous night. She was uncommonly beautiful. Her dark auburn hair perfectly complemented her creamy skin. In sleep, her dark lashes fanned across her cheeks, and he could see the faint outline of delicate blue veins on the lids of her large eyes. He remembered the deep emerald green of her eyes and how they'd flashed at him when her temper was riled. He smiled at the spray of freckles across her small nose. He liked them. Without them, her face would have looked almost unreal in its perfection. Her freckles gave her character.

Duncan hadn't forgotten the feel of her lips beneath his, either. The soft kiss had left him craving more. He was completely taken aback by his own lack of discipline. He had obviously been without a woman for too long to even consider the notion. He had neither the time nor the inclination for a female entanglement. He grinned wolfishly at the double entendre.

Whatever the case, he suspected that his attraction to her

could easily become more than a mere physical craving. Cravings were simple enough to deal with. Arren's pull on him ran deeper, and that frustrated him. He rarely lost control of his emotions or his desires, and he sensed that Arren could make him lose both. A large clap of thunder sounded overhead. Perhaps it was an omen.

He ran a hand up her arm. He felt the strength that lay beneath the surface of her fair skin and knew instinctively that Arren had an underlying determination for survival. He knew from her Gaelic, and her rhythmic Highland accent, that she hailed from the northern region of Scotland. Life in the Highlands had always been rugged. Even now, in this enlightened age, many of the traditional customs still hadn't changed. Her proprietary manner and regal bearing had given him the first clues to her background. Her seeming willingness to pay him any sum he required for his assistance gave him the second.

She shifted slightly against him, and he indulged his curiosity a little more by sliding his fingers down her arm and lifting one of her hands. He frowned. The delicate fingers fanning over his were red with calluses. He had noticed her hands were well-kept last night, but it had been too dark to see the rough places on her palms. He remembered her odd comment about his calluses speaking well of him and frowned again. He had expected the soft white hands of a privileged lady. Arren's hand indicated she was clearly used to difficult labor. The rain was falling heavily now, and he filed the observation in the back of his mind, making a mental note to consider its ramifications later.

In the distance, he heard the distinct baying of the dogs, and knew Arren's pursuers had decided to wait out the storm. He sighed, and shifted Arren's weight. Her eyes opened sleepily and she looked at him in momentary confusion.

"Remember me?" he asked.

She smiled slightly. "I was asleep."

He smiled back. "I wouldn't have known."

Her laugh ended in a distinctly unladylike yawn. "I'm sorry. I get rather disoriented when I sleep heavily. Are we leaving now?"

He nodded. "Our friends are still camped by the river. The rain is coming down hard enough to cover our tracks and our scent."

He swung down through the remaining branches, lifting her to each one beside him. She watched in silent admiration of his strength and agility. He managed the tree as easily as he had the night before. Arren watched him in fascination, acutely aware that she knew virtually nothing about this man she now trusted as her protector. What she did know, she wasn't sure she liked. He was secretive, obstinate, and unreadable, but there was a strength about him she found oddly comforting. She sensed instinctively that he could handle whatever challenges lay ahead as effortlessly as he had managed everything else.

He lifted her to the ground, planting her feet firmly in front of him. His hands closed on her shoulders and she pulled back from him slightly. He narrowed his eyes. "What's wrong?"

She winced and reminded herself to be more careful. He would ask too many questions if he saw the scars Alistar had left on her back. She met his gaze squarely. "Nothing you need to be concerned with."

He didn't miss the lift of her chin, and he suppressed a grin at her haughty dismissal. He decided for the moment to let the subject drop. The rain was falling in steady sheets now and her hair was curling riotously around her small face. Her white blouse and black vest were plastered to her skin, clearly outlining the rounded swells of her breasts. Her black wool skirt lapped up the rain, and grew heavier with each drop. She looked like a half-drowned animal, and the arrogant tone in her voice conflicted with her pitiful appearance. He shrugged. "As you wish." He motioned with his hand for her to start walking through the trees. "Let's go."

"That is north," she said in surprise. *Surely he knew that.* "Yes."

"London is south." *It was rather like talking to an obstinate child, having a conversation with this man.*

"Right again."

Exasperated, she glared at him. "Then we want to travel south."

He shook his head. "Have you forgotten that we agreed to do this my way? We're going north."

"How are we going to get to London if we travel north?"

He raked a hand through his wet hair. "Arren, I'm not going to argue every decision with you." He placed his hands on her shoulders and turned her in the direction he wanted her to go. "Walk."

She shot him an angry look over her shoulder. "All right, Gypsy. We'll walk north. But I'm warning you now, when we reach the coast, I'm not swimming to London." She stomped into the trees, listening intently for the sound of the dogs, hoping they would not have to walk far before they found shelter.

An hour passed. Arren was miserable. Every bone in her body hurt. She was still sore from her harrowing night. The muscles in her legs were cramped, and walking sent sparks of pain shooting up her spine. The thickening mud clawed at her feet, making every step a chore. The driving rain chilled her skin, and her teeth chattered almost uncontrollably as she pushed on through the dense thicket. She managed to keep the pace, however, content with the notion that there had been no sign of Alistar's dogs since they'd begun walking. She was increasingly sure she'd made the right decision when she'd asked for Duncan's help.

She reached up, and twisted her heavy braid, shivering when streams of water ran beneath the cuffs of her ruined blouse and down her arms. Resolutely, she counted her footsteps, forcing herself to keep going.

Duncan followed just behind her, and continued to study her carefully. He saw her discomfort mounting with every step she took, and his admiration for her increased. More than once, she reached up to wring the water from her plaited hair. The thick braid hung midway down her back, and he wondered how long her hair was unbound. The thought summoned another image. He shook his head, annoyed with his unruly thoughts. He had surely lost his mind somewhere in the previous night. He was tempted to turn back and look for it.

They were nearing the edge of the thicket. Heavy drops of rain stung his eyes as the treetop canopy thinned above them. They would need to find shelter soon. He mentally assessed his bearings. His cousin, Robert Dunkirk, lived less than a quarter mile beyond the thicket. Duncan had not seen Robert in years, but he knew that he and Arren would be welcome on Dunkirk land.

Outside the protection of the trees, the rain fell in torrents. As soon as they stepped from the thicket, Duncan felt a river down his spine. He put out his hand to Arren, signaling her to stop. She flinched when he touched her. He frowned at the telling action. She turned to look at him, her green eyes silently warning him not to ask the question that hovered on his lips. He frowned again. "We need to get out of the rain." He had to shout the words above the sound of the storm around them.

She nodded and wiped her wet hair off her face. "Where?"

He read the question on her lips rather than actually hearing the word. He pointed to a small hill to their left. "There's a croft over that hill. We should be able to find shelter there."

She started in the direction, but he stopped her with a hand on her arm. She turned to look back into his piercing gaze. "Do you feel well enough to go on?" His voice was a roar now above the storm.

She tugged her arm away from his hand. "I'm fine. Let's go." She turned to walk again, then let out a startled yelp when she felt her feet leave the ground. He lifted her into his arms and began walking toward the hill, cradling her against his chest. She glared at him, but didn't complain.

He walked in silence, cresting the hill with long, purposeful strides. Her fingers were cold. She slipped them as unobtrusively as possible into the fold of his shirt. Despite the dampness that had soaked through to his skin, she could still feel the heat of his flesh through his wet shirt. She wondered how he managed to stay so warm. When they reached the crest of the hill, Duncan paused and lowered her to her feet. She didn't miss his slight frown. She looked at him anxiously. "Is something wrong?" she shouted above the rain.

He shook his head, indicating the croft below them with a sweep of his hand. "All the livestock," he yelled. "There are a great many people here."

Arren turned her attention to the cluster of houses below. There were several large barns and houses, each with a welcoming billow of smoke curling from the chimney. "Perhaps it is just a crowded croft. With the evictions, it is not so uncommon."

Duncan looked at her in surprise. It was true that any number of landholders had taken to evicting their tenants. In the years following England's victory over Napoleon, sheepherding had become considerably more profitable for Scottish landholders than caring for their tenants. Greed had given way to family loyalty, and many Scots had been forced from their homes. The evictions were generally brutally executed, leaving little to the tenants but burned remains of their cottages, and slaughtered carcasses of their livestock. In many cases, tenants who resisted were imprisoned, or even hanged. The anxious look in Arren's green eyes told him she knew what it was like. He shook his head. "I know the owner of this land. His tenants have not been evicted."

She raised her eyebrows. "You know the landlord?"

He nodded briefly. "Yes. Robert would not have evicted his tenants. I am certain of it."

"Then why are there so many people?"

He shrugged, continuing to study the small croft through the driving rain. "Perhaps it is a family gathering."

Arren drew a deep breath, a brief light in her eyes. "Do you think so?"

He looked at her in surprise. "It's possible, certainly. You sound rather pleased by the notion."

"If it is a family gathering, there will be dancing and feasting for the better part of the night. Do you think we can slip into the hayloft undetected and wait out the storm where it's dry?"

He grinned at her. "I think I can do a good deal better than that."

Arren studied him warily. "What do you mean?"

"If it is a family gathering, I can almost certainly procure us an invitation."

The corner of her mouth twitched into a smile. "We are hardly dressed for such a grand occasion."

"You do not think 'soaked to the skin' is the order of the day?"

She shook her head. "Hardly. And in case it's slipped your notice—not that I'm shirking our bargain, you understand—we are growing wetter by the moment."

He nodded, and took her hand in his. "All right. I shall do what I can to get you dry. I can't promise much beyond that."

Arren fell into step behind him and allowed him to lead her down the hill. He seemed tense, cautious and watchful as they approached the small croft. At the very edge of the cluster, he tugged her inside the large door of one of the barns, and she sighed in relief, wiping the rain from her eyes. It was cool and dark inside, but the roof was secure. Simply being out of the rain was a pleasure. The scent of warm hay and animals hung in the air. Arren shivered, clutching her arms about her. Duncan looked about and pulled her toward an empty stall. She sank down gratefully into the fresh hay, and accepted the woolen horse blanket he retrieved from a pile in the corner. "Thank you," she whispered, pulling the blanket over her shoulders. "I had not realized how cold I had grown."

"You should be warm soon. I'm going to look about outside and see if I can determine what is happening here. Will you be all right by yourself for a few minutes?"

She nodded, huddling beneath the blanket. "Do you want me to go with you?"

He shook his head. "I will fare better on my own. Stay here and stay warm. I will return for you as soon as I can."

Arren watched him stride from the barn and sighed. Despite everything, Duncan made her feel safe. It was a good feeling. She snuggled down into the hay, ignoring the way it pricked her skin through her sodden clothes. She tipped her head back, allowing her eyes to drift shut. She had not heard even a hint of Alistar McDonan's dogs all morning, and despite her state of exhaustion, she felt considerably better than she had in a very long time.

When Duncan reentered the barn, she was asleep on the pile of hay. He paused to stamp the water from his boots, then lowered himself next to her, dropping the leather bag he held loosely between his fingers. Robert had been very accommodating. Duncan's secret was safe. He regretted lying to his cousin about Arren, but under the circumstances, it could not be helped. He tapped her on the shoulder. "I have returned," he said.

Her eyes flew open and she looked at him blankly, momentarily startled. Her eyes focused slowly. She pushed herself up on her elbow. "You weren't gone very long," she said.

He grinned at her. "I've been gone nearly an hour. I'm glad you rested. Are you warm enough?"

The strange light in his eyes made her shiver and she shook her head. "No," she said miserably.

Duncan laughed and slid closer to her, pulling on the blanket. She pulled back. He finally won the gentle tug-of-war and yanked the blanket free. Arren glared at him, strangely disgruntled. "Thank you," she bit out. "That was very helpful."

He grinned at her and shook his head. He had meant to pull her against him and wrap them both in the blanket so they could share body heat. "I'm going to get you warm, Duchess. Come here."

She pulled away, studying the dirty hem of her black

skirt with fascination while a sudden flurry of panic raced up her spine. "Why did you call me that?"

Duncan didn't miss the note of anxiety in her tone and he looked at her curiously, studying her bent head. The casual comment had clearly struck a mark. "Because you act like a duchess," he said in a deliberately bland tone. "I've never known a woman more demanding than you are."

She sucked in a deep breath. "There was no other reason?"

"Should there have been?" he asked carefully.

Her head jerked up. He held back an urge to pull away at the almost tangible impact of their gazes. Their noses were nearly touching, she was so close to him. Her deep green eyes locked with his for several moments. He felt a now-familiar tension pass between them. "I'm cold," she blurted out.

He blinked. Her abrupt change of mood knocked him off guard. "What?"

"I'm cold. You've taken my blanket."

He stared at her.

She pulled at the blanket. "You said you'd make me warm," she explained when he didn't release his grip on the woolen blanket.

He lifted a hand to her face. Arren watched him, hoping he wouldn't press her on her reaction to his comment. He rested his palm on her cheek. She was aware of the heat of him. Carefully, he brushed a tendril of her auburn hair from her eyes with his fingers. She leaned her face into his palm.

Encouraged, Duncan decided to take another risk. He slid his thumb tenderly over her lower lip. He watched in fascination as her eyes darkened. A flush crept up her neck, spread over her face, and slowly reached the roots of her hair. He grinned. "Are you warm now?"

Mesmerized by the look in his gold-flecked eyes, she

shook her head. He groaned and bent his head, capturing her lips in a hot kiss.

Arren was stunned. This was completely different from the way he'd kissed her that morning. His lips were ravenous. He slanted his mouth across hers again and again until she felt heat spreading from the center of her body. Her hands were trapped against his chest, and she flexed her fingers into his corded muscles, moaning deep in her throat.

The small sound inflamed him, and he reached for her, crushing her against him. He caressed her chin; she opened her mouth to him. And when she parted her teeth with a startled gasp, he drove his tongue into her mouth, moving his hand around to the back of her head to anchor her against him. He explored her sweet, hot mouth with a thoroughness that left her gasping for more. When he finally tore away from her, Arren's first thought was that she never remembered feeling so warm in her life.

They stared at each other for several long minutes. He massaged the back of her head with his strong fingers. An odd pain in his chest reminded him—he'd stopped breathing. He let out a long breath, finally breaking the silence between them.

The mood shattered. Arren was horrified. She pushed against his chest until he released her, and turned her attention to the leather bag. He shivered, and pulled the woolen blanket over his shoulder. Ignoring her startled protest, he tugged her into the wedge of his outstretched legs and draped the blanket around them both. Stubborn to the soul, he thought. She squirmed against him, trying to break free of his tight grip. The action had an unintended result. He groaned. "Sit still."

When he growled the command in her ear, she turned to look at him, a startled expression on her face. His wolfish grin got the better of her and she rolled her eyes at him in embarrassment, none-to-gently connecting an elbow with his rib cage. "Behave yourself, Gypsy. I haven't the patience for your games." She clearly wanted the subject closed. He obliged her. She turned her attention back to the bag and gasped in surprise when she finally tugged the wet lacing free. "Where did you get all this food?"

"I was right. There is a family gathering here. My friend was very accommodating."

She looked at him in surprise. "He gave you all this food? Surely he cannot afford such generosity if his only means are here in the croft."

Duncan shrugged. He had actually paid Robert heavily for the fare, but he had no wish to tell her how much money he was carrying on his person. For now, she had no real suspicions about him. He didn't want to give her any. "Robert is very generous."

"We cannot possibly accept this from him. It's probably difficult enough for him to feed his family, and this is nearly three days' worth of meals."

The scolding pleased him. Despite her obvious noble breeding, she hadn't lost her sensitivity to the problem facing those less fortunate. He was absurdly gratified by that realization. "We have no choice, Arren. We will need the food later. If you feel you must make good on it, you can send Robert some money after you accomplish your goal in London."

She seemed satisfied and she nodded. "I shall do that. Make certain you know how to reach him, Gypsy."

He rolled his eyes and accepted the piece of cheese she'd broken off for him. He suspected she wasn't going to take kindly to the notion that he'd told Robert she was his bride. He had done it for her protection, but she seemed to have a natural aversion to deceit, and while he found that rather endearing—especially in a woman—he feared it would make their journey more difficult if she insisted on making an issue of it.

She popped a piece of the hard cheese into her mouth and studied him intently. "I woul' wan' to burden hi' unneshesharily," she mumbled around the cheese.

He raised his eyes in amusement. "You're going to choke to death one day if you keep doing that."

She shrugged sheepishly and swallowed. "I said, I wouldn't want to burden him unnecessarily."

"I'll keep up with what you owe."

She nodded, seemingly satisfied. "Don't neglect the duty. It will make me cross."

Duncan stifled the urge to ask if she meant crosser than she already was, and they finished their meal, and a good part of the bottle of wine in silence. Duncan rose to check the weather. Arren carefully rewrapped the remainder of the food and secured it in the leather pouch. "Will we be able to stay the night here?" she asked carefully, hoping he would not remind her that she'd promised not to ask questions. She didn't relish the thought of setting out into the rain again.

He looked back at her and smiled absently. "We will. I have even managed to provide you with a warm bath and a borrowed change of clothing for the evening's festivities. I regret, however, that we will be forced to sleep in the barn. All the beds are full."

Arren smiled at him. "I imagine a pile of hay will be preferable to a tree limb. I shall probably be spoiled by the unexpected luxury."

Four

Arren leaned back against a broad tree trunk and watched Duncan across the firelit expanse of the large crowd. She had indeed enjoyed a long soak in a warm bath in Robert Dunkirk's house, and when his wife had handed her the soft Dunkirk plaid and a clean white blouse to wear, she had sighed contentedly, enjoying the feel of dry cloth next to her skin.

The Dunkirks had gathered to celebrate an elder's birthday, and in keeping with tradition, the ale was flowing freely. The rain had stopped earlier that afternoon, and only the lingering smell of damp earth served to remind her of the miserable morning. Even the clouds seemed prepared to partake in the festivities, and had parted to allow the stars to shine through, winking down on the happy family. The huge fire filled the air with pungent smoke, and cast an orange glow over the site. Arren watched from her vantage point as Duncan crouched down next to a small, curly-headed child, concentrating intently on what the young boy was saying. She'd shared a brief exchange with him outside Robert's house, but otherwise, she had not spoken alone to Duncan all evening.

She decided, however, that she'd learned a great deal about him watching him mill about with the Dunkirks. He was completely at his ease, almost a member of the close family, and she studied the fine set of his face in the burnished cast of the fire. He too wore a Dunkirk plaid. He was laughing at something the young boy had said, and Arren watched a bit wistfully as he tousled the child's hair affectionately. She liked the way he showed affection so readily. She liked the way he talked so comfortably with the Dunkirks. She liked the way he laughed so naturally. She smiled a bit wryly. She liked the way his kilt swung about his muscled calves, as well.

As if he'd read her sudden irreverent thought, Duncan looked up abruptly, his golden eyes locking with hers. There was a knowing look in his gaze and she blushed, tearing her eyes from his and starting down the hill to rejoin the Dunkirks. He had known she was watching him. His eyes had told her so.

Duncan sighed and pulled his attention back to Robert, feeling a bit guilty. Despite his best efforts to concentrate, his thoughts had been preoccupied with Arren all evening. She looked damned alluring in that Dunkirk plaid, and it had taken every vestige of his control to keep his distance throughout the long evening. The firelight made her hair glisten, and he knew it would be softened by their long day in the rain. It would feel like silk beneath his fingers, he was certain. He groaned inwardly, doing his best to listen to Robert's long discourse on his crop problems.

"Here now!" Robert said suddenly. "I've taken far too much of your time. I imagine you'd much rather be chasing about after your new bride than listening to me prattle on."

Duncan grinned. "The idea does have merit, Robert. I believe she'd be too embarrassed to allow me any liberties in such a large crowd, however."

Robert looked at him knowingly. "Perhaps I can arrange

a few liberties on your behalf. You do still know the Highland Karré, do you not?"

Duncan looked at him in surprise. The dance of the northern Highlands was notoriously difficult and flamboyant.
And flagrantly sensual. Duncan had mastered it several
years ago, even though it was rarely danced in the southern
part of Scotland. "What are you about, Robert?"

"You've told me your wife is from the north. Surely she
knows the Karré as well."

Duncan hesitated. He had no idea whether she knew the
difficult sequence of steps or not. "Of course," he said
blandly.

Robert grinned at him. "Then you must dance it for us,
of course. If nothing else, it will give you a chance for
some 'liberties' with your wife."

Duncan groaned and watched Robert wend his way
through the crowd toward the musicians on the far side of
the clearing. Arren would have his head for this. The ces-
sation of music claimed the crowd's attention, and Duncan
began slowly edging his way toward Arren when Robert
jumped up on a stump, calling out his name. "Friend, Duncan!" Robert shouted.

Arren looked at Duncan in surprise. He stepped a bit
closer to her and raised his eyes to meet Robert's. "What
say you, Dunkirk?" he called.

"There is a rumor about that you have mastered the Highland Karré. Is it so?"

The crowd murmured appreciatively, and Arren shifted a
bit uncomfortably as she and Duncan became the sudden
focus of attention. "It is so," Duncan announced.

"Will you and your lady dance it for us?" Robert yelled
back.

She looked at Duncan a bit frantically and started to

shake her head. Her eyes collided with his and she swallowed nervously, nearly forgetting her objections.

"Do you know it?" he asked quietly.

She nodded. "Yes, but . . ."

He held out his large hand. "Will my lady dance it with me?"

She opened her mouth to deny him at the same instant her fingers slipped into the warm cradle of his hand. He smiled and tugged her forward into the clearing. He looked back at Robert. "My lady and I will," he called.

The crowed cheered, and Arren heard the skirl of the bagpipes begin the high-spirited music. She sucked in a deep breath and looked at Duncan closely. "You'd better not embarrass me," she said quietly, raising her arm above her head in the customary pose.

"My assurance on it," he said, a twinkle in his eye. He answered her graceful pose with one of his own, and the music began.

Arren concentrated for the first several steps on the difficult sequences. She had not danced the native dance in several years, and she was horrified at the notion of performing it before such a large group of strangers. It wasn't long, however, before she noticed Duncan's effortless grace as he executed the complicated dance, and she began to truly enjoy herself, as she followed the lively rhythm of the music. She accelerated her steps, adding an additional sequence just to taunt him.

He grinned and changed the pace, readily catching on to her game. It wasn't long before they were moving so quickly that the crowd about them blurred and whizzed past. Arren had to concentrate on Duncan to keep her gaze in focus. His eyes were twinkling with amusement, and Arren laughed up at him, deftly following his lead. The music crashed around them, driving both the pace and the sequence of the dance, and he swung her about in a sudden flurry of steps that nearly caused her feet to leave the ground. At the final resounding crash of the music, she laughed and collapsed back against him, struggling to catch her breath.

Duncan pulled her close in the cradle of his arms and sighed, laughing at the crowd's uproarious applause. He pushed her gently away and bowed to her, his eyes alight with appreciation.

Arren smiled and dropped several shallow curtsies to him and to the crowd, wondering if the sudden warmth in her skin was a result of the exertion. The look in Duncan's gold-flecked eyes caused a flush to steal over her face, and she turned her eyes away, unable to meet his gaze.

The rest of the evening passed quietly, and Arren occasionally looked up to find Duncan's eyes resting on her face. She smiled at him shyly across the clearing. Her hands tingled at the memory of his warm grasp when they'd danced together.

She was seated beneath a tree, nearly asleep, when he leaned down and tapped her on the shoulder. Her eyelids drifted open lazily and she smiled at him. He smiled back. "Time to bed down for the night, Duchess. We've a long day ahead tomorrow."

She sighed and offered him her hand, allowing him to pull her up next to him. "Even our accommodations in the hay sound very appealing at the moment. I am immensely fatigued."

He looked at her closely, a bit surprised she hadn't complained more vehemently about their joint accommodations in the barn. He thought a bit wickedly that a tumble in the hay sounded more than just "appealing." He clasped her hand in his and tugged her toward the barn. "It will be a bit cold, I fear."

She shrugged. "I suspect we'll be all right if we each sleep in a stall. Robert's wife gave me some wool blankets earlier. I placed them in the barn. I do not think the small areas will be too difficult to insulate."

He shot her a sideways glance and pushed open the barn door, waiting for her to precede him inside. "At the risk of rankling your temper, Duchess, I do not think separate stalls will accomplish the task. We shall have to share warmth tonight."

She looked at him suspiciously. "Won't Robert's people find that slightly . . . unconventional?"

He paused and lit a lantern, leading the way toward the rear of the barn. "Robert is not prone to ask questions," he hedged. "I do not think too many of his family will be concerned enough to question our sleeping arrangement."

Arren followed him into the stall, waiting while he secured the lantern on a wooden hook, and spread two of the blankets on the sweet-smelling hay. His hair shone like burnished copper in the dim lantern light, and she studied him, admiring the way his white lawn shirt hugged the wide breadth of his shoulders. A memory of the way his strong, corded arms had held her securely against his warm chest caused a flutter to race down her spine, and she blushed, wondering how it would feel to sleep beside him on the soft woolen blankets. Arren twisted her fingers a bit nervously, looking about for something to do—anything other than watch him prepare their bed for the evening.

She scooped up two of the blankets and rolled them into pillows before wrapping each one in another blanket. She looked up, her gaze colliding with Duncan's. Tentatively, she extended the makeshift pillows to him, nervously running the tip of her tongue over her lower lip. "They're pillows," she said unnecessarily.

He nodded, his fingers curling into the soft blankets. "Thank you."

His voice was quiet, and Arren shivered, wrapping her arms around her middle. The stall had suddenly become too small, and she fought the urge to step away from him. Looking up, she smiled nervously. "I suppose we should sleep now."

Duncan dropped the pillows onto the soft bed and lowered his large frame, stretching out on the blankets. "I suppose we should, Duchess, but I don't think I can just yet. I'm still a bit—" he paused perceptibly, "worked up." She looked at him in surprise, and he added, "From the party."

Arren sighed gently and sank down on the hay next to him, wrapping her arms around her knees. "Of course," she said, considerably relieved that he had not pressed her about the strange tension that had settled between them since they'd danced earlier that evening. "From the party."

"It went well, I thought," he said.

Arren leaned back on her elbows, studying the flickering light of the lantern on the stable wall. "Your friends are very kind to have extended such hospitality to us." She looked at him in concern. "You do not think it will cause trouble for them later, do you?"

Duncan was stretched out on the makeshift bed, his hands linked behind his head. He regarded her frankly. "Do you mean if the men pursuing you trail us here and ask Robert questions?"

She nodded and he continued. "I think you may be assured they will stop here. Robert will not betray us, however."

"How can you be sure of that?"

He frowned at her. "He is my friend."

Arren shifted a bit uncomfortably beneath his hard glare. "I did not mean to insult you, it's just that I know these men and . . ." she trailed off, staring at him uncertainly.

"And?" he prompted gently.

"And they will stop at nothing to find me."

Duncan flexed his arms, raising his head slightly to look at her. "Don't you think it's time you told me your secret, Duchess."

She shook her head. "I cannot. I have told you before I cannot." Despite herself, her lips trembled on the last word, making her voice quaver slightly.

He sighed and pushed himself up to a sitting position, gathering her in his arms. "What have they done to you, Arren? Why are you so afraid?"

She curled her fingers into his arms and buried her face against his shoulder, inhaling a great breath of his clean, male scent. "I am sorry I'm such a coward," she whispered.

He smiled above her head. "You are not a coward."

She nodded miserably. "I am." Duncan's fingers were running gently through her hair, and she hardly noticed he had managed to work loose the pins holding her plait in place. Softly, he combed through the thick waves, and she shivered against him. Finally, Arren tipped back her head and looked at him. "He will kill me if he finds me, Duncan."

Duncan's fingers flexed in her hair. "Who?"

She stared at him for several long seconds before she shook her head. "I cannot."

He sighed and leaned over to softly kiss her forehead. "If you will not tell me who, will you tell me why?"

She shivered. Would he believe her? "He wanted to marry me. He would have done anything to make me his wife. Once I was married to him, I could never have escaped."

"You refused to marry him?"

She trembled and hugged her arms tight around him. "I tried. I tried so hard, Duncan. He would not listen to me."

"And so you fled into the night?"

She nodded. "Yes."

"Under threat of physical harm?"

"After," she said quietly.

"After?"

"After physical harm," she said softly, lifting her eyes to his.

Duncan groaned and pulled her close to him, lying back against the hay. She clung to him, seeking his warmth and comfort. He moved his large hand in soothing strokes up and down her spine, murmuring unintelligible comforts in her ear. "I am sorry," he said. "And I am sorry I pressed you. It was unfair of me."

She shook her head, burrowing against him. "It does not matter."

He sighed, settling her into the curve of his side. "Go to sleep, Duchess. I promise no one will harm you."

Arren cuddled into his side, rubbing her face on the soft lawn of his shirt. "I know it, Gypsy. You have convinced me."

Arren awoke the following morning. The sweet smell of fresh hay filled her nostrils. She sat up, wiping a hand through her tangled hair, and looked around in momentary confusion. Her mind cleared when her startled gaze collided with a pair of gold-flecked eyes. Duncan was seated next to her, carefully packing two of the wool blankets into the soft leather bag with their food supply.

He looked at her and smiled. "Good morning, Duchess."

"Good morning," she said quietly. She noticed, belatedly,

that Duncan had changed back into his dark green trousers and shirt. "Are we leaving?" she asked.

He nodded and handed her her black skirt and woolen vest. "The rain has let up for now. We will be able to cover a fair distance."

She nodded and accepted her clothes from him. She was grateful that she had taken the time to rinse them out the previous afternoon. They were still a bit damp, but no longer caked with mud. Arren rose to her feet, brushing the straw from the back of her borrowed plaid skirt. "I will change right away. We will need to return the plaids, of course."

He nodded. "We can leave as soon as you are ready."

Arren slipped into the next stall and made quick work of changing her clothes. She folded the plaid neatly before bending to pull on her heavy woolen stockings. She winced at the blisters that had formed on her feet from the pressure of her wet leather boots, but resolutely tugged her boots on. She moved toward the stall opening, wondering how far they would have to walk before Duncan allowed them to stop for the night. When she saw him saddling two horses she froze in the stable, staring angrily at his back. "What are you doing?" she demanded.

He pulled the girdle strap taut and buckled it, looking over his shoulder at her in surprise. "We're going to need horses, Duchess."

"Absolutely not," she said angrily. "Your friends have already been far too generous to us. I'd rather walk to London than take two horses they badly need."

He sighed. Finishing the task of securing the saddles before he turned to face her. He had, in fact, paid Robert handsomely for the two Shires, but shied away from revealing that to Arren. "Arren, we're on foot. The men chasing you are on horseback. We must have mounts."

Arren shook her head. She had seen too many of these crofts, too many Scots, struggling to survive on their own. Alistar McDonan had taught her that lesson well. "We cannot accept their horses—not even as a gift. It must be difficult enough for the Dunkirks to make their way here. I do not wish to contribute to that hardship."

Her compassion touched him and he sighed, clasping her shoulders in his large hands. Rubbing his fingers gently across her shoulders he looked down into her intense gaze. "Arren, I must have your trust in this matter."

She looked at him dubiously for a long moment. "I don't even know you. Why should I trust you?"

He smiled slightly. "You've trusted me with your life, yet you won't trust my judgment on this matter."

"This is different. Before, only I was involved. Robert Dunkirk's family has shown us kindness. I cannot allow you to hurt them on my behalf."

He moved his hands up to cup her face and looked down at her intently. "I share your compassion, Duchess, but I must have your trust."

She watched him closely, staring deep into his eyes, searching for any sign of insincerity. Finally, she nodded reluctantly. "Very well, but promise me you will give me a fair value on the horses so I can compensate Robert later for his loss."

He smiled and kissed her forehead. "You are a treasure, Duchess."

He turned to finish preparing their mounts, and completely missed her look of surprise. Duncan had been impressed by the quality of Robert's horses. They weren't thoroughbreds by any stretch of the imagination, but they were sturdy and strong; two qualities he knew would be needed to cross the rough Highland terrain. He had chosen an immense black one for himself, and a slightly smaller brown one for Arren. He still hadn't discussed his plans with her, hoping to avoid an argument, but he wanted to ride north to Inverness. Before he'd left Strathcraig, he'd made arrangements with a close friend in England. He and Aiden Brickston, the fifth Duke of Albrick, had been friends since childhood. They had fought in the Continental War together, and had served side by side as operatives for the British War Department. Duncan had only left England and returned to Scotland a little over a year ago when his father had died. The mess that awaited him was shocking.

When he'd made the decision to travel to England and petition the Prince Regent, he had known his adversaries would expect him to ride south. It was a two fortnight ride from his holding to London, if a man pushed hard enough. He was less likely to be intercepted, however, if he rode north and sailed from Inverness to Dover. He had contacted Aiden and arranged for his friend's yacht to be anchored at Inverness, awaiting his arrival. Duncan had been traveling a little over ten days when he intercepted Arren's flight from the dogs. His encounter with her had slowed down his pace considerably.

He still believed Inverness was the best course of action, but knew she'd argue vehemently over his choice. He finished saddling the horses and grinned. She'd dislike it almost as much as she'd dislike the thought of pretending to be his wife.

He brought the horses to where Arren was waiting for him, and smiled at her reassuringly. "It will be all right, Duchess."

She nodded and offered him her hand. "I hope so."

Duncan assisted her into her saddle, and was pleased with the effortless way she took control of the horse. He hadn't thought to ask her whether or not she knew how to ride. She was obviously at home in the saddle, and he knew the trip would be much easier on her as a result. He looked back at Arren and nodded. "You will let me know if you have difficulty keeping up?"

"I will not have difficulty keeping pace with you."

Duncan grinned at her knowingly. "All right, then. Let's go."

He preceded her out of the barn and they started down the hill. Arren looked around and drew a deep breath of the clean, moist air. The sun had finally fought through the thick clouds, and the hills were awash with color now. The heather and the rape covered the mossy hillsides in blankets of purple and yellow. The sun's warm rays glistened off the lingering raindrops and Arren looked to her left, catching her breath at the sight of the beautiful rainbow that spread across the sky. She nudged her mount forward so she was next to Duncan. She reached out to touch his arm. "Look. Over there." She pointed to the rainbow.

He turned his head and smiled. Arren was watching the rainbow in silent wonder. Even her words had been whispered, as if she feared she might startle it away. She turned back to look at him, her green eyes alight. "Isn't it beautiful?"

"Yes. It's beautiful."

His voice was so quiet, Arren looked at him. He was watching her with the oddest expression, and she decided she'd rather not risk pressing the point with him. His gold-flecked eyes were watching her a bit too closely for her own peace of mind. Instead, she asked, "Where are we going?"

He waited several long seconds before he answered. "We're going to stick to the tree line," he said, an absent note in his voice. "I don't want to be far from cover when our friends and their dogs catch up."

Arren threw an anxious glance over her shoulder. She had nearly forgotten Alistar McDonan's existence in the past several hours. "Do you think they will?"

"Yes," he answered without looking at her, and spurred his horse forward toward the trees.

They galloped along at a fairly brisk pace, and Arren lapsed into silence, considering their circumstances. He didn't seem to be at all worried. Probably because he didn't know Alistar McDonan. She now realized how foolish she'd been to think she could make the long journey on her own. At the time, there had seemed to be no other options. Nevertheless, she'd been an idiot to believe she'd escape so easily. Greed drove men to do desperate things. It had driven Alistar mad. She shouldn't have forgotten that.

Arren slanted a look at Duncan. He seemed relaxed enough, but she sensed a tenseness about him. His gold earring glinted in the sunlight, and she thought back to the previous evening, remembering the way his eyes had sparkled in the firelight, and the image of him laughing with Robert's family, just as though he hadn't a care in the world. She sighed heavily. She never remembered feeling that way.

Duncan turned his head to look at her when he heard her sigh. "Something wrong, Duchess?"

She frowned at him. "I was wondering about you."

He raised an eyebrow. "Anything I can help you with?"

She shook her head. "I don't think so. You're a very odd man. Odd in a likable sort of way, though," she hastily amended. "I was simply curious why you're that way."

He grinned at her. "I'm no more odd than you are. Has that thought occurred to you, too?"

She pursed her lips. "I can understand why you think that. Were I in your position, I would have probably drawn the same conclusion."

He grinned at the aristocratic tilt of her head. "Are you arguing that you're not odd?"

"I'm not in the least odd. In fact, I'm really rather boring. I haven't nearly the education I would like. I've seldom been anywhere other than my home, and with the exception of a few intriguing visitors, I haven't even met many interesting people. Just because you met me in highly unusual circumstances, doesn't mean you should jump to conclusions."

He laughed. She liked the sound of it. It was a full, confident laugh without a hint of malice in it. She was unused to that. "Duchess, I don't know much about you, it's true. But if I know one thing, it's that you aren't boring."

She started to answer when he abruptly pulled his horse to a stop and signaled her to be still.

Arren worried her lower lip between her teeth. "What is it?"

He held up his hand. "Quiet." The order brooked no argument and Arren fell silent. Duncan tilted his head and listened. Arren watched him anxiously. It wasn't long before she realized what had claimed his attention. In the distance, she could hear the distinct, insistent howling of dogs.

Five

Arren's eyes grew wide with fear and she looked at him anxiously. "What are we going to do?"

"We're going to ride like hell and try to outrun them. Are you up to it?"

"I'm afraid."

He nodded. "I know. There isn't hope of finding shelter until it rains again, though. Will you be all right?"

Despite herself, she flinched when the sound of Alistar's dogs carried on the breeze. Would she never be free of him? "I'll be all right."

Duncan studied her for several long seconds before he bent down and kissed her briefly. "You will tell me if you need assistance?"

She nodded. "I will."

He reined his horse around and headed for the dense protection of the trees. Arren followed, doing her best to keep his pace, trying to ignore the growing ache in her back and buttocks as the long day wore on. The pattern of wild canters through the forest alternating with brisk walks to rest the horses continued for hours. Finally, when she thought she was about to tumble from her saddle, Duncan reined to an abrupt halt in a tiny clearing deep within the thicket. She rode up next to him and waited expectantly. "You are worn out, Duchess," he said. "We'll stop now."

"Is it safe?"

He nodded. "It will begin to rain again soon. We'll be safe here until we can move again."

Duncan helped her dismount and settled down on the cold ground, pulling her into the wedge of his legs. "Go to sleep, Duchess. I'll wake you when we're ready to ride."

She sank wearily against him, too tired to argue any longer. She was asleep within minutes.

Duncan sighed and shifted her against him. In the distance, he heard the baying of the dogs, and he kept careful watch on the troubled sky, fervently hoping for more rain.

Moments later, he got his wish in the form of another heavy thundershower. Before long, lightning ripped the dark clouds and the thunder grew louder. Arren was curled up asleep beside him, and she didn't waken until a particularly loud clap of thunder shook the earth beneath them. She came awake with a startled cry and sat upright on the blanket.

"Hello," he said.

His voice startled her and she swung her head around, momentarily confused by his presence.

"Did I startle you?"

"Yes . . . No . . . It was the thunder. It's raining again."

"That means we can move on now. The rain will cover our scent."

She looked around anxiously. "Where are the dogs?"

He shrugged. "I haven't been able to hear them for some time. They're searching the region, I'm sure."

"Do you think they'll catch up with us again?"

"I don't doubt it." He studied her for a long minute. A fat raindrop landed on her nose, and he reached up to brush it away. "If you're up to it, we'd better start moving."

She rose to her feet and mumbled something as she turned to her horse.

"What did you say, Duchess?" he asked, swinging into his saddle.

Arren mounted and rode up behind him. "I said, 'And it's getting farther all the time.' We're still riding north," she pointed out.

He grinned at her. "Bothers you no end, doesn't it?"

She nodded.

"That's why I do it, you know?"

She snorted and spurred her horse ahead. At the edge of the thicket, she turned and started riding north, not daring to look back at him. The triumphant look she'd find in those golden eyes would irritate the hell out of her.

Arren lost track of time. They'd been riding for hours. The rain beat down on her bare head, and she was soaked to the skin. The darkness had begun to thicken, but she was unsure whether it was the storm or the onset of nightfall. Duncan rode behind her and they maintained a steady pace, covering a good bit of ground. She fought her fatigue and rode on, hoping he'd soon signal her to stop.

Her lingering fear of Alistar McDonan had only served to further her exhaustion, and as the night closed around them, she shivered, thinking how very close she'd come to becoming his victim.

Duncan studied her from behind. She sat her horse with an elegance and grace that was astonishing. The horseflesh he'd procured from Robert was second-rate, at best. Arren made hers look like a thoroughbred. He could tell by the slight slump of her narrow shoulders that she was growing tired, and he checked the sky, wondering vaguely what time it was. His pocket watch had gotten broken when he'd pulled Arren up into the tree the night before. The heavy thunderstorm made it impossible to rely on the sun's position for time, and he had to estimate as best he could. He also relied on his second-best indicator. The hungry rumble in his stomach told him it was well past eight o'clock in the evening, and they would need to find shelter for the night soon.

He did a mental summary of the area and decided on a low-lying area of limestone caves just to the northeast of their current location. The caves were shallow, little more than holes in the rock face, but would provide sufficient protection from the storm, and a dry place to sleep. He spurred his horse up beside Arren. "It's time to find shelter. Follow me." He didn't miss the relieved look in her eyes. He headed in the direction of the caves.

It took longer than he had estimated to reach them, and Arren was visibly exhausted by the time he saw the formation just ahead. The caves were part of an odd phenomenon. They were in one of the hilliest areas of Scotland, where the gently rolling hills of the Lowlands met the steeper, more jagged landscape of the Highlands. This particular set of caves gutted into a sheer rock face that stood among the more mountainous regions. He'd been amazed by the starkness when he first saw them. The same thought registered now. In a way, he supposed, it was a fitting gateway for the Highlands. Everything to the north lacked any traces of softness. The land was unforgiving, the weather harsh, the language coarse, and the life difficult. He sighed wearily, knowing their journey would grow harder after that night.

He turned to Arren and took her reins, smiling at her sympathetically when she handed them over. He found a relatively deep cave and led her horse under the cascade of water that sheered down the rock face, forming a waterfall at the mouth of the cave. The rain pooled below and ran into a swollen river, filling the area with the sound of rushing water.

Inside, the cave was cool and dark, and Duncan settled the horses against one wall, hoping they would emanate enough heat to take the edge off the cold. His clothes were soaked through, and a shiver raced up his spine. He removed the saddles, carefully spreading the saddle blankets on the floor. Delving into his saddlebag, he removed a thick piece of folded black wool and extended it to Arren. "Take your clothes off and wrap yourself in this."

Her eyes widened in astonishment. "What?"

"Take your clothes off." He extended the wool again.

"I will not."

She looked positively indignant and he sighed in irritation. "Arren, I haven't the time nor the disposition for theatrics. You're soaked to the skin. If you don't strip down and get dry, you'll catch pneumonia. Now take your clothes off or I'll take them off for you."

She looked at him warily. He wasn't jesting. She reached out and took the heavy wool from him, wondering briefly if she could defy his order. No, she decided, she couldn't. She retreated a little further into the darkness, glaring at him steadily. "Well at least turn around."

He managed a smile. Her embarrassment was obvious and he felt a twinge of sympathy. He turned his back and started to unbutton his shirt. Behind him, he heard Arren's sodden garments drop to the floor of the cave. There was a soft rustle when she unfolded the wool, and he resisted the urge to look over his shoulder before she told him she was ready.

"All right, you may turn around now."

He did. Arren was covered from shoulder to foot with the soft wool, and she stood in the center of the cave watching him, anxiously clutching the wool to her breasts like a suit of armor. He was exasperated. "You needn't worry so much,

Duchess. I haven't the energy to soil your reputation tonight. Now lie down on those blankets and try to get some sleep."

She looked at him a long minute. His dark green shirt was unbuttoned to the waist, and his wet trousers clung to him like a second skin. He must be horribly cold in the damp cave. "Aren't you going to sleep, too?"

He nodded. "After a while. I need to water the horses. I've got grain for tonight, but we'll have to graze them tomorrow. Just go to sleep, Arren. I'm here if you need me."

She sank gratefully to her knees on the makeshift bed he'd prepared with the horse blankets. He'd laid them across a pile of sand that had accumulated in the corner, no doubt the result of the high winds that prevailed in the area. Arren was surprised at how soft the sand was beneath her. She'd expected the ground to be hard and cold, but the pile of sand cushioned her body. She fell asleep almost as soon as her head touched the blanket.

Duncan watched her in silence. He was amazed at how well she'd managed the trek. She'd faced it all without batting an eye, and yet, as soon as he'd told her to take her clothes off, she'd nearly gotten hysterical. He sighed and led the horses to the mouth of the cave, where they could drink the cool water that pooled at the opening.

Turning back to the saddlebags, he fished out a smaller piece of wool and laid it aside, rising to shed his own clothing. He spread his sodden shirt on the floor to dry. His trousers followed. When he stood completely naked, he lifted the wool and wrapped it tightly around his waist. The cool air of the cave bit at his skin, making him shiver.

He found Arren's clothes in the corner piled in a sodden heap. He spread them carefully, hoping the heavy wool would dry by morning. He didn't want to stay in the cave more than five or six hours, at most. He knew they'd be safer if they traveled by night. It was too risky to travel much during the daylight hours. He turned to look at her again. She was curled up on the makeshift bed, her hands tucked securely beneath her cheek. He wondered for the hundredth time that day who those men were, and he tried again to ignore the simmering fury he felt over the few details she'd given him the previous night. No explanation satisfied his curiosity, and he gave up.

He moved to stand next to the horses, hoping to absorb some of their heat. Lifting one hand, he rubbed the taut muscles at the back of his neck, working steadily at the tension. He'd sustained a serious head injury during his tenure in Wellington's army, and while he'd more or less completely recovered, he still suffered from severe headaches when he grew tired.

He nearly jumped through his skin when he felt Arren's small hands settle on his shoulders. The rushing water at the mouth of the cave had disguised the sound of her movements, allowing her to sneak up behind him. Her fingers began to work the large muscles in his shoulders. She rose up on her tiptoes to whisper in his ear. "You're in pain. Why didn't you tell me?"

He dropped his hand from his neck and allowed her to continue kneading the muscles. "It's not important. It's just a headache. It'll go away."

Her thumbs smoothed a path up his neck. He dropped his head forward and groaned.

"And you think I'm stubborn, Gypsy." She dropped her hands and moved away from him. He fought the urge to sigh with disappointment. Her strong fingers had felt damn good working at his shoulders. He raised his hand and began rubbing the muscles in his neck again.

"Come here and sit down." Arren's order came from behind him and he turned his head to look at her. She'd crossed back to the blankets and was seated on the floor, waiting for him.

He raised an eyebrow. "Why?"

"So I can finish ridding you of your headache. Come here."

"Arren, it isn't important. Go back to sleep."

"Do not argue with me, Gypsy. You'll irritate me. You're too tall for me to work on your shoulders properly when you're standing. Now, come here."

He hesitated. He wasn't particularly pleased with letting her know how much his head ached. On the other hand, her fingers had begun to work magic on the tension in his shoulders. If he were rid of the pain, he would think more clearly. He walked to her side and sat down on the blankets facing her.

"Turn around."

He raised a questioning eyebrow and she sighed in exasperation, pushing on his shoulders. "Turn around. I can't reach your back like that."

He pivoted on the rug.

"Now bend your knees in front of you, cross your arms on top, and put your head down on your forearms." The dull ache in his head had expanded to a sharp pain. He was through arguing. He did as she said.

The minute her hands settled on his back, he groaned in relief. She worked at the taut muscles with an amazing strength, the heels of her hands rubbing away the tension, her fingers digging out tight knots in his shoulders. Her hands worked up and down his spine, gliding across his shoulder and smoothing up his neck. He felt the languor begin seeping through his blood. His head grew heavy on his arms. Her strong thumbs kneaded the tension in his neck, working out each knot before her fingers spread through his hair and gently massaged the back of his head.

When she finally stopped, he realized two things simultaneously. The pain in his head was completely gone, and a deep lassitude filled every fiber of his body. He knew he had only to stretch out on the wool blankets to fall asleep. He raised his head and looked at her over his shoulder. It was completely dark outside now, and the cave was pitch black. Only Arren's shoulders and head were visible above the dark wool. He could tell by the motion in her shoulders that she was breathing hard from the exertion of working on his back. He smiled and stretched out on the blanket, pulling her down with him.

She gave a startled cry and pushed against his chest. He didn't budge. He forced her head down on his chest with his hand and sighed sleepily. "Don't fight me, Duchess. I need to share your warmth."

He felt her hesitate for a minute before she relaxed against him. "You shouldn't have waited so long to tell me you were in pain," she whispered. "It wouldn't have been so bad if you'd let me do something about it earlier."

He mumbled something sleepily and she tilted her head to look at him. His deep breaths told her he'd already fallen asleep. She sighed and curled more tightly into his side, trying to fight a growing sense of panic. She was becoming too fond of this man, and that simply wouldn't do at all.

Six

Duncan woke slowly. As was his habit, he did a mental assessment of his surroundings before he opened his eyes. The sound of rushing water, the soft neighing of the horses, and the feel of Arren draped across his chest satisfied him that all was well. He opened his eyes and turned to look at the still-dark mouth of the cave.

The rain seemed to have slowed. Not even flashes of lightning relieved the darkness. He had no idea what time it was. He knew it had to be around two or three o'clock in the morning, though. It was time to move on.

Cautiously, Duncan looked down at Arren. She was sprawled across his chest, deep in sleep. He hated like hell to wake her. He flexed his shoulders, amazed that the fluid motion caused him no pain. He remembered the magical way she'd worked the tension out of his back and shoulders during the night, and he rolled his head gently from side to side. She'd accomplished what he never had been able to do on his own. It was a glorious feeling.

He slipped his arm from around her shoulders, settling her back against the blanket. He would let her sleep as long as possible. Rising, he made quick work of his clothes. He pulled on his damp trousers and shirt, grimacing as he tugged on his boots. The leather was wet and his feet protested the discomfort. The horses were standing quietly by the mouth of the cave, resting from their arduous journey the day before. He bridled first one, and then the other, softly talking to them all the while. He promised each a good meal before day's end and a private paddock with more oats and hay than they could hope to eat in their lifetimes if they held up until Inverness.

Arren had awakened shortly after he left her side, and she lay in the dark listening to his conversation with the horses. It seemed rather incongruous with his character—almost ridiculous really. She liked it, though. In truth, she liked it a lot. This gypsy was no ordinary man.

He evidently satisfied himself that the horses had agreed to his bargain and he picked up the extra blanket. She stirred sleepily when he bent and touched her shoulder.

"Wake up, Duchess. It's time to go."

She groaned. "It isn't even morning. It's still dark outside."

"I know. Get up and get dressed. I'll let you ride with me awhile so you can sleep a bit longer."

She sighed and sat up, looking around sleepily. "That isn't necessary. I'll be fine." Her authority was diminished somewhat when the words came out on a yawn.

He smiled, and turned back to the horses, deciding to argue with her later. Arren dressed quickly, thankful that he'd thought to spread out her clothes. They were almost completely dry, and not nearly as uncomfortable as they would have been if he'd left them in the wet heap on the floor. She tilted her head and listened for the rain. It was difficult to determine whether it was raining or not, over the sound of the rushing water. She sent up a fervent prayer that the rain had stopped, at least temporarily.

It hadn't. As soon as Duncan led them out of the cave, she felt the cold rain run down her back. She shivered. It was going to be a miserable night.

She didn't have time to think about it when he reached over and lifted her from her saddle onto his own. Spreading her legs on either side of the horse, he tugged her back against his chest, cutting off her startled protest with a sharp squeeze at her waist. "Relax, Duchess. I can ride faster if I don't have to worry about you falling asleep and toppling off your horse. Go back to sleep."

She thought about arguing with him, but decided against it. The swaying motion of the horse rocked her gently, and before long, she allowed her head to loll back against his shoulder. They'd traveled less than a quarter of a mile before she fell asleep again. He felt her sag against him completely and smiled, shifting her to a more comfortable position.

He spent the next several hours trying to ignore the feeling of Arren's backside wedged between his thighs, rolling against him with the motion of the horse. It felt too damn good to ignore, though, so he mentally listed all the reasons he shouldn't become involved with this woman. She was too stubborn, for one. And she had a mean streak the size of the English Channel for another.

He reached the end of the list a good deal sooner than he would have liked, and he sighed, spurring his mount into a gallop. The sun was starting to come up, and he could see where they were going more clearly. He had every intention of taking advantage of it. Arren didn't budge. Her head was leaned back against his shoulder, and she slept on. He turned to look down at her briefly. The rain had finally let up, but her hair was plastered to her head in a tangled mess. Her skin was damp and pale from the rain, and the freckles on the bridge of her nose seemed more prominent.

He smiled and thought about the women he'd known in London. They were obsessed with their appearance, worrying over the tiniest detail, following every fashion trend, spending thousands of pounds on their elaborate wardrobes. In contrast, Arren didn't seem to be the least bit mindful of how she looked. Her nails were split from the rigors of their journey together, she hadn't been able to bathe properly or wash her hair in at least three days, and while the rain had kept them relatively clean, mud splattered the edge of her skirt and caked on the toes of her leather boots.

His own appearance was no better, he knew. His beard was growing daily, his hair was unkempt, and his trousers were covered with dirt. Despite the worst of it, Arren hadn't complained. Not about any of it. She was a remarkable woman, he decided, looking at her again. Yes, there were dozens of reasons why he shouldn't allow himself to become involved with her. At the moment, though, he was having difficulty summoning any of them to mind.

Arren awoke when the horse stopped. She lifted her head from his shoulder and looked around, slightly disoriented. She barely remembered leaving the cave, and she realized now that the sun had risen in the sky. It was early morning, and they had evidently been riding for several hours. She was suddenly embarrassed and she turned to look at him apologetically. "You shouldn't have let me sleep so long. It must have been dreadfully uncomfortable for you. I could have ridden."

He shrugged. "We covered a good bit of ground. I wanted to ride as far as possible before daylight."

She looked up at the sky and saw the sun struggling to work its way through the dense clouds. "Do you think it will rain again today?"

"I hope so." He laughed at the way she wrinkled her nose. It made her freckles clump together between her eyes. He reached to brush a strand of her hair behind her ear. "I know it's uncomfortable, but it covers our tracks and our scent."

She nodded. "I know. I'd give my right arm for a hot bath, though."

He smiled. "I promise I'll do what I can."

"Oh, I wasn't complaining. Only wishing." She smiled back, somewhat embarrassed. "I can ride now, really."

He swung off the saddle and lifted her down, allowing both the horses to graze on the thick grass. They were just beyond the tree line, and Arren looked around at the spot. He had stopped at the top of a hill with an ample view of the surrounding countryside. She had no doubt he'd selected it for just that reason. She sighed. It made her feel secure to know he thought of things like that. She probably wouldn't have.

Duncan had turned his attention to her horse and untied the large leather bag. He looked inside and realized this would be their last meal on the supplies he'd bought the previous day. He handed the bag to Arren and tossed her the small piece of wool. "Spread that and we'll eat. I'll have to get us some more food this afternoon."

She winced. "Do we have to steal it?"

"How else do you propose we obtain it?"

She wrinkled her nose. "I hate doing that."

"I know. I appreciate that more than you realize."

She tilted her head to look at him. It was an odd comment, and not the first time he'd said something like that either. "Why do you say that?"

"It's difficult to explain, Duchess. As you said, some things will make more sense once we reach London." He settled himself next to her on the woolen blanket and she handed him a large piece of the cheese. He didn't miss the fact that her piece was noticeably smaller. He broke his in half and handed one portion back to her.

She shook her head and sank her teeth into her piece. "You nee' tha' more than I." She mumbled the words around the large hunk of cheese in her mouth and he started to laugh.

"I told you not to talk like that. You're going to choke to death one day."

She shrugged and swallowed the cheese. "Probably."

He finished off his part of the cheese and picked up one of the hard loaves of bread, looking at it disconsolately. He would be relieved to have fresh provisions again. There was a small town over the next crest, and he planned to situate Arren in one of the thickets and go down to the village alone. Possibly, he could procure changes of clothes for them as well.

They finished what was left of the food and Duncan stood, looking carefully over the land. There had been no sign of anyone since they'd left the cave early that morning and it bothered him. He much preferred knowing where his adversary was, to running from a phantom. He sighed and extended a hand to Arren, assisting her to her feet. She picked up the wool and shook it out, refolding it into a neat square.

"Are we going to ride more today?" she asked.

He took the wool and shook his head, turning to secure it in his saddlebag. "Not much. We need fresh provisions, and the horses need rest. There's a small village over the crest of that hill. I'll find us some food there."

"How do you know that?"

He looked at her in surprise and assisted her into her saddle. "There's bound to be food there, Arren. It shouldn't be too difficult."

She shook her head and watched him dismount. "No, I

mean, how do you know there's a village there. You always know. There's a cave or a house or a croft or a town or whatever you're looking for. How do you know that?"

"I'm familiar with the area."

She narrowed her eyes. "Why?"

He shrugged. "I just am. What difference does it make?"

It made a great deal of difference. With each mile they covered, they drew closer and closer to Arren's home. She was becoming more and more tense lest they run into someone she knew. She couldn't understand why he was so familiar with the countryside and yet completely unfamiliar to her. It bothered her immensely, and she was determined to know the truth. "I would like to know," she finally answered.

"And I would like to know a good number of things about you. I'm no more inclined to assuage your curiosity than you are to assuage mine."

Arren looked at him cautiously. "I suppose that's fair enough."

He nodded briskly and reined his horse around. "Come on, that hill is farther away than it looks on this terrain. We've a good deal of ground to cover yet."

He nudged his mount into a brisk trot, and Arren followed suit. He had been right. It took them just over an hour to reach the crest of the hill. The sun had risen higher in the sky and Arren felt a trickle of perspiration run down her back. She grimaced. At this rate, she'd be lucky if she didn't die of pneumonia before they even reached London. He reined in his horse and she stopped beside him.

She could see the small village laid out before them. It was a mining town, and the great coal mine lay just to the north of the village. Duncan did a quick survey of the area, deciding that the trees should provide her ample cover while he ventured down the hill. He nodded his head in the direction of the trees. "I'm going to leave you here with the horses and go in on foot. If anyone comes along, and I don't care who, just leave the other horse and ride like hell into the center of town. Do you understand?"

"But why?"

"Because I told you to and you promised not to argue with me."

She nodded. "Are you sure you'll be all right? What if the . . ." she stopped just short of saying a name. "What if they're down there?"

He narrowed his eyes at her. "They know what you look like, and they probably know you're traveling with a man on horseback. A stranger on foot arriving in the village shouldn't attract too much attention." She was obviously skeptical, so he added, "I'll be fine, Arren. Just stay here in the cover of the trees."

She nodded again and took the reins of his mount. He swung down and reached behind her saddle for the leather bag. She was chewing on her lip as she watched him, wondering anxiously what on earth she'd do if he got himself killed. The thought amazed her. She wasn't used to depending on anyone, and she wasn't sure she liked it now.

He lifted the bag down and swung it over his shoulder, looking up at her. "All right, ride into the thicket. I shouldn't be gone over a half hour. Whatever you do, don't come out unless someone sees you." He slapped the rump of her mount. "Now go."

Duncan watched her until she disappeared deep into the trees. He didn't like leaving her alone, but it was certainly less dangerous than taking her into town. He turned and started down the hill, praying fervently that she wouldn't do anything stupid while he was gone.

The small village was alive with activity, and Duncan

strode down the street, the empty leather bag swinging from his shoulder. There were few men about. Most of the able-bodied ones would be at the mine, he knew, but the town teemed with women and children and animals. Small dogs chased about on the streets followed by scores of dirty children. They seemed more or less oblivious to his presence, and only the women watched him with trepidation. A young girl, not more than six or seven, collided suddenly with his leg, and looked up at him in surprise. He squatted down beside her. "You should watch where you're going."

She tilted her head and looked at him. She had curly red hair and bright green eyes and he was struck with the shocking thought that Arren's children would look like that. He had no business wondering what her children would look like, he reminded himself, and tugged his unruly mind back to the matter at hand.

The child had stuck her dirty thumb into her mouth and was now staring at him. She pulled her thumb out only enough to ask, "Who are you?" before popping it back in again.

He smiled at her. "I'm a stranger here. I need to know where the baker's house is."

She turned her small head and nodded in a direction. He smiled again. "Over there?"

She nodded again.

"Thank you." He rose to his feet, and patted her on the head, heading off in the direction she'd indicated. He was aware that she stood in the center of the street staring after him, and he turned back to wave. She smiled and waved back, before taking off in the opposite direction. He shook his head. Arren's children, indeed. He had to be losing his mind to entertain a thought like that.

Duncan found the baker's house with little effort. There

were women lined up outside to purchase bread, and they watched him cautiously from beneath hooded lids. He imagined they saw few strangers in their remote location. He knew his presence would indubitably attract enough attention to be remembered if Arren's pursuers should stop here and ask questions. That was unavoidable, he supposed. He purchased six loaves of hard bread from the baker and dropped them in the bag, stopping only long enough to inquire where he could procure cheese and a bottle of wine. The baker's wife pointed him down the street, and he took off again, trying his best to keep to the shadows. The fewer people he encountered, the better it would be.

Two more stops yielded a cheese wheel and three bottles of wine, then he turned to leave. The sight across the street stopped him short. Four men, surrounded by a pack of mangy-looking dogs, were involved in an active discussion with an old woman. Duncan stepped back into the shadow of a small house and watched them carefully. The woman shook her head once, and argued something back. One of the men turned away angrily and looked up and down the street.

Duncan slipped farther back into the protection of the shadow. The dogs were yipping hungrily, chewing at their tails. The men were clearly agitated. The woman pointed angrily down the street. They brushed past her and Duncan watched them until they disappeared into the door of a seamy-looking tavern. He sighed, relaxing his grip on the leather bag. Damn! He had hoped he and Arren had eluded them temporarily. It appeared they hadn't. He wanted to get back to her immediately and ensure that she was all right, hidden in the thicket. He turned to head back down the small street and was almost to the edge of town when he stopped once more. Across the street from where he stood was a small house. A sign hung from the door stating "wool weaver."

He hesitated. There would be plaids and solid wools, and if he were lucky, he could procure a change of clothes for them both. The fit certainly wouldn't be Saville Row, of course, but in his present condition, it wouldn't take much to satisfy him. He looked around carefully. It would be a horrible risk. If the men in the tavern questioned the weaver, the man would surely remember a tall stranger buying women's clothes. On the other hand, a man's memory could usually be purchased for the right price. Duncan smiled and headed across the street.

He knocked twice on the small door before an ancient little man opened it a crack and peered out. He was clearly astonished to see a stranger on his doorstep. Duncan hastened to explain his presence. "Hello, sir. I'm traveling through, and I'd like to look at your wares. If you have them, I need a fresh shirt for myself and perhaps a new pair of trousers. I have plenty of money." He held up the leather pouch and the old man smiled a toothless grin, opening the door enough to allow Duncan through.

The gentleman wore a kilt of an undistinguishable plaid, a matching bonnet and a loosely woven shirt. He scratched his head and looked at Duncan. "Yer a big man, lad. I don't know as I have anything that'll fit ye proper."

Duncan shrugged. "I've been wearing these clothes for several days. I'm not so concerned about fit as I am about cleanliness."

The man nodded and signaled for Duncan to have a seat on the threadbare couch. He obliged.

He waited a full five minutes before his host reappeared with a pair of trousers and an ivory shirt slung over his

arm. He held the shirt to Duncan's shoulders and nodded.
"This should do. The sleeves may be short, though."

Duncan took the shirt and inspected it. It was tightly
woven of fine wool threads, extremely well-crafted, and
seemed more than large enough.

The man was holding a pair of trousers, looking at Duncan dubiously. "I don't know about these, lad. You'd best
try them on."

Duncan nodded and rose to his feet, unbuttoning his shirt.
He slipped on the ivory shirt first, immensely pleased that
it didn't scratch his skin. The man did fine work, indeed,
especially with the coarse Highland wool he would have to
use in this region. He made quick work of his trousers,
taking the wool pair from the old gentleman. They were
black with leather lacings, and buckles that fastened at mid-
calf. He slipped them on, pleased with the fit.

They were a bit tight across the corded muscles of his
thighs, but they fit through the waist and buttocks well
enough, and Lord knew, if the fashion in London was still
the same as a year ago, the bucks and dandies were lacing
themselves into breeches far tighter than these. He laced
up the front and looked at the old man gratefully. "They're
a fine fit. Exceedingly well-made."

The man nodded. "A far sight cleaner than what you had
on, too."

Duncan grinned. "Now that I think of it, I'd like to take
a present to my sister if you have something. I'll be seeing
her in a few days, and I think she'd appreciate something
of this quality."

The man smiled, clearly flattered by the compliment.
"What did you have in mind?"

Duncan appeared to concentrate for a long minute. "A long
skirt with a blouse and matching jacket would be nice."

The man looked perplexed. "Well, I have something like that. I was planning on giving it to my granddaughter for her birthday, though."

"I'll pay you well for it. You could perhaps even buy lowland wool to make another for your granddaughter."

The man appeared to consider that for a long minute before he nodded and disappeared into the back once more. He came out carrying a skirt and jacket of soft green. The blouse was the same ivory as Duncan's shirt. Duncan smiled. Arren would be pleased. He took the skirt and held it up, looking at the waist. It had leather lacings up the back, and he was fairly sure it would fit. The blouse and jacket appeared to be right, as well. He smiled at the old man and nodded, slipping the garments into the large leather bag with the food. "I'll take them all."

The man seemed to hesitate, but Duncan removed a large handful of notes from his leather pouch. Any hesitation the man had was replaced by a look of sheer astonishment. Duncan placed the notes in the man's wrinkled hand, and closed his fingers around them. "I'm sure you can buy fine wool for your granddaughter's birthday, sir. I would ask but one favor of you in return."

The man nodded and looked at the notes. "What do ye need from me now?"

"Only for you to forget that I was here—and certainly to forget any mention of my sister."

The man looked at him warily a minute, and then his face split in another toothless grin. "I've never seen ye before in my life, young man."

Duncan grinned back and turned to the door, leaving the old man happily counting his good fortune.

He climbed the hill with purposeful strides, rather pleased with his purchases. The clean clothes felt good next to his skin, and he knew Arren would be pleased that he'd returned bearing gifts.

She screamed like a banshee. He'd barely reached the tree line when she came barreling out from the thicket, throwing herself against his chest, screeching at him for all her worth. He looked down at her in astonishment as she beat her small fists against him.

"Where have you been? You shouldn't have been gone so long."

It took him several minutes to realize she was more frightened than angry, and he dropped the leather bag and wrapped his arms around her, trying to calm her down. "Arren, calm yourself. What's the matter?"

She slapped ineffectually at his chest. "I saw them. I saw them ride into town. You didn't come back!"

She was barely making any sense and he continued to hold her still against his chest, determined to wrest the truth from her.

She knew she sounded incoherent. She didn't care. Shortly after Duncan had left her, she'd seen the dogs and her adversaries ride into town. It had petrified her. When Duncan had taken so long to return, she was certain they'd discovered him. Every long minute that slipped by had seemed like an hour. When she'd finally caught her first glimpse of him coming up the hill, she didn't recognize him at first in his new clothes. Then the realization that she'd been scared out of her wits while he was stealing himself a new set of trousers from some unsuspecting family had hit her full force. By the time he'd made it up the hill, she'd worked herself into a fine fit of anger.

It took Duncan several minutes to get the story out of her. He determined that she was more frightened than angry, and she'd already calmed down a good bit by the time she finished berating him. She was clinging to him for dear life, all the while telling him she wished he'd died and hoped she'd never see him again. He smiled over her head and waited until her anger was spent. Finally, he set her away from him and kissed her on the forehead. "I'm sorry I frightened you, Duchess." He reached up to cut off her angry protest by laying his forefinger across her lips. "I'll try not to do it again."

Her green eyes glittered at him angrily, and she reached up to push his hand away. "I'm not frightened. I'm angry. You shouldn't have wasted precious time stealing clothes for yourself when we've still got a lot of ground to cover."

He grinned at her. "Would it help if I told you I brought new clothes for you, too?"

She did her best to look uninterested. She failed dismally. Her eyes strayed to the leather bag and back to his face. He was teasing her. "No."

"Then I suppose I won't give them to you." He bent to pick up the bag.

She snatched it from his hand. "There's no sense in putting your efforts to waste. Now that you've stolen them, I might as well see if they fit." She turned away, ignoring his smug laugh, and headed for the trees. "I'll be right back."

She disappeared into the thicket and Duncan smiled, turning to look down the hill. Perhaps she was not so different from other women after all. He studied the village intently, identifying the four horses and the pack of dogs at the edge of the town. The men were evidently still availing themselves of the tavern's ample supply of ale. Hopefully, they'd stay the night. Duncan turned back when he heard Arren step from the thicket.

An appreciative gleam came into his eyes. He hadn't noticed until now that she'd taken the time to work the tangles

out of her hair and replait it while he was gone. The ivory
collar of her blouse lay atop the soft green jacket and the
skirt swirled about her calves in gentle green folds. She
smiled at him shyly and crossed the distance between them.
Turning around, she presented her back to him. She held
the ends of the leather laces to her skirt in one hand. "Will
you do up my laces for me?"

He took the laces in his large hands, pulling them taut.
He tied them deftly, settling his hands gently at her waist.
She turned around, rising on her tiptoes to kiss his chin.
"Thank you. I'm sorry I yelled at you."

He grinned at her. "I'd be a lot more offended if I hadn't
guessed the reason why."

She leaned back and poked him in the chest. "Don't do
that to me again, Gypsy. It annoys me."

"Anything you say, Duchess."

She rolled her eyes and turned her attention back to the
food. His smile turned to masculine appreciation as he
watched her unpack the leather satchel. She looked damned
appealing in that outfit, and he was beginning to regret the
impulse that had prompted him to buy it for her. He'd had
enough trouble keeping his thoughts in line when she'd
looked like an urchin.

She turned and smiled at him. He groaned. Damn! He
crossed the distance between them and settled himself next
to her on the blanket. They shared one of the loaves of
bread, and drank part of the wine. He told her about seeing
the men in the village and how they'd disappeared into the
tavern. She was visibly relieved when he said he suspected
they'd stay the night there.

"I think they probably believe they're ahead of us. I hope
they'll wait until tomorrow to move on," he explained.

She nodded. "I hope so, too. Do we have much farther to ride?"

He noticed that she'd stopped asking where they were going, and grinned. "Another five days, I think. It depends on the weather."

Arren sighed and studied her hands. "Would this be a good time to ask you how we're going to get to London once we reach Scotland's north coast?"

He leaned forward and tipped her chin up. "Arren, ships travel south every day. I don't really expect you to swim."

She looked startled. The thought had obviously never occurred to her. She shocked him when she threw her arms around his neck and toppled him backwards on the blanket. "Oh that's a wonderful idea! I should have known you'd think of something like that."

He was laughing, and he placed his hands at her waist, holding her against him. "What did you think I'd do about it?"

She shrugged. "I don't know. I didn't think about it at all really. I just assumed that you . . ." she trailed off when she saw the odd light in his eyes. "Why are you looking at me like that?"

His face split in a slow grin. Arren had pushed herself up against his chest with her forearms, unwittingly aligning her pelvis in a tantalizing position with his own. His equilibrium still hadn't recovered from the earlier kiss she'd dropped on his chin, and he had a nearly insane urge to taste her mouth again. He decided to indulge it. "Why do you think?"

Her eyes took on a guarded expression. "Gypsy, I really don't think it's proper for you . . ."

He groaned and silenced her protest by locking his hand behind her head and raising his mouth to hers.

Arren froze. His lips were warm and still tasted of the sweet wine they'd shared just a few minutes before. The sun beat down on her back, and his hand moved in mesmerizing circles at the back of her head. The kiss was gentle as a whisper, sliding across her lips in a seductive caress. She sighed, and relaxed against him, surrendering to the sensation.

Duncan sensed the change in her and took full advantage. Tilting his head, he moved his lips across hers, coaxing and cajoling until she opened her mouth to him. When she did, he clasped her tightly against him and rolled to his side, trapping her beneath the weight of his body. He drove his tongue into her mouth and tasted her sweet warmth.

Duncan's tongue slid in and out of her mouth like hot, wet velvet. Arren heard herself moan deep in her throat and felt her hands slide up the breadth of his chest and lock at the back of his neck. When he groaned, she moved beneath him, silently begging for more. He willingly gave it. He moved one hand around to her midriff, sliding his fingers along the hem of her jacket. When his hand slipped beneath and rested on her stomach, she felt the scorching heat through the thin material of her blouse.

Duncan's discipline was quickly disintegrating. The sexy little noises she was making in the back of her throat were chipping away at his resolve, and when she moved against him like that . . . he groaned and drove his tongue into her mouth once more, tasting the sensitive skin behind her teeth. His hand rested on her soft stomach, and he had an overwhelming urge to feel her skin. He tugged gently at her blouse, sighing with relief when it pulled free of her waistband.

Arren gasped at his heated touch. His fingers stroked across the smooth skin of her midriff, teasing her. She pulled tighter on his neck, arching up against his touch. His callused hands felt smooth as silk sliding across her hot skin, and she squirmed beneath him. When he growled his approval, she was emboldened. Her tongue dueled restlessly with his, and he relented, allowing her to explore his hot mouth as he had explored hers. He groaned with pleasure and slid his hand farther up her rib cage. When it closed over her breast, Arren cried out and dropped her head back, arching into the caress.

The soft neighing of the horses broke through his haze of passion, and he caressed the side of her breast once, reluctantly pulling his hand away. He rested it at her waist and dropped his head between her breasts. He fought for breath. His heart was slamming against his rib cage in a painful cadence, and he found it hard to believe he'd so nearly lost all vestiges of control. He could feel the heavy beat of Arren's heart and he smiled with satisfaction. She'd enjoyed it as much as he had.

Arren was horrified. She couldn't for the life of her understand what had gotten into her. How could she ever face him again? She made to move away from him, but he held her steady with his hands and lifted his head, a grin of blatantly male satisfaction settled on his firm mouth. "Does that answer your question, Duchess, or do you need another demonstration?"

It took her a minute to remember she'd asked him why he was looking at her with that odd expression in his eyes. She felt a blush creep all the way to the roots of her hair and she pushed him away, rolling to her side. "I don't think you should have taken advantage of me like that. I don't like to be teased."

He settled a hand on her shoulder and made her turn back to face him. "I wasn't teasing, Duchess. Believe me."

His eyes were unfathomable and she turned her head away to look intently at the horses. "I think we should ride some while we have the chance."

He sighed heavily. She clearly wanted the subject dropped. "It won't go away, Duchess. You're not going to be able to ignore it forever."

She looked back at him. "We'd both be better off if we tried." Brushing his hand from her shoulder, she walked back to her horse and mounted. She waited in silence while he packed up the leather bag and secured it at the back of her saddle. When he mounted, she allowed him to take the lead. He headed north, and she followed at a comfortable distance, forcing herself to concentrate on the passing scenery. But her willful mind continued to stray to thoughts of his hand caressing her skin, and his lips gliding slowly across her own.

Seven

They rode north for two full days. Several times, Duncan lifted Arren onto his saddle and let her sleep against him. She was beginning to wonder if and when he ever slept.

The tension that had developed after their passionate exchange on the hillside soon passed, and they talked of many things. Duncan kept her entertained with stories from his childhood, telling her about his boyish exploits and how his mother had struggled to keep up with him. She didn't miss the note of admiration in his voice when he talked about his father, but it was especially evident when he talked of his grandfather. She listened intently, wondering what it was like to have such a close family. She couldn't help feeling a little jealous, and wondered again who he could be. He was such an enigmatic man. He was obviously close to his family, though she gathered most of them were no longer living. He spoke of his mother in the present tense, though, giving her the definite impression she was still alive. Yet he roamed about the countryside, without thought nor bother to anyone who might wonder where he was.

Arren had noticed he grew visibly more relaxed the farther north they traveled, while she on the other hand was becoming more tense. She had already gathered he was from lowland country, despite his flawless Gaèlic, and he was clearly more at ease the farther they rode from his homeland. Arren now lived in constant fear that they would encounter someone who knew her. They were perilously close to her home at Grayscar. Her only comfort was that Duncan deliberately kept them isolated.

In a way, their journey seemed almost unreal. Two days had gone by since they'd encountered a living soul. Once, he'd left her protected by the trees to find more food, but she hadn't personally encountered anyone since their narrow escape at the croft. Time seemed to lose all meaning. She was unsure from one day to the next what time it was, or even how long they'd been riding. She was growing sore from sitting a saddle so long, and she hoped he'd decide to stop soon.

She got her wish. Duncan reined in his horse at the top of a small crest. The position allowed him to survey the land carefully. There had been no sign of their pursuers in two full days, and he fervently hoped they'd abandoned their search for Arren. The air was warm, and it was well past noon. Arren had shed her jacket, and her blouse clung to her body, damp from perspiration. There hadn't been any rain since they'd left the small village, and though thick clouds hung overhead, nary a drop had fallen.

He looked carefully at the sky. Arren sat in silence beside him. Despite the difficult circumstances, he'd enjoyed the last two days with her immensely. He found she had a broad knowledge of the surrounding countryside, and a delightful cache of folk tales that had originated in this area. He liked to hear her tell them. The soft cadence of her voice lilted with each word, and while they usually conversed in English, she told him the stories in Gaelic. Most of them were uproariously funny, and she usually left him laughing over one tale or the next. She talked little about herself, though, and despite his attempts to draw out personal details, she generally managed to change the subject.

Always at the back of his mind, though, was the realization of his growing attraction to her. Despite her argument to the contrary, he knew full well she hadn't been unaffected by their passionate embrace. Her heart had pounded against his, and she had responded to him with all the ardor he knew she felt. When he held her in his saddle, he found himself fighting the battle of his life with his undisciplined thoughts. He longed to feel the soft heat of her skin beneath his hands again, to taste the sweet, wet inside of her mouth. He groaned and shifted in his saddle. "Oh, hell!"

Arren shot him a startled look, misinterpreting his mumbled curse. "Do you think it's going to storm again?"

He smiled ironically. "Yes. It most certainly is going to storm again."

Arren sensed his odd mood and fell silent, waiting for him to take the lead once more. To her surprise, he dismounted and walked to her side. He held up his arms to her, and she slipped from the saddle, letting him lift her to the ground. "Why are we stopping?"

He pointed to the small croft below them. "Our food store is running low. It'll be another twenty-four hours before we come to another croft. I think it's best to replenish it now."

She nodded and reached up to untie the bag. She had now gotten used to living off of stolen food. She still couldn't fight a twinge of guilt, though, and she handed him the bag with her usual warning. "Don't take more than we need."

He smiled at her and slung the bag over his shoulder, striding down the hillside.

Their brief separations were getting fairly routine. Arren led the two horses into the thicket of trees to wait for him. Once she felt securely hidden, she turned back to watch him disappear into the small croft. She didn't fight the urge to admire his physique. His shoulders were magnificently broad. He had, she was sure, the widest chest in the world. She liked the way his red-gold hair curled at his collar, and the sun-bleached streaks in his whiskers. He was devilishly handsome, and try as she might, she hadn't been able to erase the feel of him from her memory. He was a dangerous man.

She felt safer with him than she had with anyone in her life. She smiled when she recalled his brief conversation with the horses at the mouth of the cave. Few men she knew would take the time to talk to two weary horses, no matter how much they needed the animals' cooperation. She reached up and patted each horse on the nose. They looked tired.

She considered it for a minute, and then decided to unsaddle them and let them graze for a while. Duncan wouldn't be back for at least a full fifteen or twenty minutes. She didn't think he'd mind a few minutes' delay when they had to re-saddle the animals. Reaching over, she unlatched the heavy buckles and lifted down each saddle in turn.

It might have been her imagination, but she would have sworn they looked at her gratefully. She made quick work of their bridles and harnesses, and watched sympathetically as they dropped their weary heads to graze on the scrubby grass underfoot. Pulling off their blankets, she carried them back to where she'd left the saddles. On the ground, next to Duncan's saddlebags, she noticed a white piece of paper had fallen out when she'd dropped the heavy leather pouches to the ground. She stooped to pick it up, her eyes widening when she saw the signature—"Brickston."

Aiden Brickston, the Duke of Albrick, was a well-known name in Scotland. One of the Highlands' modern-day heroes was the Duke of Strathcraig. Strathcraig and his longtime friend, Aiden Brickston, had distinguished themselves during the last decade in service to the Crown. And while the Duke of Albrick was English, he and the Duke of Strathcraig had both enlisted in the 2nd Dragoons, the so-called Scots Guards, to fight in the war against Napoleon Bonaparte.

Her eyes widened a little more when she thought of why Duncan must have this letter. The Duke of Strathcraig, she remembered now, was also named Duncan. Duncan McCraig. She shook her head. It simply couldn't be. She looked anxiously over her shoulder and slipped the letter back into the saddlebag, determined not to look.

She did everything she could think of to kill time, but every few seconds her eyes strayed back to the heavy leather pouch. Could the gypsy she'd hired really be the Duke of Strathcraig? It seemed incredible. Duncan McCraig was one of the most powerful men in Scotland. He had direct access to the British Crown, he was the second largest landholder in the country, and the richest in material wealth times two. She shook her head. He simply wouldn't be traveling across country on second-rate horseflesh stealing food and clothing as he went along.

She fingered the soft wool of her skirt thoughtfully—unless of course, he wasn't stealing it at all. She had, in retrospect, never really seen him steal anything. Her eyes strayed back to the saddlebag. Curiosity got the better of her. She looked carefully down the hill. There was still no sign of him. She walked back to where the pouches lay on the ground and reached in, pulling out the letter. Glancing over her shoulder once more, she opened the paper and read:

Duncan,
    Sarah and I were both grieved to hear of the loss of your father. I had no idea things were so bad in

*Scotland now. I wish there was something more I could
do to help.*

*As you requested, I have instructed Mac to have
The Dream Seeker ready for you at Inverness. He'll
be expecting your arrival.*

*If there is anything you need from us, you know you
have only to ask. Sarah and I both look forward to
seeing you soon, and while I wish it were under better
circumstances, you have yet to meet your goddaughter.
Cana anxiously wants to meet her benevolent godfather. We'll be awaiting your visit at Albrick Park.*

                                                  Brickston

Arren quickly thrust the letter back into the saddlebag
and sat down. Good Lord! He was! He really was the Duke
of Strathcraig. She had no idea how she should feel about
that. He hadn't lied to her really. Even that ridiculous part
about being a gypsy was almost true. If her memory served
correctly he owned some twelve or thirteen holdings around
the world, and he was forever traveling between them.

She pulled her knees up to her chest and chewed on her
lip. Why on earth would the Duke of Strathcraig be traveling like this? Arren thought back to the strange circumstances in which they'd met. He'd seemed to be as much a
fugitive as she. She smiled. It certainly explained why he
appeared to know everything about anything. How he'd
managed to elude human contact for over seventy-two
hours. How he could duck in and out of areas without being
seen, and certainly how he knew exactly where they were
going all the time. It explained why he could function on
little or no sleep, how hunger and pain didn't seem to bother
him. He'd learned some hard lessons during the war.

Her mind snapped to the night in the cave when he'd

suffered from his terrible headache. She searched her memory and remembered hearing that Strathcraig had sustained a near-fatal head injury during the Continental War. All the pieces were beginning to fall into place.

She still didn't have a viable reason for why he'd agreed to this bizarre journey with her, though. She thought back over all his unexplained comments. About how gratified he'd been at her reluctance to steal food and horses and supplies. About how amazed he'd been at her compassion for the poor families they'd had to impose on. Could it be that he was one of the few Scottish lords that still took seriously his duty to his people? Arren was loath to accept the explanation. She had yet to encounter one of those men. And yet, this was the same man who'd promised two weary horses a paddock of their own.

She smiled and rocked back, still clutching her knees to her chest. The Duke of Strathcraig. How completely amazing! She could see his white shirt now as he made his way back up the hill. Now that she thought about it, she wondered why it hadn't occurred to her before. Or for that matter, why he hadn't seen fit to tell her. She hadn't seen fit to tell him certain things either, though, and she supposed it was his right to keep the secret. She grinned as he drew closer. She certainly could have some fun with it, however.

Duncan reached her side and smiled down at her. She seemed to be in an odd mood, but he didn't press her. He'd purchased enough food to last them another three days, and he wanted to get moving before the rain set in. While he'd been in the croft, heavy thunderclouds had rolled over. It seemed the sky was finally willing to relinquish the rain it had clung to for the last several days.

He dropped the food next to her. "I see you've let the horses graze."

She nodded. "I didn't think you'd mind. It's going to rain again soon, though. I suppose we should probably start moving."

"Do you want to change back into your soiled clothes?"

She looked at him in surprise. She hadn't thought of that, but she would rather wear the ruined black skirt and vest than the more comfortable green habit he'd bought her. She smiled at him and rolled to her feet, bending over to pick up her satchel. "I think I will. You must promise not to complain of the smell, however."

He smiled back. "I think I'll manage."

Arren disappeared farther into the thicket and he bent to retrieve the saddles. When he picked up his saddlebags, the white letter tumbled out and he scooped it up hastily, sliding it deep into the bag and throwing Arren an anxious look. If she knew, she'd be bloody furious. It wasn't something he was prepared to discuss with her yet.

When she returned, he'd saddled and bridled both horses and strapped the leather satchels on back. She handed him her bag, and he attached it to her saddle before turning to help her mount. She didn't miss the way he wrinkled his nose at the mildew odor that clung to her clothes. She smacked him on the head. "You promised."

He shot her an unrepentant grin and mounted his horse. "Just see that you ride downwind." He spurred his horse into a gallop and Arren followed, content to study his back and marvel at her discovery.

They rode for several hours before he stopped again late in the afternoon. She noted the look of surprise on his face and rode up next to him. Below them, nestled into the hillside, was a large croft. Duncan had said they wouldn't pass another croft for twenty-four hours. He was clearly perplexed by its presence.

"That wasn't here before."

She looked at him in surprise. "Does it matter?"

"I suppose not. I just don't like surprises." He narrowed his eyes and studied the croft intently. It was a good way away, but even from their vantage point, the unnatural buzz of activity indicated something dreadfully amiss.

He was jerked from his reverie when he heard Arren utter a strangled cry of protest at his side. He turned to look at her, stopping short when he saw her horrified expression. "What's wrong, Duchess?"

She reined her horse around and pointed to the croft. He narrowed his eyes against the sunlight and finally determined the source of unrest. His blood started to heat.

In the late afternoon sun, he could see scores of people running about in frantic agitation. Several men on horseback sat in the middle of the small ring of houses. Duncan narrowed his eyes and could see the faint glow of lit torches in their hands. Seconds later, he heard an anguished cry and saw the thatched roof of one of the small cottages erupt in flames. He turned back to Arren. Her face was white as a sheet. She turned her eyes to him. "They're burning those people out of the croft."

He heard the anguished tone in her explanation and nodded. "I know."

She looked at him. "We have to do something."

"There's nothing we can do."

He watched her eyes darken to deep green pools of anger. She glared back and wrapped the reins tighter around her hands. "The hell there isn't."

She spurred her horse and took off at a dead gallop down the steep embankment. He growled in frustration and dug his heels into the flanks of his mount, charging after her. He didn't catch her until they reached the outskirts of the

croft. She was riding at a full gallop, and he reached out
and grabbed the reins of her horse, pulling back with
enough force to stop the huge animal from thundering into
the middle of the courtyard. They were in the very center
of the chaos.

All around them, sobbing women held frightened children while furniture and belongings were tossed from cottages and strewn across the ground. Pleas of terror and the
scent of fear permeated the air. It was thick with smoke
and the coarse shouts of the men who were clearly in charge
of the burning. Duncan looked around and finally identified
the man who appeared to be leading the effort.

He sat alone on his horse, watching the bedlam. Arren
had clearly found him as well, and had started off in the
man's direction before Duncan could stop her. He spurred
his horse and rode after her, thinking to keep her from getting herself killed.

She charged up the small knoll and stopped a few feet
from the startled horseman. He turned his angry stare on
her. She glared back. "What are you doing to these poor
people?" Her voice was hard and demanding, and he raised
an eyebrow at her audacity.

"That's none of your concern, woman. It's between their
laird and them."

"You cannot simply burn these people out of their homes.
Where will they go? How will they survive?"

He didn't answer, and Duncan rode up beside Arren,
studying the man intently. As soon as he'd ridden within
fifty feet, he'd recognized him as Magnus MacKerry. Duncan had served with him briefly in the 2nd Dragoons Scots
Guards during the war. The MacKerrys had long coveted
McCraig land, but he wasn't sure what Magnus was doing
this far north. He fervently hoped Magnus's memory was

not so clear and he wouldn't recognize Duncan in return. He was relieved when he saw no spark of recognition in Magnus's eyes.

Arren turned her head to look at Duncan. "Aren't you going to do something?"

He shot her a warning look. "The laird owns this land. There's nothing we can do."

Magnus glared at her. "That's right. Now be on your way. You have no business here."

Arren squared her shoulders and glared back at him. "I have business wherever there's injustice of this nature. I demand you stop this right now."

He grew noticeably angry. "And I demand you leave this land before I have you arrested for trespassing."

She would have retorted, but felt Duncan's hand clamp onto her arm in a vise-like grip. She turned to look at him. His eyes had darkened to a deep gold, and he stared her into silence. Magnus turned his angry stare on him and eyed him suspiciously. Duncan watched a flicker of something dangerous settle in the other man's eyes. He stared at him warily. "You look familiar to me," Magnus said. "Do you hail from around here?"

Duncan shook his head, intent on getting them both out of there in one piece. There was no telling what Magnus would do if he recognized Duncan. "Nay. My wife and I are just passing through." He ignored Arren's startled expression and continued to watch Magnus.

He suspected something. Magnus turned back to Arren and watched her closely. "Is this man your husband, indeed?"

She was about to deny that he was when she felt Duncan's fingers tighten on her arm. She looked at him in surprise and lied. "Yes."

Magnus turned back to Duncan. "Then take your wife and leave this land. You're not welcome here."

Duncan nodded abruptly and tugged Arren's reins from her hands. Without sparing her a second glance, he led her horse around and nudged his own mount into a slow gallop. Hers followed suit.

They had ridden a full ten minutes before he turned to her and handed her the reins. He was furious. She took the reins gingerly from him and looked at him. He would have turned to ride again, but she stopped him with a hand on his arm. "I'm sorry if I've made you angry. I couldn't sit idly by and watch that awful man burn those poor people out of their homes. They have no place to go."

"I'm aware of that," he clipped.

She sighed in exasperation. "All he wants the land for is sheep. He's sacrificing those people for money." She squared her chin when he didn't reply. "I still think we should have done something."

He glared down at her. "It was foolhardy, Arren. Had Magnus recognized me, you could have gotten us killed."

Her eyes widened. "You knew him?"

Duncan nodded. "That's why I was forced to lie. I'm not entirely certain we could have survived the encounter if he'd known who I was."

Arren was staring at him. "Why didn't you tell me you knew him?"

"I was too busy saving your neck at the time."

"You're overreacting. We weren't in any real danger."

"Weren't we? How would you know that, Duchess?"

She chewed on her lip. "Well, I couldn't just sit there and do nothing."

He glared at her. "You should have."

She glared back. "Haven't you any compassion for these people?"

"I have plenty of compassion. I just know better than to rush headlong into circumstances I can't control."

"All right. Fine. I made a mistake. Thanks to your self-professed superiority, we both survived. Can we forget it now?"

He sighed. "It isn't that simple."

She looked at him, a question in her eyes.

"We've now agreed, in front of witnesses that we're husband and wife."

She shrugged. "It's an unfortunate lie." When he glared at her, she continued, "You told it first."

He shook his head. "I told it to save our skins. An action that wouldn't have been necessary if you hadn't put us in that position."

She looked at him quizzically. "You confuse me, Gypsy. You'll steal horses and food, yet you won't lie about something so simple. I don't understand."

He sighed. "I had intended to use the lie periodically, when necessary. But never when you were present. I certainly never intended for us to be in a position where you'd have to agree with me." He could see she still didn't understand and he frowned. "You seem to have forgotten Scottish law, Arren. When a man and a woman say they're man and wife in front of witnesses, it's a legal and binding contract. You and I are now married."

He turned his horse and galloped off, leaving a horrified Arren staring after him.

Eight

Dear God! He was right! Arren stared after him in horrified fascination. Duncan had ridden a full hundred yards ahead of her before she took off after him. She had completely forgotten the odd twist in Scottish law that allowed for marriage by mutual consent. Even though there was no official record of their union, she was legally Duncan's wife. She grimaced at his back. He was clearly none too pleased with the arrangement.

Under Scottish law, their marriage wouldn't be too difficult to undo, it was true. There would be the issue of their unconventional association, of course, but by and large, a brief petition to the Prince Regent could easily repair the damage, particularly if the marriage wasn't consummated. She suspected, however, that his anger stemmed from another source. He resented her impulsive action at the croft, and considered their bizarre marriage contract to be a direct result of her boldness. She'd seen the horrors of evictions before, however. They never failed to upset her. Her compassion for the victims ran deep. For personal reasons, she found it difficult to hold her tongue at the gross injustices committed against helpless individuals.

Arren sighed again and studied Duncan's broad back. His surly attitude was beginning to irritate her. "Gypsy!" she shouted, deciding a direct confrontation was the best course of action.

He didn't turn around. If she hadn't known better, she'd have sworn he galloped faster. She squared her shoulders and tried again. "Gypsy!"

Duncan reined in his mount so abruptly, she nearly hurtled into the back of him. They were in the middle of a small clearing. Ahead, she could see the beginnings of the rugged Highland terrain. He was leading them north through the rocks, and while she didn't dare question his reasons, she knew their pace would have to slow considerably to negotiate the rough land that lay ahead of them. When he finally turned and looked at her, his glare was unreadable. Arren fought the urge to shiver. She raised her chin instead. "There's no point in staying angry!" When he continued to stare at her, she tried again. "There have been no signs of anyone following us all day. I think we could afford to stop and eat."

His glare hardened.

She wasn't daunted. "Why don't we head for the shelter of those trees, and I'll unpack our meal?"

If possible, his voice was harder than his stare. "We haven't time to stop. We have to make use of what daylight is left. If you're hungry, it'll have to wait."

He didn't wait for her to answer, but spurred his horse into motion once again. Arren stayed where she was and glared at his retreating back. So much for a peace offering. He clearly preferred to stay angry. She flexed her shoulders and started after him. The pain in her shoulders and back, coupled with her emotional and mental fatigue, was beginning to wear on her. The sun was sinking on the horizon, and she knew it would be dark soon. She assumed he would stop when darkness set in, and consoled herself with the knowledge she wouldn't have to ride much longer. Arren finally caught up with him and settled her mount to a comfortable pace just behind him. She checked the position of the sun and estimated they had no more than an hour before it was pitch black. She fervently hoped he'd make camp soon. She was looking forward to a good night's sleep.

They rode deep into the night. Arren couldn't remember feeling more miserable. One of her brothers used to say there were four steps to misery; cold, wet, tired, and hungry. She now added pain to the list.

Even the roots of her hair ached. The biting wind sweeping over the hills added to her discomfort. Each time an icy blast wrapped around her, it cut through the thin protection of her blouse and bit at her skin. They hadn't eaten since their midday meal, and the gnawing pain in her stomach soon lodged in her head, making her temples pound in agonizing cadence with the gait of her horse. She was completely exhausted from lack of sleep and mental fatigue, and when she felt a raindrop splatter on the bridge of her nose, she nearly lost what remained of her composure.

She was riding behind Duncan, becoming increasingly infuriated with him. He seemed completely unaffected by their arduous pace. He still sat his saddle as if he'd just mounted, and he galloped ahead of her at the same maddening pace he'd established that afternoon. He hadn't spoken to her again since she'd stopped him the first time, and he never once looked back to ensure she was still beside him. She had no doubt he'd be immensely grateful if she could somehow manage to fall off her horse and kill herself.

It wasn't long before she felt the sting of a second raindrop; then another and another, until the cold, driving rain was falling in earnest. She looked at Duncan and glared. He didn't seem to be affected by the rain, either. She couldn't help but notice how his curly hair retained its re-siliency even in the pouring rain. Her thick hair was soon plastered to her head. But not his. The light red curls looked wind-tousled, but dry. Hell, he'd probably decided not to allow his hair to get wet, Arren thought cynically.

The rain clouds obscured the moon, and Arren wondered how Duncan knew where they were going. The terrain had become increasingly rough over the past few hours, but he'd kept on riding at the same relentless pace, apparently not noticing or caring that their horses were tiring.

Arren was starting to hate him. No, she decided, she'd started hating him hours ago. She had long since resorted to counting the rhythm of her horse's hooves in order to stay seated in her saddle. The temptation to throw herself to the ground and end her misery was becoming stronger with each jarring impact.

She had no idea what time it was. For that matter, nor did she care. She was well aware that she wouldn't last much longer, and Duncan showed no inclination of accom-modating her. She felt a heavy drop of rain drip from the curls at her forehead into her eye and swore beneath her breath. Even her eyelids hurt. In the distance, she heard the rumbling sound of thunder and prayed that a bolt of light-ning would strike her dead.

It nearly did. The storm was moving quickly. The rain had begun to pour down on them in torrents and Arren could barely make out Duncan's figure ahead of her. She was shivering so violently now, she had to cling to her sad-dle with one hand to keep from falling off her horse. A huge bolt of lightning lit the sky and struck the ground not two hundred yards from them. The accompanying crash of thunder sounded for all the world like a scream of pain, and Arren decided the list of misery's symptoms must surely include fear as well.

They were riding down a steep incline, and another flash of lightning briefly lit the path ahead of them. Arren could see the swollen, rushing waters of a deep burn just ahead. Duncan was headed straight for it, clearly intending to cross it. The water was moving too fast. She confirmed that fear when a third streak of lightning flashed over the water. She knew she'd be swept away as soon as her horse entered the stream.

She briefly considered warning Duncan, lest he hadn't noticed how fast the water was flowing, but decided against it. He'd never hear her over the sound of the pouring rain and deafening rush of water.

Another loud thunderclap sounded overhead, and her horse jumped in fright. She struggled briefly to maintain control, her numbed hands gripping frantically at the reins. Ahead of her, Duncan was charging into the rushing burn, clearly expecting her to follow. She suffered a brief moment of hysteria when she realized her second marriage would be even more short-lived than her first, and she plunged in after him.

As soon as the icy water closed over her legs, she felt her body go numb. The tears welled up in her eyes, and she began to sob, as much from the pain as from fear. She clung desperately to the neck of her horse, nearly lying across the saddle. The water lapped at her chin, slicing at her tender skin, and the torrential rain beat down on her back. In the darkness, she could no longer see Duncan. She wondered briefly if he'd ridden off without her. Her last conscious thought was that she wasn't going to pay him a penny for taking her on this harrowing journey, after all.

Duncan caught her just before her body hit the ground. He'd ridden his horse through the swollen burn and turned to make sure she made it across. He saw the way she was lying across the saddle, and knew exhaustion had finally taken its toll on her. He'd been acutely aware of her for the last several hours. Most of his anger over the afternoon's events had waned, and his mood had improved immeasurably as they continued to evade Arren's pursuers. He'd kept his eye carefully trained for any sign of them all afternoon, and knew they had to be considerably far behind by now.

Arren hadn't spoken to him again since he'd refused to stop and eat. He was amazed at her tenacity. If she'd asked a second time, he would have stopped. He knew she had to be physically drained from the grueling pace they were keeping. She trained her mount just behind his, however, and had remained on his flank despite the rough terrain.

He was becoming increasingly concerned about the rocky ground they were riding on, and concentrated on guiding their horses through the smoothest areas. They couldn't afford for their mounts to go lame, and he knew how easy it would be for one of the horses to turn an ankle or throw a shoe on this kind of terrain.

The rain had been an answer to a prayer. The ground was already soft from the previous day's rainfall, and he knew their horses' tracks would be clear in the mud. A heavy rainstorm would wash away all evidence that they'd traveled this way, and if his bearings were correct, would swell the burn that lay ahead, making it impossible for riders to cross it for several days. When they crested the hill he saw the steep incline to the burn.

Across the burn—not more than four hundred yards away—was a hunting lodge. He owned it. He had won it in a card game ten years prior, and had only used it twice since. It was probably in deplorable condition, but it had a roof, a fireplace, and a bed; three things that sounded damned near to paradise at the moment. They would have to cross the burn, but he saw the rushing water in a brief flash of lightning and knew they could ride safely to the other side. It would soon be impassable, however, and anyone pursuing them from this side of the river would have to wait at least two days before the water abated.

He smiled and plunged into the icy water. In minutes they would be dry, warm, fed and have a place to rest. He was feeling better already. He felt rather than saw Arren ride into the burn behind him, and made his way across so he could offer her his assistance should she need it. As soon as his horse emerged on the other side, he turned and watched her. She was clinging to the saddle for dear life. He nearly plunged in to pull her to safety, but her horse was already emerging on the sodden bank next to his own.

He barely had time to react when she toppled out of the saddle. He leaned over his saddle and grabbed her around the waist before she landed headfirst on the ground. He knew from the limp feel of her body that she'd lapsed into unconsciousness. He pulled her against him, and reached for the reins of her horse. He could see the outline of the hunting lodge just ahead, and pressed his heels into his mount, fighting a sudden wash of fatigue.

Arren's body sagged against him like a rag doll, and he felt a surge of sympathy for her. He knew she was exhausted. His surly attitude had no doubt exacerbated the problem. In retrospect, he had known that the issue of their bizarre marriage wasn't an unmitigated disaster. They could remain husband and wife until they reached London. There, a brief audience with the Prince Regent would resolve the matter. His anger had been more of a reaction to her impulsive behavior than to their circumstances.

He sighed when he lifted Arren down from his saddle.

Whatever his good intentions might be, his attraction to this woman was indisputable. She curled into him like a sleeping kitten, and he didn't resist the urge to run his hand along her womanly curves. He kicked open the door to the lodge, and stepped inside, intent on settling Arren on one of the long sofas before he tended to the horses. He was surprised to find the interior relatively clean, and he laid her down carefully, looking around for a candle.

He found one by the hearth and lit it, scowling darkly at the room now illuminated by the candle's warm glow. The large room had been recently cleaned, betraying someone's presence. The room smelled of fresh beeswax, and the soft yellow light of the candle reflected off the polished wood surfaces. He ran his finger across the mantel and confirmed what he already suspected; only a light layer of dust, not more than three or four days' worth, had settled there. There was no reason for the lodge to have been cleaned. To his knowledge, no one on his staff even knew he owned the place, yet, it was clearly still in use. Mentally, he ticked off the days on the calendar and realized with relief that the peak of the fishing season was two weeks past. Whoever had availed themselves of his hospitality was probably long departed.

He set the candle down on a low table and looked at Arren. She appeared to be sleeping soundly, and he knew he would have to get their horses out of the rain before much longer. As soon as he stepped outside, he regretted the duty. The rain was pouring down in freezing torrents. As several drops splattered on his face, he felt the sting of ice. Even this late in the spring, freezing rain was common here. He noticed with some satisfaction that the burn had risen considerably since their crossing, and prayed the rain would continue through the night, swelling the small river even more.

Duncan grabbed the reins of both horses and started for

the small stabling area at the back of the lodge. The stable was small, only three stalls, but it suited their needs. Their departed visitors had left fresh hay in the stable, and he quickly unsaddled the horses, tethering each in its own stall with a fresh bucket of water. Pulling one of the heavy wool saddle blankets over his head, he tucked the other one under his arm and stepped back out in the rain, making his way through the mud.

Arren was still asleep when Duncan reentered the lodge. She had started to shiver violently from the cold, and he dropped the sodden blanket to the floor and gently unfolded the remaining dry one over her sleeping form. He turned to the business of lighting a fire. There was wood by the hearth, and he carefully laid the logs. His clothes were soaked. He inhaled the warm air deeply, enjoying the dry smell of the burning pine.

Behind him, he heard Arren sneeze. He walked over to where she was sleeping, and looked down at her. He knew the best thing for her was a hot bath and dry clothes, but, by damn, he loathed the duty of taking her clothes off.

He grinned at the irreverent thought. It wasn't actually taking her clothes off that made him balk. He'd already done that in his head nearly a dozen times. It was withstanding the temptation that would follow he didn't relish. She sneezed again in her sleep and he shook his head. Bending down, he lifted her in his arms once again. "Come on, Duchess. Just see that you don't claw my eyes out for doing my duty toward you." He hesitated, almost expecting her to answer him. When she didn't stir, he headed for the stairs.

The single bedroom was as he remembered it. The room was completely dominated by an enormous bed that stood in one corner. He smiled when he saw it, recalling how he'd remarked on its unusual size the first time he'd seen it.

"Good Lord, Brick! Five men could sleep abreast on that mattress without ever knowing the others were present," he had said. He and the Duke of Albrick, had been traveling in Scotland when they decided to stop in at the property. Both men had stood in the doorway, staring at the bed. Duncan had made that comment, and since then, the relative sizes of beds had become a continuing discussion between them. He made a mental note to tell the duke the next time he saw him that he'd actually spent his wedding night in that bed. Brick would no doubt find it riotously funny.

Arren stirred against him and he crossed to the bed. At the moment, there was nothing funny about it. She was nearly freezing to death. So was he, for that matter. He wasted no more time on silent reverie. He built another fire, and pulled the large metal tub in front of the flame. Crossing to the window, he threw open the casement, and reached for the rope. One of the most favorable features of this particular dwelling was the placement of the cistern. The reservoir was directly below the bedroom window, and one could draw water into the room without having to carry it up the stairs. He drew several buckets, emptying them into the tub until it was over half full. He pushed the tub closer to the flame to heat, filled some kettles with water and set them over the fire to boil, and turned to strip off his sodden garments.

His clothes were wringing wet. He peeled his shirt from his cold skin, shivering in the damp air of the bedroom. It took him only minutes to disrobe, and then he could avoid the inevitable no longer. Arren had sneezed two more times since he'd carried her to the bedroom. He crossed to the bedside with some trepidation, hoping fervently that she wouldn't awaken while he was in the midst of stripping her bare. He'd seen her when she was riled, and while her fits of temper generally amused rather than irritated him, he was in no mood for female hysterics tonight.

He reached down and unbuttoned the heavy buttons of her wool vest, and laid it open, exposing the row of tiny fastenings on her white blouse.

He grimaced. Their were dozens of them, and the wet buttons clung stubbornly beneath his fingers. He finally worked them loose, and didn't resist the urge to drink in the sight of her wet camisole clinging to her full breasts. Tiny goose pimples covered her skin from the cold. Disgusted with his lack of self-discipline, he wasted no more time divesting her of the rest of her clothing. He dropped the water-soaked wool skirt to the floor, and pulled her vest and blouse free, throwing them on top. Reaching for the hem of her shift, he slipped a hand behind her and tugged it over her head. When she lay before him, clad only in her high leather boots, he looked at her for several long seconds. The sight of her lying there was so erotic, he was almost painfully aroused. He swore beneath his breath and turned his attention back to the tub, mumbling recriminations to himself. He added a kettle or two of steaming water, then tested the water with his hand, satisfied that it was warm enough. It was still a bit cool, but at the moment, he decided a cool soak would do wonders for him.

He tugged Arren's boots off, trying to ignore the demands of his body, and lifted her in his arms, carrying her to the tub. Gingerly, he lowered her into the water and slipped in behind her.

He got his first good glimpse of her back. Dear God! He tipped her forward to get a better look. He swore beneath his breath. White and red scars crisscrossed her back in a sinister pattern. Arren seemed so delicate to him. She had an underlying strength, but she reminded him of a fragile flower that had somehow survived a brutal winter storm. It was not surprising. She'd been whipped within an inch of her life, and more than once.

He reached up to gently touch one of the scars. In the flickering light of the candle, he couldn't see them as clearly as he'd like. A flash of insight told him they were the reason for her odd reaction when he touched her. He was irritated. He had believed she was afraid of him. He now realized she was just afraid, period. He frowned at the realization.

With a heavy sigh, he picked up the cake of soap and gently lathered her back. He rinsed it carefully, looking for signs that any of the scars were fresh. A few had scabs on them, but none appeared to be open. He ran a finger up her spine, and watched her squirm against his touch. Even if she had killed the villain for doing this to her, it was no more than he deserved.

Duncan finished bathing them both before he pulled her from the water and wrapped her in a large towel. Carrying her back to the bed, he settled her under the blankets. He crossed the room and pulled a long robe from the wardrobe. He slipped into it, knotting it securely at his waist, pleased that the fire was beginning to take the chill from the air.

Outside, the storm still raged, and brief flashes of lightning split the darkness. Everywhere in the room, there were indications that the house had been recently occupied. The fire was already laid, the bed linens were fresh, and the entire room had only the thin layer of dust he'd seen downstairs.

Duncan lit one of the fat candles he found in the nightstand and placed it on the mantel. He was perplexed that someone had been here. There was no reason for anyone to have used the lodge recently. It would be a brilliant stroke of luck, of course, if the previous occupants had simply left the house clean and stocked. If they returned however, he would have to cut short his plans to stay here. He couldn't risk being seen near the property.

He rubbed the taut muscles at the back of his neck in frustration. Initially, he had only intended to stay the night. He estimated the flooded burn would give them sufficient protection at least twelve hours after the storm abated. He planned to be fifteen or twenty miles north by the time the river was fordable. He seriously doubted, however, that Arren would be ready to ride in the morning. She was exhausted from the brutal pace he'd set. He looked at the window, gratified to see the sheeting rain. Perhaps they could buy a little more time.

He walked back to the bed and looked down at Arren's sleeping form. She had curled beneath the blanket. He gently brushed a lock of her hair away from her forehead. He finally admitted what he'd denied to himself since he'd seen her scars. He was cold-bloodedly furious.

Somewhere in their odd journey together, he'd gotten it into his head that it was his duty to protect her. He wasn't inclined to consider the deeper implications of that, but he deeply felt a building fury over what she'd been forced to endure. He had an insatiable desire to shake her awake and demand the name of the man who'd inflicted those scars. At the moment, he'd gladly sink his fist down the bastard's throat if she'd give him the chance.

A steady rain continued outside, but the thunder and lightning had ceased. In the dying glow of the fire, Arren's hair was a deep copper color. Her thick braid slashed across the pillow, echoing the angry red marks that marred the creamy ivory skin of her back. He fought back a fresh surge of rage. He turned to toss another log on the dying fire. Lighting another one of the long tapers on the mantel, he walked back to her side, and hesitated. At the moment, he wanted little more than the softness of the bed and a few hours' sleep, but he suspected she'd be spitting mad when she woke up and realized he'd stripped and bathed her.

For the first time in the past three hours, he managed a soft laugh. He'd never envisioned spending his wedding night worrying over what liberties he could take with his wife. He dropped his robe and slipped into the large bed beside her, wondering what she'd do when she woke up beside him.

Nine

Arren awoke with a start. She was lying on her stomach on what she wagered was the softest bed in the world. She flexed her fingers into the mattress to make sure it wasn't a cloud. The steady cadence of rain on the roof brought back memories of their exhausting ride through the storm. She vaguely remembered riding through the flooded burn, but after that, her mind was blank.

She flexed her shoulders and winced. There was an unfamiliar tightness in her back. She rolled over, intent on discovering its source. When she rolled into Duncan's sleeping form, she sat bolt upright in bed with a startled scream.

He was immediately alert. He was out of bed, adrenaline rushing through his body, before he drew his next breath. When she saw his nakedness, she screamed again. It took him several seconds to recognize the source of Arren's distress. When he did, he collapsed onto the bed laughing.

She was clutching the sheet to her breasts, watching him in poorly disguised wrath. "How dare you laugh at me!"

He struggled to control his mirth with little success. "Come now, Duchess, you needn't sound so outraged."

"This is entirely indecent."

"There's nothing indecent about it."

"You're . . . naked." She paused. When he didn't answer, she sputtered, *"I'm* naked."

He laughed harder. "I take it that displeases you?"

She glared and tossed a pillow at him. "For heaven's sake. Cover yourself."

Her order earned another peal of mirth, and she tugged helplessly at the sheet. He finally wiped the back of his hand across his eyes to catch the tears of laughter. "We're husband and wife, Duchess. What could possibly be indecent about our being in bed together on our wedding night?"

"Don't call me that!"

He grinned again and stretched his arms, linking his hands behind his head. He knew she was acutely embarrassed. He found it a riotously funny diversion in light of their current predicament. "Call you what? Duchess or wife?"

She glared at him. He could see the fire in her eyes in the darkness. "You are completely without scruples."

"Completely."

"You have no sense of honor."

"None."

She lifted the pillow in her hand and swung it at him. She grinned smugly when she heard the dull *thud* of compacted feathers connecting with his head. "And your instincts are horrid. You should have deflected that blow. I don't see how I can expect you to defend me when you . . . OH!"

Duncan had wrenched the pillow from her hand and swung it around, swatting her across the legs in the middle of her tirade. He grinned at her. "And you think *I* have bad instincts."

"That's completely unfair. You blindsided me!" She grabbed the other pillow and brought it down on his head. When he dove for her across the enormous bed, she squealed.

Duncan's hand closed briefly around her waist, but she twisted away from him, tugging the sheet with her. She was nearly to the edge of the bed when he grabbed the trailing

end of the sheet, halting her progress. She pulled once. He
didn't budge. She pulled again. He didn't yield an inch. To
her dismay, Arren felt him begin tugging on the sheet. She
gripped it tighter against her breasts, but it began to slip
from her grasp when he yanked in earnest.

She shot him a disgruntled look over her shoulder, and
nearly laughed when she met his triumphant expression. He
was kneeling in the center of the bed, both hands clasped
on the sheet. Cautiously, she released one corner and felt
the material give way. He pulled again. With her free hand
she reached down slightly, delighted when her fingers
curled into one of the large pillows. He was pulling steadily
on the sheet now, and she whirled around, throwing him off
balance when she toppled toward him. He careened backwards, and she took advantage of his momentary lack of
equilibrium. When she struck him forcibly in the chest with
the heavy pillow, he slipped off the edge of the bed and
crashed to the floor with a loud *thud* and a deep groan.

Arren grinned with satisfaction and leaned back against
the pillows. She'd wiggled comfortably into place and
pulled the covers up, just as his head appeared above the
edge of the bed. She looked over at him with a smug smile.
"Bad instincts."

There was something odd in the look he gave her. She
didn't like it. He wasn't a man to give up so easily, and it
concerned her that he was still sitting on the floor. He disappeared again without saying a word, and she craned her
neck to get a glimpse of him. The huge expanse of the bed
blocked her view, so she wiggled a little closer to the edge.
She could barely make out his hand on the floor, and she
leaned farther over for a better look.

She sighed in frustration when the view proved to be no
better, and slid even closer to the edge. He was plotting

something. She was sure of it. She rolled up on her side, nearly to the edge, hoping to catch a glimpse of him on the floor. Before she had time to react, his arm shot up in the darkness and he captured her shoulder, pushing her back against the pillows and leaping up next to her. She had time for a startled squeal before she found herself trapped against the bed by his large body.

He was braced on his elbows, his heavy thigh pinning her thighs to the bed. He looked down and grinned. "Now who has bad instincts?" He wiped the hair off her forehead with his large hands. Her skin seemed absurdly soft to him. In the dying glow of the fire, he strained his eyes. He couldn't read her expression.

She poked an accusing finger in his chest. "You do have bad instincts. It doesn't matter one whit if I do. I'm not the one offering protection on this venture."

He snorted. "It's a good thing, too. You'd have gotten us killed by now."

"You're supposed to protect me. Not the other way around." She was trying to ignore the press of his naked body against her own. She was thankful for the small barrier the covers provided between them, and fought the urge to tug them higher. She knew he'd find a sense of victory in the action.

He tilted his head and continued to study her. The playful woman he now held captive was completely different from the woman he'd traveled with for the past four days. "Do you doubt my ability to protect you, Duchess?"

"Twice in five minutes I have caught you off guard, Gypsy. Is it improbable to suspect someone else could do the same?"

"I'd react more quickly if the weapon were more dangerous than a pillow full of goose feathers."

"Should I then test your skills with a pistol or a *skean dhu?*" She slipped one hand to her side, closing her fingers on the softness of a stray pillow. She gripped it, schooling her expression to remain casual.

He grinned. "I would advise you, madam, not to try either. I may decide you are no longer worth the effort of protecting."

"I suppose I shall have to stay with . . ." she paused, tightening her grip on her weapon . . . "pillows!" She connected it with the side of his head and he let out a startled groan. She convulsed with laughter at the dumbfounded expression on his face. He really did have bad instincts.

Duncan was delighted. He was seeing a completely new side of her, and deciding he liked it. He liked it very much indeed. He growled down at her and reached out a long arm, as his hand went groping for the heavy pillow she still clutched in her fist. She thrust it away from him, but his arm was longer than hers, and they were soon involved in a tug of war over the unlikely weapon. Duncan shifted away from her slightly to gain better leverage, and she took full advantage. Scrambling to her knees, the covers forgotten, she clutched the pillow with both hands and pulled. He retaliated in kind.

They were tugging desperately at both ends when it gave way. There was the brief sound of tearing fabric, then an explosion of soft white feathers filled the air over the bed. Duncan and Arren sat facing each other, momentarily startled. The feathers rained down on them, and Arren giggled, slinging her end of the torn pillow in his direction. When a cascade of feathers erupted into the air, he started to laugh. He shook the rest of his feathers out on the bed, and pushed a handful in her direction. She pushed back. Before long they were both collapsed on the bed in a fit of laughter, while stray feathers drifted down on them.

Arren sighed contentedly, and the action sent a cascade of feathers swirling into the air. She giggled, and tried the trick again.

Duncan was lying on his side next to her, his head propped on one hand. He was fascinated. She was actively involved in trying to keep a feather afloat above her nose, apparently oblivious to him.

"Stop looking at me like that, Gypsy. You'll embarrass me."

She didn't look at him when she said it, and he smiled at her. Evidently, she hadn't forgotten his presence after all. "How can you possibly be embarrassed? You've been romping about this bed with me for the past fifteen minutes."

She turned to look at him then, and he saw the embarrassed flush in her cheeks. "That was different."

The minute her eyes connected with his, a shiver raced up his spine. All traces of laughter disappeared from his eyes. He reached out his hand and pulled a feather from her hair. "And what is it now, Duchess?"

She ran her tongue across her lips nervously and watched his eyes darken in fascination. "Duncan, I . . ." She paused, unsure. He was so close, she felt the gentle fan of his breath across her cheek. The gold flecks in his eyes glittered in the firelight, and she swallowed past an unfamiliar knot in her throat. "I . . . I would like to get dressed now."

His eyes narrowed and he shook his head. "Don't do it, Arren. Don't pull back from me like this. Not now."

She stared at him, and he didn't miss the fear in her eyes. "I . . . I can't."

He shook his head again and leaned closer, his lips were mere inches from hers. "Why are you afraid?"

Her eyes widened and she ran her tongue over her lips again. How could she tell him? Her heart slammed against her chest. Her breath was coming in shallow gasps. "Please don't."

A sudden flash of lightning ripped the darkness of the room. The crash of thunder shook the house, and Arren jumped. Her hands came up to grip his forearms. The touch was electrifying to him. Duncan felt it all the way down to his toes. Her startled gaze locked with his. He sighed heavily. The moment had passed.

Bending his head, he dropped a soft kiss on her lips before he rolled to his feet and pulled on his robe. He looped the cord at his waist and turned back to the bed. Arren had slipped beneath the covers. He bit his lip to keep from laughing. The bed was still covered with the feathers and only her face was visible above the quilts. An erotic picture flashed in his head. He allowed himself to wonder what it would have been like to bury himself in her among that snowy cloud of feathers. He groaned, and pulled his unruly imagination back to the present. "I'm going downstairs to see if there's any food in the house. There's another robe in the chest."

She nodded, watching him carefully. "Thank you."

He didn't miss her meaning. "It's not over between us Arren. You know that."

Before Arren could answer, another clap of thunder rattled the windows and she jumped nervously, closing her eyes. When she opened them seconds later, he was gone. Evidently, he hadn't expected her to reply.

Arren sighed heavily and pushed the covers off. A cascade of feathers fell to the floor, and she laughed, burying her toes in them. When their downy softness caressed her skin, she sighed deeply, recalling her tussle with him. Even now, she didn't know what had possessed her.

But she found his reaction even more perplexing than

her own behavior. He had seemed to enjoy the encounter as much as she. He hadn't been even remotely irritated. She found it inconsistent with his previous demeanor. The thought elicited another giggle. If she thought his behavior odd, he surely must have thought she'd gone mad.

She sighed again and stooped to sweep up the feathers with her hands. She tidied the room as best she could by pulling the heavy quilt from the top of the bed and encasing the feathers in its folds. She tossed it to one corner of the room and crossed to the large wooden chest by the fire. A brief inspection yielded the robe he had promised. She slid into its voluminous folds. It was obviously a gentleman's garment. The sleeves hung a good six inches longer than her hands, and the hem dragged the floor by another foot and a half. She fiddled with it, trying several different ways to make it fit, before finally giving up and shrugging out of it. She wondered if he'd conspired to leave her with nothing to wear.

She turned back to the chest, and examined the contents again. Toward the bottom she discovered a white lawn shirt of equally huge proportions and a large piece of soft wool plaid. She smiled. These had possibilities.

She pulled the shirt on first, and rolled the cuffs four or five times until her hands extended beyond the length of the sleeves. The garment hung well past her thighs. She buttoned it all the way to the throat, and inspected herself in the mirror. It would serve very nicely as a sleeping gown, and she decided she would carry it with her when they left this place.

At the thought, her eyes widened, and she looked at herself in the mirror. The gypsy was beginning to have an effect on her. She had never stolen anything in her life until she'd come on this journey with him. Now she thought nothing of making off with another man's property. She grinned and turned her shoulder, inspecting the fit of the shirt from another angle. In this case, she would excuse it as defending her honor. As long as she carried a sleeping gown with her, Duncan could give her no valid argument why she shouldn't wear it.

Satisfied, she picked up the plaid. Crossing to the fire, she held it to the light and studied its pattern. It was a hunting plaid, comprised mostly of dark green and deep yellow threads. She recognized it as a McCraig pattern and smiled. Duncan would probably choke when he saw her wearing it.

Turning back to the mirror, Arren pulled the plaid deftly over her shoulder and pleated the remaining material into a skirt. Tucking the waistband into itself, she looked at her reflection and smiled. In the thirty-five years that traditional tartan dress had been outlawed in Scotland by the British Crown, many Highlanders had forgotten or lost the art of wearing plaids in the traditional manner. Fashioning the pleats was a complicated task, and now, most Highlanders preferred presewn kilts to the large pieces of seamless cloth that required hand pleating.

Arren had learned the art at the age of sixteen, largely for the satisfaction of spiting her father. He'd been on one of his usual tirades about her inadequacies when he'd suggested that she couldn't even pleat a plaid properly. It didn't seem to matter that he couldn't either.

She'd spent the next six days practicing the craft. Nanny had shown her how to fashion the pleats, and Arren worked at it for countless hours until she'd mastered it. She'd taken great satisfaction in wearing her plaid to dinner that evening. Her father hadn't noticed. She hadn't bothered to point it out.

She did keep up the art, however. She generally wore the traditional costume at the highland festivals and clan meetings, and through the years, she'd mastered it completely. She could now execute the complicated procedure in a matter of seconds. She turned and inspected her reflection, immensely pleased with the result.

The rain was beginning to pour again, and she sighed, wondering how long they could enjoy the shelter of the house. At the moment, the thought of riding out in the rain again was rather overwhelming.

She brushed it aside and turned her attention to her hair. She wrinkled her nose in distaste when she inspected the thick plait. The soft curls on the top of her head had dried fairly well, but the braid was matted and tangled. She fished back in the chest and discovered an ivory comb. As she began the arduous process of untangling her long auburn hair, her thoughts drifted to Duncan. He seemed always to be in perfect control. It took a good deal to rile his temper. She grimaced when the comb snagged in a knot of her hair. She pulled it free and looked at herself in the mirror. But, good Lord, he was surly when he was angry.

She pulled the comb through her damp hair a few more times and laid it down on the chest. Tilting her head, she studied her reflection. Duncan confused her. Her reaction to him confused her more. She wanted to believe that her attraction to him was due only to their odd circumstances and proximity. Try as she might, though, she couldn't bring herself to accept that.

He was different from any other man she'd ever known. Self-assured. Confident. Strong and capable, yet without a need to dominate her. He didn't need to belittle her to build himself up. He was determined, but patient. She chewed on her lip a minute before adding "devilishly handsome" to her growing list of his qualities. Yes, "Gypsy" Duncan was a remarkable man. And the truth was, he scared her to death.

Ten

Duncan slammed the wheel of cheese down on the wooden butcher's block. Good Lord, that woman was infuriating. She was the most complicated, annoying, unpredictable—he paused and plunked a bottle of wine next to the cheese—damned attractive woman he'd ever known. She was beginning to get under his skin.

He sighed heavily and began searching for glasses. He found them on a top shelf in the pantry, and with them he discovered plates, silverware and table linens. He added them to the growing pile on the butcher's block and returned to the pantry to examine the supply of salted meats.

There he found the note. Attached with a nail to the back door of the pantry, was a large white envelope addressed to "His Grace, the Duke of Strathcraig." Duncan grabbed the envelope and tore it off the nail. He checked over his shoulder. Arren was still upstairs doing God only knew what. The wax seal on the back belonged to the Marquess of Glenmore, the previous owner of the lodge. It was newly sealed, the paper not yet yellowed with age. He carefully split the seal and removed the heavy vellum note. The message made him smile.

Your Grace,
 I think it horribly rude of you to have cheated me

*out of this property and neglect it so thoroughly. I have
kept proper count these last ten years, and to date,
you have only deigned visit here twice. As the fishing
is excellent, the hunting better, and the location ideal,
I have taken the liberty of keeping the holding in
proper condition by using it once a year.*

*Each year I leave you this note. Each year, you
never arrive to read it. I suppose that means I will
return again next spring and make use of this very fine
estate you so readily neglect.*

Yours,
Glenmore.

Duncan smiled again and folded the note back into the
envelope. He would have to remember to thank Glenmore
when this bloody ordeal was over. Turning his attention
back to the pantry, he found a large portion of salt-cured
salmon and he carried it, along with the vellum letter, back
to the butcher's block.

A loud crash of thunder interrupted his thoughts, and he
shifted his eyes to the ceiling, wondering what on earth was
taking Arren so long. He decided to give her five more
minutes before he went looking for her.

Fifteen minutes later, she joined him downstairs. He had
moved restlessly back and forth between the kitchen and
the large entry room. Three times he had started for the
stairs. Three times, he'd talked himself out of it. She had
wanted her privacy when he left the room. If she needed
him, she would call.

He was standing in front of the fire when she descended
the stairs. Her long hair hung in damp waves to well below
the center of her back. The curling tendrils at the top of
her head framed her small face, and she was covered nearly

head-to-foot in a large piece of McCraig plaid—his plaid. An odd reaction began somewhere in the pit of his stomach and worked its way to his heart. He watched her walk down the stairs and felt the tightness settle in his chest. She seemed so perfectly suited to his plaid. He liked it. He liked it a lot.

She didn't like the way he was staring at her at all. He seemed to be rooted to his spot in front of the fire. She hesitated at the bottom of the stairs, unsure about his odd mood.

Another crash of thunder broke the tension. Arren gave a startled cry and Duncan crossed the room to stand in front of her. "Are you afraid of thunderstorms, Duchess?"

She looked up at him. His gaze was intense, and she had trouble meeting it. "Of course not." Her scornful denial was belied by her instinctive reaction to another loud crash.

He reached out to adjust the plaid at her shoulder. "Not many people can still craft a plaid by hand. I'm duly impressed."

He caught the startled light in her eyes before she smiled at him broadly. She seemed absurdly pleased with the simple compliment. "Thank you. It took me hours to learn this. I didn't think I'd ever master it."

He nodded. "It isn't nearly as easy as it looks."

She smiled again. Somehow it didn't surprise her that he would know the complicated procedure. He seemed capable of just about anything. It pleased her immensely however that he was perfectly comfortable complimenting her ability without boasting of his own. Yes, he was a remarkable man. A loud clap of thunder interrupted her reverie, and she started visibly. She reached for his arm.

He grinned at her when her small fingers clamped into his forearm. "For someone who isn't frightened by thunder, you certainly give a convincing performance." He nearly laughed when she jumped again as lightning split the darkness. Taking her hand, he pulled her toward the kitchen. "Come on. It's a good bit quieter in here."

He was right. The stone walls of the kitchen filtered the rumbling thunder much better than the rest of the house. Arren sifted through the pile of food and utensils on the table. "You found quite a bit of food here. Do you have any idea who lives here?"

He reached for the vellum note on the butcher's block, handing it to her. "Read this."

She examined the envelope, her eyes widening. "Good Lord, Gypsy. You've tampered with the Duke of Strathcraig's personal correspondence. Do you know who he is?"

Duncan shrugged and picked up a knife, slicing small wedges of the salted salmon.

Arren continued, unable to resist goading him just a bit. "Strathcraig is the second wealthiest landholder in Scotland. His estates are larger and more productive than any other except the Grayscar holdings."

Duncan looked up and popped a piece of salmon in her mouth.

She chewed on it. "He hash direc' accesh to the Regen'."

He grinned at her. "I told you not to talk and chew at the same time. It isn't at all proper etiquette." He slipped a piece of the salmon into his mouth and went to work on the cheese.

She glared at him and finished her piece of the fish. "I said, 'He has direct access to the Regent.' "

Duncan shrugged and tossed her a piece of cheese. "Does that matter to you?"

She rolled her eyes at him and bit off a piece of the cheese. She chewed on it for a long minute before she answered. "Of course it matters. You've tampered with his mail for heaven's sake. How do you think he's going to feel about that?"

"I don't think he'll mind so very much. Read the note."

"Just because you read it doesn't mean I have to. I don't relish the thought of angering Strathcraig."

He looked up and grinned at her. "Arren, if it will make you feel any better, I'll reseal the note when you're done. When I'm finished with the wax, His Grace will never know it's been opened." She looked at him dubiously and he added, "Besides, according to that, he never comes here anyway. I doubt he'll ever even read it."

"What do you mean?"

He sighed and pulled the letter from the envelope, handing it to her. "Arren, just read the letter."

"You're sure you can reseal this?"

"I'm sure."

She didn't doubt it. Lord knew he could do just about everything else. Finally, curiosity got the better of her, and she opened the note.

He watched her carefully while she read it. They were on dangerous ground, and he hated like hell to deceive her, but common sense warned him not to divulge the whole truth to her just yet. She finished the letter and looked up at him, a sparkle in her green eyes. "I read somewhere that gypsies are supposed to be terribly lucky. I suppose it must be true."

He started to laugh. "Arren, in less than a fortnight, we've been chased by dogs, nearly drowned, rained on, practically frozen, and forcibly married. I find one empty hunting lodge with stale cheese and salted fish and you decide I'm lucky."

She grinned and reached for another piece of the salmon. "I'm warm, dry, rested, and well-fed. That's all the way from misery."

He raised an eyebrow at her and she quickly explained the comment by repeating her brother's explanation. Other than the brief explanation Arren had given him in Robert Dunkirk's barn, it was the first time Duncan had heard her mention anything about her family or her background. He hesitated, hoping she'd give him more detail. She took a long drink of her wine and obliged his curiosity. "Donald was a loner. Even as a child. He liked to go out to the edge of our land and watch the ships on the horizon. He would sit up there for hours at a time. It used to make my father furious."

Duncan didn't miss the sadness that crept into her eyes and he held his breath, waiting for her to go on.

"Even as a child, Donald was always very unhappy. After Mother died, he drew back into himself. He and my father grew farther and farther apart." She paused and took another long drink of wine. "Still, it was no excuse for him to kill himself."

She downed the rest of the glass and Duncan sat perfectly still, watching her. The simple statement spoke volumes. She was still deeply pained by her past, and he knew instinctively she wouldn't give him any more details tonight. He mentally recorded the story and decided to examine it later.

She leveled her gaze to his and gave him a tremulous smile. "I'm sorry. I didn't mean to bore you with maudlin tales of my past."

He shook his head. "You didn't."

She reached over, grabbed a piece of the cheese, and bit off a large hunk. "Are you goin' to reseal tha' letter now."

He grinned at her knowingly and she shot him a quelling look before she shrugged and swallowed the cheese. "Old habits die hard." She paused. "Well, are you?"

He picked up the letter and the envelope in one hand,

and a clean knife in the other. He motioned her to precede him back into the entry room. "Come on, Duchess. I'll assuage your curiosity."

He walked over to the fire and seated himself on the hearth. "Come here and stand behind my shoulder."

She did. He handed her the letter and told her to replace it in the envelope. Arren watched in fascination as he heated the blade over the flame. After several long minutes, he pulled it out and carefully wiped the soot off the blade until it was perfectly clean. He reached for the envelope, and she placed it in his large hand.

Bending closer to the fire, he carefully aligned the wax seal on the envelope. Arren leaned over his shoulder, watching him intently. He suppressed a grin. He certainly was going to a lot of trouble to reseal his own damn letter!

He applied the hot knife to the split in the seal and held it there long enough to soften the wax. Deftly, he slid the blade clear and used the point to fuse the edges of the wax together. When he was finished he fanned it in the air several times to let it cool, and then handed it to Arren for her inspection.

She was fascinated. The seal looked completely unbroken. Not even the faintest crack showed in the wax. She lifted admiring eyes to his. "How did you do that?"

He shrugged. "Years of practice."

"I knew it. You're in the habit of tampering with other people's mail."

"Guilty."

She laughed at him. "And you're not the least bit ashamed of it either, are you?"

He grinned back. "Not the least. Actually, I picked up that trick because a friend of mine told me it would impress my lady friends."

She looked down at the seal again, admiring his handi-work. "He was right. It does."

He nodded. "It's good to know. I've never tried it for that purpose before."

"Well, let's hope the Duke of Strathcraig is just as im-pressed."

"If it works, he won't even notice."

"You'd better hope not. I think he'd be greatly displeased to find out we've been here."

He tilted his head and looked at her. "What makes you think so?"

She shrugged. "Even in the north we've heard things. He's the first Duke of Strathcraig, you know."

Duncan turned to add another log on the fire, unable to watch her during the discourse. "Is that so?" he asked over his shoulder.

Arren seated herself on the long sofa, tucked her feet under her knees, and resisted the urge to laugh at him. "Yes. He lived in England for the better part of the last fifteen years. As far as I know, he earned the ducal coronet for some act of heroism on behalf of the English Crown. No one knows any details, really."

Duncan sat down on the hearth and turned to watch her carefully. "Why not?"

She shrugged. "I don't know. His father was very re-spected, though. I hope he lives up to the legacy."

Duncan smiled. "I hope so, too."

She yawned and turned her attention to the window. The rain was still coming down in torrents, and occasional flashes of lightning slashed through the darkness. The flick-ering warmth of the fire, coupled with the wine she'd con-sumed at dinner and her lingering fatigue were beginning to take their toll. Her eyelids were growing heavy, and she yawned again, settling deeper into the sofa. "How long do you think we can stay here?"

Duncan didn't miss the hopeful note in her voice. He knew she was exhausted. He had no doubt she dreaded the thought of leaving the warmth of the lodge. In truth, he didn't relish it himself. He rose and walked to the window, watching the driving rain. Tiny beads of ice clinked against the glass. It was a good sign. "I think we can afford at least until morning. The burn's fully in flood. It may even keep us isolated a while longer." When she didn't answer, he turned from the window. She'd fallen fast asleep on the sofa.

Duncan carried Arren upstairs again and settled her in the bed. He pulled off the plaid, folded it neatly, and laid it by the bed. He smiled at the sight of her attired only in his shirt, and he pulled the covers up over her shoulders. "I'll have answers from you yet, Duchess," he whispered. "Don't ever doubt it."

He left the room, intent on taking further stock of the house.

Duncan spent the next several hours inspecting the lodge. In reality, he suspected they would have almost thirty-six hours before the swollen burn receded enough to allow their pursuers to cross. Fleeing had never appealed to him in the past, and he resented the thought of it now. He planned to keep every available option open.

Whoever those men were, they were dogging Arren's path. By now, they would have learned she was traveling with him, and they would be looking for a couple. It was becoming more and more difficult to evade them at every turn, and Duncan's patience had run out.

A brief inspection of the kitchen yielded an ample supply of cheeses and salted meats to last them until they reached Inverness. He smiled to himself. Arren would be relieved to know they wouldn't have to steal any more food. He hadn't really stolen any of it, of course. He'd actually paid handsomely for it all. Arren had merely assumed it was stolen.

He rubbed the taut muscles at the back of his neck and turned to look out the window. She was an amazing contradiction. Frightened of thunderstorms, but courageous enough to flee alone into the night when threatened. She was secretive, mysterious. Yet she was open with her emotions. She laughed and cried easily, loved to argue, and had a God-awful temper.

He raised a hand and stroked the whiskers on his chin. He hadn't shaved in over a fortnight, and his beard had become quite full. The thought made him smile. Given his present appearance, it wasn't so difficult to believe Arren hadn't a clue who he was. He regretted the deception more and more each day.

His eyes widened with a sudden realization. He trusted her. Completely. It was a startling thought. He didn't come by the emotion easily. It was odd indeed that he would trust her so readily after only a few days.

He shook off his silent reverie and turned his attention back to the matter at hand. Within another hour, he'd packed and prepared two bundles of provisions, including enough food to last them until Inverness—together with two fresh changes of clothes. Arren would have to make do with a pair of boy's breeches he found in one of the trunks. One of the Earl of Glenmore's guests must have left them behind. They each had fresh shirts, though. Small comforts were becoming more and more important.

He carried the bundles upstairs to the bedroom and placed them by the door. Arren was curled up beneath the blankets, oblivious to his presence, and the storm that raged outside. He shook his head and continued his inspection of the room. The east wall provided what he sought.

The walls of the original structure were stone. Glenmore had done several renovations, however, and in the interest of warmth, he'd had wood paneling added to the walls. The paneling was attached to heavy wooden beams spaced approximately six feet apart. The fit would be tight, but effective.

He carefully pried one of the panels away from its supporting beams, taking care not to split the wood. The space between the stone wall and the panel was less than two feet deep. He studied it carefully.

Arren would be able to hide in the space with no problem. He grinned ruefully. She'd probably gripe to high heaven about it, too. He examined the panel again, testing its weight carefully. Satisfied, he set it to the side and turned back to the window. It was still dark outside. He'd lost all track of time since they'd come to the lodge. He looked at the clock on the mantel, and strained his eyes in the darkness to determine the time. It was just after four o'clock in the morning. He yawned. The rain continued to fall in steady torrents, and he sighed, leaning his hand against the window frame, praying for the rain to continue.

Eleven

It stopped. Duncan opened his eyes and listened intently. The rain had definitely stopped. He was sitting on the long sofa in the bedroom where he'd temporarily dozed off. The sudden silence startled him.

He squinted as he looked out the window. The sun was creeping over the horizon, and the trees glistened with the previous night's rain. Duncan sighed wearily and shifted his eyes to the bed. Arren was still curled beneath the blankets, fast asleep. He studied her for a long minute. Her hair was spread across the pillows. For the moment at least, she seemed unafraid.

He rose to his feet and stretched the muscles in his shoulders and back. Mentally, he ticked off the days since he'd left Strathcraig. It was probably Thursday, though he wasn't prepared to wager on it. In either case, they were a good four days out from Inverness at least. According to his arrangements with the Duke of Albrick, Aiden's yacht should already be moored there awaiting his arrival.

He smiled to himself. He doubted seriously that Aiden's crew would take kindly to the thought of having Arren on board. He still hadn't decided what he'd do when they reached Inverness and he was forced to explain how and why they'd be boarding the yacht. The vessel was an engineering marvel, and it would be difficult to convince Arren that he'd managed to procure free passage for them. She'd have to be gullible to believe a tale like that. He shrugged, and winced at the tight knots in his shoulders. He would simply have to think of something plausible when they arrived at Inverness. For now, they had four days and a pack of hungry dogs to contend with.

Duncan walked to the side of the bed and studied Arren's sleeping form. It was a miracle that she'd held up so well. He knew she'd been miserable. The rain had helped them elude her pursuers, but had severely hindered their progress and comfort. It was a wonder neither of them had developed pneumonia from the cold, wet weather.

Carefully, he reached down and brushed a lock of her deep red hair from her forehead. She yawned sleepily and turned her face into his hand with a contented sigh. He smiled. She'd be horrified if she knew she'd done that. "Duchess . . . Duchess, wake up."

Her eyes slitted open and she glared at him. "What do you want?"

He raised an eyebrow. Her voice sounded raw. "You sound like you swallowed a frog."

"Thank you!" She raised a hand and rubbed at her throat gingerly, and groaned at the dry parched feeling. She had a bad cold.

"Do you feel all right?"

She opened her eyes and glared at him again. "Of course I feel all right," she snapped. "Why shouldn't I? Just because I've ridden for three days in freezing rain without any sleep is no reason why I shouldn't feel on top of the bloody world." She sat up in bed and her head swam from the pressure between her ears. Raising her hand, she massaged her temples and groaned again.

Duncan laid his hand on her shoulder and pushed her

back down on the bed. Tugging the covers up to her chin, he grinned at her. "No play time for you today, Duchess. You're staying in bed."

"I thought you said it was time to get up." The words were barely above a whisper this time, and Arren didn't bother to open her eyes.

Duncan laid his hand across her forehead. She definitely had a fever. "It was. I've changed my mind."

She sniffled loudly and pushed herself up with one hand. "If it's time to go, it's time to go. I won't have you slowed down because of me."

"And I won't have you dead because of me. I'd have a hell of a time explaining that to the authorities." He pushed her back on the bed.

She sat up again. "Then why don't you go on without me. You've gotten me this far, I'll pay you for your journey when I reach London."

He pushed her down. "By God, you're stubborn! I can't very well abandon my wife in the middle of nowhere, now can I?"

Her eyes flew open and she started to raise herself back up. He pulled her hand out from under her and she flopped back against the pillow. "I see you've forgotten that detail."

She grimaced. "I didn't forget. I was hoping you had."

He shook his head. "Not a chance, Duchess. Not while there's still unfinished business between us."

She closed her eyes again and hoped he would think the sudden blush that suffused her cheeks was attributable to her fever. She coughed once and groaned, rolling to her side. "I feel rotten."

"I know. I'm sorry."

She sniffled and rubbed her cheek against the pillow. "We can't afford to stay here any longer. The rain's stopped. I'll be all right in another hour or two. Perhaps we can leave then." She didn't really believe it, but hoped she could convince herself it was true.

Duncan sighed and sat down on the side of the bed, reaching out to run his large hand gently up and down her spine. She moaned at the exquisite feeling and curled against him. "No. We'll stay here for now, Duchess. What you need is another twenty-four hours in bed."

She shook her head. "We can't do that."

"The burn will stay properly flooded at least that long. It'll give us adequate protection until tomorrow morning."

Arren rolled to her stomach to give him better access to her spine. "But that's not what you planned, is it?"

"I had hoped to gain some ground today if we could. But I have an alternative arrangement in mind. In the long run, it's probably better."

She moaned and squirmed against the firm ministrations of his fingers. It felt so damn good to be in this bed, warm, dry, and at least safe for the moment. In some corner of her mind, she knew Duncan wanted to move on today, but her body cringed at the idea of facing another day in the saddle. Turning her head to the side, she opened one eye and looked at him. He was staring out the window, seemingly lost in thought. She sniffled, trying to ignore the raw feeling in her throat. "Gypsy . . ."

He turned his head and looked at her. "Hmm?"

"Thank you."

He smiled slightly and continued the mesmerizing movement of his hand along her spine. "Go to sleep, Duchess. We'll talk about it later."

Arren dropped her head back onto the pillow, mumbling something unintelligible about his autocratic attitude. It took less than a minute before she was asleep.

Duncan tucked the covers around her shoulders and rose from the bed, his decision made. He had hoped they could leave the lodge this morning, but Arren's health clearly prevented it. He wasn't willing to risk making her sicker than she already was. She groaned in her sleep and rolled back onto her side. He shook his head. If he'd goaded her, she probably would have ridden today just to spite him.

Satisfied that what Arren needed most was rest, he turned his attention to his preparations for the arrival of Arren's pursuers. In a way, he rather relished the thought. Once he came face to face with them, he'd have a better feel for what he was dealing with. He didn't like this game of cat and mouse they were playing, and he felt it was high time he turned the tables.

He walked down and surveyed the burn. It was still flooded well above crossing level, and would probably remain so until at least the following morning. He squinted his eyes and looked up at the cloudless blue sky. It was shaping up to be a relatively warm spring day, though. That wouldn't help matters any.

He walked back to the barn to check on the horses. He hadn't had time to look them over and brush them properly when he and Arren had arrived, and he spent the better part of the morning lavishing much-needed attention on each of them. They showed only slight signs of fatigue. One had a bit of heat in a tendon, and the other had a loose shoe. He tended to both problems, aware that they, too, would benefit from the much-needed rest.

It was noon before he returned to the house again. He'd worked up a proper sweat in the stables and his stomach was rumbling. When he threw open the door of the lodge, he froze, his expression moving rapidly from surprise to anger.

Arren was in the middle of the large entry room, her voluminous shirt tied at the waist, clad in the boy's breeches he'd bundled the previous night. She'd wrapped her hair in a soft piece of wool to hold it off her face, and she was bent over a steaming tub of soapy water, a pile of sodden laundry next to her on the floor.

"What the hell are you doing?"

She looked up and smiled, wiping the sweat from her forehead with the back of one soap-covered hand. "Washing the clothes. We don't have many, you know. They needed cleaning."

He scowled. Her voice still sounded like silk over gravel. "You're supposed to be in bed," he clipped.

She leaned back again and shrugged. "You were working. Why shouldn't I?"

"Because you're the one who's sick. Dammit, Arren, you're going to make yourself seriously ill if you don't get some rest."

She reached back into the water and wrung the white shirt, sending soapy streams running down her elbow. "I already told you, I'll be fine. There's really nothing to worry about. I just want . . ." She yelped when she felt his fingers curl into the back of her waistband and lift her off the floor. He tossed her briefly in the air, and caught her against his chest. His arms locked around her like steel bands. "Put me down!"

He glared down at her. "I don't want to have this discussion again. Do you understand?"

She struggled briefly, trying to break free of his grasp, but he was already halfway up the stairs before she realized the futility of it. He carried her down the hall in angry strides, ignoring her rambling protests. He kicked open the door. What he saw made him swear darkly beneath his breath. Arren had unwrapped each of his carefully tied bundles, taking all the clothes and the two woolen blankets downstairs. She'd stripped the bed and heaped the laundry in the center of the room, no doubt with the intent of washing that, too. He looked at the bed. She'd already put fresh linens on it, and the pillows lay in neat order against the massive headboard. Only the one they'd burst the night before was missing.

He sighed and carried her to the bed, dropping her down on the soft mattress. Glaring at her for a long minute, he crossed the room to stoke the dying embers of the fire.

"For heaven's sake, Gypsy! It already feels like an oven in here now. What are you . . ." She cut off the protest when he turned his head and glared at her. Arren sat up on the side of the bed and watched him warily. She really did feel unwell, but she hadn't been able to listen to him working in the stable and simply lie in the bed all morning. Scrubbing out the laundry had been a way to keep her mind and body occupied and her thoughts away from her mounting fears. Evidently he didn't understand that.

Duncan took a deep breath and turned from the fire. Arren was watching him, trepidation in her eyes. He walked back to her side, dropping to one knee in front of her. He ignored her look of surprise and tugged at her boots. The soggy leather gave way, and he pulled the boots off, and dropped them to the floor. He paused briefly and massaged the ball of each small foot with his thumbs. Arren moaned and closed her eyes.

Duncan stood up and pulled her to her feet only long enough to peel off her breeches, despite her protests, and help her crawl back into bed. Arren slipped between the sheets and sighed when he pulled the heavy quilts up to her chin. He really didn't understand that it was hot in the room. She thought to explain it to him, but a sudden chill raced up her spine.

Duncan could feel the sweat running down his back. It was a bloody furnace in here, but he hadn't missed the pallor of Arren's skin, or the nearly scalding heat of her hands. Her fever was running fairly high, and he knew she'd soon be suffering from a severe case of chills. His eyes narrowed when she shivered and clasped the blankets closer. He had to resist the urge to remind her that he'd warned this would happen. He sat down on the side of the bed and watched her instead.

Arren was growing nervous. He clearly had no intention of leaving, and she was starting to become uncomfortable under his steady stare. "Why are you staring at me like that, Gypsy?"

He narrowed his eyes. "What makes you think like you do, Duchess?"

She tilted her head to one side. It was an odd question. "What do you mean?"

"I mean what makes you push so hard. You feel ill. It's written all over your face. So why the hell are you running about doing the damned laundry."

She shrugged and would have turned away from his piercing eyes, but he reached up and grasped her chin, forcing her to meet his gaze. "Why, Duchess?"

"It was just something to do. Why are you making a monumental . . ."

He squeezed her chin, interrupting her. "Why?"

He watched with something akin to amazement as her lip wobbled slowly. He could feel the tremor in her chin and realized she was close to tears. He'd never really seen her cry before, not in any circumstances, and he sure as hell hoped she wouldn't start now.

One tear slid down her cheek before she squared her jaw and reached up to push his hand away. "I'm afraid."

He blinked. She'd delivered the statement so matter-of-factly, it took him a moment to absorb it. "Why?" he asked again, his tone much softer this time.

Her eyes widened in amazement. "They're out there. They're going to find me. And when they do, not even you can stop them."

Duncan shook his head and leaned forward, pulling her against his chest. He tucked her head securely in the crook of his shoulder and sighed. "Arren, you're worn out. You don't feel well, and you're letting it cloud your judgment. Nothing's going to happen."

She pushed ineffectually against his chest before surrendering to the secure feeling he gave her when he held her there. "How can you say that? You don't know. You don't know any of it."

He reached up and ran his fingers soothingly through the long tresses of her auburn hair. "Only because you haven't told me."

She sniffled pitifully. "I can't."

"Arren, I have everything under control. I have up until now, haven't I?"

She nodded against him and sniffed again.

"Then why are you so worried?"

"It was different before. We were moving. I didn't have to think about it then."

He rolled his eyes, she was barely making sense, and he knew her confusion was attributable more to her fever and her fatigue than anything else. "You don't have to think about it now if you go back to sleep."

She shook her head. "We're trapped here."

"We are not."

"Yes, we are. And it's my fault."

He pushed her away from him slightly so he could see her face. She looked miserable. "Arren, lie down. I want to show you something."

She looked at him suspiciously but leaned back on the bed. "What?"

He rose from the bedside and crossed the room to the panel he'd removed and inspected last night. Lifting it down carefully, he showed her the space inside. "Do you know what this is?"

She shook her head.

"It's the space between the old stone walls of the house and the modern paneling. I discovered it last night. Do you know what we're going to use it for?"

She shook her head again.

"When the burn is no longer flooded and your friends get here, you're going to hide in this space. I'm going to go downstairs and get rid of them. Once they're convinced you're not here, they'll continue riding north." He paused to see if she was still listening. "They'll be ahead of us, Arren. We'll have all the time we need to reach Inverness."

She shook her head. "You can't possibly face them alone. How are you going to do that?"

He rolled his eyes and replaced the panel. "For God's sake, Arren! Just go back to sleep and trust me on this. I'll handle it."

She snuggled farther back into the pillows, fighting a yawn. "I'm still afraid."

He walked to her side of the bed and smoothed the sweat-dampened hair off her forehead. "Nothing's going to happen to you. Just go to sleep."

She shook her head, and he watched her eyelids droop. "You shouldn't make promises you can't keep, Gypsy."

Duncan waited a long minute before he answered. Her eyes had drifted shut, and he saw her chest rise and fall with the slow deep breaths of sleep. "I never do, Duchess."

Twelve

Duncan removed the small gold loop from his ear and dropped it in the trunk. Checking his reflection in the mirror, he studied it carefully. He wore the white wool shirt he'd purchased from the weaver a few days back. He smiled and brushed an imaginary piece of lint from the shoulder. In truth, he was glad Arren had washed it. He had pleated the large McCraig plaid that Arren had found in the chest at his waist and secured it midway down with a bone and gold pin. His hair was freshly washed and combed, though he'd decided to leave his whiskers. A fur sporran hung jauntily at his waist, and he tucked a jeweled handled *skean dhu* into the top of his stocking. The soft leather boots he wore completed the look and he eyed it critically.

"I think this is a very stupid idea, Gypsy."

Arren's voice came from behind him where she was sitting up in the bed. God's truth, she sounded worse than she had yesterday morning, but she claimed the twenty-four-hour rest had worked wonders. Her fever had broken during the night, and he'd satisfied himself that she was no worse off than a stuffed head and a hoarse throat.

He turned his head and grinned over his shoulder. "I think I play the part of the nobleman on retreat rather well, don't you?"

Arren suppressed a smile. Actually, he was awful at it.

He didn't fit the image of any nobleman she knew. She was glad he was looking the other way and couldn't see the mischievous glint in her eye. "No one in their right mind is going to believe you're the Duke of Strathcraig."

He continued studying his reflection in the mirror, and tugged the loose black cravat at his neck a little tighter. "You'll have to hope I can do a better job of convincing them than I can you, Duchess." Duncan didn't dare turn around and look at her. He was likely to burst out laughing if he saw the skeptical look he knew he'd find on her face. He continued fiddling with his cravat instead. "I think we should go over the plan once more."

Arren sighed and leaned back against the pillows. When she'd awakened early this morning, Duncan had taken great pains to walk her through the house and explain in detail what he planned to do. They'd repeated the details at least a dozen times. She was beginning to understand why he had been so successful as an operative for the British War Department. Nothing escaped his attention. He wanted to be damned sure nothing escaped hers, either.

She sighed again. "You're going to help me into the space behind the panel when you see them approaching."

"Don't you think this would be as good a time as any to give me their names?" he interrupted.

Arren glared at his back. They'd been over this a dozen times as well. She wasn't entirely sure what they'd tell him until they got here, and she wasn't inclined to give away more than she had to. "You're on retreat, remember? You aren't supposed to know who they are."

Duncan cast her an exasperated look. "All right. Go on."

"You'll help me into the panel and loosely hammer the nails so I needn't worry about it falling off." She'd tried leaving that detail out once, and he'd made her repeat it three or four times so she wouldn't forget it again.

"That's right." He bent to adjust his stockings and boots. "And you're to stay there until when?"

"Until you come to get me out."

"Or?"

She puckered her brow. That wasn't part of the original plan. "There is no or."

He turned around and looked at her intently. "That's right. There is no 'or.' Under no circumstances whatsoever are you to leave that panel. Understood?"

"But, Duncan, what if . . ."

"No circumstances. Nothing's going to go wrong. There are no ifs."

She watched him speculatively. He was pretty damn sure of himself. In a way, she was rather glad. She found his arrogance rather calming in an odd sort of way. Duncan interrupted her reverie. "All right, what's next?"

"You'll go downstairs and attempt to convince them that you're the Duke of Strathcraig and you're on retreat here."

He overlooked her deliberate effort to goad him and nodded, waiting for her to continue.

"They may search the house, but once they leave, you'll come upstairs and let me out."

He nodded and walked over to sit down facing her on the side of the bed. He hadn't missed the way she was worrying the edge of the quilt with her hands, and he knew she was still exceedingly agitated. He grasped the quilt and pulled it free, his gold-flecked eyes staring intently into hers. "There's nothing to worry about, Arren. I've promised you nothing's going to happen to you."

She sank her teeth into her lip to prevent it from trembling. "You don't know that."

He tugged her against him, and wrapped his arms around her, cradling her gently to his chest. "I do know that. You have to trust me, Duchess."

She shuddered once, drawing a deep breath against his neck. She'd have given half of all she owned to stay right here, isolated and secure. It wasn't possible, though, and she resolutely pushed away from him, unwilling to surrender to her need for comfort. "How long do you think we have?"

Duncan studied her for a long minute before turning to check the position of the sun through the window. She was a perplexing woman. He didn't know who these bastards were that had worked her into such a state of unmitigated terror, but he had a good mind to kill the lot of them and be done with it. He squinted his eyes against the bright light and gauged the sun's distance. "It's about half-past seven o'clock. I think they'll be here in an hour or so."

"Did you think the burn would lower this quickly?"

He shrugged and looked back at her. "It was shallow to begin with. There wasn't much of an embankment to trap deep water. It flooded the area around it and dissipated."

She nodded and resolutely changed the subject. "I'd like to have a bath and get dressed now."

He reached up and brushed a strand of hair behind her ear. He found it riotously funny that she persisted in throwing him out of his own bedroom. He refrained from pointing that out to her, however. "Do you want something to eat?"

She shook her head. "I'm not very hungry."

"All right. You have time for a bath if you don't linger. I've already drawn the water for you. It should be hot by now."

"Thank you."

Suddenly, he reached up and caught her face between his hands. He was tired of the inane conversation, tired of combating the walls she erected around herself for protection, and especially tired of fighting the attraction between them. Her gaze flew to his, burning a path to his soul, and he breathed her name on a sigh, lowering his lips to hers for a long, hot, possessive kiss.

Arren was stunned. Duncan hadn't touched her since their first night in the house, and she'd long accepted that any desire he felt for her had evidently cooled. She'd almost succeeded in convincing herself she wanted it that way, until she'd felt his lips settle on hers in this searing kiss. She sighed and leaned into him, wrapping her arms around his neck. She couldn't have fought her need to be close to him even if she'd wanted to.

Duncan groaned his pleasure at her small surrender and moved one arm around her back to anchor her to him. His hand still rested at her cheek, and he moved his thumb down to her chin, forcing open her mouth. When her lips parted to give him access, he swept his tongue into her hot, sweet mouth and drank in the taste of her. He could feel his temperature rising, and knew this had to stop. If he didn't pull away now, he wouldn't be able to.

He lost any shred of reason he still possessed when he felt Arren's tongue duel restlessly with his. He growled his approval and allowed her to explore the inside of his mouth. Her tongue was hot and wet and he sucked on it, wringing a moan from deep in her throat. Duncan trailed his hand softly down the side of her face, across her shoulder, and over her collarbone, finally settling on the swell of her breast. She swelled to fill his palm and he groaned, gently kneading the soft mound with his fingers.

In the pit of her stomach Arren could feel a knot expanding. His touch was magic, filled with sensual promise, and she longed as she never had in her life to surrender to it.

She moaned deep in her throat and leaned fully against him, as she let her hands splay across his wide shoulders.

Duncan sighed and lifted his head, running his finger gently over her swollen mouth when she whimpered in protest. Arren's emerald green eyes were locked with his and he stared into them, seeking answers.

She was spellbound by the gold fire in his gaze. The tiny gold flecks in his eyes intensified and bored into her, leaving her vulnerable and exposed. She blinked, shielding her emotions from him. Duncan watched the shutters drop back into place and sighed again. "Arren, this thing between us can't be ignored much longer."

She pushed against his chest and broke the embrace, ignoring the heated blush she felt creeping up her face. "There is no thing between us. We're trapped in unusual circumstances. Once those circumstances cease to exist, everything will return to normal."

Duncan stared at her a minute longer, fighting an urge to haul her back into his arms and erase the ridiculous notion. He very much doubted the attraction between them would be so easily remedied. Arren didn't sound particularly convinced, either, but her desperation to believe it was beginning to wear on his patience. He leaned his face down just inches from hers, his gold-flecked gaze locking with her cool green one. "I hope you do a better job convincing yourself of that than you've done of convincing me, Duchess."

Arren stared after him as he left the room. It took her several long minutes after the door clicked shut to make herself move. Throwing off the covers, she pulled herself out of bed and crossed to the large mirror. She looked a mess. Her hair was rumpled from her fitful sleep the night before, and her lips were still swollen and warm from Duncan's kiss.

She trembled, **and** raised her finger to run it gingerly over her mouth, **remem**bering how his touch had scalded her there. As much as she wanted to deny it, she knew he was right. The attraction between them was potent. He had only to touch her to make her come alive, but her reaction to him was as frightening to him as it was powerful. If she allowed it, he could hold her captive with that power. The thought made her shiver. No, that wouldn't happen ever again. No matter what it cost her, she wouldn't permit it.

Arren tugged her heavy thoughts back to the present with some difficulty. No matter how hard she tried to concentrate on her bath, her unruly mind continued to stray to a pair of intense gold-flecked eyes. She felt the goose pimples raise on her flesh and sighed in irritation. The sooner they reached London, the better off they both would be.

She was finishing her plait when he knocked and entered the room. She turned to him, her eyes locking with his. He saw the way she clamped her teeth into her lower lip and he cursed beneath his breath. The more he saw of Arren's courageous and fiery spirit, the angrier he became at the men she was fleeing. They had the power to put that terrified look in her eyes, and he relished the thought of his coming confrontation with them. He was determined to know the truth of her association with them before the end of the morning, and if it meant he had to beat them to a bloody pulp, he wouldn't much mind the duty. "It's time, Duchess. They'll be crossing the burn soon."

She nodded and started toward the panel.

"Arren." She froze when he called her name. "Are you sure you don't want to tell me what this is all about?"

She shook her head. "You'll know soon enough, Gypsy. I'm sure they'll tell you their side."

"I'd rather hear yours."

Her lip trembled again and she turned away from him, unable to meet his gaze. "You'd better help me into the panel now or your plan will be spoiled."

He sighed and crossed the room, lifting down the heavy wooden panel. Arren stepped inside the tiny space and leaned back against the stone wall. He frowned. "I'm sorry it isn't going to be very comfortable in there."

"Just don't make me stay here long."

He nodded. "I won't. Remember, Arren, no matter what happens, you aren't to make a sound."

"I remember."

He stared into her eyes a second longer, then bent to drop a quick kiss on her forehead. "You'll be fine. I promise."

She nodded, and he replaced the panel, driving the four nails into place. He studied the panel closely, satisfying himself there were no traces of it having been removed. Then he tapped on it once to reassure her. He smiled when she tapped back.

Duncan had cut a tiny slit in the panel to let the light and air through, and Arren could see his broad back as he walked from the room. She settled back against the wall, trying to ignore the cramped conditions of her hiding place, while she waited.

It went on forever. Duncan stood at one of the windows in the entry room, studying the four men crossing the burn. The water was still fairly high, and it took them a long time to ford the swollen stream. He frowned. They were scurrilous-looking. He had only to recall the way Arren's eyes clouded with fear when she thought of them, to make his blood start to heat. Even from this distance, he could see that their horses were fine quality. They had cost a good deal of money, and it gave some indication that her adversaries were wealthy.

They all wore the same dirty blue plaid and he stared at the pattern intently, trying to place it. A memory snapped in place, and the corner of his mouth tugged down into a scowl. McDonan.

Alistar McDonan was a dirty son of a bitch. His clan was spread across the northern Highlands, and he was widely known to be obsessed with power and greed. There were stories about his cruelties to his tenants and workers that made Duncan's flesh crawl. Remembering the white scars on Arren's back, he felt a muscle begin to twitch in his jaw. The four men were working their way steadily up the hill now, and Duncan could see them clearly. Alistar was not among them. He'd no doubt sent them to do the work for him, and Duncan's fingers curled into a tight fist. He longed to sink it down their throats. The knowledge that he likely wouldn't have the chance, scalded him with disappointment.

They were nearing the lodge now, and he stepped back from the window, not wanting them to see him as they approached.

He made them knock twice before he opened the door, doing his best not to look murderous when he greeted them. "I assume you gentlemen have a valid reason for trespassing on my land."

The four men studied him with some surprise. One stepped closer to the door. "Who are you?" he asked.

Duncan crossed his arms and leaned nonchalantly against the door frame. He towered head and shoulders over the tallest of them, and the longer he looked at them, the more irritated he became. He raised an eyebrow at the insolent question and stared down at the man who'd asked it, silently reveling when the man fidgeted nervously before him. "I am the Duke of Strathcraig. This is my land. You are trespassing."

They clearly didn't believe him. Duncan waited expectantly for their answer. A hawkish-looking man stepped forward and narrowed his eyes at him. "My name is Euan McDonan. I'm Lord Alistar McDonan's brother. We have been traveling for several days in pursuit of a criminal. We have reason to believe she may be hiding here."

Duncan's lips turned into a cynical smile. "You've allowed a woman to elude you?" He made it clear he found the notion ridiculous, and Euan McDonan glared at him, taking another step forward.

"I'm going to have to ask your permission to search the premises."

The request brooked no arguments, but Duncan didn't budge from the doorway. "I was under the impression that property was still private in the Highlands. Has this changed?"

Euan fidgeted. "Strathcraig lands are over fifty miles south of here. I'm not entirely certain you can produce evidence that you own this particular holding, Your Grace." He sneered the title and leaned back, waiting for Duncan to respond.

Duncan reached down and slipped a gold ring from his finger, holding it up to Euan's eye level. All four men blanched visibly at the Royal crest. It was well known in Scotland that the Duke of Strathcraig lived within the favor of the Prince Regent. Strathcraig was the only noble in the Highlands who would possess a Royal crest. Duncan slipped it back on his finger and glared at the four men. He had been careful to conceal the ring from Arren for fear she'd realize who he was. He had no such trepidations now. "I'm not going to tell you again to get off my land."

Euan squared his shoulders. "I'm sorry for the inconvenience, Your Grace, but I must insist. The woman we seek has stolen a considerable sum from my brother. We believe she was also involved in the death of her former husband, our cousin. She could be hiding here without your knowledge."

Duncan knew he couldn't refuse without raising their suspicion, and while he'd rather they not search the house, he was certain they wouldn't find anything to indicate Arren's presence. He leaned aside, leaving them just enough room to enter single file. "Five minutes, gentlemen."

Euan turned to one of the men and sent him to investigate in the stables. The other two spread out through the small lodge. Satisfied, Euan leaned back against the door and studied Duncan. "What brings you to this part of the Highlands so long after the salmon have run, Your Grace?"

Duncan narrowed his eyes. Euan was still suspicious. He shrugged. "Retreat. I find the rigors of running an estate exhausting at times."

Euan nodded. "Alistar and I find the same. The bloody tenant problems would drive any man daft."

Duncan swallowed a disgusted reply and nodded. God, he longed to pummel this man! "Particularly in light of the current economic circumstances."

Euan snorted his agreement. "Greedy lot they are. Every one of them believes you owe them a living."

Duncan turned away, unable to look at him any longer. Euan embodied all that he loathed about the state of Scotland's landholders. "This woman you seek, was she a tenant?"

Euan made a disgruntled sound and pushed himself away from the door frame to settle on the long sofa. "No. She lives adjacent to McDonan lands. She has something precious that belongs to us, however, and Alistar is prepared to go to any lengths to get it back."

The casual statement sounded more like a threat than an

explanation, and Duncan felt a cold knot of anger settling in his gut. He heard the door open behind him and turned to see one of Euan's men returning from the stable.

"There are two horses in the stables, My Lord," he told Euan.

Euan turned his gaze to Duncan. "Do you have need of two horses here, Your Grace?"

"One belongs to my caretaker. He lives six furlongs down the river and houses his mount here. It's part of his remuneration for tending the property in my absence."

The explanation was plausible, and Euan nodded, aware he wouldn't be able to push Duncan any further on that issue. The other two men were coming down the steps, and Duncan resisted the urge to look at them. He continued to glare at Euan instead.

"There's nothing there, My Lord. Only His Grace's things."

Euan nodded reluctantly and looked back at Duncan, eying him suspiciously. He was far from convinced, but knew he couldn't confront the Duke of Strathcraig on his own property. "Very well, Your Grace. I thank you for your cooperation. I imagine she's eluded us again."

Duncan nodded. "Evidently."

Euan bristled at the smirk in Duncan's tone and rose to his feet. "We'll be leaving now. I'm sure if you see anyone suspicious, you'll notify the authorities?"

Duncan inclined his head. "Of course. I hope you have better luck finding your errant woman."

He couldn't resist the goading comment and he had to suppress a satisfied grin when he saw Euan's shoulders stiffen. He still wanted to pummel him, but he felt better, knowing that Arren's adversaries were no more ominous than these four bastards. He'd certainly faced worse in the past, and no doubt would again.

The four men filed out the door, and Euan paused, his hand on the door latch. "Your Grace, how much longer do you intend your retreat to last?"

Duncan shrugged. "Several more days at least."

Euan nodded thoughtfully. "Enjoy your holiday, then. Thank you again."

He stepped out the door and pulled it shut behind him. Duncan listened intently. He heard retreating footsteps and the sound of men mounting and riding away. He stood stock still. It took a full two minutes before he heard a fourth set of footsteps walk from the door and mount. The horse galloped away and Duncan smiled. Euan had stayed behind to listen intently at the door for Duncan's actions after their departure. If he'd heard voices, he would have known there was someone else present in the lodge. Duncan shook his head and started up the stairs to free Arren from her cramped hiding space. He slipped the gold ring from his finger, and dropped it in his sporran. Euan McDonan was an idiot, and if his brother wanted Arren badly enough, he'd have to find someone considerably more competent to track her down.

Arren stood frozen behind the panel, listening to the heavy footsteps coming up the stairs. She'd been able to hear a good deal of the conversation, and her nerves had calmed when she realized how firmly under control Duncan kept the situation. She had known only a brief moment of panic when Euan's cousins were in the room searching beneath the bed and in the heavy trunk, but they had clearly been out of their league with Duncan, and she'd released a long sigh of relief when she heard them return downstairs.

She heard Euan and his cousins ride away and she sagged against the wall with relief, waiting for Duncan to come free her. It didn't occur to her until she heard him coming up the stairs that he might have believed the story Euan had told him. She hadn't missed their conversation about the tenants, and while she was certain Duncan had merely used the discourse to distract Euan, she couldn't be sure he had discounted Euan's story about her. The thought occurred to her that she'd given him no reason to think otherwise, and if he believed she'd stolen something from Alistar McDonan, and—God forbid—killed her own husband, he'd be ready to turn her over to Euan.

She shivered at the thought and wondered vaguely what she would do if he was angry at her. She sank her teeth nervously into her lip as the panel lifted down and the sunlight filled her cramped hiding space.

Dear Lord! He looked bloody furious!

Thirteen

Duncan lowered the panel and glared down at her. She ran her tongue nervously over her lips and struggled to hold his gaze. "They're gone?" she whispered the question and watched him cautiously.

He nodded, wrapped his hands around her waist and lifted her out of the space, plunking her down in front of him. "Arren, why the hell didn't you tell me?"

She bristled visibly. "Because it isn't true. I didn't kill my husband, and I didn't steal anything from Alistar McDonan."

He growled something unintelligible and raked his hand through his curly red-gold hair. "Oh for God's sake! I never entertained the thought that you had. I want to know why you didn't tell me that Euan McDonan and those three bastards he's with were the ones trailing you."

Her eyes widened and she stared at him in surprise. "You didn't believe him?"

He glared at her. "Of course I didn't believe him. You're no more capable of killing your own husband than you are of flying. You haven't answered my question."

Arren stifled a hysterical giggle and raised a hand to her temple. Dear Lord! He believed her.

"I'm waiting."

She raised her eyes to his. "I didn't think you'd believe me."

He raised an eyebrow. "Why shouldn't I?"

"Alistar McDonan is a powerful man. Hasn't it occurred to you that I must have done something fairly potent to make him expend this much energy to apprehend me?"

Duncan shrugged. "Alistar McDonan is a greedy, power-hungry son of a bitch who'd chase a salmon upstream if he thought he could gain from it. Why didn't you tell me, Arren?"

She shook her head. She could hardly credit that he was more concerned over her failure to tell him who, rather than why. "I didn't think it was important."

He groaned. "We've been running at an inhuman pace for nearly half a fortnight from men who couldn't find themselves in the dark, much less anything else. You didn't think that was important?"

She looked indignant. "They've done a fairly good job of keeping up with us so far."

"Only because I was more concerned about covering ground than eluding them. They're bloody imbeciles, Arren. If they had brains in their heads, they'd have noticed your hair in the brush on the table." He paused and waved his hand in the direction of the incriminating brush. "Or they'd have thought to ask me why my bath water was scented with rape petals." He pointed to the now-tepid water in the tub where the bright yellow petals were clearly visible. "If I'd known what I was dealing with, we could have been rid of them miles ago."

She looked at him angrily. "Well, forgive me for not knowing that. I was frightened." She paused. "I still am."

Duncan sighed and pulled her against him. She resisted only briefly before she surrendered and wrapped her arms around his waist, clinging to him. "There's nothing to be afraid of, Duchess. Believe me, Euan McDonan poses no threat to you."

She squeezed her arms around his waist a little tighter when she felt a shiver race up her spine. Duncan felt it, too, and cradled her against him. Arren shook her head. "You don't understand. You don't know what they're capable of."

Duncan sighed heavily and raised a hand, stroking it gently over her hair. "Arren . . ." He waited for her to look up at him. "What did they do to put that look of fear in your eyes?"

The question was intense and she stared at him, running her tongue nervously across her lips. He groaned and lowered his lips to hers for a hard kiss that left her breathless. It was over before it began. Arren had to blink several times to regain her equilibrium. Duncan rubbed his thumb slowly across her lower lip and stared down at her. "One day, Duchess, you're going to understand that I take care of what's mine."

She looked at him cautiously, unsure how to interpret the odd statement. She pulled away, deciding to break the mood instead. Crossing to the bed, she toyed idly with the quilts. "If Euan is gone, does that mean we're leaving now as well?"

He sighed in exasperation and consented to the change of subject. "No. They're watching the house."

She looked at him in surprise. "How do you know that?"

"Come here." He motioned her toward the shuttered window and she walked to stand beside him. Cracking the shutter just enough to see out, he pointed toward the thicket of trees to their west. "Watch."

Arren watched the thicket for several minutes, unsure what she was supposed to see. A sudden glint in the trees caught her eye and she turned to look at him. He nodded. "There's nothing in the thicket to reflect the sunlight like that. It's probably one of the fittings on their saddles." He didn't think it wise to tell her it was more likely the barrel of a revolver.

She turned back to look at the thicket again and several seconds later, saw another glint. Arren stepped back from the window and looked at him admiringly. "That's amazing. How do you do that?"

His surprised gaze met hers. "Do what?"

"Know things like that. You always know things like that. You always know where we are. You know how to provide for us. How do you do that?"

He shrugged. "I used to be a spy."

Arren started to laugh. It was true of course, now that she thought of it, she simply hadn't expected him to be so blunt about it. "You seem to be a man of many talents, Gypsy. Is there anything you haven't done?"

He raked his eyes over her meaningfully, clearly implying that there were quite a few things he hadn't done, with her, in particular. She stopped laughing abruptly, blushing all the way to the roots of her hair. "You're shameless, Gypsy. You shouldn't taunt me like that."

He shot her a slow grin. "I've told you before, Duchess, I'm not taunting."

She turned her head back to the window. "So if they're watching us, what are we going to do?"

"Outfox them, of course."

Arren smiled at his arrogance. "Of course."

"I'm going downstairs to make some preparations, Duchess. Why don't you get some more rest. You're still not entirely recovered."

Arren turned around to face him, laying her hand gently on his chest. He drew a quick breath and forgot to let it out. "Gypsy . . . I haven't thanked you."

He raised an eyebrow. "For what?"

"For believing me. I've given you no reason to."

"On the contrary. You've given me every reason."

She furrowed her brow in confusion. He was so perplexing, she found it difficult to trace his moods from one moment to the next. "You confuse me."

He grinned at her. "It's only fair. You confuse me, too."

She returned his smile and tapped him on the chest. "I promise it will all make sense to you when we reach London."

He nodded and turned toward the door. "Get some rest, Arren. It may be the last chance you have to sleep in a bed for a while." He pulled open the door and hesitated, turning back to her. "Arren?"

She looked around from the window. His hand was on the door and he was watching her intently. "Yes?"

"Answer one question for me."

"All right."

"Is there any reason why our marriage isn't valid?"

She raised her eyebrows in surprise and shook her head. "No."

He nodded. "Thank you."

He stepped outside the door and pulled it shut behind him. Arren drew her brows together and studied it as if its heavy wooden panels had suddenly become the most fascinating thing in the world. She hadn't expected him to react as he had, and it perplexed her. She wasn't at all comfortable with the way she'd come to rely on him. She knew their time together would be over once they reached London. She found herself beginning to dread the thought.

Arren shook her head. She walked to the bed, and pulled back the covers. She simply had to convince herself that whatever attraction she had for him was a temporary infatuation brought on by their enforced proximity. She couldn't allow it to be anything more. She sighed and slipped between the sheets. Duke of Strathcraig or not, it was still impossible. It would be much simpler, though, if she didn't melt every time he touched her—or come alive each time he entered the room.

Arren felt a tear slide down her cheek, and cursed, swiping at it angrily. She blinked several times, preventing any more tears from escaping, and snuggled into the pillows. The sooner she realized the futility of her wayward thoughts, the easier it would be to say good-bye when the time came. She would have almost believed it if she hadn't dreamed about him when she finally fell asleep.

Duncan pulled the knot tight, testing its strength. After he'd left Arren alone, he'd gone downstairs to make arrangements for their departure. It was just after eleven o'clock in the morning, and he had no intention of leaving before dark. It would give Arren a few more hours of much-needed sleep before they set off again. He sighed heavily. The next leg of their journey would be brutal, but with any luck, they could reach Inverness in three days. Once they boarded *The Dream Seeker,* he would sit her down and have a long talk with her. He had no intention of waiting until they reached London to hear her explanation.

He bent down and picked up the long rope of knotted linens. He'd torn long strips of the bed linens and knotted them together carefully. He was certain Euan McDonan would be watching the front door. They would have to escape from the upstairs window to avoid detection. There would be one brief moment of danger when they'd have to cross the open space between the stables and the lodge, but he was fairly certain they could manage it with little or no difficulty if they timed it correctly.

Duncan tossed the knotted rope in a corner of the entry room and rubbed the taut muscles at the back of his neck. He was developing another headache and he wondered what he'd have to do to convince Arren to get rid of it for him as she had the last time. He grimaced. He wasn't entirely certain he could survive the experience this time. He shook his head and stretched out on the couch, closing his eyes. He fell into a fitful sleep, not even trying to ignore the picture of her flashing, emerald green eyes that dominated his dreams.

It was dusk when Arren awoke. She stirred in the large bed, momentarily disoriented. She finally remembered where she was, and sat up, squinting her eyes in the near darkness. She could tell by the soft light seeping in from behind the shuttered windows that the sun had sunk low on the horizon. She yawned, fighting the urge to drop back onto the bed. She actually felt much better than she had in days, and only hoped it meant her health was nearly restored. Throwing off the covers resolutely, she adjusted her clothes and headed downstairs to find Duncan.

She knew the minute she saw him that he was in pain. He was reclining on the sofa, his arm thrown over his eyes. He was perfectly still, seemingly asleep, but the tight lines around his mouth betrayed his discomfort. She frowned at his profile and crossed to his side. Lord, he was stubborn! "You should have awakened me, Gypsy. Your head's paining you, isn't it?"

He groaned. She interpreted it as agreement. She bent over and lifted his arm from his forehead, wincing sympathetically when she saw the pain etched in his gold-flecked eyes. "Can you sit up?"

He squinted, trying to focus his gaze. Damn, he hurt! "Arren, I can't . . ."

She cut off his protest when she laid her cool hand on his forehead. He'd meant to tell her he couldn't sit through another one of her tender ministrations, but he lost the thought when he felt her hand. She kneaded his forehead gently, kneeling down beside him. "If you can just sit up, I can help you."

The position of the sun outside the window told him it would be dark in a few hours. It would help immensely if he weren't fighting this dreadful pain when they started again. He groaned and rolled to a sitting position, ignoring the wave of nausea it caused. She shifted to sit beside him on the sofa and urged him gently down on the floor. He slid off the edge of the sofa, and gingerly lowered himself, pulling his knees up in front of him. He crossed his arms and dropped his head as she'd instructed him before, and sighed with pleasure when her hands settled on his wide shoulders.

Arren worked steadily on the taut muscles, kneading away the tension. In the cave, it had been too dark to really see him, and only now did she notice the jagged scar that ran up his neck and disappeared into his thick hair. Her fingers worked their way through his curly locks, and she massaged his head with her fingertips.

He groaned. It felt wonderful. It felt better than wonderful. He lolled his head to one side and groaned again when her thumbs worked at the taut muscles in his neck. Arren ran one finger over his scar and studied it carefully. It should have killed him. It was really miraculous that he hadn't died as a result of that wound.

She moved her hands over his shoulders, satisfying herself that the tension had ebbed away. He dropped his head back so he could see her. She smiled at him gently. "Do you feel better?"

"Immeasurably. How on earth do you do that?"

She shifted uncomfortably. "My father used to suffer from headaches. I learned early that it soothed his temper."

Duncan narrowed his eyes and watched her closely. Summoning what remained of his energy, he pushed himself up next to her on the sofa. She would have turned her head away if he hadn't caught her chin between his strong fingers. He looked down at her, disturbed by the clouds he saw in the green depths of her eyes. "Please don't ask," she pleaded with him.

He longed to. More than he wanted to draw his next breath he wanted to know why he saw so much pain in the green depths of her gaze. Instead he kissed her softly, and pulled her gently against him.

The kiss was comforting. Arren leaned against him, unwilling to break the tender contact. When he raised his lips from hers and tucked her head against his chest, she sighed. He cradled her there for a long while, running his fingers through her hair. She shuddered and pulled away, smoothing her clothes in embarrassment.

Duncan turned his attention to the window. The sun had sunk low on the horizon, and he knew they had less than an hour before dark. He looked back at Arren and smiled. "We should eat something now. We'll be leaving in about an hour."

She nodded and rose from the sofa. "I'll prepare it."

He watched her disappear into the kitchen. He raised his hand, massaging the muscles at the back of his neck. His headache was completely gone. Considering they had sometimes lasted days on end, it was amazing Arren could rid him of them so easily. He frowned and thought back on her cryptic comment about her father. Some of the scars on her back had been years old. She'd probably been abused as a child. The thought made him seethe. There were few things he despised more than men who found satisfaction in cruelty to children and animals. It made his stomach turn to think what Arren's childhood must have been like.

He remembered that some of those scars hadn't been but a few months old and his stomach turned again. His fingers clenched into a fist. He swore softly. They were trapped in an intolerable situation, and he was beginning to resent his helplessness. He was used to being in control, making things happen. He sighed heavily and stood up, heading for the bedroom to change back into his traveling clothes. Arren had already donned the breeches and shirt he'd found for her before she came downstairs. They'd be leaving within the next half hour. It was none too soon.

Fourteen

"Hold onto the harness and don't look down." Duncan whispered the words in Arren's ear as he lowered himself out the window on the knotted rope. He had created a harness for Arren so she could follow him down without worrying about falling. Only when he'd shown her the rope had she informed him she was afraid of heights. He had reminded her she wasn't afraid of anything. Besides, they had no other choice. Arren reluctantly agreed to the escape, but pointed out to him she'd never forgive him if she fell and broke her neck.

"Of all the things you should be worried about, my looking down isn't one of them," she whispered back, trying to gauge the distance between her perch on the window ledge and the ground.

Duncan braced his feet against the house and reached up to take hold of her chin, forcing her eyes to meet his. "Don't look at the ground," he reminded.

She sighed in disgust. "As if I'd bloody want to. Get me down from here in one piece, Gypsy."

He grinned. In the darkness, she saw the white slant of his teeth. "I haven't failed you yet, Duchess. Come on."

"There's a first time for everything," she mumbled and followed him over the ledge. She was surprised to find that it really wasn't so bad. The first several slips of the harness

were relatively easy. Duncan pushed away from the wall,
lowering himself a little more each time, and then tugged
on the rope, signaling her to follow. It was only when she
turned to look at the ground, intent on seeing how much
farther they had to go, that she grew terribly dizzy.

"Arren!"

She heard Duncan's growl from behind her and obedi-
ently snapped her head back around.

They reached the ground in less than thirty seconds. Arren would have sworn it took at least an hour and a half.
Duncan had her untied from the makeshift harness and
pulled back against the protective shadow of the wall in the
blink of an eye. She glared up at him. He grinned back.
"All right, Duchess. This is the hard part."

"The *hard* part? What are we going to do now? Fly?"

He smiled at the indignation in her tone. She was back
in fine form, evidently fully recovered from her cold. Only
when she was healthy could she sound that indignant. He
shook his head and leaned closer to whisper in her ear. "We
have to cross the courtyard to get to the stables. It's cloudy
tonight, and as long as the moon stays hidden, we should
be all right. Stay close to me though. We'll have to move
as quickly as we can."

Arren nodded and slipped her hand in his. He waited for
the clouds to blot out the moon then took off at a dead run.
The wind had picked up considerably and the clouds were
moving rapidly overhead. Arren tripped once, nearly falling,
but Duncan's hold remained firm. He pulled her into the
shadow of the stable just as the clouds broke and the moon
illuminated the courtyard. She sagged against the barn in
relief.

Duncan handed her one of the bundles he'd carried on
his shoulder and motioned for her to follow him. Keeping

to the edge of the barn, they worked their way around the corner and slipped inside. It was dark in the barn. Arren paused a minute to let her eyes adjust.

Duncan heard her startled gasp in time to spin around and watch her swing her bundle instinctively at the man stepping from the shadow inside the door. The man crumpled into unconsciousness. Arren dropped her heavy bundle to the ground and stared down at the limp body in horrified fascination. Duncan had to stifle the urge to laugh. He crossed the space between them and leaned down to get a closer look at Arren's victim. The moon shone brightly through a crack in the barn door. When he turned the man's head, he found himself face to face with Euan McDonan. The man was out cold. Duncan turned and grinned at Arren. Her hands flew to her mouth when she saw Euan's face. Duncan cut off a piece of their rope and used it to bind Euan's hands loosely behind his back. He left the man neatly trussed, like a chicken. Duncan stood, retrieving her bundle for her.

He placed it firmly in her hand and leaned over to whisper, "Not bad, Duchess. Though I'll confess I would've liked a shot at him myself."

Arren raised her eyes to meet his and finally saw the humor in the situation. Her bundle contained one of the bottles of wine Duncan had packed earlier. Evidently, the bottle had connected with Euan's head when she'd swung it at him. She stifled a hysterical giggle. Good Lord! He'd be furious with her when he realized what had happened. God willing, it wouldn't be for a while yet.

She looked down at his unconscious form before looking at Duncan again. "It couldn't have happened to a nicer man."

He grinned and pulled her with him to saddle the horses.

"Did you know he'd be in here?" she whispered.

Duncan pulled the buckle tight on his saddle. He turned to fasten hers. "I suspected one of them might be."

"You should have warned me."

He grinned at her and hoisted her into her saddle, pausing to secure her bundle on the back. "Then you wouldn't have had the satisfaction of knocking him unconscious."

She grinned down at him and tapped him on the shoulder. "See that you don't anger me, Gypsy. You could be next."

He swung up into his saddle and reached for her reins. "I'll certainly keep it in mind." He smiled at her and pulled her mount around next to his. "Now stay close to me and don't say anything until I give you your reins back."

She nodded, curling her fingers around her saddle while he led her through the barn door. They rode in silence for several minutes before Duncan reined in his horse. He pulled her mount next to his. Handing her the reins, he looked down at her carefully. She wore only the long-sleeved wool shirt—from the hunting lodge—tucked into her soft breeches. "Are you cold?"

She shook her head. "Not yet."

He reached behind him and pulled the familiar piece of black wool from his saddlebag. Unfolding it, he wrapped it around her shoulders, tucking it securely beneath her arms to form a makeshift jacket. "It's going to be rough from here on out. I'd like to reach Inverness in three days."

She nodded. She wondered what could be rough compared to what they'd been through before.

He raised his hand and brushed a lock of hair from her forehead. "Tell me if you need to stop."

She nodded again. "All right."

Duncan bent down and dropped a quick kiss on her lips. "When we reach London, remind me to tell you how much I admire your tenacity." He turned his mount and galloped down the hill, leaving Arren to follow as best she could. She stared at his retreating back and wondered at the comment. How odd that he hadn't yet realized what a horrid coward she was. She shrugged and charged after him.

The pace was grueling. They alternately cantered, then walked to avoid tiring the horses. Duncan stopped only twice in the next twenty-four hours. Both times, they ate, fed and watered the horses, and tended to their personal needs in the minimum possible time. The horses were at the edge of their endurance, and Arren was exhausted. She clung to the saddle, struggling to stay awake. She knew the sooner they reached Inverness, the sooner they'd be on their way to England.

Duncan continued to throw furtive glances over his shoulder, to ensure she was all right. By nightfall the following evening, he knew she was wearing thin. He slowed just enough so he could reach her. He pulled her from her saddle and onto his own, reaching for the reins to her mount. She protested sleepily, moving against him.

"Go to sleep, Arren."

"Don't you need sleep, too?" She was so tired the words were slightly slurred.

"No. Go to sleep."

"But you have to be tired. You haven't . . ." The words trailed off and she sagged against him, falling into a deep exhausted slumber.

Duncan smiled and settled her more comfortably against him. He slowed the weary horses to a walk. It was really amazing she'd lasted as long as she had. He breathed in the scent of her hair and wondered how she managed to smell so good after twenty-four brutal hours in the saddle. He wrapped his arm more tightly around her waist, doing his best to make her as comfortable as possible. Arren sighed in her sleep and her head lolled back against his shoulder.

Duncan turned his head slightly to look down at her delicate features, highlighted in the rosy glow of the setting sun. In less than two days, they'd be aboard *The Dream Seeker* on their way to London. For the first time, he allowed himself to consider what would happen when they got there. He had business to conduct with the Regent, of course. If that went according to plan, he could return to Strathcraig secure in the knowledge that he'd seen to the well-being of his clansmen.

But what of Arren? Their time together had been so intense, it was difficult now to picture his life without her. He knew her so well, and yet, there was so much he didn't know. She had yet to confide her reasons for her journey. He didn't even know her maiden name. He knew only that she'd been widowed, and that Alistar McDonan wanted her very badly. He was certain the solution, at least in Arren's mind, lay in London.

The longer he thought about it, the more anxious he became to reach Inverness. His attraction to Arren ran deeper than he was willing to think about at the moment. He knew, in the back of his mind, that only when his own responsibility was fulfilled would he be free to pursue his feelings for her. He sighed heavily. He also knew that despite the problems he foresaw, he was unwilling to consider life without her.

Duncan spurred his mount into a gallop, as he held Arren securely against him. It promised to be a long night.

Arren stirred in the saddle and opened her eyes. The sun was glistening on the early morning dew. It took her a minute to remember that she was astride Duncan's horse. She realized they must have ridden through the night. She stirred again and he reined in his mount. "Good morning, Duchess."

She turned to look at him. He looked tired. She was fairly certain he hadn't slept at all in the last two nights unless he'd stopped while she slept. "Have we been riding all night?"

He nodded.

She reached up to brush a lock of his hair off his forehead. "I'm sorry. You shouldn't have let me sleep so long. It must have been beastly uncomfortable for you."

He grinned at her. "I had you completely at my mercy. How could I be uncomfortable?" He swung down from the saddle, reaching up to assist her down.

She blushed, but ignored the suggestive comment. Only when her feet touched the ground did she realize how sore she was. She had to cling to his shoulders a good while until the circulation returned to her feet.

He watched her sympathetically. He knew her knees must feel like jelly. In truth, he didn't feel particularly wonderful himself. He kept his hands at her waist until she looked at him gratefully and released her grip on his shoulders.

"Thank you, Gypsy. I'm fine now."

"Are you sure?"

She tested her weight gingerly and winced. "I'll survive."

He nodded. "Why don't you head for the thicket and stretch out some of that soreness."

Arren looked at him gratefully and limped toward the small grove of trees to their left. Duncan watched her make her way stiffly to the thicket and grimaced in sympathy. He knew she probably had saddle sores, aching legs, and cramped back muscles. He didn't envy her the next day and a half. They'd have to spend most of it in the saddle. It would probably be torturous.

* * *

It was. They had shared a brief meal and started off again after a few hours' rest at the clearing. Arren had visibly blanched when he'd helped her mount. She insisted she was well enough to ride, though, and he set a gentle pace, keeping a careful eye on her and their mounts.

The sun grew hot, and Arren loosened the black wool, cramming it into the bundle on the back of her saddle. Every muscle in her body ached, and she rode up beside Duncan, intent on talking to him. She hoped conversation would make the day seem shorter and take her mind off the pain in her back and legs.

She asked him questions about the countryside they were passing through, and he indulged her, finally goading her into telling him some more of the folk stories she'd shared with him before. Arren shot him a mischievous look when he made the request. "And what would you like to hear, Gypsy? Tales of romance or tales of adventure."

"Adventure, of course."

Arren smiled. "I shall tell you one of the Highlands' greatest legends, then. 'Tis about our friend and former host, the Duke of Strathcraig." It might have been her imagination, but she could have sworn his horse missed a step when she said it.

He shot her a sideways glance and grinned. "All right. But make sure you entertain me with it. I'll lose patience if it isn't full of daring exploits and heroic deeds."

"Ah, but it is." Arren promptly switched to a lilting Gaelic and launched into the tale, unable to look at him through most of it. "His Grace the Duke of Strathcraig is known for his courage and heroism. Yet those who know him best have told stories of his arrogance and temper.

"In his younger years, he lived in the border country, calling neither the Lowlands nor the Highlands his home. Strathcraig land is vast, carved by many rivers and covered in fields of heather and rape. It is said that the snow blankets the hills of Strathcraig in just such a way that the castle seems surrounded in a quilt of white.

"As a youth, the young laird built a reputation for his success at gaming. 'Twas once said that he could toss a caber over a furlong when the mood caught him just so—though I, myself, never believed it. 'Tis well known, however, that he caught the biggest salmon in Scotland—over seventy-five pounds it was—but his golden heart made him free her when he discovered she was plump with roe. 'Twould be a crime, he explained, to slay such a magnificent beast. No one doubted the young laird's word, of course. If he said he'd captured the fish, then it surely must be so."

Arren paused and cast a sideways glance at him. The corner of his mouth tugged into a slight smile.

"He sounds like a remarkable fellow," Duncan remarked.

"Aye, he is. And that's not even half the story. At ten and eight years of age, he left the border country to serve the British monarch. 'Twas there that he distinguished himself on behalf of Scotland.

"A strange thing it is, though, that no one knows much of what he did. Many of our lads fought at his side in the war against the Emperor Napoleon. They returned with stories of his fearless exploits and his courage in battle.

" 'Twas there that he was nearly mortally wounded on behalf of the British Royal Crown. He was knighted and returned home a hero after four long years on the continent.

"Many of the details were lost after his years in the war. We know only that he returned to England where he took up a frivolous lifestyle. 'Tis widely believed there was a woman involved. There's no other explanation for why he didn't return home to Strathcraig.

"She was said to have the fairest blond hair and the bluest eyes of any woman on earth, and she snared the young laird's heart just as he'd snared the monster salmon so many years before.

"He was quite pleased, they say, by the swing of her step and the tilt of her head, not to mention her rather remarkable talents for . . ." Arren trailed off, shooting him a speculative glance.

He was watching her in open amusement, fascinated by the fanciful story. "Her talents for what?"

She smiled slightly. "I think, Gypsy, that you can well imagine what the London beauty's talents were rumored to be without an explanation from me. In any case, 'tis rumored that he was greatly taken with her.

"He showered her with gifts, traveling to exotic locations to procure them. Some have even said that his exploits on her behalf surpassed the feats of Hercules.

"But alas, she broke the young laird's heart, and he reportedly buried himself in gambling and drinking to help rid his mind of her memory.

"Some have said he became quite debauched in those years, but I, myself, have never believed it.

"In truth, no one is entirely certain what he did during those years, but he distinguished himself so richly to the Prince Regent, that His Highness elevated his noble standing from Laird to Duke. And quite a feat that is, too, I would add.

"His detractors say he's arrogant and bad-tempered, but most believe he is merely heartbroken over the loss of the fair-haired Englishwoman who trod on his heart and rejected his suit."

Duncan was laughing outright by the time she finished the tale. It was outrageously inaccurate, of course, as most of the folk tales were, and he found it riotously funny. He dearly hoped he'd be able to persuade her to repeat it to his friend, the Duke of Albrick, when they reached England. "Arren, that can't possibly be true."

She grinned at him. She'd actually embellished the tale only slightly, relaying mostly only the story as she'd learned it. " 'Tis not my place to comment on the rightness or wrongness of His Grace's legend. I have only repeated what those who know better have told me."

He laughed again. "Well, I'm certain His Grace would probably like to straighten out a few details."

Arren dropped the Highland Gaelic she'd used to tell the story and switched back to English. "I think it's a rather nice story. It's very heroic."

"I'm not entirely sure the Duke would like to know his exploits have been boiled down to some fanciful *affaire de coeur* with a 'fair-haired, blue-eyed Englishwoman.' "

Arren suppressed a smile. "How would you know, Gypsy? Perhaps it's true after all."

He shot her a grin. "Yes, perhaps it is."

"I would very much like to meet His Grace. He must be a fascinating person."

"What makes you think so?"

"He's traveled all over the world, been to exotic places, and met some of the most interesting people. He must be very well educated."

Duncan shifted a little in his saddle so he could watch her. "I would imagine that's likely."

"They say he's horribly arrogant, though," she continued, not daring to look at him. "And I imagine he's probably dreadfully pompous to listen to."

"You don't know that. Perhaps he isn't that way at all."

"Oh come now, Gypsy. He's the second largest land-holder in Scotland. He holds the ear of the Prince Regent. He's been overindulged and pampered his entire life. How on earth would you expect him to be?"

"What do money and power have to do with being pompous?"

"A great deal in my experience. Perhaps I wouldn't much like to meet him after all. He is more from the lowland country, you know. He isn't likely to be a very hardy fellow. I imagine he'd have trouble surviving outside the pampered environment he lives in." Arren couldn't resist the barb. She watched Duncan out of the corner of her eye, and nearly burst out laughing when he drew himself up in his saddle. She would have to remember to apologize for that grossly unfair remark later.

Duncan smiled slightly to himself. God knew what she'd do when she learned the truth. She'd either be mortified beyond belief, or she'd be so outrageously angry at him for letting her sound foolish, her eyes would shoot those emerald daggers at him he liked so well. He felt the corner of his mouth tug into a slow grin. God, the woman pleased him!

Duncan checked the position of the sun and saw that it was nearly midday. He had kept careful watch for signs of anyone following them, and was satisfied they had completely eluded Euan McDonan and his men. McDonan would expect Arren to be traveling south, and was no doubt riding headlong toward London even now. They were still a day and a half outside Inverness, and he made the decision to stop and rest. The horses were exhausted, and they and their riders, would benefit greatly from a few hours' respite.

They crested a small hill and he slowed their pace, looking at Arren. "We'll stop here and eat. The horses need rest."

She smiled at him and reined in her mount. "When the horses need rest, you're willing to stop, but when I am the one who needs it, you make us go on. What am I to think of that, Gypsy?"

He leaned forward and grinned. "That it wouldn't be nearly as pleasurable for me to carry your horse in my saddle. I rather enjoy the feel of you there."

She blushed and turned away. How she wished he wouldn't say those ridiculous things. She didn't like blushing. It made her feel like a bloody idiot, and if he were not to persist in embarrassing her, she wouldn't have to contend with it. Arren started to slide from the saddle, but Duncan was already at her side to assist her. He lifted her down, holding her until she found her footing again.

She was grateful the day had gone by as quickly as it had. Even though they were still riding at a tremendous pace over the rocky terrain, Duncan seemed completely at his ease. His nonchalance had a calming effect on her, and she thought for the thousandth time how grateful she was for her chance encounter with him, what now seemed a century ago. She sighed, decided her legs were steady enough, and released her grip on his shoulders. "Thank you. I'm fine now."

He nodded and turned to loosen the saddles and harnesses so the horses could graze more comfortably. He tethered them in a sun-dappled grassy field, then saw to his own comfort and Arren's. He spread the black wool on the ground, and Arren sat down on it gingerly, sore from the long hours in the saddle. The sun had risen high in the sky, warming the day considerably. She lay back on the woolen blanket, watching the clouds drift overhead.

Duncan dropped down beside her, the bundle of food in his hand. "What are you dreaming about, Duchess?"

She shot him a lazy smile. "A soft bed, a hot bath, a warm meal and a new gown."

He laughed. "The latter indubitably being as important as all the rest?"

"Of course. The bed, the bath, and the meal wouldn't mean nearly as much without the gown."

Duncan reached over and gently removed a stray piece of grass from her hair. "Shall I promise you then that you'll have all four when we reach Inverness?"

She turned her attention back to the clouds. "You once told me, Gypsy, that you don't make promises you can't keep. Beware you don't tempt me now and taunt me later."

He leaned over and ran his forefinger softly over her lips. "I could say the same of you, Duchess."

She reached up and curled her fingers around his hand, holding it still. "Duncan, I . . ."

He cut off her protest. "Not now, Arren. What I wish to say cannot be settled with a few minutes idle conversation. We'll discuss it later." He dropped his hand and turned his attention to the food, delving into the bag for a large piece of cheese and a bottle of wine.

Arren was struck by the sudden thought that this was their last real day together on this odd journey. Tomorrow, they would reach Inverness where, according to the note she'd found in Duncan's saddlebags, they would board the Duke of Albrick's yacht. Things would be different then, she knew, and she couldn't quite keep a feeling of regret from creeping into her thoughts. She resolutely pushed it aside. "Do you think Euan is following us?" she asked.

He shook his head and broke off a chunk of the cheese,

handing it to her. "There hasn't been any sign of them since we left the lodge."

She popped the cheese in her mouth. "Where do you shupposh the' are?"

He cast her a sideways grin when she mumbled the question around the piece of cheese. She swallowed it, smiling at him sheepishly. "Where do you suppose they are?" she repeated.

He shrugged. "I would imagine they've either returned to Donglass to inform Alistar of their failure, or they're riding south, thinking to intercept you on the way to London."

She shook her head and swallowed another piece of cheese. "They don't know I'm going to London."

He raised his eyebrows in surprise. "Where do they believe you're headed?"

"I don't know. Anywhere, I suppose. But they have no reason to suspect I'm going to London."

Duncan sighed in exasperation. "Arren, I'm growing tired of this."

She chewed on her lip and studied him for a long moment. There was really no reason now not to tell him at least part of the details. He had, after all, not believed Euan's story. He had trusted her despite her refusal to disclose the full truth to him. She drew a deep breath and looked out over the countryside. "My former husband was a very wealthy man."

Duncan froze. He hadn't expected her to relent now any more than she had in the past. He had made the simple statement and then raised the bottle of wine, intent on finishing off the last swallow. When Arren made the comment about her husband, he froze, with his arm still stretched across his bent knee, and the wine bottle dangling from his fingers. He was afraid to breathe lest he startle her into silence once more.

Arren was concentrating on the softly rolling hills along the horizon. She hardly noticed he had gone stock still beside her. "For that matter, so was my father," she continued. "My husband owned vast estates in the northern Highlands, and a good stretch of his land was adjacent to my father's. There were several disputed boundaries, however, and my brother Donald convinced Papa that my marriage to Lawrence would solve whatever problems existed. Papa agreed.

"I was married when I was seventeen years old. Lawrence was eight years older than I, and I had managed to romanticize him at the time. My home life was not what one would call ideal, and I envisioned Lawrence as a gallant man who would carry me away and fall madly in love with me."

She paused and smiled bitterly. "It was a childish fantasy at best. Lawrence never had any such intentions. My marriage was . . ." She paused, looking for the best word, ". . . tolerable. It was better, certainly, than living with my father had been. Lawrence died in a hunting accident six years later. We were childless, so there was an open dispute over who would inherit the land and the fortune. According to Scottish law, of course, I was entitled to whatever had been part of the marriage contract. That meant I became sole possessor of the boundary lands that separated Lawrence's estate from Papa's."

She sighed. "Everyone was angry. Papa wanted the lands. Lawrence's family wanted the lands. No one wanted me to have them, and yet no one wanted me to be their responsibility, either. For three more years, the dispute went back and forth. I had a small staff I took with me from Lawrence's house, and we lived in one of the crofts on a remote part of the boundary. But it soon became difficult for us to survive.

"All I had was the land. There wasn't any money. We had to grow our own food, and barter for clothing and supplies.

"I think we would have made it, though, if it hadn't been for Alistar McDonan. The McDonans were related to Lawrence's family by marriage. Alistar wanted it all. He wanted the title, he wanted the money, and he wanted the land. He plagued me unmercifully. He tried everything from formal suit to outright threats.

"When I wouldn't marry him, he became furious. He threatened the merchants so no one would trade with us. He ruined our small crops. I'm sure it is he who fed tainted grain to our sheep, killing them all.

"I was becoming desperate. I had to let what remained of my staff go. Only Nanny stayed with me. It was then we received word that my father was dying and wanted me to return home. After the death of my brothers, I was Papa's only heir, and according to Scottish law, I stood to inherit everything.

"Nanny and I returned home, and my father died five months later. Alistar McDonan became obsessed with greed. Alistar's first wife was Lawrence's sister, and he had already seized Lawrence's land in Margaret's name. Lawrence's family was in disarray, and unable to dispute Alistar's claim to the estate. When my father died, and Alistar realized he could own not only the border land, but all my father's wealth and land as well, he was relentless. He would stop at nothing to force me to marry him.

"Finally, I fled in desperation. My mother's uncle lived in a remote holding a fortnight's ride south of my father's home. Nanny helped me arrange an extended visit there, and I traveled to see them, hoping to arrange for passage to London while I was there. They betrayed me, though, and informed Alistar that I was staying with them. When

Euan and his cousins showed up to haul me back, I fled into the night. I eluded them for twenty-four hours, but they were tracking me on horseback. I was on foot. The following evening, they would have run me down had you not appeared to interrupt my flight."

She finished the story and brushed at an imaginary spot of dirt on her trousers, afraid to look at him. She had only left out a few pertinent details. She'd given him almost all the relevant facts save the names that protected her anonymity. She still believed he would be at great risk, as would she, if he knew who she really was.

Duncan watched her in silence. He knew she'd left out many of the painful details, giving him only a rough outline of the story. He had spent too long studying people not to have a fairly certain idea what some of those details were. He'd seen the scars on her shoulders and back, and would now wager any sum of money her father had inflicted them. He was also prepared to guess, that part of Alistar McDonan's strategy to make Arren his wife accounted for the fresher wounds he had seen there.

He had heard the bitterly sad way she'd spoken of her uncle's betrayal. He had seen the tension in the way she wrung her hands as she had when she'd talked of Donald's suicide. Her marriage had been disillusioning, and she was still pained over it.

Unwittingly, she had allowed him a glimpse into her soul. He longed for a clearer look. He wanted to help heal her lingering scars more than he'd ever wanted anything in his life, and yet, their circumstances prevented it. She had been as honest, if not more so, with him as he had been with her. And while he still didn't know why she was fleeing to England, he understood that somehow, London meant safety to her. He was feeling more and more driven to provide her with that. He threw back his head and finished the swallow of wine.

Arren was watching him surreptitiously. He hadn't said a word, and she wasn't certain whether or not he believed the story. He finished off the wine and finally turned to look at her, an unfathomable look in his eyes. He reached up to tuck a stray tendril of her hair behind her ear, allowing his palm to linger against her face. She held his hand close to her cheek and raised her eyes to his.

His gold-flecked gaze was intense, boring into her, seeking answers to the questions she'd left dangling. She shook her head slowly. "Please don't ask me."

He nodded and rubbed his thumb reassuringly along her cheekbone. "You'll tell me when you're ready."

She smiled gratefully, and he bent his head to drop a soft kiss on her lips. She opened to him, enjoying the taste of his mouth, still flavored from the wine, rubbing in the lightest caress over hers. When he finally raised his head, she sighed softly.

Duncan was filled with a fervent desire to reach Inverness. He rose to his feet, extending his hand to Arren, pulling her up beside him. She brushed off the seat of her breeches and bent down to retrieve the black wool. "How much longer before we reach Inverness?" she asked, handing it to him.

He had resaddled her horse, and was securing what remained of the bundled food behind her saddle. He took the folded wool and slipped it under the bundle, pulling the cord taut. "A day and a half. Less if the wind stays at our backs. We should be there by nightfall tomorrow." He looked at her carefully. "Are you all right to ride?"

She nodded. "I am for now."

"You'll tell me if you need assistance?"

She nodded again. "Of course. You'd ride off and leave me if I didn't."

He furrowed his brow and studied her while he tightened his own saddle. "I'm sorry it's so uncomfortable."

She looked at him in surprise and slipped the harness over her horse's nose, talking to her mount gently. "I've been uncomfortable before. I'm all right."

He attached his harness and reached over to fasten hers, handing her the reins. "I'll do what I can to make it up to you in Inverness."

She smiled at him. "Why all this concern, Gypsy?"

He sighed and lifted her into the saddle, looking up at her. "I've pushed you unmercifully hard, Arren. No woman should have to endure what you have these past several days." He silently added that no woman should have to endure what she had in her lifetime, but didn't think she'd appreciate it if he said it out loud.

A teasing look had crept back in her eyes, and she swatted him gently on the shoulder with the end of her reins. "But it's been such a wonderful adventure. I've met a gypsy, a former spy, a thief, a master of disguise, and gotten married to him all in a fortnight. It will make a wonderful legend."

He swung into his saddle and grinned at her. "You're rather lucky to have met a man like me, you know. No one else could have provided you with so much to tell your grandchildren about."

He thought perhaps a sudden cloud passed across her eyes, but she masked it before he could be sure. "There'll be no grandchildren if we don't reach Inverness."

He nodded and reined his horse around. "I'll set the pace. Stop me if you need to."

He charged down the hill without awaiting her answer.

Fifteen

They rode in silence for the rest of the day. Arren sensed that Duncan became more and more tense as they approached Inverness. Instead of intruding on his thoughts, she concentrated on ignoring the throbbing pain in her backside. The afternoon passed slowly for her, and she was surprised when he missed several opportunities to stop as the sun sank lower in the sky.

The sky had darkened to a deep rose when she realized he intended to ride through the night again. Arren shifted miserably in the saddle, trying to make herself more comfortable, and followed his pace. Thinking back, she began to wonder how he functioned without sleep. He had never in her presence, slept more than three or four hours at a time, if that, and often he would go days on end without resting. He seemed to slow his pace only when she needed him to, and then it was generally with reluctance.

She frowned and studied the wide expanse of his back. It was nearly impossible to imagine what her life would be like without him. When they reached London, he would, she imagined, petition the Prince Regent to terminate their circumstantial marriage. It shouldn't be difficult for the Duke of Strathcraig to earn favor for the request, and then they would go their separate ways. It was odd, almost painful, to contemplate. Arren realized, between one beat of her heart and the next, that she was in love with him.

The thought so took her by surprise that she reined in her horse and stared at Duncan's back in open fascination. Dear God! Why on earth hadn't she realized it before, and what the devil was she going to do about it?

Duncan had ridden nearly fifteen yards before he realized Arren was no longer behind him. He reined in his mount abruptly and turned to see if she was all right. She was sitting back a ways, clinging to the reins of her horse, staring at him. "Arren? Are you all right?" He nudged his mount forward, riding up next to her.

She had the oddest expression on her face. She didn't answer him. "Arren? Is something wrong?"

She blinked several times. "No!"

Her denial was vehement and he raised an eyebrow, studying her intently. "Are you sure?"

"I . . . yes . . . no . . . I . . . I don't know." She shook her head, unable to look at him. "Shouldn't we move on."

"Are you all right to keep riding?"

"Yes, of course." She had no desire to continue the bizarre conversation and spurred her mount forward, only to be stopped by his hand.

Her behavior was odd at best, and he was determined to know its source. "Perhaps you should ride with me for a while."

"No! I'm fine. Let's just go."

"Arren . . ."

She cut off his protest and threw him a quick glance over her shoulder. Why hadn't she noticed before how sinfully handsome he was? "Let's go, Gypsy. I tire of this." She nudged her mount forward, breaking free of his hand, and he followed at a comfortable distance, studying her thoughtfully.

Arren was horrified. How could she have allowed this to happen? It would make their parting in London nearly unbearable for her. She cursed herself for not having prevented it. It all seemed so obvious now. Suddenly she understood why she reacted as she did every time he touched her. Why she felt as though her insides came unglued when he shot her those teasing glances.

The thought occurred to her that she had struggled desperately to elude him for precisely this reason. She had known from the beginning that she couldn't allow herself to fall in love with him. In doing so, she'd given him the very power over her she feared most. He could hurt her badly now, and probably would, but with the realization came a certain power.

If the pain she knew would follow was inevitable, there was no reason to resist what she felt for him. Duncan had made it clear he desired her. When she thought about it, he'd made it abundantly clear. She had always pulled away, afraid of allowing the intimacy, but now, her reason ceased to exist. In truth, she loved the feel of his hands and mouth, and she longed to deepen her intimacy with him.

The trip from Inverness to England would take three-and-a-half days if the weather was good. Once they docked at Dover, it was less than a day's journey to London. Within a week, she would no longer be his wife—would, in fact, no longer be his responsibility. She would return to her home and he would return to his, and there was every likelihood they would never see each other again. She had less than one week to spend with the man she knew she'd love forever. The thought was liberating to her long-suppressed emotions.

Duncan watched her carefully from a distance. Something was dreadfully wrong. Arren had seemed stunned, even disoriented, when she'd reined in her mount so abruptly. She had made it clear she didn't wish to talk to him about it. Until now, he had respected her silence. It was beginning to irritate him. He sighed heavily and spurred his mount forward, intent on riding alongside her. Perhaps he could convince her to talk to him.

Her smile caught him so off guard he nearly fell from his saddle. He cast her a speculative glance. "Your mood has certainly improved."

Her smile widened slightly and she just barely resisted the urge to reach over and rumple his red-gold hair. She nodded instead. "Other than a few muscle aches, I feel wonderful."

He raised an eyebrow, adjusting himself in his saddle so he could see her more clearly. "May I ask what brought on this sudden good humor?"

She laughed, and he felt it all the way down to his toes. "I think you'd be shocked if I told you, Gypsy." The sun had sunk low on the horizon she could barely see ahead of her now. "Are we stopping for the night?"

"I had thought to ride through if we keep the pace slow for the horses. I'd be glad to carry you on my saddle, though, if you'd like."

Arren decided she'd like that very much indeed, and reined in her horse. She felt suddenly reckless, more so than she remembered feeling in years, and she threw what remained of her caution to the wind. When he slowed next to her she reached over and handed him her reins. "I'm growing tired. Would you mind if I rode with you?"

His eyes narrowed suspiciously, but he didn't comment. He took her reins in one hand and reached out to lift her onto his saddle with the other. Arren settled herself in the wedge of his legs, squirming against him for good measure. He groaned. She smiled.

"Sit still, Arren."

"I will. I wanted to get comfortable." She squirmed again.

He thought to tell her she was making him damned uncomfortable, but decided to let it pass. Her mood was strange, and he sensed he would be wise to leave well enough alone.

Arren leaned back against his chest and reached up to take her reins from his hand. "I'll hold these for a while."

He released them without comment and they rode on in silence. The sun was now completely gone, and the darkness was deepening quickly. Arren was glad the cloud cover was not as thick as it had been in nights past, and the light of the moon lit their way a little more clearly.

Duncan seemed content to ride in silence, and she sighed, enjoying the feel of his strong arm wrapped securely around her waist. They had ridden nearly an hour before she felt herself growing sleepy again. The thought occurred to her that he hadn't slept in days, and she was struck with a concern for his well-being. "Duncan?"

"Hmm?"

"How long has it been since you last slept?"

He shrugged, and she liked the way his warm chest moved against her back. "I don't know. Three or four days, I think."

"We should stop and rest. You can't go on like this."

He sighed, his warm breath fanning across the top of her hair. "I'm fine, Arren. If we ride through the night, we'll be in Inverness by this time tomorrow."

"I know, but it couldn't hurt to stop for a few hours. If you push yourself like this, you'll get another headache."

He decided not to tell her the pain in the back of his neck had been mounting steadily since early that afternoon. "I'm fine, Arren. Just go to sleep."

"But, Duncan, I really think we should stop. I don't want

you to be in pain." She turned in the saddle to look at him, and she furrowed her brow when she saw the tight lines around his mouth. She suddenly understood why she'd sensed a change in him over the course of the afternoon. He was already in agony. Damn, but the man was hard-headed! "Stop this horse right now!"

He glared at her. "Arren, I am not stopping. Shut up and go to sleep."

She wasn't daunted. "Dammit, Gypsy, I said stop!"

"No!"

Arren reached up and grabbed the reins in front of his hand, giving them a mighty tug. His horse reared to a stop, nearly throwing them both in the process. He cursed loudly under his breath and she shot him a smug smile.

"What the hell are you doing?" he demanded.

"You're already in pain, aren't you?"

"It doesn't matter," he growled.

He would have nudged his horse back into a trot, but she tugged on the reins again. "We aren't going any farther tonight. Not until I rid you of that headache."

He gave an exasperated grunt. "Arren, this is ridiculous. I hadn't planned on stopping tonight and I'm not going to. End of discussion."

She glared at him and slid from the saddle before he had the chance to stop her. "Then you'll have to leave me here."

"What the devil's gotten into you?"

"This trek of ours is far from over, and when we reach Inverness, I dare say you'll need your wits about you. I'm not about to allow you to get me killed simply because you're too by-damn stubborn to take care of yourself. Now get down."

He had to resist the urge to laugh. She was glaring up at him with her hands firmly planted on her slender hips. From his lofty vantage point he could see the way her eyes shot green sparks at him in the moonlight. He paused, and considered briefly the ramifications of stopping for the night.

She was right, of course, about Inverness. If anyone were trying to prevent his departure from Scotland, they would either be awaiting him on the border, or they would be expecting his arrival in Inverness. It wouldn't do for his concentration to be lessened by the pain in his head. Much as he wished the affliction wasn't plaguing him, he couldn't ignore it. The fact that it only affected him when he was immensely tired didn't do much to ease the throbbing ache he now felt. The temptation of allowing her to work the tension out of his neck and shoulders was powerful. He sighed heavily, sliding to the ground.

Arren smiled smugly, and poked him in the chest. "You'll not regret this, Gypsy. Sit down."

He glared at her. "If we're stopping, the horses need to be unsaddled and unharnessed."

She reached up and pulled the black wool from the back of her saddle. "I'll do it. Sit down."

"Lord, you're autocratic."

"You seem to have forgotten, Gypsy, that I am paying you to take me to London. Until we get there you're in my employ. Sit down!"

He groaned and spread the black wool with a sharp flick of his wrist. He sank to the ground, laying his head back and closing his eyes in pain. He could hear Arren unbuckling the saddles and harness and whispering softly to the huge animals. He would have smiled if he hadn't thought his head would split open. She seemed so fragile, and yet she managed the huge beasts with as much strength as she managed everything else.

It took her less than five minutes to tend to the horses. She removed the heavy saddles and bags and dropped them to the ground, leading the horses to a grassy area where she looped their reins around separate trees. She returned quickly to his side, more concerned than she cared to admit to him about the excruciating pain she knew he must be feeling.

He was stretched out on the blanket, his arm thrown across his eyes to shield them from the light of the moon. She sank to her knees next to him and placed her small hands on his chest, carefully unbuttoning his shirt.

He drew in a surprised breath, but didn't move his arm to look at her. "What are you doing?"

She did her best to keep her voice calm. "Unbuttoning your shirt so I can work on your shoulders properly."

He seemed to accept the explanation, and she continued the task, silently marveling at the warmth of his skin and the muscled hardness of his chest. She tugged the shirt free of his waistband, spreading it wide on either side of him. She looked for several long seconds at the expanse of his body. She realized she'd never really looked at him before. Red-blond hair covered the expanse of his chest, disappearing into the waistband of his trousers. She barely resisted the urge to run her fingers along the flat muscles of his stomach.

"Seen enough?"

She jumped visibly when he whispered the question. She tore her eyes away. His arm still lay across his forehead. He couldn't see the flush that covered her delicate features. "I was only wondering if you could roll over."

He groaned and moved his arm, his eyes meeting hers in the bright glow of the moonlight. "Have you any idea what it does to me when you touch me like this?"

She shook her head and nervously ran her tongue across her lips. "No."

"I didn't think so." He rolled to his stomach, crossed his arms beneath his head, and waited.

Arren studied his back. She could see the tension in the corded muscles and felt a twinge of sympathy. Scattered haphazardly along his back were flat scars of varying sizes she knew were wounds from bullets and knives and swords. He'd no doubt sustained them during his service to the Crown. The angry mark that ran up his neck seemed almost swollen in the moonlight, and she longed to soothe it away, removing the pain she could see in the taut lines of his body.

Duncan was still waiting for her to touch him. She sat beside him, seemingly mesmerized by the sight of his naked back. "Arren?"

He felt her startled motion beside him, and heard her sigh. "I was merely wondering how to do this when you're lying down."

He groaned. "If I sit up, it'll likely make me sick."

Arren chewed her lip and looked at him thoughtfully. There seemed to be but one solution, and she decided, under the circumstances, it wasn't such a terrible predicament. She shifted closer, throwing one leg over his back so she sat astride his hips. She settled herself down on him and smiled softly when she heard him groan.

For long minutes, Arren stroked her hands over his skin. Working at the tight muscles with her palms, she soothed away his tension. She leaned over him, kneading his taut flesh, with firm, sure strokes of her fingers.

Duncan could feel the pain ebbing out of his back. Every movement of her hands loosened the knots and cords that bound him. He felt his muscles relaxing beneath the firm ministrations of her fingers. It was an exquisite feeling. Even the gentle pressure of her thighs astride his hips added to his lassitude. He sighed with pleasure, surrendering to the sensation.

Arren knew the minute he fell asleep. His deep sigh echoed the shudder that ran up his spine, and she felt what remained of his tension drain out of him. She smiled and moved to his side, stretching out on the ground next to him. Dear Lord, how she loved this man! She knew he was deep in sleep, and didn't resist the urge to run her fingers caressingly over his firm flesh. She found a private pleasure in the realization that surely he had the broadest back in the world.

Arren stared at him for long moments, enjoying the sight of his sun-bronzed skin awash with moonlight. The quiet neighing of the horses, coupled with the heavy scent of the warm spring breeze, lulled her senses. So many nights, the winds had been cold and unforgiving, but this was one of those rare evenings when the breezes warmed the earth and the scents of spring hung in the air. Arren sighed and nestled her hands beneath her face, a ghost of a smile on her lips. On a night like this, when the moon cast a glow of fairy dust over the earth, nearly anything seemed possible. She could almost make herself believe there was a future for them.

Sixteen

Duncan awoke with a start. He was lying on his stomach. A warm spring breeze caressed his back. He inhaled deeply, taking stock of his surroundings. He finally realized what had awakened him and rolled to his back. Arren was asleep at his side. She'd turned in her sleep and laid her hand across his back. The soft contact had startled him into awareness. He propped his head on his hand and looked at her.

Moonlight washed over her, and he studied her intently. In sleep, her face was free of the anxieties that often lurked beneath the surface of her delicate features. The thick plait of her hair lay across her shoulder. He reached out to touch it. Her hair was soft, almost like warm silk. It clung to his hand as if it were alive.

Arren sighed and shifted slightly in her sleep. Duncan smiled and gently smoothed the stray tendrils of her hair that curled riotously around her face. She looked absurdly beautiful lying there. Only the small spray of freckles on the delicate bridge of her nose made her look real. His eyes roamed over her face, drinking in the way her dark lashes fanned over her cheeks, the full curve of her lips, and the tilt of her aristocratic chin.

When his eyes moved lower, he nearly groaned at the taunting way her shirt gaped open, giving him an ample view of the gentle rise and fall of her breasts. He ached for her. He felt himself reacting physically and sighed, dropping to his back once more. He suddenly felt like a schoolboy in the throes of adolescent lust. He had only to look at her to feel himself growing warm.

His movement woke her. Arren sighed lazily and opened her eyes. He was lying on his back, his strong arms crossed beneath his head. In the moonlight, his naked skin looked almost like marble. She couldn't resist the urge to touch him. She reached out, gently touching the curve of his rib cage with her fingertips. She felt his sharply indrawn breath, and froze.

Her touch scalded him. Duncan rolled to his side. His gaze met hers. Her eyes were wide and unreadable, her hand still frozen in place. She too, had stopped breathing. Duncan raised his hand, his gaze never leaving hers, and gently laid it alongside her face. Her eyes widened slightly, but she didn't pull away. Encouraged, he took another risk.

He ran his thumb over her lower lip in the softest of caresses. When her mouth opened to the pressure of his finger, he groaned and lowered his lips to hers. The kiss was rife with long-suppressed desire. Duncan's hand moved to her shoulder, pushing her down beneath him, and his mouth slanted across hers with demanding persistence. Arren didn't wait for him to deepen the kiss. Wrapping her hands around his neck, she pushed her tongue into his mouth with a soft whimper of desire.

He groaned her name and rolled to his back, pulling her with him. She explored his mouth tentatively at first, unsure of what he expected. Duncan didn't hesitate to show her. He sucked on her tongue, pulling it fully into his mouth and opened to her, allowing her to leisurely explore the hot, wet taste of him.

The feeling was exquisite. His mouth was so gloriously

hot, and Arren moaned, splaying her hands across his naked chest. Duncan was fast becoming dissatisfied with the barriers between them. His hands were at her waist, anchoring her to him, and he tugged at the fabric of her wool shirt. It pulled free, and Arren moaned with pleasure when his hands caressed her warm flesh. He ran his fingers along her spine, sending a shiver all the way to her toes.

He finally tore his mouth from hers and moved lower down the delicate curve of her neck. "God, Arren, you're so beautiful." His lips settled in the sensitive hollow at the base of her throat and she moaned something unintelligible. Duncan locked his leg around both of hers and rolled her onto her back. She sighed with pleasure as the weight of him pinned her to the ground, and opened her mouth, silently begging for his kiss.

He denied her only long enough to kiss each of her closed eyelids and bring one hand around to the buttons of her shirt. His mouth covered hers. He thrust his tongue between her lips, reveling in the soft sounds she made deep in her throat.

His fingers worked at her buttons, exposing tiny inches of flesh as each pulled free. She could feel the heat of his hand between her breasts and she squirmed against him, anxious to feel his naked skin next to hers. She had denied her feelings too long. In the warm breeze of the evening, her sanity fled. She could not have denied him now even if she'd wished to.

He peeled back her shirt and raised his head to drink in the sight of her. Her breath was coming in fitful gasps. He watched the rapid rise and fall of her breasts in fascination. He raised his hand and circled the coral bud of one breast with his forefinger.

Arren arched into his hand. "Duncan, please . . ."

He couldn't deny her. He covered the full mound of her breast with his hand, groaning with pleasure when he felt the nipple peak against his palm. With exquisite tenderness, he kissed her high cheekbones, the delicate curve of her neck. Then his lips slid lower to the rounded curve of her breast.

Arren's hands clung to his shoulders. She felt a tight knot expanding somewhere below her stomach and she squirmed against him in pleasure. He moved his head lower, deliberately scraping his teeth across the sensitized nipple. She cried out even as her breast swelled to his touch.

He raised his other hand and caressed her, loving the way her nipple puckered toward him. He leaned over and licked the nipple tenderly, raising his head just long enough to allow the warm breeze to blow across the wet peak. It hardened even more. He whispered something unintelligible against her flesh and covered the engorged bud with his lips.

When he began to suckle, Arren came unglued. The tight knot at the core of her feminine desire was expanding. She felt it spread down her legs into her toes. She cried out his name and clung to him.

Duncan was inflamed by her reaction to his touch. He laved the nipple with his tongue before sliding his lips along her sensitized flesh to give her other breast the same loving attention. Her breath was coming in painful gasps and she ran her fingers across his shoulders. Duncan tore his mouth away to look at her.

She whimpered in protest at the broken contact, opening her eyes to find his gold-flecked ones staring down at her. He seemed to be having as much trouble breathing as she was. She gloried in the thought. She brought one hand around to touch the taut flesh on his chest. He drew a sharp breath, catching her hand to hold it still.

"Arren . . ."

He seemed to hesitate. She felt a cold thread of panic begin to weave its way through the haze of passion.

"Arren, if we don't stop now, I won't be able to."

She sighed in relief. "I don't want you to."

He groaned and dropped his forehead to hers, closing his eyes. "Do you know what you're saying to me, sweetheart?"

She moved against him, anxious for the feel of his lips once more. "Please, Gypsy. I can't deny any longer that I want this."

Duncan raised his eyes and studied her. For the briefest of seconds, Arren feared he'd reject what she offered, but he stroked his long fingers over the soft curve of her lips and stared down into her green eyes. "Arren, you're my wife in name only. If I make love to you, you'll be my wife in every sense of the word. Tell me that's what you want."

She didn't hesitate. She wrapped her arms around his neck and tugged his head down to hers. "More than I want to go on breathing, Duncan."

He groaned and reached for her hand. Carefully, his eyes never leaving hers, he slipped her husband's ring from her finger. Arren ran her tongue nervously across her lips and watched him slide the ring into the pocket of his breeches. With a satisfied sigh, he bent his head and covered her mouth with his in a kiss that was blatantly possessive. His tongue drove in and out of her soft mouth, while his hands touched her everywhere at once. He caressed the soft curve of her breasts, rubbing his thumbs across her hardened nipples. He ran his hands over her smooth stomach, delving his forefinger into her navel. She cried out and arched against him. He chuckled delightedly.

Arren was fast losing control. Her hands roamed over his hard flesh, her nails raked across his shoulders. When his fingers slid along the waistband of her trousers, she squirmed against him, silently demanding that he end her torment. He wouldn't be rushed.

Duncan splayed one hand at the small of her back and dropped his mouth to the hollow between her breasts. The movements she was making against him were driving him mad, and he felt the pressure building in his loins. He ached with his need to fill her with his flesh, but was driven even more by a desire to see her find fulfillment at his touch. He worked the buttons of her breeches loose and moved his hands to her hips, drawing back to push the soft trousers down her legs.

In seconds, she lay naked before him. She was exquisite. He hesitated, longing to touch her, unwilling to stop looking at her. Arren's eyes flew open and she raised her hands to cover her breasts, acutely embarrassed. He reached out and grabbed her hands, gently tugging them away. "Don't. Don't be embarrassed, Duchess. You're perfect."

She looked at him, and he could see the trepidation in her eyes. Tenderly, he took one of her hands and guided it to the source of his manhood. Her fingers touched him there, and she could feel his hardness even through the fabric of his trousers. Her startled eyes flew to his, and he smiled at her. "See what you do to me, Arren. I ache for you."

She tried to pull her hand away, but he anchored it there, watching her intently. "Don't be embarrassed, sweetheart. You should be proud of the power you have over me."

"I . . . I don't know what to do."

He smiled and raised one hand to her breast. "Follow your heart."

She drew a deep breath and moved her hand against him, fascinated when his eyes closed and he groaned with pleasure. Emboldened, she slid her other hand along the hard plane of his back, while she worked at the buttons of his breeches. The material strained against his hardened flesh, and her trembling fingers tugged at the buttons. She finally worked them loose, and gasped in surprise when the hardened evidence of his desire surged against her fingers.

Duncan groaned and reached down to anchor her hand around him. He couldn't stand the exquisite torture much longer. He was becoming desperate to bury himself inside her. His lips covered hers in another long, hot kiss, and he ran his hands over her hips in feverish desire.

Arren pushed at the waistband of his breeches. Duncan tore his mouth from hers, rolling away long enough to pull them free. She reached for him and he covered her with his naked body, his mouth taking possession of hers once more. She whimpered, caressing his narrow hips, arching into his kiss. Duncan groaned and moved his head to the soft plane of her stomach.

When his hand slid along the curve of her hip, Arren turned into his caress. He stroked her gently, sliding his fingers across the sensitive skin of her thigh. She froze when his hand slipped between her thighs and he raised his head to look at her. "Darling, please. Open for me. I won't hurt you."

The rough stubble of his beard inflamed the sensitized flesh of her tender belly and she realized she couldn't—no, wouldn't—deny him. Her heart belonged to this man. She wanted him to possess her completely. Arren spread her thighs with a soft sigh. He groaned, his hot hand stroking her warm flesh. When his fingers found the moist evidence of her desire, he lost what remained of his fragile self-control.

"Oh, God, Arren!" The words came out on a groan. "You're so hot for me. So wet." He slid one finger deep inside her and groaned again. Her body clung tightly to his finger. He moved over her, feeling the painful hardness in his groin expand. "Sweetheart, you're so tight. Has it been so long for you?"

Her eyes flew open in confusion and he met her startled gaze. Before she could answer, he shook his head and moved his lips over hers. "I have no right to ask that."

His mouth covered hers again, and she lost what chance she had to explain. She kissed him back with all the desire she had so long suppressed and he growled with pleasure, moving his finger inside of her.

His thumb found her most sensitive spot, and when he rubbed it across the bud that controlled her desire, her hips arched into his hand, her breath coming in painful sobs. "Please, Gypsy . . . now."

"Call me Duncan."

He moved his fingers again and she cried out. "Oh God! Duncan, please!"

It was a demand, and he could deny her no longer. He surged into her with a forceful thrust, then went perfectly still when he felt the fragile barrier of her virginity tear and give way. Arren cried out in pain and clung to his shoulders. Her legs wrapped around his hips, locking him against her even as she demanded he get off her.

Duncan was frozen somewhere between blinding desire and arrogant bliss. She had been married. How could he have known? And yet, his heart nearly exploded with the realization that no other man had touched her so intimately. He murmured soothing words in her ear, stroking her softly with his hands. Her tight inner muscles clenched around him and he ached to slam himself into her hot, wet sheath again and again until he found his release and poured himself inside of her.

Arren was squirming beneath him, trying to move away

from the unfamiliar feeling of his flesh expanding in her womb.

"Darling, don't move. Just give me a minute. The pain will stop soon." He whispered the words, all the while praying they were true. Dear God, she felt wonderful!

"You're hurting me!"

"Just hold still."

She drew several deep breaths. In truth, the raw feeling had passed, and she could feel the knot in her stomach expanding again. Duncan kissed her tenderly, stroking his hand lovingly along the line of her rib cage. He told her how beautiful she was. He kissed her closed eyes and whispered how much he admired their deep green color. His hand moved lower. He moved his lips to the line of her jaw and told her how he loved the way her chin tilted when she was angry.

His fingers moved across her stomach and Arren whimpered. Duncan sighed against her mouth, covering her lips in a long, hot kiss, and his hand slid between their joined bodies, stroking her until she reached the peak of desire once again. As Arren arched against him, a shudder ran down her spine. He pulled back slightly, then thrust forward again, embedding his shaft deep inside her.

She moaned and clung to him. He could stand it no longer. He repeated the motion again, and then again. Arren sucked at his lower lip. Her hands clung to his shoulders. As soon as he felt her tight inner muscles clench around him, signaling her release, he cried out her name and thrust deep inside her, pouring himself into her womb.

Arren clung to him for long minutes, uncertain whether or not she'd died from the exquisite pleasure. He lay atop her, and his ragged breathing fanned across the gentle swell of her breasts. His hand moved along the length of her body and she clung to him, stunned by the force of what they'd shared.

Duncan couldn't move. Twice he told himself he was crushing her and should roll away. Twice his body refused to respond. His head lay on her breast, and he remained as he was, buried deep inside her. Against his ear he could hear the erratic beat of her heart pounding. Her hands still lay nestled in his hair. Never before had he felt so sated.

He thought about the word and rejected it as inadequate. He was satisfied, yet he still yearned for her. He felt filled and complete. His passion had been slaked, yet something deep inside of him still clung to her. In his mind he scrolled through an entire list of emotions, rejecting each one as too shallow to fully relay what he felt.

Then he smiled against her breast. He loved her. It seemed startling now that he hadn't realized it before. He loved her. He repeated it to himself, smiling at the way the word filled his heart. Yes, she was a part of him, completely and fully his other half. He chastened himself for not having recognized his tangled emotions earlier. Summoning what strength he still possessed, he raised his head to look at her, intent on telling her how deeply he loved her.

She had fallen asleep, with her hands still embedded in the curls of his hair. He smiled again and rolled to his side, pulling Arren firmly against his chest. He reached down and pulled the edge of the black wool over their entwined bodies, promising himself he'd tell her in the morning.

Seventeen

Arren stretched languorously in her sleep, her thoughts fleeing almost immediately to Duncan. Her eyes flew open, and his first words captivated her.

"I adore you." He was propped on his elbow, staring down at her. He ran one finger lovingly along the curve of her collarbone.

Arren's eyes widened momentarily and she stared at him, unsure of herself and of him. He smiled and leaned down to kiss her lingeringly. The soft touch of his lips sent sparks along her spine and she shivered.

"Are you cold, sweetheart?"

She shook her head. "No. I'm fine."

He pulled her into the curve of his body anyway. The naked contact startled her. She had to resist the urge to pull away. Arren worried her lower lip with her teeth and waited for Duncan to speak. He seemed completely relaxed. His callused palm moved up and down the line of her back in a slow caress. He laid his head back against the blanket, staring at the stars overhead.

Arren could feel the anxiety working its way up her spine. Why in the name of heaven, didn't he say something?

Duncan sighed. He would be perfectly content to lie just so for the rest of the night, but he knew it would be daylight before long. They had a long ride ahead of them. He was unwilling, however, to break the tender silence, and he continued lovingly to stroke the soft satin of her skin.

Arren could stand it no more. The tension was unbearable. She muttered something unintelligible and rolled away from him. She made it only as far as the edge of the blanket before his arm clamped around her waist and his heavy thigh pinned hers to the ground. "Where are you going in such a hurry, Duchess?"

She pushed futilely at his arm. "Don't call me that!"

He raised an eyebrow at her tone, and tugged her more securely beneath him. His eyes bored into hers. He saw the familiar shutters drop back into place and he groaned. "What's the matter, Arren?"

"Nothing's the matter. I just want to get dressed."

He held her still and shook his head. "You're not going anywhere until you tell me what this is all about."

She stiffened beneath him. As if he didn't bloody well know. "I don't have to tell you anything. Let me up."

He growled in irritation and shifted his weight, pinning her fully beneath him. "After what we just shared, you damn well do have to tell me. I'm not going to let you throw the walls up between us again, Arren."

Her eyes widened slightly. He saw the fear in them and swore beneath his breath. "I'm not going to hurt you, sweetheart. Surely you know that now."

She hesitated only briefly. She did know that. It wasn't fair to let him think otherwise. "I do."

He sighed and smoothed the hair away from her face with his hands. His forearms were braced on either side of her shoulders, and his hard body covered hers completely. She was having trouble thinking clearly, with his naked flesh blanketing her own. She swallowed.

"Arren, what's wrong?"

She looked at him in surprise. "Don't you want an explanation?"

He looked momentarily confused before his face split in a supremely masculine grin. Hell, yes, he wanted one. Arren had been married before. Until last night, she'd worn that son of a bitch's ring. Yet he knew she was untouched. No other man had made love to her. The thought made his heart swell until it was almost painful, but he realized Arren was extremely anxious over his reaction.

Duncan reached up and ran his thumb over the full curve of her mouth. "Yes, I want to know." He saw the way her eyes clouded and shook his head. "But I think you should know that I'm so damned ecstatic, I could fly if I wanted to."

She blinked. Did he mean that? "You are?"

His grin was shameless. "I realize it sounds horribly arrogant, but there's little in the world that makes a man feel more satisfied than to know a woman belongs to him alone." He saw the anxiety in her face and studied her carefully. "Arren, don't you believe that?"

"I deceived you."

He shrugged. "I suppose. Did you lie to me about your marriage?"

She shook her head. "Lawrence and I were married as I told you."

He waited. She chewed on her lip a bit more. "I . . . Duncan, did I please you?"

He raised an eyebrow. "Do you need to ask me that?"

She nodded.

"Arren, for God's sake! If I'd been more pleased, I'd be dead. How could you doubt that?"

"Do you have to know? Can't we just forget about it." She supposed she sounded rather desperate. She certainly felt that way.

He sighed. He was losing patience. "Arren, the sun's going to be up in another two hours or so. I would like to be well on the way to Inverness by then. But so help me, if I have to lie here with you all day, you're going to tell me what's bothering you."

She sank her teeth into her lower lip and shifted uncomfortably beneath him. "It's . . . humiliating."

He narrowed his eyes. He had a distinct feeling Arren was about to tell him something that would work him into a blue rage at her former husband. He nearly regretted the fact that the bastard was already dead. He took a deep, calming breath. "Sweetheart, there's nothing you can tell me that will make me think less of you. Do you understand that?"

He looked at her closely. She didn't believe him. He tried again. "What did that son of a bitch do to you?"

Arren shivered against him and reached up to pull his head down to her breast. It would be easier if she didn't have to look at him during the telling of it. He resisted only slightly before fitting his head comfortably in the curve of her shoulder. Her heart beat steadily against his ear. Arren's hands moved absently through the thick curls of his hair. He wondered if she was going to tell him after all.

Her voice was barely above a whisper when she spoke. "I saw a good bit of Lawrence before we were married. He visited with my brother, Donald, frequently. I fancied myself desperately in love with him."

Duncan felt a shard of irrational jealously lodge in his heart. He dismissed it, as he waited for her to continue.

"It was all an adolescent daydream, of course. Lawrence was very handsome, almost beautiful, really. I could hardly credit that he wanted to marry me. It all seemed horribly romantic.

"Donald had convinced my father that the disputed lands

on the boundary were not so important to our family, and that we would do well to barter with Lawrence. Papa and Donald negotiated a rather large financial settlement for me. Lawrence paid my father, in exchange for the rights to the land and my hand in marriage.

"At the time, I believed Lawrence really loved me. He had paid a huge sum for my troth, and I knew the lands were not worth nearly so much. I spent the three months before my wedding in a haze of blissful ignorance. Lawrence and I were married in my father's chapel with all the pomp and ceremony a young bride could desire."

Arren paused and stroked her hand absently across his shoulder. Duncan lay perfectly still, hardly daring to breathe. She sighed heavily. "It wasn't until my wedding night that I learned the truth. I was shy, of course, and incredibly nervous. My mother died when I was very young, so no one had taken the time to explain the way of things to me. I asked Nanny, but she merely explained that Lawrence would tell me everything and that I should trust him."

She shuddered. "I shall never forget lying in my bed waiting for him. The wedding banquet had gone on for hours, and Lawrence had been drinking heavily the entire evening. It seemed to take him an extraordinarily long time to come to me.

"When he finally entered the room, I had nearly fallen asleep. I remember thinking he was the handsomest man alive when I saw him in his long velvet dressing gown. He came in the room and shut the door, and I waited for him to join me in the bed. He crossed the room and stood by the window, staring out at his estate.

"I said, 'Lawrence, aren't you going to kiss me?' And I'll never forget, he looked at me with the hardest glint in his eyes. He sneered, 'God, you are an innocent, aren't you?'

"I was confused, so I waited for him to continue. He said, 'Don't you know I have everything I want from you. I have the lands, and I have the respectability of a wife. That's the only reason I married you.'

"I remember feeling rather desperate then. He sounded so angry with me. 'But, Lawrence, I love you,' I said. He walked over to the bed and leaned down so his face was just inches from mine. I could smell the liquor on his breath. His eyes glittered in the darkness. For the first time, he looked really evil to me.

"To the day I die, I'll never forget what he told me. His lip curled in the most awful sneer, and he said, 'I only left Donald's side because he insisted I should tell you the truth. Very well, wife, let me spell it out for you. I have no intention of touching you, now or ever. I married you for the land, and for Donald.'

"I told him I didn't understand. He grunted something distasteful and leaned closer to me. 'Donald isn't my friend, wife,' he said. 'He's my lover.'

"I was horrified. I shall never forget how bitterly I wept that entire night. I didn't fully understand the implications of what Lawrence told me until later, but I felt so . . . devastated.

"He had sobered up by the next morning. He came to my room early to crawl in bed with me. I remember shrinking away from him for fear he'd touch me. He laughed at me derisively and explained he'd only come to me so the servants wouldn't know he'd spent the night in Donald's bed instead of mine. I was terribly afraid of him. I asked what he planned to do about supplying an heir. He would, after all, need an heir to inherit his land and his title.

"He explained that he'd pay one of his cousins to see to the duty when the time came. Once I became pregnant, he could send the 'young buck,' as he called him, away where he couldn't betray him. Lawrence never did touch me, and blissfully, he never felt the time was right to start a family. Donald visited us several times a week, and I was so humiliated, I didn't dare tell anyone. One season turned into the next, and eventually, I accepted the truth. Lawrence was never physically cruel to me, and I lived in relative solitude while we were married. He died in a hunting accident six years later. My brother Donald killed himself two months after Lawrence's death."

Duncan had remained perfectly still during the entire story, fighting a cold knot of anger that was slowly building in his gut. He realized his fingers were clamped tightly on her shoulder, and he mentally forced them to relax. He silently fought for control, knowing Arren needed his reassurance more than he needed to express his rage. He took several deep breaths, waiting for his temper to abate.

"Duncan?"

He heard the anxiety in her voice and clenched his jaw tighter. "Hmmm?"

"What is it about me that's so repulsive my own husband would prefer to pleasure himself with a man rather than touch me?"

He could wait no longer. Anger be damned! He surged up on his forearms, his eyes glittering down into hers. "Dammit, Arren, don't you ever believe that! Do you understand me?"

Good Lord! He looked furious. Her eyes widened in disbelief and he groaned, grasping her face in his hands and lowering his mouth to hers for a hard, hot kiss. He raised his head and stroked the side of her face. "Arren, your husband and your brother were a couple of regular bastards for what they did to you, and so help me, if I *ever* hear you accept the blame for that again, I'll throttle you."

A shudder coursed through her and she wrapped her arms around his waist, seeking his warmth. She needed his reassurance desperately. "Duncan . . . please make love to me."

He groaned and kissed her again, more gently this time. When he finally raised his head, they were both breathing heavily. His lips lingered at the corner of her mouth and he lifted his head to stare down into her eyes. "Nothing would give me more pleasure."

He whispered the words lovingly. She raised her lips to his once more. Duncan made love to her as the sun rose over the horizon. He adored her with his mouth and his hands, giving her all the words of praise she longed to hear. When he slipped inside her silken warmth, he groaned with pleasure and kissed her deeply, matching the primitive movement of his hips with the strokes of his tongue.

Arren surrendered to the sensual storm, and clung to him, giving him all she had to offer. After the waves of exquisite pleasure passed, Duncan collapsed on top of her, soothing her feverish skin with his callused hands. She was fast becoming an obsession for him. He realized suddenly, that he had not yet told her he loved her, and he tilted his head to look at her.

Her green eyes were heavy-lidded with lingering passion. She met his gaze with a sleepy yawn. She looked positively wanton. A smile tugged at the corner of his mouth and he leaned up, kissing her softly on her still-swollen lips. He lingered over the curve of her upper lip before he raised his head and smiled at her. "Arren, I want you to . . ."

She cut off his statement by laying a finger across his lips and shaking her head. "Please don't say anything." She stroked her hand along the stubble at his jaw. "We'll settle it all when we reach London."

He stared at her a long minute, not entirely willing to concede. Her eyes pleaded with him silently. He sighed. At the moment, he couldn't deny her the moon if she wanted it.

Duncan nodded. "All right, but I'm warning you, Arren. I'll not let you erect the barriers between us again."

She smiled at him gratefully. "Didn't you say you wanted to be on the way to Inverness by now?"

He graced her with a lazy grin. "I was distracted." She blushed. He laughed and rolled to his feet, stretching his arms above his head. Arren didn't even resist the urge to look at his magnificent naked body. He looked down at her knowingly. "Quit ogling me, wife. Get dressed." Her face turned scarlet, and he bent over, tossing her the trousers and shirt she'd worn the day before. He shot her a slow grin, slung his own clothes over his shoulder, and strode into the thicket, leaving Arren alone to dress.

She sighed in relief. Arren pulled on her shirt, and buttoned it thoughtfully, thinking back over their conversation. She was exhausted. He hadn't reacted at all the way she'd thought he would. He never ceased to amaze her. She pulled on her trousers, wincing slightly at the unfamiliar discomfort between her legs. She wanted a bath. She looked at the horses and grimaced. It promised to be a long day.

Duncan reemerged from the thicket, buttoning his shirt. He watched Arren's profile as she fastened the tack on both horses and smiled, glad he'd given her the privacy he'd sensed she wanted. Her emotions were raw, leaving her vulnerable and exposed. He knew it would be unwise to push her too hard. Arren hadn't heard him step from the thicket. When he walked up behind her, she started visibly.

Duncan settled his hands on her shoulders. "Are you ready?"

She turned to face him and nodded. "I'd feel better if I had a bath, though."

He grinned, throwing the heavy saddles in place and pulling the buckles taut. "You smell terrible."

She glared at him and poked his back. "You're no prize yourself, Gypsy."

Duncan started to laugh. "Madam, are you suggesting that you find me offensive?"

She shook her head and turned to her horse, waiting for him to assist her into the saddle. "Not at all. I would merely have you admit that perhaps our good fortune in eluding Euan McDonan is attributable to our mutual . . ." She paused, settling herself in her saddle with a slight wince, ". . . aroma."

He laughed again and swung onto his horse. "I should think it would make us easier to locate."

She cast a glance at him. "Certainly. But who would want to?"

He turned in the saddle and studied her for a long minute. Her eyes were sparkling in the early morning sunlight. She seemed more at ease than she had in days. A slightly haunted look lingered in the emerald depths of her gaze, but she had resisted the urge to force him away again. He knew the courage it had cost her, and he loved her all the more for it. Suddenly, he began to resent the deception between them with a vehemence that surprised him. She might not be prepared to reveal all her secrets, but he sure as hell didn't have to keep his. He reined his horse around, trotting up beside her. "Arren . . ."

She shook her head, cutting him off. "Please don't. There are so many things between us. Can't we please leave it alone until London?"

He leaned over and kissed her gently. "All right, Duchess. You may have your way until we reach England. I promise you, though, I'll have answers from you in London."

She nodded. "Thank you."

Duncan tilted his head and looked at her for a long moment. "Arren, do you feel well enough to ride today? I know I hurt you last night."

Her face flushed a delicate coral. "I have no wish to discuss it, Gypsy. We're wasting time."

He reached up and tucked a stray tendril behind her ear—his now-habitual gesture of affection. "Next time, I promise you a bath, a fire, and a warm bed."

She wondered if her face could flame any brighter, and she spurred her horse around, glaring at him once for good measure. "I'll race you to Inverness!" she challenged, charging down the hill before he could respond.

He followed her down the hill.

They rode in silence the better part of the morning. Duncan followed Arren at a comfortable pace, watching her closely. Her auburn hair trailed behind her. The warm sun was highlighting the depth of its color. He was surprised at the depth of his feelings for her. He had always believed love was an emotion that touched a different sort of man. Even when his friend the Duke of Albrick had fallen victim to the elusive emotion, Duncan had insisted no woman could hold that kind of power over him.

But Arren wasn't just any woman. From the bits and pieces she'd told him of her past, he knew she had a remarkable will to survive. She had left out what he guessed were crucial details about her childhood, but the scars he'd seen on her back, coupled with the few mentions of her father, had given him a relatively clear picture of what her life had been like. The circumstances of her marriage, her enforced fight for survival following her husband's death, and the fear that had sent her fleeing into the night, were horrifying.

And yet Arren had not simply survived, she had flourished. He remembered the first night he'd met her. He'd seen her as a fragile flower fighting to survive a brutal winter storm. The analogy was fitting. She bloomed amidst the frozen, unforgiving background of her past and emerged as an exotic and rare blossom. He smiled at the poetic picture. No one could have convinced him he'd start thinking so melodramatically. No one could have convinced him he'd love a woman like Arren.

He settled back in his saddle, a grin of masculine appreciation settling on his lips. He followed her, content to merely look at her for the next several hours. Only when the sun had risen high in the sky did he decide they should stop and eat. Arren had been riding stiffly for at least the past hour, and he knew she was beastly uncomfortable. He spurred his mount forward, intent on riding alongside her.

She could feel the perspiration running down her spine. God, how she longed for a bath! She was covered in grime and dirt, her hair was damp with sweat, and her white wool shirt clung to her body, scratching her sensitive skin. Every muscle in her body ached. She had consoled herself for the last several miles with the knowledge that if all went well, she would soon be aboard the Duke of Albrick's yacht. If it had a bed, clean bath water, and a change of clothes, it would be heavenly. She heard Duncan closing the distance between them, and sent up a quick prayer that he'd decided to stop. She slowed her pace, waiting for him to reach her.

When he did, he shot her a sympathetic grin. "There's a burn just beyond those trees." He indicated the direction with his hand. "If we stop there and eat, you can wash up some."

She smiled at him gratefully and allowed him to take the lead.

The cool rush of water looked for all the world like a piece of paradise. Arren reined in her mount and slipped from the saddle before Duncan could reach her side. She wasted no time kneeling at the edge of the burn and plunging her sun-heated face into the cold water. It felt wonderful. She sighed and raised her head, blotting her eyes carefully with her hands. She was horrified at the wet streaks of grime that ran down her hands and wrists. She plunged her fingers into the water, scrubbing at them vigorously. She doused her face several more times before she was completely satisfied and turned to rise from the edge.

Duncan was reclined on the grassy bank, watching her intently. Water dripped from her chin and hair. She resembled a half-drowned animal. He smiled at her. She looked beautiful.

She smiled back. "Don't you want to try it? It feels wonderful." She walked to his side and sank to the grass next to him. The day was unusually warm. Arren tipped her head back, raising her face to the sun. A gentle buzzing grabbed her attention, and she opened one eye to see a fat fly circling about her head. She swatted at it once, but it returned, continuing its annoying rhythm.

She gasped visibly when Duncan's hand shot out in front of her face and seized the offending insect. He grinned at her and held out his hand, slowly opening his fingers. When the fly buzzed free and fled toward the thicket, Arren laughed. "You've probably scared him to death."

"Probably." He paused and broke off a piece of the cheese. "But he won't come back, I'll wager."

She nodded, gratefully accepting the piece of cheese he

handed her. "That's really an amazing trick. It's not far behind the wax seal bit you do."

He smiled at her. "You think so?"

"Of course. It shows magnificent reflexes."

"I distinctly recall you telling me I had bad reflexes," he answered, referring, she knew, to their brief tussle with the pillows.

Arren shook her head. *"Instincts.* I said you had bad instincts, not reflexes." She popped the cheese into her mouth, not waiting for his answer. "I've eaten sho much cheese thesh pas' few weeksh, I thin' I'll shoon turn into one."

He laughed and handed her the bottle of wine he'd opened. "Especially if you insist on talking while you chew it."

She smiled and drank a long swallow of the wine, handing the bottle back to him and stretching out on the warm grass. "It isn't at all gallant for you to tease me like that, you know. I really do know how to eat properly."

He tipped his head back and drank from the bottle before he looked back at her. "You could have fooled me. When we reach London, I'll no doubt have to give you lessons in proper etiquette."

She rolled to her side and propped her head on her elbow, studying him intently. "And what do you know of it, Gypsy?"

Duncan realized she'd given him a perfect opportunity to dispel some of her misconceptions. "A good deal more than you suspect. Arren, there's something . . ."

She shook her head abruptly. "You promised me."

"But, Arren, this is . . ."

"No. You promised. We're not going to discuss any of it until we reach England."

He sighed heavily and grumbled something unintelligible, rising to walk down to the burn. Arren watched him through sleepy eyes. She liked the way he walked. He carried himself with an air of confidence that reflected his character. At all costs, he would protect what was his. It was no wonder she always felt safe with him. When he dipped his head in the burn, his red-gold curls darkened and tiny beads of water clung to his hair. He slung them off—the way a huge dog she used to have, would shake water out of his fur. Arren barely stifled a giggle.

Duncan caught her smiling at him and smiled back. Returning to her side, he extended his hand and helped her to her feet. "Are you ready, Duchess?"

She groaned. "Yes. Though I'll admit I'm growing weary of that saddle."

He nodded. "I know you are. I wish there was something I could do to make it more comfortable for you."

She shrugged philosophically. "I'll be all right. I've survived worse."

He hated it when she said things like that. He silently promised himself that before too much longer, he'd see to it she had every comfort money could provide. Duncan walked with her to where her horse stood drinking the cool water from the burn. He helped her mount, before bringing his own horse around and hoisting his tired body into the saddle beside her.

Eighteen

Inverness lay spread before them, a sea of flickering lights and activity. Duncan reined in his horse on a small knoll overlooking the busy port city. Arren rode alongside and sighed wearily. It was well after midnight, and they'd been traveling nonstop since the episode by the clearing earlier that afternoon. She thought of the incident and managed a slight smile. Fatigue was getting the better of her, and at the moment, she was unable to see anything humorous about being astride this horse.

Duncan looked at her sympathetically and lifted her onto his saddle without a word. She nearly collapsed against him. He started down the hill, cautiously alert. He had known from the beginning that he could run into trouble in Inverness. If anyone, especially some of his neighboring landholders, wanted to prevent his journey to London, they would have dispatched men to Inverness to wait for him. He was unwilling to take any unnecessary risks when Arren's safety was at issue.

He had decided to approach the city from the southern road. The road was busily trafficked and lined with inns and taverns. It would, he hoped, provide enough activity to prevent their arrival from looking out of the ordinary. He bypassed three of the seedier-looking inns, knowing that as they drew closer to the city, the establishments would grow nicer and more expensive. His first order of business was to stable the horses where he could have his secretary retrieve them later. He and Arren would then be free to arrive in Inverness on foot, keeping to the safety of the shadows.

He chose an inn with a relatively inviting-looking stable and rode into the courtyard. Arren looked at him, a question in her eyes. He smiled. "I'm going to see to the horses. I think it will be best if we arrive in Inverness on foot."

She nodded wearily and allowed him to help her dismount. She had to cling to him for several minutes until she found her footing again. Her knees felt like jelly from the long afternoon she'd spent in the saddle. Duncan reached into his saddlebag and removed his leather money pouch, no longer making any effort to hide it from her. He looked at her, prepared to explain, but she shook her head. "I grow weary of this conversation, Gypsy. See to the horses' comfort so you can see to mine."

He grinned at the order and dropped a quick kiss on her forehead. "Stay right here. Don't move. I'm going inside to make arrangements with the innkeeper. If anything suspicious happens, come to me immediately."

She nodded and leaned back against the saddle, watching him stride into the inn. The courtyard was relatively deserted. A pair of young lovers stood in one dark corner, oblivious to her presence, and an old man sat on one of the low benches beneath the window. A few dogs and stray animals milled about, but there seemed to be nothing untoward about her surroundings.

As soon as she had arrived at that conclusion, she saw the group of uniformed officers deep in conversation by the stables. She shrank back between the horses and watched them cautiously. They were magistrates, not port police, though one of the gentlemen wore a blue and yellow uniform she didn't recognize. They seemed to be extremely agitated over something the man in blue was telling them, and she wondered wildly if Alistar had really sent the police after her.

She was so absorbed in watching them, she didn't hear Duncan come from the inn and walk up behind her. When he touched her, she started visibly, whirling around to face him. Her hands automatically twisted in the fabric of his shirt, and she raised her frightened gaze to his.

"What's wrong?" he asked.

"Look by the stables."

He turned his head slightly and narrowed his eyes, watching the conversation closely.

Arren twisted her hands tighter in his shirt. "Do you think they're looking for me?"

He shook his head but didn't look down. "No. They're looking for me."

Arren blinked twice. It had simply never occurred to her that he had a reason for traveling across the country as he had, and she felt suddenly very stupid. For God's sake! If he were really the Duke of Strathcraig, he would have traveled in a comfortable carriage, staying in posh inns along the way. He wouldn't be standing here with her, badly in need of a bath and a good night's rest, hiding from the police.

She refused to entertain the notion that he could have done something truly worthy of arrest. She trusted him completely, and whatever the complication, there was a simple explanation for it. She leaned against his chest and shivered. It was growing colder again, and she was suddenly almost too tired to keep her eyes open.

"Arren, I didn't commit a crime."

Her eyes flew to his and even in the darkness, she could

see the intense gold flecks in his gaze. "I didn't think you had."

He released a long breath. He had felt her tremble and merely assumed she had jumped to that conclusion. He should have known better. "You're trembling," he persisted.

"I'm cold," she argued logically.

He smiled and wrapped his arms around her. "I was afraid you'd jumped to the wrong conclusion. It wouldn't have been difficult considering the level of secrecy between us."

She snuggled closer to him. "Secrecy you've been stubbornly trying to dispel for two days." She shook her head. "I'm sure there's a very good reason you're being hunted by the magistrates of six different localities, and, I assume, the port police. If you want to tell me, you will."

He laughed softly. "Actually there is a very good reason. Thank you for believing that."

She mumbled something unintelligible and tipped her head to look at him. "For heaven's sake! If you posed a threat to me, you certainly would have done something before now. At the moment, the only threat I face immediately is dying from exhaustion."

He didn't miss the demand in her voice and kissed her softly. He raised his head and smoothed a tendril of her hair off her forehead. "All right, Duchess, I'll take care of you. I promise I'll explain everything once we're on board."

She nodded and allowed him to lead her through the darkest part of the courtyard, well out of sight of the magistrates. He explained as they walked down the road the arrangements he'd made for the horses, and she smiled in the darkness, remembering his conversation with them in the cave. He'd promised them a paddock of their own, and all the comforts they could desire for the rest of their lives if they provided safe transport to Inverness. He was evidently a man of his word.

Arren began to feel better with each step. Some of the stiffness in her legs and back began to abate as she stretched the cramped muscles. She could see the glistening lights of the city drawing nearer. The moon lit their way, and Duncan continued to point things out to her along the road, more to keep her mind off the distance they were walking than anything else.

They had only a brief scare when a group of uniformed horseman approached from the direction of the city. Duncan pulled her quickly into the shadow of a tavern and waited for the men to pass. There were eight of them, and Arren recognized that at least three uniforms were different from the ones she'd seen at the inn. Duncan had evidently managed to offend the better part of the country.

After the horses passed, Duncan pulled her back out onto the road, and they began walking again. They reached Inverness in a little under an hour. Even in the early hours of the morning, there were people everywhere. Merchants were unloading crates and barrels of stock from the huge ships that arrived and embarked daily in the port. Arren was fascinated by the colors and smells. Huge caravans of exotic goods moved up and down the crowded streets, and everywhere there was noise. Drunken seamen teetered about, stumbling from tavern to tavern, and Arren willingly settled against Duncan's side when he wrapped his arm around her shoulders.

They worked their way steadily toward the docks, and Duncan continued to scan the crowd for signs of danger. He pulled Arren along with the crowd, careful to avoid the port police who milled about in silent vigilance. They finally reached the docks, and Duncan tugged Arren behind a protective barrier of stacked cargo. His eyes scanned the ships docked off the coast, and he nearly fainted with relief when he saw the familiar lines of *The Dream Seeker* moored less than three hundred yards out.

Arren heard his sigh and looked at him inquisitively.

"There it is." He pointed to the yacht's low-slung form silhouetted against the dark sky.

"How are we going to get there?" she whispered.

He sighed again. "That's going to be a problem. I instructed them to moor off coast and wait for me. I didn't want the port police using their dock rights to search the yacht."

"How had you planned to get aboard?"

"I was going to swim out."

"So why can't we swim now?"

He looked at her in surprise. "Arren, it's over three hundred yards away."

She shrugged. "Can't you swim that far?"

"Of course I can. You can't."

She shot him a disgusted look. "How the hell do you know?"

"Well, can you?"

"I can."

He sighed wearily. "Arren, I'm serious. Don't be stubborn with me."

"I'm not. And it's awfully arrogant of you to believe I can't do it. Just because I'm a woman doesn't mean I don't know how to swim."

"How on earth would you have learned to swim?"

"We had a large loch near my home. I used to sneak down there late at night and swim. The cool water took the sting out of the . . ." She trailed off, her startled eyes flying to his. She was appalled at what she'd nearly revealed.

Duncan swallowed a retort and closed his eyes. She had been about to tell him the cool water took the sting out of the lashes she'd received from her father. He'd have bet his life on it. He opened his eyes and looked at her, leaning down to drop a hard, brief kiss on her lips. "I'm sorry."

She shrugged, knowing he understood. "It doesn't matter now. Are we going or not?"

"Are you sure you can make it?"

"If you ask me that again, I'm going to take offense."

He nodded before pushing her down on the ground, and tugging off her boots. "All right, but stay close to me, and for God's sake tell me if you grow weary. I don't want you to drown."

He made quick work of her boots before pulling off his own and tossing them aside. He'd kept the saddlebags from the horses and he opened them, carefully emptying the contents on the ground. Arren watched him sort through them. He brushed the remainder of the food and wine aside. He took the heavy vellum note she'd seen the day she'd waited for him on the hillside, and tucked it into his money pouch, securing the pouch inside his shirt. Discarding the large pieces of wool, he sifted through the remaining contents. He brushed aside the extra clothes, satisfied there was nothing else they needed, but stopped short when he heard Arren's sharply indrawn breath.

He looked at her, and saw the stricken look on her face. She was staring at the garment in his hand, and he looked down at it. He held the green riding skirt and jacket he'd purchased for her. He had been about to throw it aside with the rest of the garments but she looked at him imploringly.

"Arren, it's too heavy."

She nodded. "I know."

"It'll get wet, and the wool will draw tight."

She nodded again. "I know."

"You won't be able to wear it."

She didn't answer. He grumbled something unintelligible and folded the skirt carefully, securing it inside his shirt. He tucked the jacket beneath it and looked at her. She smiled gratefully.

Duncan pulled her to her feet and they picked their way down to the edge of the dark water. It was going to be ice cold, and he knew their most serious threat would be muscle cramps. He turned to Arren and needlessly adjusted her shirt on her shoulders. "It's going to be cold. Be careful you keep your muscles stretched so you don't get cramps, and for God's sake stay close to me." She nodded briefly and he sighed. "Arren, are you sure about this?"

"You are the most exasperating man, Gypsy. Is there a bed aboard that yacht?"

He nodded in surprise. "Several. Why?"

"Is there likely to be hot bath water?"

He nodded again. "Yes."

"Are they going to feed us?"

"I'm sure they will."

"Can I have a fresh change of clothes?"

He smiled, beginning to comprehend. "There's a wardrobe full of gowns that should just about fit you."

She sighed and pushed him toward the water. "Then I'd walk across the desert barefoot if I had to."

He grinned and stepped into the water that lapped against the coast.

Arren felt the need to gasp when the icy water closed over her feet. Blissfully, they numbed almost immediately. She waded out behind Duncan as far as she could, and then began to swim. He swam just in front of her, throwing cautious glances over his shoulder to ensure she was all right.

The first hundred feet or so were fairly easy. Before long, however, Arren's arms began to ache with the effort of sluicing through the frigid waters. Duncan did his best to create a tow for her, but each stroke became more and more difficult. Before long, she had to count out a rhythm just to remain afloat.

She refused to look at *The Dream Seeker* for fear the distance would intimidate her. Instead, she studied the movement of his arms and shoulders in the water, doing her best to keep pace. Twice, she lagged behind, and both times he cast a furtive glance over his shoulder and slowed his rhythm. They were nearly inching along by the time she heard the lapping of the water against the hull of the yacht. Duncan wrapped his fingers around the anchor rope, sighing in relief, and reached back to pull Arren up next to him. She fainted the moment he lifted her against his side.

He smiled down at her, holding her steadily against him. She was indeed a remarkable woman. Duncan turned his attention to the task of getting them on board. Mac MacPhereson, the captain of Aiden's yacht, was supposed to have left a rope ladder over the side in anticipation of his arrival. It would be difficult to climb if he had to carry Arren, but he'd be damned if he was going to awaken her now. He pulled her with him, careful to keep her head above the water as he moved along the side of the hull, searching for the ladder. He found it midway along the starboard bow.

Duncan reached into the top of his stocking. His fingers closed around the jeweled handle of his *skean dhu*. He removed the small knife and pulled up a length of the rope ladder that hung beneath the water level. Cutting off an ample piece, he fashioned a harness for Arren and secured her carefully against his chest. She never stirred. Cautiously, he began the slow ascent up the ladder, hoping one of the crewmen would discover him before long.

Jake Smythe came to his rescue. The burly seaman was at the railing, reaching down for Arren before Duncan climbed midway. He carefully handed Arren up to Jake, and made quick work of the rest of the ladder. The moment his feet landed on the deck of *The Dream Seeker,* he felt a surge of relief. They had made it after all.

Duncan turned to Jake and lifted Arren into his arms, cradling her close to his chest. "Thank you, Jake. I doubt I could have made the climb without your help."

The seaman shrugged. "Captain Mac said we were to keep an eye out for ye." He paused. "Didn't say nothing 'bout the woman, though."

Duncan grinned. Jake looked about as pleased as a schoolboy trying to stare down a plate of spinach pie. Duncan knew a heart of gold lurked beneath the enormous man's crusty demeanor, however. "Come on, Jake, it won't be so bad. There have been women on board before."

Jake snorted. "Only one that's never been a problem is the Duchess. All the rest were trouble from the start."

Duncan knew Jake was referring to Aiden's wife, Sarah. She'd managed through some miracle to completely win over every member of her husband's staff. Evidently, even burly Jake Smythe wasn't immune to the young Duchess of Albrick's charms. "I don't think you'll be having any trouble from this one, Jake. It looks as though she'll sleep all the way to England."

"Welcome aboard, Your Grace."

The voice came from behind him, and Duncan turned on his heel to find himself face to face with Mac MacPhereson. Mac was the permanent captain of *The Dream Seeker.* He'd been in Aiden's service for over twenty years. He looked

every bit the part of a sea captain, his red curly hair and
beard streaked by the salt and the sun. He was old as the
hills, his face weathered from the long days he spent on
the deck of the yacht. He had a real first name, too, but
they'd all long forgotten it. "Hello, Mac. You're a sight for
sore eyes!"

"So are you, lad. I was beginning to worry."

A brisk wind whipped across the deck, and Duncan shivered in his wet clothes. "It's a long story."

Mac nodded. "I'm sure you'll want a bath and a change
of clothes before you tell it. Follow me."

Duncan lifted Arren a little higher against his chest and
followed Mac along the deck. He smiled. Aiden's staff was
exceedingly well trained. Not a member of the crew had so
much as blinked over his strange arrival. Mac had yet to
ask who Arren was or why she was with him. The crew
had received instructions from Aiden to await Duncan's arrival off the coast of Inverness. He could have showed up
with an elephant in tow and not a one of them would have
thought it odd.

Mac led him down to the second level, and Duncan sighed
with pleasure when his bare feet sank into the warm carpet.
The yacht was luxuriously appointed, pampering its passen-
gers to the point of sinful excess. Duncan thought, not for
the first time, how glad he was Aiden shared his passion for
comfort. Both men had survived without even simple neces-
sities, many times more than they wished to recount. As a
result, neither believed in needless deprivation.

Mac threw open the door to the main cabin and looked
at Duncan. "Will you be needing more than one cabin, Your
Grace?"

Duncan shook his head. "I know your curiosity is nearly
killing you, Mac."

The captain grinned. "I've been in His Grace's service too long to be fazed much by oddities. We have a good deal to talk about though. You'll join me soon?"

Duncan stepped inside and laid Arren down on the bed. "I'll be up in less than an hour."

Mac nodded and pulled the door silently shut behind him.

Nineteen

Duncan peeled his sodden shirt off his back and shivered. The air in the cabin was warmed by a bright fire in the small hearth, and tiny goose pimples spread over his flesh. A knock at the door sounded, and Duncan barked out the command to enter. Two of the crewmen entered the room with four buckets of steaming water. They made quick work of filling the tub in the bathing closet, and Duncan thanked them as they laid out fresh towels on the long sofa before withdrawing from the cabin.

Duncan shivered again and tugged at the buttons on his trousers. He dropped his sodden clothes in a heap on the floor, turning his attention to Arren. She still lay unconscious on the bed, with her wet clothes clinging to her body. He stripped off her shirt and trousers, and grimaced when he saw the angry red saddle sores on the backs of her thighs. Lifting her close to his chest, he strode to the tub, sinking down in the water behind her.

Arren's head lolled back against his shoulder, and he smiled, remembering how he'd bathed her the first night in the hunting lodge. He silently promised himself they'd soon do this when Arren wasn't unconscious from fatigue.

Another memory jarred him, and he tipped her forward over his arm to look at her back. There had been several recent scabs the last time he'd looked, and he ran his fingers over them now, satisfied that they had continued to heal. He traced the tip of his forefinger over a particularly angry-looking one and sighed heavily, fighting a fresh wash of rage.

Gently, he undid Arren's plait, working his fingers through the thick, wet waves of her hair. She sighed in her sleep and leaned back against his chest. He groaned and continued the task of bathing her.

It was the closest thing to exquisitely painful torture that he had ever experienced. He ran his hands over her body, lathering her with the small cake of soap, trying to ignore the effect it was having on him. At least he wasn't cold any longer. He rinsed out her hair carefully, wrinkling his nose at the streaks of dirt that ran down her back. They were both filthy, and he lingered in the warm water only long enough to get them as clean as possible. He lifted Arren against him and stood, dumping one more bucket of water over their heads. Another shiver raced up his spine.

He wrapped a huge towel around her body, and looped another one over her wet hair. He toweled the long auburn tresses as best he could, before tucking her gently between the quilts. She sighed, and snuggled into the soft pillows. Duncan smiled at her and brushed a damp tendril of hair behind her ear. He grabbed a fresh towel and briskly rubbed at his skin.

The wardrobe along the far wall yielded a fresh change of clothes, and he slipped into a pair of Saville Row tailored breeches, thankful yet again that he and Aiden were so close in size. He pulled on a fresh shirt, sighing with pleasure as the soft lawn floated over his body. He cast a glance back at Arren and grinned. She probably wouldn't know what to do with herself when she saw the wardrobe full of Sarah's gowns. They should just about fit, though he suspected the sleeves would be a little short, and the waist a tad too large.

He looked at the sodden pile of his clothes and fished out the green riding outfit she'd wanted him to save. It was in sorry shape. Spreading it as carefully as possible over the fire grate to dry, he ran his hand through his wet hair once more, and reached over to snuff out the candles. Only the fire lit the room now, and the soft glow flickered over her sleeping form. He smiled and stopped to tuck the quilts more securely around her shoulders. Silently, he left the room to seek out Mac.

He found him at the helm. "Hello, Mac."

The older man turned and greeted him. "Hello, Your Grace. I trust you feel better?"

Duncan stepped forward and leaned on the railing. "Much. I was in sorry need of a bath."

Mac smiled. "I take it it's been a rough journey."

"Aye it has. I left Strathcraig nearly two fortnights ago. I'd have been here sooner if it hadn't been for Arren."

Mac pulled out his pipe and lit it, taking a long draw and exhaling the plume of smoke. "Will the lady be traveling with you to England?"

Duncan looked at him and grinned. "I should hope so. She's my wife, Mac."

The captain raised an eyebrow. "It's been an interesting journey indeed."

Duncan started to laugh and recounted the broader details of how he'd met Arren and their trip together. "I can't tell you how relieved I was to finally arrive and find you waiting, Mac."

Mac sighed. "I'm afraid I have some bad news to relate, Your Grace."

"I'm not certain I want to hear this."

"It's especially complicated now that Her Grace is involved. My belated congratulations, by the way."

Duncan nodded and watched Mac draw on his pipe. "What's the problem, Mac?"

"Shortly after we arrived, the port police paid us a visit. It seems some of your adversaries are smarter than you gave them credit for. We've been embargoed in port indefinitely. No one comes aboard and no one goes ashore until further notice. We're allowed one weekly shore trip for supplies, but they watch us fairly close." He leaned back against the railing and exhaled another long plume of smoke.

Duncan rubbed at the tension in the back of his neck. "Does Brick know?" he asked, knowing full well Aiden would be enraged.

Mac shook his head. "It seemed unnecessary to rile His Grace's temper until we heard from you."

"So now what?"

"Well, Jake Smythe has a cousin who works as cook on one of the British cargo ships that's been in port the last few days. They're waiting on a shipment from the south, and expect to embark in the next day or so."

"And?"

"And, Jake has talked to his cousin—George is his name—and arranged for you to have passage." Mac paused. "He hadn't counted on the woman."

Duncan slammed the flat of his palm on the railing. "Damn! I thought we were done with this game of cat and mouse we've been playing."

Mac shrugged. "Greed's a powerful thing, Your Grace. There's many who'd sleep easier if they thought they could prevent you from gaining the ear of the Regent."

"I know. I'm worried about Arren, though. She's exhausted, Mac. It's been a rough journey for us both."

"It'll be another four days on board until you reach Dover. With the embargo on us, we'll not be able to notify His Grace you're on your way."

Duncan nodded. "That means we'll have to arrange our own transportation from Dover to Albrick Park. If these bastards were smart enough to embargo us here, they'll likely be waiting for me in Dover."

"What do you want to do?"

"Hell if I know. I don't want to do anything until tomorrow, though. I can't move Arren until morning."

Mac nodded. "I'll have Jake talk to his cousin and see if he'll agree to take you both on board. You realize, of course, you're going to be stowaways? You'll have to remain hidden until you reach Dover."

Duncan uttered a brief laugh. "We'll probably both sleep the whole trip. If he has a warm bed for us, we'll be better off than we've been in days."

"All right, Your Grace, I'll see what we can do."

Mac bade him good night and disappeared along the deck. Duncan turned his attention back to the starry sky, silently thinking about the journey that lay ahead. He sighed heavily and turned back toward the cabin where Arren was still sleeping. He hoped a good night's rest would make things look better in the morning. A brisk wind whipped across the deck, and he heard the distinct sound of thunder in the distance. It appeared things would get worse before they got better.

He found Arren still curled up in the bed, and he stripped off his clothes. Sinking down next to her, he pulled the covers over his bare body.

"Gypsy?"

He smiled in the near darkness. "I should hope so," he answered, stretching out his arm and pulling her toward him. "If it's some other man, I'll have to kill him in the morning."

She giggled and curled against his side, sharing her warmth. "You're cold."

"I know. Am I making you uncomfortable?"

"No. Am I making you warm?"

He grinned and kissed her forehead. "Always."

She poked him in the ribs and yawned sleepily. "Are we on our way to England yet?"

He sighed. He didn't have the heart to tell her. "Not yet. Perhaps in the morning."

"What are we waiting for?"

"It's a long story, Arren, I'll tell you in the morning?"

She trailed her fingers up his chest, enjoying the feel of his cool, muscled skin. "Gypsy?"

"Hmmm?"

"Do you remember what you promised me last night when we . . ." she trailed off, too embarrassed to finish the question.

"When we made love?" he teased. "I promised you a lot of things, which one are you interested in now."

"You said next time, it would be in a soft bed with a warm fire after we'd both bathed properly."

Duncan sucked in a long breath and forgot to let it out. Arren leaned over him and dropped a kiss on his chest, her dark hair fanning around them both in a silken cloud. "I'm clean." She kissed the hollow in his throat. "You're clean." She moved lower and dipped her tongue into his navel. "The bed is soft."

Duncan felt his chest contract painfully when she rasped her fingernails over his flat male nipples. "And last time I looked," she whispered, "the fire was still warm. So what are we waiting for?"

It was the same question she'd posed before. He groaned deep in his throat. "Arren, are you sure?"

She looked up, a sly smile settled on the generous curve of her lips. Her dark green eyes met his and sparkled in the firelight. "Oh yes. I'm very sure."

Duncan rolled over, pushing her down beneath him. His lips came down on hers in a ravenous kiss, and he plundered the sweet inside of her mouth. Arren moaned with pleasure and clung to him, and together they forgot everything but the passion between them.

Duncan awoke to a number of realizations. Rain beat against the cabin window, betraying the onset of the storm he'd heard in the distance. The pitch and roll of the yacht indicated that the winds were high and the waters had grown rough. Arren was draped across his chest, her nails digging into the skin of his forearms. She was trembling violently, obviously petrified. "Arren, what's wrong?"

"We're going to sink." Another crash of thunder shook the cabin and she started, sinking her fingers deeper into his flesh.

He smiled and ran his hand soothingly up her back. If Aiden heard her say that, he'd be horrified. He had designed this ship himself, and it had withstood far worse than a simple spring thunderstorm. Duncan remembered that thundershowers frightened Arren. He'd always found that strangely endearing in a woman who feared little else. "We aren't going to sink."

The ship pitched again and she tossed back her head to stare at him knowingly. "Care to wager on that."

He grinned. "We're not going to sink. And for God's sake don't tell Brick you thought so when we get to England."

She puckered her brow in confusion. "Who on earth is Brick?"

"The gentleman who owns this yacht. He wouldn't be very pleased if he knew you had so little faith in it."

Arren quickly realized he was referring to the Duke of Albrick and couldn't resist the opportunity to goad him a bit. "You mean you plan on confronting this gentleman and telling him we've stolen passage on his ship. You're even more witless than I gave you credit for, Gypsy."

Duncan sighed. "Arren, I didn't steal passage on this yacht. I know the man who owns it. I'd tell you more if you weren't so stubborn about it, by God."

She looked at him and smiled. "Mystery preserves the fire in a relationship." She yelped in surprise and slapped his hand away when it came up to tease her breast. "Though I don't know why I worry about it with you."

Duncan grinned wolfishly and strained his eyes at the clock on the mantel and checked the time. It was just after four in the morning. He imagined they would have to make arrangements soon if they hoped to use the cover of darkness to disembark from *The Dream Seeker*. He sighed and kissed Arren briefly on the lips. "Go back to sleep, Arren. We're in no danger of sinking. I need to go on deck for a few minutes."

She watched him as he rolled from the bed and tugged on his trousers. "Is something wrong?"

He sighed. "Yes and no. Get some rest and I'll tell you about it when I know all the details." He reached into the wardrobe and pulled out a heavy oilskin cloak to keep himself dry in the driving rain.

She nodded and dropped back against the pillows, trying not to tremble when a loud crash of thunder shook the cabin. Duncan's hand was on the door and she called after him, "If this ship sinks, Gypsy, I'll hunt you down in hell and make you settle our wager."

He threw her a slow grin and slipped from the room, making his way to the deck to find Mac.

Mac and Jake were conferring near the stern, and Duncan worked his way through the pouring rain to their sides. Mac looked at him and nodded. "It's all set, Your Grace. Jake's cousin has agreed to take you and the Duchess on board. We've already paid his price out of the money His Grace sent along. One of the galley boys laid ill and had to be taken ashore. You can hide in the lad's cabin until you reach the coast of England."

Duncan wiped his wet hair off his forehead. The rain was falling in steady torrents now, and he had to shout to be heard. "Where is the ship?"

Jake pointed to his left. "Four hundred yards out. I'll row you over."

"When do we leave?"

Mac pulled out his pocket watch and checked the time. "It's just after four now. It'll be daylight in a few hours. I suggest you leave as soon as possible."

Duncan sighed and wiped the dripping water from his brow. "All right, I'll get Arren ready. Where do you want to meet us, Jake?"

"Aft port."

Duncan nodded. "Fifteen minutes."

He turned to leave and fought his way back along the rain-soaked deck. He wished to God he didn't have to bring her out in this! He sighed heavily and went below, slinging the water from his curly hair once more.

Arren was sitting up in bed brushing her hair when he reentered the cabin. He dreaded having to tell her. "You were supposed to be asleep."

She shrugged. "I wanted to look nice for my burial at sea. I still think we're going to sink."

He grimaced. She wasn't likely to be overly thrilled about the rowboat either. He crossed the room and settled himself on the edge of the bed. "Arren . . ."

She put down the brush and smiled at him. "We're leaving, aren't we?"

Duncan raised an eyebrow. "How do you know that?"

She shrugged. "Perhaps I'm fey. It would be too much to hope that we could travel to England in this kind of comfort." She paused and winked at him. "It would spoil our record of adventure."

He shook his head and leaned down to kiss her. "I don't think we'll be too bad off on the ship we'll be boarding." He briefly explained the arrangements to her.

"How are we getting there?"

He grimaced. "That's the worst part. Jake's going to row us over. I'll do the best I can to keep you dry, but it's raining fairly hard out there."

She made a sound that was half laugh, half groan. "After all you've dragged me through to date, you're worried about keeping me dry. For heaven's sake, worry about keeping me from drowning. Worry about keeping the damn rowboat afloat, but don't worry about keeping me dry!"

He laughed, loving her for her courage. "All right, Duchess. We're leaving in fifteen minutes. There are fresh clothes for you in the wardrobe." He paused and cast a glance at the colorful array. "And much as I know you'd like one of the gowns, I suggest you stick with the breeches. I know Sarah well enough to know there must be a pair in there somewhere. Bundle whatever you think you'll need in one of the clean towels. It'll be useful later. There's an extra oilskin in the wardrobe, too. Bring it along."

Arren snapped her hand to her forehead in a salute. "Aye aye, Captain."

He grinned at her, reaching for the door. "And don't worry. I do enough of that for both of us."

He slipped out into the corridor, still smiling. She was a piece of work, all right.

Jake Smythe waited for them on the deck. Arren had emerged from the cabin a scant five minutes after he left. Duncan had made his way to the galley to bundle a wheel of hard cheese and a bottle of wine. Despite the fact that they'd spend their journey in a galley cabin, he preferred not to take risks. He returned to the corridor to find Arren waiting for him outside the cabin, a small bundle tucked beneath her arm. He wagered it contained a certain green wool riding habit.

He smiled and pulled her oilskin cloak over her shoulders. She was comfortably attired in a pair of soft, champagne-colored breeches and a blouson ivory shirt. She had found a pair of riding boots to replace the ones she'd discarded before their long swim out to the yacht. Her hair was neatly plaited, and she waited for him, fighting a yawn of fatigue.

Satisfied that the cloak would keep her at least somewhat dry, he took her hand and led her to the deck. They found Jake standing by the rope ladder. He looked at Duncan and nodded. "I'll go down first, Your Grace, so I can assist Her Grace to alight."

Arren raised her eyebrows at the use of their titles. It hadn't really occurred to her until just that moment that she was now the Duchess of Strathcraig. She suddenly found it riotously funny and shot Duncan a teasing glance. "You're getting rather good at this impersonation of nobility," she whispered as Jake started down the ladder. "I'm not so certain I can carry it off, though."

He started to answer, and cursed beneath his breath when Jake called up to them. He walked with Arren to the side of the railing and tossed the two bundles down to Jake. The rain was falling steadily, and he helped her gingerly over the side. "Watch your grasp. The rope is slippery from the rain."

She nodded and started down the long ladder. He released a breath when he saw Jake lift her down into the small boat. Then Duncan started down after her.

The journey out to the larger ship was exhausting. Duncan cradled Arren against his chest, keeping her face inside his oilskin cloak to shelter her from the rain. The cold rain beat down on them, intensified by the biting wind. The boat pitched and tossed on the rough waters, slowing their progress. Each time the thunder crashed overhead, Arren's grip tightened around his waist. By the time the larger craft was in sight, she'd nearly cut off his circulation.

Jake found a rope ladder similar to the one they'd used on *The Dream Seeker* and pulled alongside it. His cousin's face appeared at the railing, and he signaled them to begin their ascent. Duncan handed Arren up first, watching her carefully as she struggled with the unstructured ladder. He looped both bundles together and tied them to his waist beneath his heavy cloak. As soon as he saw George Smythe lift Arren over the railing, he thanked Jake and hurried up after her.

The small rowboat soon disappeared into the night. Duncan swung his leg over the railing of the larger vessel, and pulled Arren protectively against his side.

George motioned for them to follow him, signaling them to remain silent. There was a brief scare when they passed a sleeping night watchman, but in minutes, George had them safely below deck. They worked their way quickly to the galley deck, following George's lead. He checked over his shoulder two or three times to ensure they hadn't been spotted, and then threw open a cabin door revealing a small basin, a tiny trunk, and blissfully, a sleeping cot. Duncan smiled and pulled Arren inside. "Thank you, George," he whispered.

The large man nodded and slipped the key to the door into Duncan's palm. "I'll see that you're fed as best I can. I'll let you know as soon as we lay anchor off the coast of England."

Duncan nodded and took the key. "We'll be fine."

"Stay quiet, and don't open the door lest you know it's me. I'll knock twice."

"All right."

"Try to get some sleep now. I don't think we'll be leaving until at least this afternoon. Make sure you lock the door after me."

Duncan nodded and slipped the key in the lock, throwing it home after George shut the door. Arren had already peeled off her soaked oilskin cloak, and dropped it in one corner. She knelt beside the tiny trunk, untying the bundles he'd carried aboard. She found the wheel of cheese and bottle of wine he'd packed and placed them on the chest.

He watched as she untied hers, smiling in fascination. She pulled out the green wool skirt and jacket he'd expected and laid them aside. There was a candle, a tiny comb, a fresh shirt, and a separate bundle wrapped in a piece of cotton. She peeled back the cotton and removed a tiny box of phosphorous fire sticks. She inspected them closely for dampness, satisfied that they were still workable. Peeling back the cotton a little further, Duncan saw something glint in the faint light that showed beneath the door. He walked to her side, curious.

She smiled up at him and held the object out for his inspection. "You see, Gypsy, you're having an effect on me," she whispered. "I've stolen His Grace's candlestick."

Duncan sank down on the low cot and started to laugh, trying to ignore Arren's indignant glare. Finally, he raked a hand through his still-damp hair and grinned at her. "Of all things on that ship you could have stolen, you took one of the candlesticks." He reached out, grabbed it, and inspected it in the dim light seeping under the door. "Not even an expensive one at that."

She snatched it back, and plunked it down on the trunk. "I didn't want to take an expensive one. He might have missed it." She picked up the candle, ignoring Duncan's almost silent chuckle, and forced it into the candlestick. Gingerly, she ignited one of the fire starters and lit the fat candle. A warm orange glow filled the room. She turned back to him, a triumphant gleam in her eyes. "There. You see. If it hadn't been for my resourcefulness, we'd have been here in the dark."

He reached out and ruffled his fingers through her hair. "I could think of some very interesting things we could do in the dark," he teased.

She reached up and smacked his hand away. "You're completely shameless. Do you know that?"

He grinned. "I thought we established that long ago."

Arren glared at him briefly before turning to survey their surroundings. They were rather dismal, really. Even in the warm glow of the candlelight, the walls were sadly in need of fresh paint. There was no porthole, and the only source of light was the narrow crack beneath the door. The tiny water basin was chipped and stained, and the floors were long overdue for cleaning and polish. She leaned back against the cot and sighed. At least they were isolated from the storm. Except for the pitch and tilt of the floor, the tiny cabin was protected by the hull of the large vessel. Unless the storm grew a good deal worse, the sound would never reach their small haven.

Twenty

It was deafening. Duncan awoke from a light slumber and found Arren clinging to him in fear. The storm outside had worsened considerably, and the cabin was permeated with sounds of inanimate pain. The ship tossed about on the water like an unfortunate animal, trapped in the jaws of an angry dog, every wave beating at the hull in relentless fury. He could hear the straining sounds of ropes and sails, fighting against frigid winds and the rending power of the driving rain.

Directly overhead, he heard the shouts of the crew as they struggled to control the vessel, as it sprawled about like a giant creature of the sea. The small candle in their cabin had gutted low, and the tiny flame flickered on the drowning wick. An enormous wave beat against the side of the ship, relentlessly pitching their cabin about. Arren's nails dug into his shoulders in fear. He smiled, and wrapped his arms about her waist.

She was terrified. Duncan had persuaded her to lie down with him on the small cot and rest for a while. She had awakened gradually to the sound of the storm. Every crash of the waves, and rumble of thunder, made the walls creak and the floor groan, and at any moment, she expected the vessel to be rent down the middle, throwing them into the tempest. She clung to him, fighting a wash of terror until even her breathing became a chore. When she felt his arms wrap around her, she shuddered against him, choking out a silent sob of fear.

He lifted his hands and stroked her hair soothingly, trying to ease some of the tension in her slender shoulders. "Arren, it's all right. We'll be fine." Another wave crashed on the hull, and the room pitched violently. Her grip tightened on him. He tried again. "Sweetheart, there's nothing to worry about. This ship is built to survive storms much worse than this."

It wasn't helping. In her shoulders and back Arren felt the tense muscles draw taut with every roll of the ship. She drew deep, shaky breaths against him, feeling like a coward and cursing herself for it. He must think her a fool. She jerked reflexively when a loud crash of thunder was followed by the sound of splitting wood above their heads.

Duncan rubbed his hands along her spine, trying his best to comfort her fear. "Arren, I'm not going to let anything happen to you." He stifled a curse when he heard another crash of water beat at the hull. "What can I do to make you feel safe?"

She raised her stricken green eyes to his, her unbound auburn hair spreading across his chest in a silken wave. The candle flickered one last time before drowning in its tiny sea of wax, and the room was plunged into blackness. Even the light beneath the door had all but gone out, and only the tiniest sliver of light severed the opaque darkness.

In the faint light, her eyes seemed to glow into his, and he met their gaze, watching her intently. She shivered against him, fear and anxiety driving her. Clenching her hands into his shoulders she raised her face closer to his and he heard the labored sound of her shallow breathing. She slid one hand from his shoulder to trace the curve of his whiskered jaw. "Make love to me, Gypsy."

The order brooked no arguments. Duncan thrust his hand into her hair, his fingers closing on her scalp. He pulled her more firmly atop him and tugged her head down to his, his lips capturing hers in a hot, possessive kiss. Arren whimpered and ground her mouth against his, clutching his face with her small hands.

Duncan's hands moved restlessly up and down the length of her back, and he groaned when Arren began tearing at the buttons of his shirt. She pulled the material back, burying her hands in the soft, warm hair that covered his chest. Her lips moved frantically against his, even as her hands roamed his bare torso, scorching his flesh.

Duncan tugged at her shirt, anxious to feel his hands on her naked skin. The shirt pulled free and he slid his hands underneath, tearing at the fragile chemise. It gave way as his strong fingers rent the material, and he groaned deep in his chest, his hands roaming from her back to the taut flesh along her ribs.

Arren was fast becoming desperate. The storm crashed above them, and she longed to black out the terror of the raging storm above them, in a storm of sensuality. Her movements became restless, and she arched against him, wrenching another groan from his throat. Duncan clasped his hands at her waist, rolling her to her back. He came down on top of her, his heavy thigh pinning her in place. When he pulled at the buttons of her shirt, she moaned with pleasure and arched into his touch. "Make me forget, Gypsy," she cried, pulling his head down to hers once more.

They climaxed together. Arren's screams mingled with the crashing thunder. Afterward, Duncan lay for long minutes, absently running his hands along her slick skin. Arren's heart pounded against his ear, and he could feel her hands tangling in his curly red hair.

"I think you killed me," she whispered.

He summoned what energy he had left and smiled, rolling to his side. Arren turned into him, wrapping her arms around his waist and pillowing her head on his chest. He stroked his hands through her hair, gently working through the tangled tresses. She moved her head against his hand, all but purring in satisfaction. "Arren?"

"Hmm?"

He grinned. She sounded completely exhausted. It did wonders for his ego. "The storm has passed. We're moving now."

She stirred against him and trailed her fingers down his chest. Her yawn was distinctly unladylike. "All these years I've been afraid of thunderstorms. If only I knew, I would . . ." Her voice trailed off and she mumbled something unintelligible, and Duncan felt her go limp against him.

He shifted her carefully, tucking her more securely into the curve of his arm. The ship still rocked and pitched a good deal on the rough water, but he could tell from the gentle creaking and twisting he heard overhead that they had set sail and were headed farther out to sea. If all went well, they should be anchored off the coast of England in less than five days.

He stroked his hand absently along Arren's back, wondering for the hundredth time what secrets still lay between them. Arren seemed tense, almost afraid, the closer they drew to England, and yet, she evidently still believed everything would be put right once they arrived in London. He considered a number of possibilities, rejecting each in turn, and sighed. She was a complicated woman. But, God help her, she was *his* complicated woman, and there wasn't a law nor a man in the world he'd allow to change that.

Duncan closed his eyes and allowed his mind to drift into a light slumber, keeping an ear tuned to the door and the activity above. Their circumstances seemed relatively secure, but he wasn't a man to take chances. He especially wasn't a man to take chances when Arren's safety might be at risk. As much as his body clamored for sleep, his mind knew better, and he lay quietly beside her, listening to her deep, even breaths. Only the lap of the waves on the hull and the creaking of the ship broke the silence in their small haven. He hoped the peace would last until they reached England.

Arren's eyes popped open and she looked around, momentarily disoriented. The tiny cabin was lit by the glow of a fat candle she had procured from George Smythe. She found Duncan seated on the floor, his back against the wall of the cabin. His forearms rested on his bent knees, his large hands dangling before him, and his head was tipped back against the wall. His eyes were closed, and except for the tight lines around his mouth, he appeared to be asleep.

The pain in his head had intensified over the past several hours from lack of sleep. They had been aboard for three, possibly four, days—somewhere he'd lost count. Arren had slept a good deal of the time, but Duncan dozed only fitfully, unwilling to lower his guard. His fatigue was so acute, he was afraid he'd sleep like the dead if he allowed himself to drift off.

Instead, he'd taken his position along the wall of the minuscule cabin and spent the time concentrating on what they'd do once they reached London. In his mind, he planned how they'd get ashore from the large vessel to the coast of Dover. He considered options for their subsequent journey to Albrick Park. He figured the odds on whether his adversaries had enlisted the Dover port police. He thought carefully about how he intended to approach Albrick Park. He thought about Arren.

Actually, he thought about Arren more than all the rest combined, but was unwilling to admit it. Their conversation had been limited to the short periods when she was actually awake. Those generally centered around the meals George brought them each morning and evening. An uneasy tension had settled between them after the night of the storm, and the longer Duncan pondered the problem, the more it aggravated him.

He couldn't for the life of him piece together the puzzle Arren presented. The fragmented information she had shared with him did little to shed light on her possible reasons for her journey to London. She insisted that the mystery must remain between the two of them.

He sighed, and pondered the details yet again. He knew she came from a wealthy background. Her father had been a landholder, evidently of considerable wealth. Her former husband had paid handsomely for her hand in marriage and undisputed title to a parcel of land. The land must be of considerable worth. After her husband's death, Arren had inherited the land, and, Duncan surmised, she had fled her husband's home to live with a skeleton staff. When her father died, Alistar McDonan had entered the picture. Arren was without protection following her father's death, and Alistar had brought considerable pressure to bear on Arren to marry him.

He paused, rubbing the tight muscles in his neck. There was a detail that nagged at him. Something he thought perhaps he'd overlooked. He searched his memory for it carefully, annoyed that it eluded him. Finally he reversed his train of thought, going over each issue in turn until he found it. There was another brother. He distinctly remembered Arren referring to Donald as one of her brothers. That meant there was at least one more, if not several.

He worried over the detail in his mind. She hadn't made any other references that he could recount. So who was the bastard, and better yet, *where* was he? He evidently hadn't been on hand to protect his sister when she'd fled from Euan McDonan in the dead of the night.

Duncan felt the dull pounding in his temples escalate at the thought. He frowned. The cabin had suddenly grown smaller and more restrictive. The longer he pondered the mystery, the more it worried him. Arren had deftly avoided any attempts he'd made to broach the subject, and the closer they drew to England, the more withdrawn she became. At this point, even fighting with her would be preferable to her enforced moratorium on all but the most inane conversation.

"Does your head ache?"

Her soft voice floated across the cabin. He gritted his teeth against the throbbing in his temples and said, "No."

She sat up in the bed, pushing herself up against the pillow. "Have you slept at all?"

"Some."

"It does hurt, doesn't it?"

He opened his eyes and turned his head to look at her. "Quit worrying about my damn head and go back to sleep."

She shook her head. "I don't want to."

"Then what do you want?"

Arren's eyes widened at the waspish tone in his voice. She shrugged. "I don't know. Why are you so irritated?"

"Why the hell do you think I'm irritated?" He had closed

his eyes and tipped his head back against the wall. The question was barely above a whisper, removing some of its sting.

Arren rolled her feet to the floor and reached for his shirt. It lay in a crumpled heap next to the bed, and she pulled it on to cover her nakedness. When she stood, it fell well below her thighs, and she deftly rolled up the sleeves, and came to his side. He didn't open his eyes. She sighed, and sank down next to him, mimicking his position. "I think," she said in answer to his question, "that you've been cooped up in here too long and you'll feel much better when we reach England."

He grunted something unintelligible and Arren shot him a sideways glance. "Are you sure you don't have a headache?"

He turned his head to look at her abruptly, ignoring the flash of pain it caused in his temples. "Yes, dammit, I have a headache. And, no, I don't want you to rid me of it."

Her eyes widened at his vehemence, and she ran her tongue nervously across her lips. "Why don't you at least stretch out and get some sleep? You haven't really slept in days, have you?"

He glared at her. "No, I haven't slept in days, and I don't want to now."

Arren squared her shoulders and looked at him indignantly. "Well, I don't see what good it's doing either of us for you to sit here and be angry. It isn't my fault you have a headache."

He sighed wearily and reached out to tuck a tendril of her hair behind her ear. "That's where you're wrong, Duchess. It is your fault. The whole bloody thing is damn well your fault." The fatigue in his voice softened the rebuke slightly.

She looked at him in confusion, furrowing her forehead. Reaching up, she laid a hand on his forearm. "Duncan, I . . ."

He shook his head, interrupting her. "No. Every time we start to have this discussion, you put a stop to it. Not this time. I love you, dammit, and you love me. Whether you want to admit it or not, it's true. And I'm sick to death of this game we're playing."

Arren looked stricken. Her eyes widened, momentarily giving him a glimpse of her soul. Just as quickly, the shutters dropped back into place. She shook her head, dropping her hand from his arm. "No you don't. You can't. I can't."

He reached over and grabbed her shoulders. "Arren, I can't keep playing this game where you throw dragons in my path to see if I can destroy them. As soon as I kill one, you produce another."

She pulled away from him. "I told you you'll understand everything once we reach England."

He was fast losing his patience. "Why?"

"You just will. You promised me we wouldn't discuss it."

He sighed in exasperation. "Dammit, Arren, you're my wife. What the hell is there to discuss?"

"I'm not really your wife. Once you petition the Prince Regent, he'll undo the marriage. It was only a common-law ceremony. We didn't even register it." She suspected she was beginning to sound desperate.

A dangerous glint flared in his eyes. "After all we've been through, after you've given me your body," he paused to let the blunt words sink in, "you want me to petition the Prince Regent for a termination."

She shook her head. "You'll have to."

"Arren, this is ridiculous."

"You don't understand."

"That's the first thing you've gotten right since we started this conversation. You're damn right I don't understand!"

She looked at him nervously, unsure what to do. "Duncan, please . . ." she trailed off, carefully watching the angry glint in his eye. "Please . . ."

He drew a deep, calming breath and dropped his head into his hands, waiting for his temper to abate. "I'm sorry. I shouldn't have lost my temper."

Arren felt the relief seep into her blood and slid across the room to his side once more. "At the risk of reawakening the beast within . . ." she waited for him to look at her. "Are you sure you don't want me to work on your headache?"

He groaned and dropped his head forward, turning to give her access to his broad shoulders. The instant her hands touched him, he turned his head to look at her. "Nothing's going to take you from me, Arren. I mean that."

"I hope so," she whispered.

Twenty-one

Twelve hours later, they anchored off the coast of England. Duncan had stretched out on the low cot and faded into a light slumber when he felt the vessel stop moving. The heavy vibration of metal against hull signaled the lowering of the anchor. He exhaled a heavy sigh. He hadn't told Arren what he'd planned to do when they reached Dover. He hoped they would be able to go ashore with the crew. He would have to rely on George for information about the docks.

Any number of scurrilous characters could be awaiting his arrival. If so, he and Arren wouldn't be able to go directly ashore. Instead, they'd have to swim ashore at a point farther up the coast. Unfortunately, the only route from there was straight up the cliffs.

A brief knock sounded at the door, and Duncan slipped from the cot, careful not to disturb Arren. He opened it, and George Smythe stepped inside, shutting the door behind him and turning the key in the lock. He looked rather frantic. Duncan frowned. "What's the matter, George?"

The seaman shook his head. "Bad news, Your Grace. There's a group of men what claims they're revenue cutters. The cap'ain is checking their credentials now. They want to come on board." He shot a meaningful look at Arren. "And they want to look for the two of you."

Duncan swore under his breath. "What time is it?"

"Three o'clock in the mornin' and no moon. Black as pitch it is. Trouble is, sir, I could disguise you as a member of the crew all right, but there's nothing I can do with the both of ye."

Duncan nodded. "I know, George. What do you want us to do?"

George shuffled his feet. "We're going to have to lower ye over the side, Your Grace. There ain't no other way."

"How far out are we?"

"A good five hundred yards. I don't know what you'll do about the Duchess."

"Are we up shore from Dover."

"Aye, right parallel to the cliffs."

Duncan sighed and raked a hand through his hair. "We'll be all right, George. Can you give us a few minutes to get ready?"

"Only five, Your Grace. I suspect they'll be aboard soon."

"That'll be plenty."

George left the room, pulling the door shut behind him. Duncan turned to wake Arren. She was already pulling on her trousers behind him. "Arren, are you going to be all right?"

"Gypsy, have I yet failed to fulfill a task you've given me?"

He grinned and walked across the tiny cabin, dropping a quick kiss on her forehead. Deftly, he buttoned her shirt to the throat. "Not a one. I'll make you a promise, though."

She raised an eyebrow. "Another one?"

He nodded. "This time tomorrow you'll be near a warm fire, in a soft bed, having enjoyed a hot bath."

She frowned and poked him in the chest. "I tend to get

myself in trouble when that particular combination of events occurs."

He grinned and swatted her behind. "I'm counting on it. Pack."

Arren quickly rewrapped her bundle, placing the green wool skirt and jacket in the center. When she picked up the candlestick, Duncan shot her an amused look, but she stared him into silence, wrapping it tight in the center of the small parcel. She tied the ends and rose to her feet, ready to leave with him.

Duncan was tying the two bundles together over his shoulder when George knocked on the door. He took Arren's hand, opened the door, and stepped outside. "We're ready, George."

"All right, Your Grace, follow me."

They crept along the dimly lit corridors, making their way carefully to the bow of the vessel. They climbed up three sets of ladders before they emerged onto the deck. It was pitch black. Arren had to blink several times before her eyes adjusted to the darkness. She reached out a hand and curled her fingers into the back of Duncan's white shirt, allowing him to lead her along the deck.

They worked their way across piles of coiled rope and rigging, to the starboard railing. A burly-looking seaman waited for them, a long coil of rope slung over his shoulder. George hurried forward and exchanged words with the man. He turned back and handed one end of the rope to Duncan. "All right, Your Grace, we'll send you down first, so's you'll be there to catch Her Grace when she reaches the water."

Duncan nodded and looped the rope around his waist several times. He slung one leg over the railing and looked back at George. "I won't forget this, George."

George grinned. "If you don't get going, won't any of us forget this. We'll all be in the brig by mornin'."

Duncan shot Arren a reassuring glance and disappeared over the side of the ship. She watched him go, shivering in the early morning air. A cool fog surrounded the ship, obscuring her view of the coast, and she strained her eyes in the darkness, trying to gauge the distance. George had said it was nearly five hundred yards. Five hundred bloody yards! She'd probably drown.

"All right, Your Grace, it's your turn." George held the rope out to her expectantly, and she saw that Duncan had already knotted the harness before he sent it back up.

She felt a smile tug at the corner of her mouth, stepping into the harness and pulling it up under her arms. She walked to the railing, and allowed George to lift her over the side. "Good-bye, George."

"Good-bye, Your Grace. Don't forget to hold onto the rope."

Arren wrapped her hands around the rope just above the harness. The rope twisted as she sank down into the mist, twirling her around in dizzying circles. Duncan's hands gripped her waist and he lowered her into the water.

"Oh! It's cold." Arren shivered as the icy water closed around her shoulders.

He grinned at her and deftly untied the rope, tugging on it firmly. He watched it slide upward until it disappeared in the mist. Arren was treading water beside him, trying to adjust to the ice-cold water. "All right, Duchess, we've a long way to go. Pace yourself, and stay close to me."

She shivered. Her muscles were already beginning to cramp. Duncan struck out first, sluicing his way through the black water. She followed as best she could, trying to ignore the numbness in her fingers and toes.

Desperate to think of something other than the stitch in her side, she turned her attention to Duncan and the odd argument they'd had in the cabin. He was vastly irritated with her, but she knew with a sinking sensation in her heart that he'd understand before long. She would soon have to tell him the full story, and once he understood the gravity of their circumstances, he wouldn't hesitate to petition the Prince Regent to terminate their marriage.

She was beginning to run short of breath, and she stretched her arms as best she could, to work out the painful cramp in her side. Gauging her distance from him, she sank her head back into the water and swam a bit longer before she let her thoughts drift back to the argument. She knew Duncan believed he loved her. But she'd been grossly unfair to him. She knew far more about who he was than he thought. He couldn't possibly understand until he had the whole story, and she'd been terrified to tell him.

Arren looked up and checked his distance from her. She was still swimming directly behind him. Drawing a deep breath, she pushed on. She hadn't realized, until they'd argued, why she hadn't told him the truth before they reached Inverness. She had convinced herself he might not take her if he knew, but today, she'd finally admitted the truth. The brief time she'd spent with him had been one of the happiest times of her life.

It seemed odd now. Their journey had been exhausting, both mentally and physically. Duncan had pushed her harder, demanded more from her, and settled for less than any other person in her life. When she thought about it, it was nearly a miracle they'd survived. She would have either been apprehended by Euan McDonan, or died trying to get away if it hadn't been for Duncan's protection—she owed him her life. After she told him the truth, he'd have no need for it.

She sighed, and ignored the pain in her arms and legs. She was growing more and more exhausted with every stroke. Her body had finally acclimated to the icy water, but her toes and fingers were still numb from the cold. She looked ahead of her, easily making out his white shirt in the darkness. She resorted to counting her strokes and breaths, fighting the fatigue that threatened to drown her.

The sand took her by surprise. It seemed they'd been swimming for hours when suddenly, she felt him pulling her toward him and the wonderful feel of sand beneath her feet. Duncan paused only long enough to kiss her, the salt on his lips mingling with hers. "Are you all right?" he whispered.

"Except that my toes are frozen off, I've a dreadful stitch in my side, and my hair is in knots, I'm on top of the world."

He laughed and swung her into his arms, carrying her ashore. They sat down on the beach, and he untied one of the bundles, pulling out their boots. The sun was creeping over the horizon, burning at the thin layer of fog. He handed her her boots, and bent to tug on his own. "It'll be daylight soon. I'm glad we wore pale clothes."

She tugged on her boots and looked at him in confusion. "What are you talking about?"

He finished pulling on his own boots and bent to help her with her own. "We're going to climb the cliffs. Our pale-colored clothing will make us blend in with the chalk."

"We're going to what?"

"That's the only way out—straight up the cliffs."

"Are you insane?" She looked over her shoulder at the towering white cliffs behind them. "We can't climb those."

He grinned at her. "Of course we can. All you have to do is follow me."

"For God's sake! It's a ninety-degree angle. We'd have to scale straight up the cliff face."

He tilted his head and looked at her carefully. "It's really not so bad, Arren. I've done it before. All you have to do is find one foothold at a time."

She glared at him and swiped the water off her forehead. "You can bloody well find the footholds yourself. I am *not* climbing that damn cliff."

He grinned at her. "You've been hanging about me too long. Your language is atrocious."

She snorted. "At least I haven't lost my mind like you have. I'm not the one who wants to scale the cliff face."

He was busily unwrapping the other bundle to pull out a long length of rope when the candlestick fell out on the sand. "No, but you're the one who's carted this candlestick across the continent."

She snatched it from him. "Only because I wish to return it. I don't care if it is inexpensive, the owner has a right to it."

"Believe me Arren," he paused and pulled a tight knot in the rope, "he won't care about the candlestick."

"Well I care. And don't you bother making that harness because I'm not going up that cliff with you."

He tossed her one of the bundles to retie while he calmly continued to fashion the harness. "And just how do you hope to hunt down our host to return his property?"

"You're the one who knows him. All you have to do is tell me where he lives and I'll gladly return his candlestick."

He tugged on another knot. "I'm sure he'll be thrilled to have it back. Now Arren, I'm going to loop this over your shoulders, and I want you to make sure it's comfortable."

"Have you listened to a word I've said?"

He gave her a blank look. "Of course. When we reach London, you want to return the candlestick. Now try this on."

She glared at him and poked his shoulder, shoving him back on the sand. "Not about the damn candlestick, you cad, about the cliff."

He grinned and reached for her abruptly, pulling her down on top of him. "Yes I have. But I know you well enough to know you're trying to cover fear with bluster."

She pushed up against his chest with her forearms. "I'm not afraid, and it isn't bluster. I'm just not stupid enough to climb that cliff."

He reached up and grasped her long braid, twisting it around his hand. "Then perhaps you'd like to explain to me why you're trembling."

"Because I'm cold."

"That's a problem I can solve," he said suggestively.

She glared at him. "But you can't solve the cliff."

He sobered suddenly. "You know I would if there were any other way. We don't have a choice, Duchess."

She drummed her fingers on his chest, and he watched her glance speculatively at the cliff. "You say you've done this before."

He nodded. "Several times."

"This same cliff?"

"This one and a few others."

"I take it you did all this while you were a spy?" she teased.

"Yes. I was pretty damn good at it too."

She looked back at the cliff. "How long will it take to get to the top?"

He shrugged. "An hour. Maybe two."

She rolled to her side and cast him a disgruntled look.

"All right. But I'll only climb for an hour. If it takes longer, you'll have to carry me up the rest of the way."

He grinned at her and rolled to his feet, extending his hand to help her up. She stood up beside him and he wrapped an arm around her waist, anchoring her to him. "That's just one of the things I love about you, Duchess. You're so accommodating."

She glared at him. "You have nerve. I've ridden days on end without sleep. I've gone weeks without a bath. I've survived off a diet of cheese and stale bread. I've done your laundry, tended your horses, mended your clothes, prepared your meals, warmed your bloody bed, and you suggest that I'm not accommodating."

He bent his head to capture her lips in a hard kiss. "And you're so even-tempered, too."

She poked his chest. "And I suppose you're the easiest man in the world to get along with."

"That's what they tell me."

"Well they tell you wrong."

He shot her a wink, and looked down at her. In the heat of the argument, he'd managed to slip the harness over her head and under her arms without her notice. He looked immensely pleased with himself. "Is it comfortable?"

She grumbled something about rope burn, and she tugged at the harness. "It'll do. If I fall and kill myself, I swear I'll haunt you for the rest of your life."

He stopped suddenly and lifted his hand to her face. "Don't you know you already will, Duchess?"

Her mood changed quickly with his soft comment and he watched the melancholy seep back into her expression. Reaching down, he smoothed away a frown at the corner of her mouth with his thumb. "Please don't, Duchess. The woman I love was here just a few moments ago and I get to see her so rarely."

She stared up at him, her teeth sinking into her lower lip. Suddenly, the sun broke through the clouds and flooded the beach with an orange light. Arren felt her heart break with the realization that this could well be their last day together. Resolutely, she squared her shoulders and looked up at him. He was watching her intently. She reached up and brushed a wet lock of his hair off his forehead. "All right, Gypsy. Let's climb this damn cliff. But there'll be hell to pay if you fail to get me to the top in the hour you promised."

Twenty-two

It took nearly seven hours. Duncan led the way up the face of the cliff, finding each handhold and pulling himself up so Arren could follow. At first, the cliff seemed jagged enough, and the climbing wasn't nearly so bad as she'd thought it would be. But the further they climbed, the smoother the rock face became. Before long, Arren was slipping her hand into impossibly small crevices, pulling herself up with little more than her fingertips.

She refused to look down, knowing full well it would make her dizzy if she did. Instead, she concentrated on his boots, following him carefully. She felt the awful cramps in her neck and arms as they inched their way up the rock face, and twice she had a nearly insane urge to release her hold and plummet to the earth below, thereby ending her misery. But Duncan encouraged her, helping her up when a reach was particularly far, periodically tugging on the rope to make sure she followed him. And they climbed.

The sun had risen high in the sky as they neared the top, and trickles of sweat ran down her spine. In less than twelve hours she'd been nearly frozen to death and about to roast alive. Even if she survived this bloody ordeal, she'd probably die of pneumonia. She wiped the sweat off her forehead, and hoisted herself up another level.

Duncan cautioned a glance at the top. They were close.

Just a few more minutes and he could pull himself over the edge and reach down to assist her. He looked down and saw her wipe the sweat from her brow. Good Lord, but he loved this woman. He searched for the next toehold and pulled himself up. And by damn he wasn't going to let her slip away from him—no matter how hard she tried.

He groaned with relief when he reached up and his hand landed on the edge of the cliff. Cautiously, so as not to jar her hold, he hoisted himself over the edge and reached down to extend his hand to her. Her sweat-slick hand closed around his forearm, and he lifted her up from the rock face, pulling her up beside him.

They collapsed together on the ground. Both of them were breathing heavily, more from the adrenaline flowing through their bodies than from the physical exertion. Every muscle in her body ached, and she groaned, rubbing the blisters on her fingers. "That's the longest hour I've ever spent."

He tilted his head and grinned at her. "I lied. You wouldn't have done it if you'd known."

She glared at him. "You *knew!*"

"Of course I knew. I'd climbed it before. Remember?"

She reached over and swatted his arm. "Charlatan! Remind me never to believe another word you say."

He smiled at her and pushed himself up on his elbow. "But look over the edge. It'll give you a sense of satisfaction."

She looked at him dubiously. He nodded his encouragement, and Arren cautiously crawled her way to the edge of the cliff. The sight made her dizzy. Dear God, it was a long way down. She groaned and fell back on the ground beside him.

"Don't you feel like you've accomplished something, Duchess?"

"No! I feel exhausted."

Duncan laughed and rolled to his feet. Stretching his arms above him to pull at the tight muscles in his back. He reached down and untied his end of the harness, pulled Arren to her feet, and removed hers as well. With the bundles slung over his shoulder, he held out his hand to her expectantly.

She took it cautiously, allowing him to tug her toward the road. "Where are we going?"

He grinned at her. "To return your candlestick. Besides, I promised you a bed, a bath, and a fire."

"We're walking?"

"Do you have a better idea." He pulled her out onto the road and they traveled along in silence for a while.

"How far are we going?"

He looked at her cautiously. "Until we can get a ride." That seemed logical enough and Arren fell into step with him.

After an hour, the wet leather of her boots started to blister her feet. She was beginning to realize that no ride was forthcoming. She stopped walking. "Why can't we sit down until a ride comes along?"

He paused to look at her. "Because I want to get there before nightfall."

Arren eyed him suspiciously. By her calculations it wasn't even eleven o'clock in the morning. "How far away is this place we're headed, Gypsy?"

He winced. "You really don't want to know, Arren."

"Duncan."

There was a warning note in her voice and he took her hand and pulled her forward again. "It's a little over ten miles."

"How much over?"

He looked at her sheepishly. "All right it's twenty miles over ten miles."

She stopped again and glared at him. "Thirty miles? We're going to walk thirty miles? Are you out of your mind?" She paused. "What am I saying? Of course you're out of your mind."

Duncan grabbed her shoulders, turning her in the direction they were headed. He pointed with his finger to a crossroad about two hundred yards away. "Look. That's the main road. With any luck, we can get a ride from a passing carriage."

She turned around to glare at him. "You'd better hope so. You're going to have one hell of a backache if you have to carry me thirty miles." She turned and stalked down the road, leaving Duncan to follow her.

They reached the crossroad and walked a good way north before they were finally able to hitch a ride on the back of a farmer's cart. The horse was old, and slow, and the wagon rolled along at a snail's pace. Duncan and Arren sat in the back of the wagon, neither mentioning that it smelled suspiciously like manure. They rode in silence for three hours, and Arren felt her eyes drooping in the hot afternoon sun. She was hungry as well, but she knew Duncan had disposed of the cheese before they left the ship early that morning.

He watched her head bobbing up and down and took mercy on her. Pulling her across the wagon, he pillowed her head on his chest. It wasn't five minutes before she drifted to sleep. Duncan continued to scan the road for signs of trouble. His ever-watchful eye took in each passerby, each carriage along the way. They were so damn close, he was hardly willing to make what could be a fatal error now.

The farmer stopped at a small crossroad and turned to look at Duncan. "I'll be turnin' off here. You and the lady'll have to walk a bit."

Duncan nodded. "Thank you for your kindness. We'll be

fine." He nudged Arren awake and helped her alight. She yawned sleepily as they watched the farmer disappear over the hill. "Come on, Duchess. Let's go."

She yawned again and slid her hand into his, stumbling along after him. They walked for hours. Arren lost track of how many crossroads they passed. She could feel her skin burning under the hot sun, and her feet were raw with blisters. Her stomach growled occasionally, reminding her she hadn't eaten since the night before, and, Lord help her, she smelled rotten. Between the sweat that ran down her back, the long-evaporated sea water and the farmer's manure, she stank to high heaven. Her only consolation was that Duncan did, too.

The sun had begun to descend in the sky by the time they procured another ride. This time, a traveling merchant picked them up. They settled themselves in the back of the wagon, their feet dangling off the back. Arren fought the urge to pull her boots off, well aware that her feet would swell and she'd never get them back on. The merchant's pace was not much better than the farmer's, and it was slowed considerably by his frequent stops at taverns and inns where he made deliveries. It was growing dark when he pulled into the courtyard of an inn and announced he would be staying the night here. Duncan thanked him and helped Arren down.

She took his hand again, and they started off once more. He knew they were within four or five miles of Albrick Park. There could be a problem breaching Aiden's relatively tight security system, but once he and Arren got onto the estate, they would be in the clear. He pulled her along, knowing that her physical and mental exhaustion were beginning to get the better of her.

She didn't speak at all. Instead, she counted footsteps,

exhaustedly trudging along beside him. Twice her ankles twisted beneath her from pure fatigue. She didn't have the courage to ask him how much farther they had to go. She knew she'd die on the spot if he said some God-awful distance.

Duncan watched her carefully through the corner of his eye. She was dead tired, and finally, he couldn't push her any harder. He shifted the bundles to his back, stopping abruptly. Arren barely summoned enough energy to raise her head and look at him. He smiled at her gently and bent down, lifting her into his arms.

Her head dropped against his chest and she mumbled something into his shirt.

"What did you say, Duchess?"

She moved her head sleepily. "I said, 'I didn't really expect you to carry me thirty miles. I simply' "—the words trailed off in a sleepy yawn and Arren drifted to sleep against him.

He smiled, shifting her weight. Ahead, he could see the line of trees that marked the edge of Aiden's estate. At the moment, they looked like the gates of paradise. He trudged along the road, pausing to shift Arren against him several times, and finally, he reached the edge of the long drive of Albrick Park. He paused, shifting Arren once more before he started the long walk.

He didn't walk more than fifty yards before he saw the grooms riding toward him. He stopped and sighed in relief. Brick's security system was intact, ready to pounce on an intruder in less than a heartbeat. He stopped and waited for the four men to approach. He didn't recognize any of them.

The rider at the front appeared to be in charge of the small contingency. Duncan's suspicion was confirmed when the groom addressed him. "This is Albrick property, sir. Have you business here?"

Duncan grinned—polite as all get-out and no doubt mean as hell. "Difficult though it may be to believe, gentlemen, I am the Duke of Strathcraig. I need to see His Grace."

The four men looked at him suspiciously. "Do you have identification?"

Duncan nodded. "In my shirt front. It's in the money pouch."

One of the grooms dismounted and walked over to him, reaching into his shirt to pull out the small leather bag. Duncan shifted Arren again, holding her tightly against his chest. The groom pulled open the small leather pouch and peered inside. "The vellum will tell you all you need to know," Duncan explained.

The man pulled out the now-crumpled piece of heavy paper and handed it up to the first groom who'd spoken. He opened it and looked at it carefully in the light of his torch. His eyes widened slightly and he dismounted, walking over to Duncan. "I'm sorry we didn't recognize you, Your Grace. We weren't expecting you to arrive on foot."

Duncan grimaced. "Nor were you expecting me to smell like a pig, either, I'd wager."

The groom grinned and pulled the horse around. "We'll escort you and the lady back to the house. Would you like me to hold her while you mount?"

Duncan shook his head, unwilling to surrender his hold on her. Instead, he lifted her onto the saddle, and steadied her with one hand while he swung up behind her.

The groom handed him the reins, and turned to swing up behind one of his riders. Passing the vellum note back to Duncan, he looked at Arren's sleeping form and smiled sympathetically. "Don't you worry, Your Grace. I'm sure Mr. Burroughs will have you and the lady settled with a hot bath, a soft bed and a warm fire in no time at all."

Duncan was almost too tired to appreciate the irony. Almost. "God, I hope so!"

They rode up the long drive, approaching the massive doors in less than ten minutes. Duncan cast a quick glance at the flagstaff. Aiden's pennant was flying, indicating he was in residence at Albrick Park. The head groom dismounted and walked around to hold Duncan's mount steady while he slipped to the ground, lifting Arren down into his arms. He held her securely against his chest and strode up the long stairs.

One of the grooms rushed forward to knock on the heavy door, and Duncan smiled at him gratefully. The door was opened almost immediately by a rather startled footman in Albrick livery, and a staid butler came hurrying down the stairs to see who could possibly be calling on the Duke of Albrick at this hour of the night.

Duncan leaned against the door frame, Arren still clutched to his chest. "Hello, Burroughs," he said with a half smile.

The old man looked momentarily startled before he recognized Duncan. "Good God in Heaven, it's you, sir! We've been dreadfully worried." He turned to one of the footmen and fired off a rapid list of orders. Duncan vaguely understood something about rooms and baths and food being prepared, and he leaned his head back against the door frame, his eyes drifting shut in exhaustion. "There has to be a fire, Burroughs. I promised her a fire."

Twenty-three

The Duke of Albrick leaned back against the pillows, his hand tracing absent circles on his wife's bare shoulder. Sarah was asleep beside him, and he tilted his head to stare out the window, his mind turning for the countless time in the last fortnight to his friend, the Duke of Strathcraig

They had expected Duncan's arrival weeks ago. As time slipped by with no word, Aiden was becoming increasingly agitated. He knew, from his communications with Duncan, that he had expected the journey to be difficult, but it had been over three months since Aiden had received his last letter.

Sarah sighed and moved against him, molding herself more closely to his side. He smiled gently and stroked her hair. For the last three weeks, Sarah had insisted that Duncan's room remain ready for his arrival. The linens were changed daily, the fire burned continuously, and the kitchen staff kept a constant supply of hot water ready to fill his bath. She had done everything possible to conceal her growing concern from Aiden, but he knew his wife too well. Sarah cared deeply for Duncan, and Aiden was well aware that her agitation grew with each passing day.

He narrowed his eyes, staring at the moon and scrolling through the possibilities in his mind. "Where the hell are you, Duncan?"

The soft knock sounded at the door almost in response to his whispered question. Aiden frowned and slowly detached himself from Sarah's side, swinging his feet to the floor. He didn't bother to pull on his robe, knowing that only his valet would dare disturb them at this hour. He crossed the room. His feet sank into the thick carpet. He cracked the door open enough to see his valet standing in the corridor. "What's wrong, Kirkwell?"

"It's the Duke of Strathcraig, Your Grace. He's just arrived."

"Thank God! I'll be right down."

Aiden would have shut the door, but his valet held out his hand. "There's something else, Your Grace. He's got a woman with him, Burroughs wants to know if you'd like a separate room prepared."

Aiden's brow furrowed. Duncan had said nothing about traveling with a female companion. "Did His Grace say he wanted another room?"

Kirkwell shook his head. "He doesn't seem entirely capable of making that decision right now. He keeps mumbling something about a fire."

Aiden nodded. "Tell Mr. Burroughs to wait for me. I'll be right there."

He shut the door and crossed the room to his wardrobe for a fresh pair of trousers.

"What's the matter, Aiden?"

Sarah's voice came from behind him, and he stepped into his trousers, turning to look at her. "Duncan's here."

Sarah sat bolt upright in the bed and tossed the covers off. "Oh, thank heaven! I was so worried." She swung her feet to the floor and crossed the room to Aiden's side. "I'm going with you."

He curled his fingers around her shoulders and dropped

a quick kiss on her forehead. "You're welcome to, darling. But even if Duncan is my closest friend, I'd much prefer you put some clothes on first."

Sarah giggled. She had completely forgotten she was stark naked, and imagined it would cause somewhat of a stir with the house staff. "I'm certain Mr. Burroughs would be most appalled."

Aiden smiled and kissed her again, swatting her bare behind playfully. "Get dressed, wife. I'll meet you downstairs."

Sarah smiled at him and turned to reach for her robe. Aiden was halfway to the door when she called after him. "Aiden . . ."

He looked back, his hand on the door handle. "Yes?"

"I know how worried you've been. I'm glad he's all right."

He smiled at her and pulled the door open. "So am I."

Aiden tugged the door shut behind him and hurried down the corridor, ignoring the slight chill of the house that touched his bare chest. Even this late in the spring, the evenings still grew cold, and the stone walls and marble floors of Albrick Park did little to protect against the chill. He reached the top of the stairs and saw the hum of activity in his foyer. It took him only a few minutes to identify Duncan among the throng of servants. He was the scurrilous-looking one.

Duncan still stood with his back against the door frame, his head tilted back in exhaustion. He held Arren against his chest, her unconscious body sagging in his arms.

"Good God!"

Duncan heard Aiden's voice and opened his eyes. Aiden came striding down the stairs toward him.

"Duncan, where the hell have you been?"

Duncan managed a weary smile as he watched his friend approach. "Damned good to see you, too, Brick."

Aiden strode across the foyer, his forehead bowing as he took in Duncan's appearance. "We expected you weeks ago. My last communication from Mac arrived over two fortnights back. I . . ." Aiden reached his side and paused. "Good Lord! You smell rank."

Duncan exhaled an exhausted sigh. "Under normal circumstances, I'd answer that with something appropriately sarcastic. I don't think I'm capable of that at the moment, however. I . . ."

"Duncan!" Sarah came flying down the long staircase, her unbound hair flying out behind her. She'd pulled on her velvet dressing gown, and she ran down the stairs, her bare feet slapping against the polished marble. "Oh Duncan!" She reached his side and threw her arms around his neck, completely unconcerned with the horrendous odor that emanated from him. "We've been so worried!" She kissed his cheek, and stepped back, swiping at her tears with the back of her hand. For the first time, she looked down at Arren. "Is she all right?"

He nodded. "Just exhausted. We're both in desperate need of sleep."

Sarah reached up and touched his beard, frowning at the deep circles under his eyes. "I'm sorry. We shouldn't have made you stand here so long." She turned to Aiden. "Aiden, carry . . ." she paused and looked back at Duncan. "What's her name, Duncan?"

He sighed and shifted Arren against him. "Arren."

Sarah nodded. "Aiden, carry Arren upstairs for Duncan and let's get them settled."

Aiden stepped forward, casting her an amused glance. "Let's get them bathed first. They smell horrid."

"Aiden!" She shot him a disparaging look. "Help him!"

Aiden reached out his arms to lift Arren. Duncan looked

up at him, their eyes locking. He seemed incapable of letting her go.

"Duncan," Aiden's voice was soft with sympathy. "She's safe now. Let me take her."

Duncan appeared momentarily disoriented before he sighed in relief and dropped his arms. Sarah reached out and linked her arm through his, leading him toward the stairs. "We've already prepared your room. What you need now is a solid night's rest."

Duncan trudged wearily up the stairs. All the exhaustion of the past few days seemed to seep in on him at once. Aiden followed them, holding Arren, and studying her carefully. Whoever this woman was, Duncan had evidently worn himself out protecting her. It was undoubtedly one hell of a story.

Sarah turned down the long corridor and threw open the doors to one of the elegantly appointed staterooms. Inside, three footmen were hastily filling the large tub in the bathing closet, while a fourth saw to the fire. "Aiden, we'll put Arren in here. Lay her on the bed and Emily and I will take care of her. You and Mr. Kirkwell can see to Duncan."

Duncan looked about to protest, but Sarah crossed the room and opened the connecting door. "You'll be right next door, Duncan."

Aiden lay Arren on the bed, and looked down at her. "Sarah, can you and Emily manage all right?"

"Yes. Don't worry about it. We need to get them settled as soon as possible. He's nearly dead from exhaustion."

Aiden nodded and walked across the room, placing both hands on Duncan's shoulders and shoving him through the door. Behind him, he heard Sarah dismiss the servants and send for her lady's maid and his valet. He pushed Duncan down on the bed so his feet dangled over the side, and bent to tug his boots off. "So who the devil is she, Dunc?"

"She's my wife."

Aiden looked up in surprise, in time to see Duncan fall back on the bed in exhaustion. His eyes closed, and he lapsed into a deep, unconscious sleep before he landed on the covers. Aiden heard the door open, and he turned his head to see Kirkwell coming toward him with a pile of towels and a long velvet dressing gown slung over his shoulder.

"I don't think he looks so good, Your Grace. Kind of peaked."

Aiden nodded and pulled Duncan's other boot free, curling his mouth in distaste at the sight of his blistered, swollen feet. "He's in rough shape, all right. Let's see if we can get him shaved and bathed before we settle him in for the night."

"From the looks of him, I suspect he'll sleep through the day tomorrow as well."

Aiden reached down and lifted Duncan's arm, hoisting him onto his shoulder. He carried him across the room to the large bathing closet and lowered him as gingerly as possible into the steaming bath. Kirkwell dropped the towels and moved to his side, gingerly raising Duncan's face. "I'll shave off his beard, Your Grace, but we'll have to soak his face or he'll be devilishly sore in the morning."

Aiden nodded and gripped the back of Duncan's hair. He dipped his face forward into the warm water twice, wetting the thick red-gold whiskers. Duncan groaned in his sleep, and his head fell back against the edge of the tub. "All right, Kirkwell, shave them off. I'll see if I can cut through this dirt."

They worked together a good long while, pausing only

to comment on Duncan's disheveled condition. When they finally had him cleaned and shaven, Aiden lifted Duncan to a standing position, allowing Kirkwell to dump the tepid rinse water over his head. The soapy lather ran down his arms and legs, and Kirkwell toweled him off, waiting for Aiden to lift him from the tub before he finished the job.

They slid his arms inside the long velvet robe, and Aiden hoisted him over his shoulders once again, striding for the connecting door. "Based on his earlier reaction, I don't think he'd like to awaken and not find his wife beside him."

"Aye, Your Grace." Kirkwell rushed forward and pulled open the door. "He seems a bit protective about the Duchess."

Aiden strode through the short corridor, leaving Kirkwell to straighten the other room. He kicked on the connecting door with his toe. "Sarah, open the door."

Emily swung it open, and curtsied to him, withdrawing from the room with a bundle of wet towels and sodden garments. Sarah stood by the bed, pulling the covers over Arren's shoulders. She turned and looked at him in surprise. "You're going to put him in here?"

Aiden nodded and walked to the bed, lowering Duncan beside Arren. "I think it'd be best if they were near each other. He might react if he awoke and she wasn't with him."

Sarah nodded and helped Aiden settle Duncan in the bed, tactfully turning her head when he pulled the velvet robe free and slid his body beneath the blankets.

"Did he tell you who she is?"

Aiden pulled the covers up, smiling when Duncan turned in his sleep and slung his arm across Arren's waist. "She's his wife." He looked at Sarah and laughed at her dumbfounded expression. "That's all I could get out of him before he collapsed." He raked a hand through his hair.

"Whoever she is, they've been through hell getting here. What kind of shape was she in?"

"Oh Aiden, it was awful. Her feet were blistered raw. She had the most horrid saddle sores on the backs of her thighs." Sarah paused and looked at him. "And there were terrible lash marks on her back. Some of them are fairly fresh."

He sighed and walked to Sarah's side, taking her hand. "He wasn't much better. No new scars as well as I could determine, though. I suppose we'll have to wait until morning to get the story out of them."

Sarah followed him across the room and turned back when they reached the door. The moonlight spilled across the bed, highlighting Arren's auburn hair. "I shall have to find something for her to wear. I told Emily to burn her clothes."

Aiden tugged on her hand. "You can worry about it in the morning. Kirkwell is right. They'll probably sleep through the day tomorrow."

He pulled her through the door and shut it behind them, wrapping his arm around Sarah's shoulders and leading her back to their bedroom. "Aiden?" She turned her head to look at him.

"Hmm?"

"Why do you suppose he didn't wait for you to have them picked up in Dover?"

He shook his head. "I don't know. But there were chalk stains on his trousers. I think they probably had to climb the cliffs."

"Climb them! Is that possible?"

"He and I have done it before. Two or three times, in fact."

Sarah sighed, remembering the days when Aiden and

Duncan were actively involved with the British War Department. She had spent weeks at a time agonizing over their whereabouts, and occasionally he would relay a detail about their various activities. Each time, she became more and more aware how glad she was that she hadn't known at the time. She shivered and wrapped her arm more firmly about her husband's waist. "What could have prevented them from coming ashore at the docks?"

"I don't know. I suspect Duncan's problems may have followed him from Scotland. We won't know for sure until he can stay awake long enough to tell us."

They reached their room and Aiden pushed open the door. Sarah raised up on her tiptoes to kiss him briefly on the lips. "I'll join you in a minute. I want to check on the baby."

He raised his eyebrows. "Sarah, Cana's fine. Nanny's with her."

"I know. I've just suddenly become very grateful that I don't have to worry about you like I used to. I want to go look in on her and count my blessings for a minute."

He smiled and took her hand, pulling the door to their room shut once more. "Come on. I'll go with you."

She leaned her head against his shoulder, and they walked hand in hand to the nursery.

Duncan awoke only once in the night. He raised his head on the pillow, staring into the warm glow of the fire. He felt Arren curled beside him and he sighed contentedly, tightening his hold on her slightly. For the first time in weeks, he knew they were completely safe. Protected by the stone walls of Albrick Park, nothing could threaten them here. He dropped his head back, allowing his eyes to drift shut. They were cocooned in a haven of warmth and security. Everything and everyone that threatened them lay beyond the gates of Albrick Park. At the moment, the only dragon left was the one Arren kept between them.

He fell asleep, thinking he'd slay that dragon too, just as soon as he could stay awake long enough.

Twenty-four

Aiden crossed his legs on his desk and leaned back in his chair. He was seated in the library of Albrick Park, watching the rain glide down the windows in steady sheets. His secretary had just left, having completed the week's correspondence. Aiden sighed and reached for his cup of coffee. It was late afternoon, and Kirkwell had looked in on Duncan and Arren twice. They were still completely unconscious.

The heavy door opened and Sarah came in, holding Cana against her shoulder. "Hello, darling. Did you finish up with Mr. Robertson?" she asked.

Aiden nodded and rose from his chair, crossing the room to take his daughter in his arms. Cana giggled delightedly and curled her fingers on the side of his face. He laughed, pulling her hand away. "Yes. There was a considerable amount of correspondence on the mining problem. I think we've worked through the bulk of it, though. What have you been up to this afternoon?"

Sarah sighed and settled herself on the long sofa, making room for Aiden beside her. He sat down, resting his feet on the coffee table. "You mean besides dying with curiosity?" She reached up and flipped a towel over his shoulder. "Careful, she'll drool all over your jacket."

He smiled at Cana and tipped her away from his shoulder,

cradling her head in his large hand. "It's all right, isn't it Cana? You've ruined plenty of your papa's jackets before."

Sarah snorted. "Well that particular one arrived just last week. Let's try to make it last."

Cana giggled again and sucked on Aiden's finger. "I think she's cutting her teeth," he said.

Sarah nodded. "I noticed that last week. I can't believe how quickly she's growing."

"Before we know it, she'll be breaking the hearts of every man in London."

"Um-hmm. Her father will have spoiled her rotten, too."

Aiden grinned at her. "If I had half a dozen more, I wouldn't be able to spoil her so completely."

Sarah shot him a disparaging glance. "You'll be just as bad with all of them. We'll have a whole pack of hellions running about, if you have your way."

He grinned again and leaned down so his mouth was just inches from hers. "But think of the fun we'll have creating that uncontrollable horde."

"You have a one-track mind, Aiden Brickston."

"Um-hmm," he mumbled, his lips capturing hers for a long, satisfying kiss.

Neither of them heard the door swing open. "Oh for God's sake! Some things never change." Duncan was standing in the doorway, his hands planted on his hips, a sarcastic smile on his face.

Aiden raised his head and looked up abruptly. "Dunc! You're awake."

Duncan strolled into the room, pausing to pour himself a cup of coffee. "Clearly. I feel immeasurably better, too. Thank you for the clothes, Brick."

Aiden smiled. He had left a clean pair of trousers, a fresh shirt and cravat, and polished boots for Duncan by the bed.

Sarah had left several gowns for Arren, and they'd disposed of all the tattered, dirty clothes the two had arrived in. "I hardly thought you'd want to walk around in that mess you showed up wearing on your back."

Duncan nodded and crossed the room to look down at Cana. He reached out and stroked her cheek with his finger. "I saw the gowns you left for Arren, Sarah. Thank you for that." He looked up at her. "Is this my baby?"

Sarah laughed. "I think Aiden may want to dispute that with you." She reached over and lifted Cana from Aiden's lap. "Come here, sweetheart." Sarah carried the baby to Duncan's side and held her up to him. "Cana, this is your godfather. You may call him Uncle Duncan from now on. If you smile at him just right, he'll be another man you can add to your list of conquests."

Cana responded with a chortle of laughter and Duncan smiled down at her, mesmerized. Her large purple eyes sparkled at him and he reached up his large hands, taking her carefully from Sarah and holding her against his shoulder. "Thank God she looks like you, Sarah. It would have been a tragedy if she'd gotten her father's scurrilous looks."

Sarah smiled and patted the baby's back. "She got her father's charm though. One smile and she has the world at her feet."

Duncan grinned as he settled himself in the large chair facing the sofa, and shifted Cana against his wide shoulder. "She'll undoubtedly rule London when she's old enough."

Sarah lifted Duncan's coffee cup from the beverage cart and set it on the low table beside him. "Yes. And I'm sure Aiden will be calling you in from Scotland to help ward off the dandies lined up on our doorstep."

Aiden laughed. "I'm not sure either one of us will be up to the task."

"Well between her father and her godfather, I doubt any of those poor young men will stand a chance," Sarah answered.

Cana snuggled her head against Duncan's shoulder and curled her tiny fingers around his thumb. He smiled at her. "I think Brick's right. We're in tremendous trouble."

Sarah laughed, shaking her head. "I'm going to talk to Mrs. Whittle about supper. Duncan, do you think Arren will be eating with us?"

He shook his head. "I don't think so. She'll probably want something later though."

"I'll make sure there'll be something ready for her." Sarah crossed to the door, leaving Aiden and Duncan alone to talk. Only when she reached it did she look back and smile. The two of them made quite an incongruous picture sitting there. They were both large, powerful-looking men. Yet Aiden still had the towel slung over his shoulder, and Duncan sat in the chair, with his legs spread before him, Cana cuddled against his wide chest. Yes, her daughter had made yet another conquest. She smiled again and pulled the door shut behind her.

Aiden sighed and pulled the towel from his shoulder, tossing it to Duncan. "Here. You'll want this, unless you want her to drool all over your shirt."

Duncan shrugged and slung the towel over his free shoulder, shifting Cana so her face rested against it. "It's your shirt."

Aiden laughed. "I'm glad to see the past eleven months haven't changed you much. You're still the shiftless fop you've always been."

Duncan grinned. "That's damned ungrateful after all the spots I've helped you out of, Brick."

"I seem to remember you complained a good bit about it, too."

Duncan raised his coffee to his lips and took a long sip. "Only when the situation warranted. I wanted to make sure you were duly appreciative of what you put me through."

Aiden laughed. "You wanted to make sure I would pay up later. I haven't known you all my life without learning some things."

Duncan nodded and rubbed his hand absently along the baby's back. His mood became more serious. "Things were much simpler, then."

Aiden sighed and leaned forward, his forearms resting on his knees. "I can't tell you how sorry we were to hear about the death of your father, Duncan. I wish we could have been there for you."

Duncan smiled sadly. "He would have understood, Aiden. It happened too soon after Cana's birth for Sarah to travel."

"How's your mother holding up."

"She's surviving. My cousin Ian is at the castle taking care of her. She misses my father dreadfully."

Aiden nodded. "I imagine she does. I know how close they were."

Silence fell between them, and Aiden watched Duncan resettle Cana against his shoulder. She was nearly asleep, and his friend seemed completely absorbed in watching her small head bob against his chest. "Duncan . . ."

He looked up.

"Are you going to tell me what this is all about?"

Duncan sighed heavily. "I'm sorry, Brick. There's so much to tell, I'm not sure where to start."

Aiden rose and poured himself another cup of coffee. "Let's start with your last letter. What brings you to England under such adverse circumstances?"

Duncan nodded, raising his own cup to take a long swallow. "The conditions in Scotland are horrendous, Brick. Poverty is rampant. Since the war ended, a good many of the landholders have discovered that herding sheep is more profitable than caring for tenants."

"Is Strathcraig in financial trouble?"

Duncan shook his head and took another sip of his coffee. "We have the mine. As it happens, most of my clansmen are in fairly good shape. The problem is outside pressure from the other landholders."

"To convert your land?"

"To take my land."

"Are you serious?"

"I wish to God I wasn't, but greed's a powerful motive."

"There are landholders who want to seize Strathcraig land?" Aiden asked in surprise.

Duncan nodded and shifted Cana to his other shoulder. She curled against him, properly drooling down the front of his shirt. "The boundaries in the Highlands are mostly established by tradition. All that separates one estate from the other are trees and rivers and hillsides. In the last few years, there has been a marked increase in border disputes by landholders who want to expand their territory."

"Have you lost anything?"

"Not yet. But I'm growing damned tired of having to hold the bastards at bay. Essentially what they're doing is burning their tenants out of their homes and off their farms so they can convert the land to sheep pasture."

"Where do they go?"

"That's a big part of the problem. There's nowhere for them to go. A lot have fled to England. Some have gone to the Americas. Some have even gone farther afield. You can't imagine what it's like until you see their faces. I won't let my clansmen live in fear like that."

"I can understand that. What's your goal in London?"

"I want the Regent to establish official boundaries for my estate. I can't protect every Highlander as much as I'd like, but I can damn well protect my own."

"That shouldn't be overly difficult. I'm certain the Regent will see you."

"So am I. That's why I contacted you initially, but things have changed. It seems I'm not the only Scottish landholder with a conscience. I've been working steadily to form an alliance against the gradual raping and stripping of our lands. A lot of landholders stand to lose a lot of money if I succeed."

"Do you think the Regent will be willing to step in?"

Duncan shrugged. "It's difficult to say. Whether they like it or not, every Highland noble is a Royal subject, but the Regent will have trouble dictating what landholders can do with their own property. Ideally, he'll be willing to declare a moratorium on further seizures through border disputes, though."

"Good God, Dunc! It sounds like something straight out of the Norman conquest."

"Close. There have actually been some reports of invading armies of clansmen, though I've never seen it myself. At any rate, the closer we grow to solving some of these problems, the stiffer the opposition. By the time I decided to travel to England, I knew I'd have to outrun my adversaries."

"That's why you wanted *The Dream Seeker* moored at Inverness."

"Right. I'd originally planned to make it there in a fortnight."

"What detained you?"

A smile tugged at the corner of Duncan's mouth. "I met Arren."

"Ah. I suppose this is where the real adventure begins."

"I'll tell you, Brick, if I hadn't lived it myself, I'd never believe it was possible." Duncan related the entire story beginning with his interruption of Arren's flight from Euan McDonan, explaining the circumstances of their bizarre marriage, and the details of their grueling journey to Inverness.

Aiden exhaled a long sigh. "You're right. It is an incredible story. But once you reached Inverness, why didn't you contact Mac?"

"We did."

Aiden raised an eyebrow. *The Dream Seeker's* not in port at Dover."

Duncan explained what happened once they boarded the yacht. He didn't miss the angry glint in Aiden's eyes when he told him the ship had been detained.

"This is intolerable!" Aiden's voice was explosive, and Cana stirred awake against Duncan's shoulder.

Duncan concentrated for a minute on settling her down. When she drifted back to sleep, he turned his attention back to Aiden. "Take it easy, Brick. Once they know I've escaped the country anyway, they'll have no more reason to hold Mac."

Aiden grumbled something under his breath. "They've no damn reason to hold him now. I'll have the magistrate's head for this."

"You'll have to do more than that if you want justice."

"How do you mean?"

"I counted eight, maybe nine, different magistrate uniforms before we left Inverness. That's not including the port police there or the revenue cutters in Dover."

Aiden's breath came out in a low whistle. "You have managed to make a lot of enemies. Is that why you came ashore via the cliffs?"

Duncan raised an eyebrow. "How did you know?"

"Give me some credit for my powers of investigation. I used to be quite an expert, you know. There were chalk stains on your trousers, and white dust under your fingernails. It was a fairly accurate sign."

Duncan nodded. "They tried to board our ship early yesterday morning. George Smythe lowered us over the side and we swam ashore. The only way out was up."

"Don't tell me you made Arren climb with you."

Duncan nodded. "There wasn't an option. It was amazing, Brick. I don't know a woman alive who could have done it. Anyway, we reached the top and walked to the main road. We were able to catch two rides on the way, but we had to walk most of it. The rest, you know." He settled back in his chair and watched Aiden carefully.

"There's something I don't understand, Duncan. What are Arren's reasons for needing to travel to London that way?"

"You've got me there. She's only given me bits and pieces of information. It has something to do with Alistar McDonan, though, you can count on that."

Aiden nodded. "That would seem likely. What do you know so far?"

Duncan quickly related what Arren had told him. "There are too many pieces that don't fit, Brick," he finished.

Aiden stretched his legs and rubbed his shoulder absently. He'd sustained an injury there several years ago, and it bothered him when the weather was bad. "What about the scars on her back?" He noted Duncan's look of surprise. "Sarah told me," he explained.

Duncan nodded. "I'm relatively certain she got most of

them from her father. I'd be willing to wager the fresher ones were a gift from McDonan."

"I'd wager you're right on that. It would explain some of her terror, anyway. So what do you plan to do about it?"

Duncan shook his head in frustration. "She's convinced there's some insurmountable problem to be solved. I can't do anything until she tells me what it is."

Aiden paused and drank another long sip from his coffee cup, studying Duncan carefully. "I take it you two are . . . really married?"

"In every sense of the word, but it's a common-law marriage, though, and Arren insists I'll petition the Prince Regent to end it once I know the truth."

"Will you?"

"Hell no!"

Aiden laughed and rubbed his shoulder again, the action sparking a sudden memory. "By the way, when was the last time you slept?"

Duncan shrugged. "I can't remember. I never felt like I could let my guard down."

"So how's your head?"

Duncan groaned, understanding Aiden's question. "Hurts like hell when I get exhausted. Arren does the most wonderful thing with her fingers though."

Aiden raised an eyebrow. "Then I take it having her along has at least made your somewhat arduous journey a bit more . . ." he paused suggestively, ". . . exciting?"

"God, you're a cad! If I didn't know you better, I'd hit you for that remark."

Aiden raised an eyebrow. "Evidently this is a bit more than a physical attraction."

Duncan grinned, realizing he'd been trapped. "I see you

haven't lost your touch for interrogation. All right, I'm bloody well head-over-heels in love with her."

Aiden sighed and looked closely at his friend. He decided love agreed with him. "So tell me about the new Duchess of Strathcraig. What's she like?"

Duncan pursed his lips thoughtfully. "It's hard to say. She's such a contradiction."

"In what way?"

"She's so fragile. She hurts easily."

"Overly sensitive?"

Duncan shook his head. "She's got a temper that would shame Attila the Hun."

"She's a shrew."

"With a compassionate streak the width of the English Channel."

"She's softhearted."

Duncan gave a short laugh. "Make her mad and she'll rip your head off without batting an eye."

"She overreacts to things."

"No. She's incredibly reasonable. She'll respond to logic better than just about any woman I've ever met."

"She's a bluestocking."

"Far from it. There isn't a boring bone in her body. She's got an amazingly vibrant personality."

Aiden was having to fight to suppress a smile. Duncan was completely oblivious to his line of questioning and continued to take the bait. "She's the frivolous type."

"Don't be ridiculous, Brick. I've told you what her life is like."

"She takes things too seriously."

"Not at all. She can be uproariously funny. Especially when she starts telling all those Highland folk tales."

"She's incapable of intensity."

"You wouldn't believe her ability to concentrate. I was amazed at her fortitude."

Aiden was laughing outright now. Duncan was the picture of a love-struck adolescent.

"What's so funny, Brick?"

Aiden drew a long breath, his voice filled with mirth. "So tell me, Duncan, what's she like?"

Duncan looked momentarily confused before his face split in a slow grin. "All right, I confess! I've turned into a besotted fool. But I seem to remember a time when you weren't your usual acerbic cynical self as a result of your infatuation with a certain Lady Sarah Erridge."

Aiden laughed again. "Guilty as charged! It's simply nice to know I'm not the only one who's fallen victim to a female power."

Cana stirred against Duncan's shoulder and he looked down at her. Their boisterous laughter had awakened her, and her face was puckered in an angry pout. He smiled at the infant before holding her out to Aiden. "Here, see to the other female whose power has taken you hostage. I'm going to check on my wife."

Aiden lifted Cana into his arms, and grinned when she let out a healthy squawl. "If that isn't just like you to cut out when circumstances turn sour."

Duncan walked to the door, looking back at Aiden. "You've always been the responsible one, remember?"

"I suppose some things will never change."

Cana let out another lusty yell and Duncan pulled open the door. "And you said I smelled bad!" He turned to go, and found himself face to face with Arren.

She stood outside the library door with Sarah. Her hair was neatly plaited, and she wore a pale yellow gown that molded to her graceful figure. Her eyes were sparkling green and she smiled at him, nearly knocking the breath from his lungs.

Sarah broke the tension. "Look who's awake."

Duncan smiled. "Hello, darling."

Arren smiled back tentatively. "Hello."

Saran grinned at them and pushed her way past Duncan into the library. "I hear my daughter crying. Excuse me."

Duncan raised his hand and tucked a tendril of Arren's hair behind her ear, bending down to kiss her gently. "How are you feeling?"

"I feel fine. Thank you."

He smiled. "You look wonderful."

Arren couldn't suppress a giggle. "You're just not used to seeing me without dirt up to my eyebrows and tattered clothes hanging on my back."

He grinned. "It's a marked improvement, I might add."

She poked him in the chest. "You don't look so bad yourself." She produced the candlestick from behind her back. "Now, are you going to properly introduce me, or will I have to do it myself?"

He laughed and pulled her toward the door. Sarah was carrying Cana against her shoulder, and she smiled at them as she slipped past. "Don't start without me, Duncan. I've waited all day to hear this story. I'll be extremely cross if you cheat me out of it."

He smiled. "We'll wait."

Sarah left the room and Duncan pushed Arren forward. Aiden was standing in the center of the room studying them intently. He stepped forward and extended his hand to her. "Hello, Your Grace. I'm the Duke of Albrick."

She smiled at him and held out the candlestick. "I'm pleased to make your acquaintance, Your Grace. I'd like to return this. I stole it from your yacht."

Aiden laughed, taking the candlestick from her. "I'm relieved to have its return. I'm sure I would have missed it."

She shot Duncan a triumphant look. "There. You see. And you complained."

He groaned and sank down on the sofa, reaching for Arren's hand. He tugged her down beside him, settling her comfortably in the curve of his arm. "I don't think Aiden seriously expected you to make me carry that thing up the cliffs of Dover."

Aiden set the candlestick down on the mantel, grinned, and crossed the room to sit in the chair opposite them. He crossed his long legs and studied the couple before him. Duncan had been right about Arren's inherent vibrance. She had a certain depth of character that was evident even now. Aiden smiled at her. "So tell me, Arren, what kind of woman risks her life and her husband's ire to return a candlestick?"

She looked cautiously out the corner of her eye at Duncan. His expression was unreadable. "It's rather a long story, Your Grace."

He held up his hand. "I insist you call me Aiden. Duncan is the closest thing I have to family. I don't think there's any need for formalities."

She shifted uncomfortably, smiling at him slightly. "I really did it just to irritate him."

Duncan groaned. "It worked, too."

Aiden laughed, and looked at Duncan. "I like this woman."

Duncan shook his head. "You like her because she gets the better of me."

"Why else?"

The door opened and Sarah entered the room again. "Did I miss anything?"

She would have walked past Aiden and settled herself in

the other chair, but he grabbed her hand and pulled her onto his lap. "Where's Cana?"

"I put her down for a nap. Aiden, this is most improper."

He shrugged. "Indulge me."

She smiled at him, wiggling her way to a more comfortable position. "All right, Duncan, I want to hear the entire story. From the beginning."

Duncan shifted slightly away from Arren so he could see her more clearly. "I've already told Brick my side of things." He ignored Sarah's disgruntled stare. "Arren has to fill in the rest of the details."

She looked at him uncomfortably. "Where do you want me to start?"

"Sarah wants you to start at the beginning."

"You aren't going to like this."

He settled back against the corner of the sofa. "Try me."

She sighed and leaned back. "All right. But don't interrupt me."

Duncan shot Aiden an amused look at the proprietary note in her voice and Arren began the story. She started with the death of her father, and with Alistar McDonan's unwanted advances. She ended with their arrival at Albrick Park.

Sarah was horrified. "Oh my God! How did you survive all that?"

"I wouldn't have if Duncan hadn't helped me." She looked at him. "I owe you my life."

Aiden was stroking Sarah's back absently. "Arren?" He waited for her to look at him. "There's something I don't understand."

"Yes?"

"Alistar McDonan wants your former husband's land and your father's land. Is that correct?"

She nodded. "Yes."

"And you fled from him to avoid marrying him?"

"That's right."

"So why was it worth risking your life to reach London? What's there that will help you?"

Arren looked anxiously at Duncan. He had leaned forward, a look of intense concentration on his face. She chewed on her lip slightly. "I need an audience with the Regent."

Aiden raised an eyebrow. "Did you think he'd grant you one so readily?"

She looked back at Duncan again. "Of course he will. I'm not only the Duchess of Strathcraig. I'm also the Duchess of Grayscar."

Twenty-five

Duncan stared at her. "Good God, Arren! Why didn't you tell me?"

She glared back. "I told you you wouldn't like it."

Sarah stared at both of them in confusion. "I don't understand. Arren, was your former husband the Duke of Grayscar?"

She shook her head. "No. Lawrence was a Baron. My father was the Duke."

Sarah furrowed her brow. "Then how did you end up with the title?"

Aiden reached up and tugged on her braided hair. "You've forgotten your Highland law, darling. If there's no male heir to the title, the oldest daughter will inherit it."

Arren nodded. "That's right. And that's why Alistar McDonan wants to force me to marry him. With the land I obtained from my marriage to Lawrence, and the Grayscar estates, I'm the largest landholder in Scotland."

"So what do you want from the Regent?" Sarah asked.

Arren sighed. "Protection, of course. As a titled landholder, I'm a Royal subject. I have the right to Royal protection. If the Regent prohibits the marriage, Alistar can't marry me."

Sarah persisted. "But how could he do that?"

Arren chewed on her lip. "He could forbid the consolidation of Royal land. The Grayscar estate is so large, it would make any alliance with another landholder unduly powerful."

Sarah nodded. "I see. That explains why the McDonans wanted to prevent you from leaving Grayscar property."

Aiden sighed, pushing Sarah to her feet. "It also explains why Arren believes she can't remain married to Duncan. Doesn't it?"

Arren looked at him, a pained look in her green eyes and nodded. He stood, taking Sarah's hand. "Come on, darling. They have a lot to talk about." He tugged her to the door before she could retort.

Arren watched the door click shut behind them before she summoned enough courage to look at Duncan again. "I never tried to mislead you."

He sighed in exasperation and rubbed the taut muscles in his neck. "Arren, let's get one thing straight before this conversation goes any farther. Alistar McDonan be damned, you're my wife, and I'm not going to let anyone change that."

She wrung her hands in agitation. "Haven't you heard a word I said? It isn't possible. Now that we're here, don't you understand that?"

"What I understand is that you've got this all worked out in that stubborn head of yours. I understand that you've decided your only hope is to place your lands under Royal protectorate. And I understand that you think that the Regent's policy will force us apart."

"Duncan, please be reasonable. There's no other way. I have to appeal to the Regent."

"Dammit Arren, this is completely illogical!" He rose from the sofa and walked to stare out the window. "Do you know who I am?"

"Yes. You're the Duke of Strathcraig."

"How long have you known that?"

Arren brushed at an invisible speck of dust on her gown. "I'm afraid I've been terribly unfair to you. I've known since the day after we were married." Briefly, she told him how she'd found the vellum note in his saddlebag.

Duncan braced his hand on the windowpane. "Even so, you don't believe I'm capable of protecting you from the likes of Alistar McDonan."

"Duncan you don't understand what he's capable of. He killed Lawrence. I'm sure of it. And he killed my older brother Mason, as well."

He sighed and turned from the window, walking back to her side. "Arren, I want you to tell me the whole story. Start from the very beginning, and don't leave anything out this time."

She nodded. "What do you know of my father?"

"I know he was a mean son of a bitch who'd sell his soul to the devil if he thought he could turn a profit."

"That's fairly accurate. He really wasn't so bad, though, until Mason died."

"Mason was your oldest brother?"

"Yes. He was sixteen years older than I. I was twenty-one when he died. My mother had died years earlier, of course."

"You said Alistar killed him."

"He had him killed, actually. We were told Mason had joined the 2nd Dragoons—your unit, I believe?"

Duncan nodded. "That's right."

"But he didn't. While I was married to Lawrence, several of his guests had fought in the Dragoons. They confirmed what I already suspected. Mason never fought in the war. His disappearance coincided with the disappearance of Alistar's cousin, Edward."

Duncan's brow furrowed. "If memory serves, Edward

McDonan was the heir to his father's title. When he died, his cousin—Alistar—became the Earl."

Arren nodded. "That's right. He killed his cousin Edward, too, though no one's ever proved it."

"And you believe he had Mason murdered."

She nodded. "He was positioning himself to take Grayscar land long before my father's death."

"So after Lawrence's untimely death, he stepped up his efforts."

"Duncan, it became unbearable, and if I didn't believe he was capable of anything before, I certainly do now."

He leaned forward and looked at her intently. Her green eyes had darkened until they were nearly black. "Arren, I'm going to ask you a direct question. I want a direct answer."

"All right."

"Who put those marks on your back?"

Her eyes widened in surprise. "How do you know?"

He raked a hand through his hair. "Oh for God's sake, Arren! I'm your husband. How do you think I know?"

She blushed and ignored the question. "Most of them came from my father. Alistar McDonan gave me the rest."

Duncan swore under his breath. "Just as soon as I can get my hands on him, I'm going to skin the bastard alive."

Arren reached out and laid her hand on his forearm. "Duncan, don't you see? Alistar McDonan is going to do whatever it takes to own my land."

He sighed heavily. "Arren, don't you believe I am capable of protecting you from him?"

"It isn't that. Once the Regent places the land under protectorate, I can't be married to you."

"Arren, you *are* married to me. The Regent isn't going to do anything with Grayscar land. We'll administer it together."

"But that's impossible. The estates aren't even adjoining."

"For the love of God, this isn't the eleventh century! What the hell difference does that make?"

"What do you expect to do? Administer the largest estate in Scotland from over seven hundred miles away."

He shrugged. "There's no reason why we can't spend time at both estates. This entire conversation is ridiculous."

She looked at him, her eyes wide in disbelief. "You don't understand."

"Arren, I haven't understood this from the beginning."

She sighed. "There's no other answer. I don't know how else to explain it to you."

He rose from the sofa and stared down at her. "I've learned a lot about you in the last two weeks. But if I've learned one thing, it's that you won't listen to reason when you've already made up your mind."

She looked at him curiously. "What are you talking about?"

"I'm talking about you and me—that is to say, you and me together. You've decided there's no way this will work. I've decided I'm not going to let you have your way."

"What are you going to do?" She eyed him somewhat warily, and he looked down at her, the gold flecks in his eyes growing intense.

He leaned down and stared into her eyes. "I'm going to marry you all over again."

Arren blinked. "Why?"

"Because you keep throwing this common marriage in my face. Every time we have this conversation, you point out that as soon as I petition the Regent, we'll both be free."

"We will."

"Is that what you want, Arren?"

He saw a brief flash of something indecipherable in her

eyes before she turned her head away. "It doesn't matter what I want."

Duncan grabbed her chin and pulled her head around, forcing her to meet his gaze. His voice was barely above a whisper. "Doesn't it?"

Her eyes widened slightly. "What do you mean?"

"Isn't this what you wanted all along, Arren? Didn't you console yourself with the knowledge that once we reached London, you'd be free of me?"

"No! It wasn't that way at all. I . . ."

"Didn't you believe when you let me make love to you that your previous marriage would protect you from scandal after our marriage was dismissed?"

"No! I swear, I . . ."

"And didn't you manipulate me into bringing you to England by whatever means possible—even to the extent that you surrendered your innocence to me in exchange for safe passage."

"No!"

Duncan leaned closer to her, his fingers curling around her shoulders, his voice dropping to a dangerous whisper. "Then tell me what you want, Arren. Say the word and I'll escort you to London this afternoon. You'll never have to see me again."

She chewed on her lip, watching him intently. "I can't."

"You can't what? Tell me, Arren."

"I . . . there's no choice. The Regent is my only hope."

Duncan swore under his breath and walked away from her, slamming his palm on the windowpane. "By damn you're stubborn!" He sighed heavily, drawing several deep, calming breaths. When he turned to face her again, Arren had buried her face in her hands. "All right, Arren. I'm not going to push you any harder. I warn you, though, I'll not let this subject drop."

She raised her face to look at him. He didn't miss the haunted look in the green depths of her eyes. "Duncan, I . . ."

He shook his head, cutting off her protest. "I'm through with this conversation. You are incapable of thinking rationally. I'm unwilling to pressure you."

She studied him, seeking answers in his gold-flecked eyes. "I never wanted to hurt you, but you cannot protect me forever." When he didn't answer, she began to fidget uncomfortably. He seemed to be looking directly through her, and finally, she could stand the silence no more. "When are we leaving for London?"

He raised an eyebrow and leaned back against the window frame. "We're not going to London."

"But you just said you'd decided to terminate our marriage after all."

"I didn't say that. I said I was through discussing the possibility."

"But, Duncan, you can't mean to . . ."

"Oh yes, I do mean to."

She stared at him a while longer, and finally, he walked over to stand in front of her again, thoughtfully studying the top of her head. "Perhaps it would be a good idea if you went upstairs and rested awhile, Arren."

She raised her head and eyed him suspiciously. "Why?"

"Because you're getting married this evening, and as your husband, I want you to be especially well rested on your wedding night."

Twenty-six

In a borrowed dress, Arren walked down the long corridor to where Duncan awaited her at the top of the stairs. She tugged a bit nervously at her sleeve and addressed him, "May I say, Your Grace, you look quite respectable for a gypsy." He was wearing a Strathcraig dress plaid, neatly pleated at his waist. His black velvet jacket and ivory cravat set off the strong line of his chin. A gold buckle held his plaid in place on his shoulder, and his bonnet sat at a jaunty angle atop his red-gold hair.

He grinned and dropped a quick kiss on her forehead. "I have something for you," he said, delving into his jacket-front pocket with his fingers. Finally he came out with quite the largest emerald ring she'd ever seen. He lifted her left hand and slid the ring home on her finger.

She looked at him in surprise. "How did you manage to get this so quickly?"

He smiled at her. "I ordered it ahead." He laughed at her suspicious expression and explained, "I paid George Smythe to send a courier to my jeweler in London. It arrived this afternoon. Do you like it?"

Arren looked from the ring, to Duncan, and back again. "Yes, of course I like it. It's just that you . . ." she trailed off and he raised an eyebrow.

"Yes?"

". . . you ordered it before you even knew, didn't you?"

He knew she referred to her identity as the Duchess of Grayscar, but deliberately chose to misunderstand her. He raised his hand and traced a finger along her cheek. "I've always known you were going to be my wife, Arren."

She shook her head. "That's not what I meant."

"I know what you meant. But it doesn't matter now, any more than it mattered then. One day, I'll make you believe that."

She looked at him, wondering if the fear showed in her eyes. "Would it help if I told you I want to believe it?"

He nodded. "It does."

Arren drew a deep breath. "Then I do."

He grinned. "Remember those words. I want you to repeat them in a few minutes." He took her hand and pulled it through the crook of his arm, leading her down the stairs. He stopped again when they reached the bottom. "Arren, are you all right?"

"No. I'm scared to death."

He laughed and tucked a tendril of her hair behind her ear. "I know you. You function best under pressure."

She managed a smile. "You'd better hope so."

They walked the rest of the way to the chapel in silence. Duncan didn't miss the way her small fingers gripped his forearm. He smiled, and covered her hand with his own. At the door of the chapel, Arren stopped and looked at him expectantly. "Isn't Aiden going to give me away?"

He shook his head. "No. Sarah and Brick are already inside with Reverend Staunton. I'm going to walk you down the aisle myself."

"Duncan that's highly irregular."

He sighed heavily. Good Lord! Arren was going to pick a fight with him just before their own bloody wedding. "Arren, no one's going to give you away because you already belong to me. I can't very well give you to myself, now can I?"

Well that was certainly hard to refute, but she still wasn't ready to back down. "What are the vows?"

He blinked. "What?"

"The vows. What are the vows?"

"What do you mean, what are the vows? We're using the traditional ones, of course."

She reached down and adjusted one of the blooms of heather in her bouquet before she met his gaze again. "All right. But I'm not going to promise to obey you."

He groaned and pulled her hand through his arm again. "You foul this up, Arren, and I swear I'll throttle you!"

She smiled at him sweetly when he swung the door open. "Why would you expect me to do a thing like that?"

He shot her a warning look and started down the aisle. Both of them were oblivious to the amused look Aiden was giving them. He and Sarah stood at the front of the chapel, waiting for Duncan and Arren to make their way down the aisle. Aiden couldn't suppress a grin of satisfaction. They were going to fight all the way to the altar.

"I mean it, Arren," Duncan continued, "don't even think about it."

She smiled at him again. "I wouldn't dare."

He didn't even realize they'd reached the front until she shot him an amused look. He glared at her. If Reverend Staunton thought their behavior a bit odd, he certainly didn't give that impression. Instead, he opened his prayer book and began the ceremony. Duncan had a brief scare when they exchanged their vows and Arren hesitated noticeably before she promised to obey him. He squeezed her fingers so tight, he wouldn't have been surprised if he'd heard the bones crack. She finally relented.

They exchanged their vows and Duncan raised her hand, sliding a gold band home on her third finger. She looked at him in surprise when he pressed into her palm a larger band with three tiny emeralds encrusted in the top. He extended his left hand to her and waited for her to slide the ring onto his finger. Her brow knitted in confusion. It was highly irregular for gentlemen to wear wedding bands, but Duncan smiled at her reassuringly, and she pushed the ring over his knuckle and it nestled at the base of his finger.

Duncan took her hand in his again and turned back to Reverend Staunton. He finished the brief ceremony, and Duncan leaned down to kiss Arren lingeringly. Aiden felt Sarah's head tip against his shoulder and he turned to look at her, not surprised at all to see she'd cried through the entire ceremony. He smiled and took her hand in his.

Duncan finally raised his head. Arren ignored her blush and went up on tiptoe to hiss in his ear, "I don't think I should have to keep that vow to obey you when I made it under duress."

He threw back his head and laughed, pulling her back down the aisle. "I'll simply have to do what I can to break that will of yours."

She poked him in the ribs. "You'll not succeed, you know?"

Aiden smiled and watched them disappear. He turned and thanked Reverend Staunton and tugged on Sarah's hand. They walked slowly down the aisle and she turned her teary eyes to look at him. "Didn't you think it was a beautiful ceremony, Aiden?"

He laughed and pulled the chapel door shut. "If you don't count the fact that they argued through most of it."

"Oh they did not! I thought it was dreadfully romantic."

He smiled at her and dropped an indulgent kiss on her forehead. "Sarah," he said patiently, "you think it's romantic when the foxhounds are in heat."

She gave him a disgruntled look and poked his ribs. "Aiden Brickston, that isn't a bit polite."

His face split in a slow grin. "Probably not. But then, neither are the thoughts I'm having about you right now either."

Sarah glared at him. "Why did I marry you?"

He pulled her into his arms for a long, satisfying kiss. "Because you couldn't keep your hands off me."

She sighed and leaned against him, raising her lips to his. "Well, there's that," she whispered just before he kissed her again.

Duncan hadn't stopped walking since they'd left the chapel and Arren looked at him in surprise when they reached the foot of the stairs. "Aren't we going to dine with Aiden and Sarah?"

He shook his head and led her up the staircase. "I've arranged for us to dine in our rooms. I'd rather have you to myself so I can have my wicked way with you."

She groaned. "I knew that was the only reason you married me."

He looked at her and grinned. "Well it sure as hell doesn't hurt that I get hot just looking at you."

"Duncan!"

He pulled her toward their staterooms. "Well I do."

"You shouldn't say things like that. It's improper."

"Arren, I may be a lot of things, but proper isn't among

them." They reached the door of her room and he pushed it open, leading her inside.

The room was filled with the soft warm glow of the fire and a half-dozen candles. A lavish tray of food sat on the low table by the fire, and a bottle of champagne rested comfortably in a silver bowl of ice. Arren's eyes roamed about the room, trying to discern what had changed since she'd last seen it. When her gaze reached the bed, she let out a low gasp of surprise.

It was covered with feathers. She had a sudden vivid memory of the first night they'd spent in the hunting lodge and her hand flew to her mouth. She turned to look at him, her eyes shooting fiery green sparks. "Duncan! How could you do this?"

He grinned at her shamelessly. "I love it when your eyes shoot fire like that."

"Duncan!"

There was a demand in her voice and he bent down and kissed her briefly. "How could I do what?" he asked innocently.

"You know very well what I mean."

He traced his finger along her lower lip, smiling in satisfaction when she barely trapped the moan in the back of her throat. "You see, I have this fantasy. I spent my first wedding night with you on a bed covered with feathers. The memory of what might have been has plagued me ever since."

She looked mortified. His finger was tracing the whorl of her ear and she found it increasingly more difficult to concentrate. "But Duncan, everyone will know."

He laughed deep in his chest. "Well of course, they'll know," he whispered, reaching up his thumb and pressing it between her lips.

The moan escaped her this time, and she leaned against

him, her fingers resting against his chest. "But how will I be able to face Sarah and Aiden in the morning?"

He traced the line of her teeth with his thumb. "Aiden has a very well-trained staff. No one but his valet knows about the feathers. I'm sure he won't repeat it." He knew damned well it was a baldfaced lie. There wasn't a person in the household who wouldn't know by morning.

Arren was through arguing. His fingers were wreaking havoc with her insides, and she realized, suddenly, how much she craved his touch. Sliding her fingers along the plane of his chest and over his broad shoulders, she delved them into the thick, curly hair at the nape of his neck and tugged his head down to hers. "And what exactly does this fantasy of yours involve, Gypsy?" she whispered against his mouth.

He groaned and answered her with a hot, wet kiss. His lips slanted possessively over hers, and he wrapped his arms around her, hauling her up against the hard length of his body.

Arren sighed with pleasure and sucked on his lower lip. His tongue plunged into her sweet mouth and plundered her with a dark, sensual promise of things to come. She returned his kiss full measure. She slid her hands along the width of his shoulders, and back down his chest, sliding them into the lapels of his velvet jacket.

When her fingers caressed his warm skin through the thin fabric of his shirt, he suddenly found the barriers between them too restrictive. His fingers ran up and down the length of her back, and he groaned. "Arren, there are so many damn buttons."

She froze and pushed at his chest. "You don't have to undo my gown. I'll get it."

He looked at her curiously, releasing his hold on her only

slightly. "I don't mind, sweetheart. It's just going to be torture to only bare one inch of you at a time."

She pushed harder on his chest, and he watched the rest
of her passion drain from her eyes. "Please. I'll do it."

He reached up and held her chin firmly with his fingers,
studying her intently, seeking to determine what had caused
her odd change of mood. "Arren, what's wrong?"

She caught her breath and stared at him. "I . . . I don't
want you to see my scars."

Duncan drew a deep breath and pulled her back against
him, stroking her hair. He gently pulled the pins from her
tiara and veil. He lifted it and dropped it on the plush carpet.
One by one, he released the curls of her heavy auburn hair
from their elegant coiffure. The pins tumbled to the floor,
and he ran his fingers through her thick tresses, tenderly
brushing out the tangles.

Arren clung to him, too embarrassed to meet his gaze.
She knew he must think her a fool. He'd seen her scars
before, of course. There was no logical reason why he
shouldn't see them now, but she was strangely unwilling to
show him her imperfections. She buried her face on his
shoulder instead.

Duncan sighed and kissed her hair, his hot breath fanning
against her ear. "Arren?" He waited for her to raise her
head and look at him. "Undress me."

Her eyes widened slightly and she stared at him.

He took her hands and guided them to his chest. "Just
take off my jacket and shirt, sweetheart. Just that."

She licked her lips nervously and moved her fingers to
the jeweled pin that held his plaid at his shoulder. She fumbled with it slightly, but worked it loose, and dropped it to
the floor with her veil. His plaid fell away from his shoulder
and she looked at him for reassurance.

"Take off my jacket, Arren."

He whispered the command and her fingers slid to the lapels, pushing them over his wide shoulders and down his arms. He shrugged out of it, and it dropped with a soft *plop* on the carpet. He took her hands once more and guided them to the buttons of his shirt.

Arren had to concentrate on each one. They clung stubbornly to the fabric of his shirt, and her fingers fumbled with them several times before she pulled them free. Duncan reached up and pulled his shirt from his wide shoulders, baring his chest.

The red-gold hair on his chest gleamed copper in the firelight and Arren stared at him in fascination. She was certain he had quite the widest chest in the world. Duncan raised a hand and gently caressed the side of her face. "Arren, what do you see when you look at me?"

She raised her eyes to his in confusion. "What do you mean?"

"Sweetheart, I'm covered with scars. Don't you see them?"

She finally understood and shook her head. "Your scars are different. They're marks of honor and courage."

He smiled at her gently and reached for her hand. "Not all of them." He guided her hand to a flat, smooth scar on his shoulder. "You see this one?"

She nodded.

"I got that one when I was eight years old. Brick bet me he could shoot an apple from my shoulder with an arrow at one hundred paces. He lost." He noticed her slight smile and slid her hand to another scar on his rib cage. "And this one I got during a drunken brawl with a fellow who had cheated at cards."

She moved her hand along his chest, settling on a long

scar that ran just above his navel. She raised her eyes to him curiously. "I got that one learning to fence."

She moved her fingers tentatively to another one just above his heart.

"That one was from a bullet."

Arren looked at him suddenly and he wrapped his arms around her again, and said, "Darling, you have no reason to be ashamed of your scars. They're your father's mark of shame. Not yours."

Arren swallowed, mustering her courage. She raised her eyes to his once more, her fingers twirling in the hair of his chest. He wondered briefly if she had any idea what she was doing to him. "Duncan?" she whispered.

"Yes."

"Undress me."

He groaned and seized her mouth in a carnal kiss, as his fingers moved to the long row of pearl buttons. He undid each one, baring one inch of her back at a time. His lips roamed hungrily over hers, his tongue caressing her in heated, wet strokes. Arren's hands moved restlessly over his naked shoulders, and she raked his skin with her nails, moaning deep in her throat as his fingers continued to scald her back.

She sucked on his tongue, eliciting a growl from deep in his chest, and four more buttons popped loose. Arren arched into him, pressing her body against his, and moved her hands down the hard length of his back to the waistband of his pleated kilt. As her fingers tripped along the edge of his plaid, he tugged at the buttons of her gown. She moaned in relief when he opened the gown halfway and splayed his hand against her back. Only the thin gauze of her chemise separated his fingers from her naked skin and she pulled on his lower lip with insistent urgency.

Duncan could stand it no more. He tore his mouth from hers, drawing deep breaths of the cool night air. Arren whimpered in protest at the broken contact. "God, Arren! Do you have any idea what you're doing to me?"

She leaned against him but he stayed her with his hands, turning her around so he could see her back. He made quick work of the rest of the buttons, shoving the gown from her shoulders. It slid down her arms and collapsed in a silken puddle at her feet. She sighed in relief and tried to turn back to him again. He held her still and tugged her chemise up bit by bit until he held the hem. All the while he was lavishing loving attention on the arch of her neck, the whorl of her ear, and the shapely curve of her shoulder, with his mouth.

Arren's head lolled back against him and she felt a shiver race over her spine. He stepped back and pulled the chemise over her head, baring her back to him. The white scars were barely visible in the firelight, but he felt her tense slightly against him. He soothed the tautness from her shoulders with his strong hands, lowering his lips to her spine.

Gently, he caressed the nape of her neck with his mouth. "I love your skin," he whispered against her, sliding his hands around to cup her breasts. "You're so soft." His fingers kneaded the opulent curves of her breasts. "So warm." His lips slid lower against her spine, and she cried out, reaching up to hold his hands more firmly to her breasts. Her nipples were tight and hard and straining for his touch, and when he rasped his thumbs over them, she thought to die of pleasure.

Duncan kissed a wet path down her spine to the small of her back and up again. His lips moved over her scars, caressing each one in turn. When he finally reached the sensitive nape of her neck, Arren strained into his touch. "Duncan, please!"

He turned her around and she reached up, capturing his mouth with her own. Her hands slid down the length of his chest, rasping over his flat male nipples, and moved almost frantically to the waistband of his plaid. She tugged at it, and the pleats came free. Unfastening the sporran that held his kilt in place, she dropped it to the floor, and the plaid pooled around them in a soft, woolen puddle. His undergarments followed. And Arren knelt before him, sliding off his stockings and shoes before she rose and pressed her body against his.

The feeling of her naked flesh against his was exquisite. He moved against her, reveling in the way her soft curves molded to the harder plain of his body. He kissed her deeply, letting his hands slide down her back, over the smooth curve of her buttocks, as he lifted her against him.

She felt his hardness pressing against her belly and sank her teeth into his lower lip. The tight knot in the pit of her stomach was expanding, and she felt tiny tremors racing down her legs. Desperate to be closer to him, she wrapped one leg around the length of his and arched into him. He groaned. "Dear God, Arren! You're driving me mad."

She pulled back slightly, her breath coming in fitful gasps. "It is no worse than what you're doing to me, Gypsy."

He closed his eyes, released a deep breath and swung her into his arms, carrying her to the bed. When Duncan settled her among the feathers, she nearly cried out at the erotic sensation. As Duncan stared at her, the soft down caressed her body, sending tiny shivers down her spine. She writhed against the feathers, seeking to end the pleasant torment.

He stood looking down at her, fighting for control. Already his loins ached to fill her, and he rubbed the taut muscles at the back of his neck, taking in the erotic picture she made spread upon the feathers. Slowly, he reached out his hand and deftly untied her garters. When his hands slid seductively along her legs, removing first one and then the other silk stocking, she cried out and reached for him.

He braced his forearms on either side of her and lowered his body onto hers. The movement sent a small bevy of feathers whirling about them and Arren gasped when she felt his hard length cover her body. He groaned with pleasure and buried his lips on hers. She clung to him, writhing against his hardness. Her whole body tingled with the desire to be touched by his hands, his mouth, and she pressed into him, wordlessly conveying her need.

Duncan stroked his hands along her sides, his fingers stopping to knead her sensitive flesh. He could feel her nails digging into his shoulders and he tore his mouth from hers, trailing it over the curve of her jaw. His tongue shot into her ear and he closed his teeth over her earlobe, smiling when he heard her moan. "Tell me your fantasies, Arren. What are all your wicked desires?"

She raked her hands along his back, then her fingers curled into the firm curve of his buttocks. He groaned with pleasure and she turned her face to his, seeking his kiss. When he resisted, she forced her eyes open and stared into his gold-flecked gaze. His eyes were glazed with passion, and she felt some odd spark of feminine power course through her when she realized he was as aroused as she. She trailed one hand back along the curve of his rib cage, smiling with satisfaction when she felt his stomach muscles clench. He shut his eyes and arched his head back, and she rasped her tongue over the curve of his throat. His sharp intake of breath encouraged her further. Gently laving the gentle hollow at the base of his throat with her tongue, she scraped her nail over his hard male nipple. Sliding her fingers further up his chest, over the curve of his shoulder, and into the thick, red-gold curls at his nape, she pulled his head down so her mouth was inches from his ear. "I have a wicked desire, Gypsy, to feel your lips on every inch of my body."

A spasm shot through him, and he felt a painful groan wrench from his chest. "Oh God!" He dropped his head to the hollow between her breasts and caressed it frantically with his lips. He could feel Arren's heart slamming against her chest, and knew his own was surely about to explode. She clutched at his head and guided his mouth over the curve of her breast. He lingered there only long enough to hear her whispered command, before he closed his lips over the puckered nipple and began to suckle.

Arren writhed against him, the soft motions of her pelvis inflaming him to a fevered pitch. He sucked hard on her nipple, kneading her other breast with his hand before his mouth replaced his fingers there, and he lavished the same attention on the swollen flesh.

Arren's hands clung to his hair. She was pressing his mouth to her, and she moved feverishly among the feathers, sending them cascading over their bodies. As her skin became slick with desire, the tiny white down clung to her, erotically soothing her hot skin.

Duncan held her still against him, his lips trailing a wet line across the soft swell of her stomach. When his tongue delved into her navel, he felt her hands clench in his hair. He moved his mouth lower, deliberately scraping the sensitive triangle of auburn hair with his teeth. Arren writhed in his hands, her body taut as a bowstring. "That's it sweetheart, let your body sing to me."

Her breath was coming in sobs and she arched into him,

gasping for breath when his lips slid along the sensitive skin of her thigh. Her body was slick with sweat, and her hands clung to him feverishly, demanding his touch.

Duncan stroked the soft plane of her stomach with his hands, and moved his lips along the sensitized skin of her inner thigh. She gasped. Her hips bucked against his hands and he raised his head, his gaze locking with hers. Her green eyes smoldered with her need for him and he stroked her thighs with his hands, willing her to open herself. "Open yourself for me, Arren. Let me pleasure you."

She arched her head back and spread her thighs, allowing him access to her most sensitive place. He sighed, and lowered his mouth, kissing her with searing intimacy. Arren cried out in shocked pleasure when his tongue pressed against her.

When Duncan felt her hot, wet, core of passion, he thought he would go insane. He moved his mouth over her soft feminine heat, sucking at the sensitive nub until he felt her body tremble against him. "God, sweetheart, you taste so good. You're so hot for me."

He pressed his tongue high into her heat and she clung to him. "Duncan!" His name came out on a sob, and suddenly, he could stand it no longer. Rising over her, he ground his lips onto hers.

Arren tasted the flavor of her passion on his lips and moaned. Her fingers curled around the hard, rigid shaft of his desire. She caressed him with her fingers, and she felt the tight spring in her lower body wind even tighter. He moved his tongue in and out of her mouth in a sensual, promising rhythm, and Arren tugged him closer to her feminine opening.

When he felt the tip of his hardened shaft pressing at the

moist center of her body, he lost what remained of his control and embedded himself inside of her.

Arren cried out and arched to meet his thrust, taking all of him into her tight, hot sheath.

"God, you're so tight. You feel so damn good."

She raked her fingers over his shoulders, as her body writhed against his. The tiny white feathers cascaded around them, and she clung to him. "Gypsy, end this torment!"

He reached out and grabbed a handful of the soft feathers, running them gently over her skin, his eyes meeting hers. "I love you, Arren." The words were a soft groan, and then he buried his lips in the hollow between her breasts and began to move.

Arren forced him to quicken the pace, wrapping her silken thighs around his hips and rising to meet each thrust. He felt his loins tightening from the exquisite pressure and slid his hand between their joined bodies to heighten her passion.

When his fingers seared her most sensitive spot, Arren shattered. Her nails dug into his shoulders, her thighs clenched around him, and he felt her body begin to rock and shake with the mind-shattering contractions that signaled her release. The slender thread that held his desire in check snapped in two and he slammed himself into her, burying his seed deep inside her.

He collapsed, utterly replete, his passion slaked, his heart filled.

Duncan awoke deep in the night when Arren rolled away from him in her sleep, sending a cascade of feathers swirling into the air. He smiled, and followed her. She was stretched out on her stomach. Her long hair fanned out over the blankets, and her arms were tucked securely beneath her pillow. He splayed his hand on her naked back and gently caressed her spine. He probably would have gone back to sleep if she hadn't started to move against the tender ministrations of his callused palm. When she all but purred in her sleep, he decided he wasn't a damn bit tired.

Arren awoke to the most exquisite sensations, and it took her a minute to realize Duncan was sliding his hands up and down her back in slow, sensual strokes. She moaned, and the strong pads of his thumbs slid along the taut muscles of her lower back. She moved slowly with the rhythm of his hands, reveling in the glorious feeling of his hands on her skin and the snowy white down caressing her body.

Duncan heard her soft sigh of pleasure and chuckled, bending down so his lips rested against her ear. "Now you know what it does to me when you touch me like this."

She smiled sleepily and turned her head to look at him. "I had *your* interests at heart, My Lord. I'll wager you haven't yet thought about *mine.*"

When he heard her use his title, he paused momentarily and brushed her hair out of the way, continuing the deep, soothing strokes. "Arren, do you remember sliding the ring on my finger during the ceremony this evening?"

It seemed a ridiculous question, particularly at the moment, but his hands were sliding along the sensitive skin of her rib cage and she was hardly inclined to argue with him. "Of course." She sighed, and squirmed again. "I meant to ask you why you had me do that."

His thumbs kneaded gently at her shoulder blades. "Because you wear my ring as a symbol that you belong to me." He shifted his hands to her other shoulder. "And I wear yours as a symbol that I belong to you."

Arren turned her head and looked at him again. She could

only see him out of the corner of her eye, and it made it difficult to read his expression. "That's important to you?"

He might have taken offense at the question except that it was accompanied by another breathless sigh of pleasure. Moving his hands back along her sides, he stroked at her ribs, sliding under her to cup and knead her breasts. "Yes. It's important to me. And in our bed, I don't want you to use my title."

Arren decided that comment was worth breaking the languor that had settled permanently in her body, and she pushed herself up on one elbow so she could see him clearly. The movement sent a mound of the white feathers drifting to the floor. "What do you mean?"

He leaned back slightly and looked at her, his fingers trailing softly up and down her spine. "When we're in bed together, here of all places, I do not want you subjugated to me. You are my wife, and as such, my equal."

She raised an eyebrow and studied him curiously. "I don't think I understand."

He sighed and shifted his position to lean with his back against the headboard. He decided the issue should be addressed, despite the growing ache in his loins brought on by the feel of her soft skin in his hands for the last quarter hour. He pulled Arren around and tugged her into the wedge of his legs, wrapping his arms securely around her. He rested his chin on the top of her head and smiled, tenderly removing the white down that had lodged in her auburn hair. "I think, Duchess, that you have some false notions about the nature of normal marriages."

Arren drew her brows together in confusion. She could feel his hardness pressing against her backside, and she was certain he was aroused. Why he wanted to have this conversation now was beyond her. "I would think that shouldn't be too difficult for you to understand. My mother died when I was five years old, and my father never remarried. My marriage to Lawrence was a nightmare, and I would hardly call the time we've been together normal."

He smiled and hugged her closer. "Don't be combative. I'm not criticizing you."

"Then what are you doing?"

"I'm merely pointing out that in some things you would do well to trust my judgment."

"Of course. You, having been married so many times before, would clearly know every detail about it."

He grinned. God the woman was obstinate! He reached up and stroked her hair softly. "Quit arguing with me. You'll like this."

"How do you know?"

"Because you're the one who nearly refused to take her vows if you had to promise to obey me."

"I'm still not happy about that. I think it was very high-handed of you."

"That's what I mean."

She made a small sound of exasperation. *"What's* what you mean? You aren't making a whit of sense, you know."

He tugged on her hair to silence her. "A few minutes ago, you used my title. It implies that you are somehow less important, or subject to me. I want you to know you have my promise it will never be that way between us. Especially not in bed."

"Why especially?"

"Because here, we're vulnerable. I'm as vulnerable to you as you are to me. I'll not have that become a weapon between us."

She turned around to get a better look at him and leaned

with one hand on the corded muscles of his thigh. "But Duncan, when you make love to me, its . . ."

He reached up and covered her mouth with his hand, shaking his head. "No. Sometimes I make love to you. Sometimes, I hope you will make love to me." He saw her eyes widen and he grinned, removing his hand to kiss her briefly before raising his gaze to hers once more. "Generally, I prefer us to make love together."

Something strange flickered in the green depths of her eyes, and before she could stop it, a tear slipped from the corner and trickled down the side of her face. He reached his hand up and caught it with his thumb, studying her curiously. "I didn't mean to make you cry."

She shook her head, unable to tear her eyes away from his gold-flecked gaze. "You didn't."

He looked curiously at the wet tear on the pad of his thumb, and she smiled, kissing it away. "I only cry one tear at a time. That's not really crying."

He tilted his head and studied her intently. "Have you never cried in your life, Arren?"

She shook her head. "Crying is only worth doing if there's someone to listen."

Duncan was filled with a sudden, nearly uncontrollable urge to weep for her. He crushed her to him instead. "Oh God, sweetheart! I'm so sorry."

He rocked her gently for several long minutes, whispering endearments in her ear. Arren sensed he needed the comfort more than she, and leaned into him. He did sound somewhat shaken, though, and Arren tipped her head back to look at him, trailing her fingers over his face. "Duncan, it doesn't matter now. I'm happier with you than I ever have been in my life."

His hand shook when he ran his fingers through the curtain of her hair, and he looked down at her. "Happier, but not happy?"

A cloud passed over her eyes and she turned them away. "I thought we'd agreed not to discuss this again."

He trailed his fingers over the line of her jaw, smiling to himself. Arren was not yet ready to admit her feelings for him, and she clearly still believed their marriage was folly. The fact that it distressed her so much made his heart swell. He had more than passed the halfway mark. He tugged on her hair until she turned her face back to his. He had been growing steadily more uncomfortable from the ache in his groin, and each time she shifted against him, he had to fight the urge to groan. He grinned at her. "As long as we're both awake, then, have you a better suggestion on how we can pass the time?"

His smile made her heart flip over in her breast. She wondered if he had any idea how much she longed to tell him how she felt. She loved him so desperately, and yet, fear made the words lodge in the back of her throat. Duncan McCraig was a fine man. He deserved a fine woman in exchange, and try as she might, Arren couldn't place herself in the role. She realized he was still waiting for an answer to his rather suggestive question, and reached up to trace his mouth with her forefinger. Leaning closer to him, she felt his hardened manhood press intimately against her thigh and she smiled a wickedly feminine smile. Reaching down, she curled her fingers around a handful of the soft white feathers and raised them to her lips, blowing on them gently. They drifted across his chest, resting erotically among the curly red-gold hair. "I suppose I could practice using this new power you've given me." She pressed a kiss in the center of his chest, and grinned in satisfaction when she felt his heart slam against the spot and begin racing erratically.

Arren raised her head and met his gaze, her smoldering green eyes glittering in the firelight. "I do remember you saying you'd like me to make love to you?"

He seemed to have stopped breathing completely. He nodded and reached out his hand to her. She caught it and pushed it back down at his side, leaning over him again. She raised another handful of feathers and trailed them across the taut muscles of his stomach, feeling suddenly powerful at the way his abdomen clenched beneath her hand. "Then relax, Gypsy. I am anxious to show you I'm up to the task."

Duncan groaned and sank deep beneath the covers. Another cascade of white down whirled above their bodies, fluttering silently to the floor amid Arren's quiet giggles.

Twenty-seven

Arren rolled over in her sleep and her hand splayed across his cool, empty pillow. She opened her eyes, slowly, groaning at the bright, morning light that spread over the bed. Duncan was gone, and she looked at his pillow twice before she saw the white note tucked among a bloom of heather he'd pulled from her bouquet She smiled, reaching for it. She realized she'd never seen his handwriting before, and decided it matched his personality perfectly. It was strong and bold, with tiny flourishes on the ends of some letters, yet intensely masculine. She ran her fingers over the crisp letters, sighing deeply.

Tearing her thoughts from Duncan, she forced herself to concentrate on the piece of white vellum. It read:

Duchess,
   I rose early to go riding with Brick. I didn't have the heart to awaken you. Sleep as long as you like. No one's expecting you up today if you are overtired. I love you.

Gypsy

Arren smiled again. Overtired indeed! What a braggart. She could nearly see the arrogant tilt of his head as he'd written the shameless note. She would simply have to prove him wrong.

She gripped the edge of the blankets and tossed them off, groaning when a cascade of feathers flew into the air, spreading aimlessly about the floor. The room was an unholy mess, with clothes and feathers strewn about recklessly. The house staff would likely be appalled. She sighed, and straightened up their discarded clothes from the previous evening, slipping into a long velvet robe she found in the wardrobe. Only when she crossed the room and settled herself at the dressing table did she get her first good look at herself.

She had to laugh. It was certainly no wonder he hadn't awakened her this morning. She looked like chickens had roosted in her hair during the night. She had a brief memory of the tiny white down nestled in the hair on his chest and suppressed a shiver, picking up the brush and running it vigorously through her long, tangled curls. Satisfied that all the feathers were freed from her hair, she braided it into a thick plait, and tied it with a deep green ribbon.

Turning around, she looked at the room in dismay. She longed for a bath, but was hesitant to call for hot water lest the servants see the feathers strewn across the bed. Duncan had promised her only Aiden's valet knew, and she'd be too mortified to let anyone else in on the secret. She crossed to the bathing closet and tested the water in the large tub with her fingers. It was tepid at best, but she tugged open her robe anyway, preferring the cold water to an embarrassing encounter with Aiden's staff.

Arren bathed quickly in the cool water, trying not to remember the feel of Duncan's hands on her body as she slid the cake of soap over her skin. She shivered, and stood up in the cool air of the room, reaching for the dry fluffy towel that rested on the hearth. It was blissfully warm from the lingering heat of the fire. She wrapped herself in it as she stepped out of the cool bath water.

The bath made her feel immeasurably better, and she delved into the wardrobe for something to wear. She smiled when her fingers curled into a pair of soft, butter-colored breeches. Sarah must have provided them yesterday with the gowns she'd sent, and Arren pulled them out, deciding they suited her mood. She tugged them on over a pair of cotton pantaloons, cuddling into their snug fit. Another search through the closet for a shirt proved fruitless, though, and she nearly despaired before she remembered that Duncan's clothes were in the adjoining room.

She walked through the short connecting corridor, cautiously checking the other room before she entered. She didn't think Aiden's staff would take kindly to the sight of her wearing nothing but the butter-colored trousers. The room was empty and she entered it, shivering in the cool air. The wardrobe proved to be a treasure trove of fine lawn shirts, and she selected one in a deep shade of rust and tugged it on, satisfied that the roomy fit adequately disguised her rather scandalous state of undress.

She buttoned it all the way to the collar, turning to check her reflection in the mirror. Satisfied, she returned to her own room and tugged on a pair of soft black slippers to complete the outfit. It was grossly unconventional, she knew, but it suited her mood much better than a gown this morning. She had generally run about Grayscar in plaids and stockings, and much as she admired the rich gowns Sarah had lent her, the trousers were certainly more comfortable. She sighed and pulled open the heavy door, wondering when the valet would come and remove the evidence of those embarrassing feathers.

The corridor was deserted except for the same maid she'd seen polishing the same piece of furniture the previous day. Arren smiled at her and started down the long hall, intent on finding Duncan and telling him how arrogant she'd thought his note to be. When she reached the top of the long staircase, she froze.

There was no one about. Only one footman was on duty, and he stood well off to the side, almost completely out of sight. She strained her eyes to get a better look at him and decided the warm sunlight pouring in through the casements had nearly put him to sleep. He was probably the sole watchman from the previous night, and was simply waiting to be relieved for the day. She looked around, casting a speculative glance over her shoulder. The maid had disappeared somewhere farther down the hall, and there were still no other servants in sight.

Her eyes slid to the polished wooden banister. The huge house was completely quiet. Only the relentless ticking of the hall clock punctuated the silence. She looked over her shoulder again, satisfied that no one was about, and she took a tentative step toward the banister.

Duncan was fascinated. He had risen early to ride with Aiden so they could map out a strategy for contacting the Regent. When they returned to the house, Aiden had gone directly to his office to dispatch a communication to his contact in London, and Duncan had sat down in a corner of the foyer to remove a pebble that had lodged itself in his boot. When he tugged his boot back on and stood up, he saw Arren at the top of the stairs.

He was immediately struck by the rather seductive picture she made in the snug trousers and blouson shirt, and he barely resisted the urge to call up to her, ordering her to go change. He didn't doubt she would ignore him if he did, so he watched her instead.

Her behavior was suspicious. She seemed to be looking for someone, expecting at any moment to be caught in some highly shameless act. From his vantage point, he could see her clearly, but he knew she wouldn't see him unless she leaned over the banister and looked below. When she took a step forward, he expected her to descend the long staircase. He thought to call out to her again, alerting her to his presence.

Her name lodged in his throat when he saw her toss one leg over the wide wooden railing. She gripped the sides of the banister with her fingers, and positioned herself firmly astride it. His face split in a slow appreciative grin. The little tart was going to slide down the bloody banister. Unable to resist, he stole around the edge and positioned himself at the bottom, hoping she wouldn't see him.

She didn't. Arren clung to the banister, throwing one last glance down the long hallway. Satisfied it was too early for anyone to be about, she released her grip, hoping the lone footman wouldn't wake and see her shameless behavior. She flew down the length of the banister, deciding it was a thoroughly exhilarating feeling. She was immensely pleased she'd gotten away with it until she'd nearly reached the bottom and felt a pair of strong hands curl around her waist.

Duncan stopped her just before she could slip off the end. He leaned down so he could whisper in her ear, "God you're a hussy!"

She giggled slightly and squirmed until he let her down. He didn't let go of her waist though, and she turned to face him, settling her hands against his chest. Raising up on her tiptoes, she kissed him soundly, a bright smile on her lips.

She pulled back and patted his shoulder. "It's the company I've been keeping."

He raised an eyebrow. "Madam, are you suggesting I've had a corruptive influence on you?"

"I'm not the one with a fetish for feathers. Remember?"

He grinned wickedly and kissed her again.

"Oh God!" Aiden's voice interrupted their embrace, but Duncan took his time raising his mouth from hers. Arren's face flamed with embarrassment. Aiden grinned at the two of them. "Must you behave so shamelessly in my house? You'll embarrass the staff."

Duncan started to laugh. "If you haven't worked all the embarrassment out of them by now, you're losing your touch."

Arren poked him in the chest, warning him to be silent. Mustering what remained of her dignity, she stepped away and patted her hair back into place. At least Aiden hadn't seen her slide down the banister. "Good morning, Your Grace. How was your ride?"

He smiled at her. "I thought we'd agreed to dispense with the formalities, and it was fine except that Duncan still can't keep up with me."

Duncan grunted. "You're a bloody liar, Brick. I outpaced you on three of those steeples."

"Only because I acted the gentleman and let you have the better horseflesh."

"Aiden, don't lie to Arren. She's likely to believe you." Sarah's voice sounded from the top of the stairs, and Arren turned to see her coming toward them.

She sighed in relief when she noticed Sarah's soft champagne-colored trousers and deep blue shirt. She felt suddenly much more at ease. "Your husband was simply trying to excuse Duncan's poor horsemanship."

Duncan swatted her on the behind and she yelped.

Aiden started to laugh, as he went walking up the remaining few stairs to greet Sarah with a brief kiss. "You're going to have to do something about that, Dunc. You can't have your wife tossing you about like that."

It was Duncan's turn to laugh. "Oh and yours doesn't?"

Sarah gave them both a disgruntled look and slipped her arm through Arren's, pulling her toward the dining room. "Arren and I are going to have breakfast. The two of you are welcome to join us after you've changed," she announced.

Arren shot Duncan an amused glance and followed Sarah across the wide foyer. They had almost reached the door when she heard Duncan's voice from the top of the stairs. "Arren!"

She turned to look at him. "Yes?"

Aiden stood at his side and Duncan shot Arren a devilish look. "There's a feather in your hair." He didn't wait for her reaction, but turned and mounted the last two stairs and disappeared down the hall with Aiden.

Arren's horrified gaze flew to Sarah. "Is there?!"

Sarah looked at her passively and shook her head. "He was just teasing you. There isn't."

Arren eyed her speculatively, but decided she was simply being overly self-conscious. She sighed and stepped into the dining room, suddenly remembering she and Duncan had never eaten their supper last night. She was ravenously hungry.

Duncan and Aiden joined them a few minutes later, and the four of them ate a leisurely meal, laughing good-naturedly at each other. Sarah rose first, excusing herself to check on Cana, and Aiden leaned back in his chair, picking up his pipe from the long buffet table. A footman stepped forward to light it for him, and he took a long draw, slowly exhaling a plume of smoke into the air.

Duncan rolled his eyes. "You're just like an old man with that thing. I can't believe you've taken to smoking a pipe."

Aiden grinned. "Sarah made me quit smoking cheroots. She said they stank up the house."

Duncan nodded. "She was right, too. Those things were vile."

"So I took up a pipe. I only smoke it after meals."

Duncan snorted. "You still look like you're a hundred years old."

"Wait until you're back at Strathcraig with a baby on your knee. You'll start feeling mighty settled yourself."

Duncan laughed. "You're probably right."

Arren rose suddenly from the table, and her chair nearly tottered backwards. The footman stepped hurriedly forward and righted it for her, and she shot him a grateful smile. Unable to meet Duncan's gaze, she looked at Aiden. "If you'll excuse me, I think I'll leave you gentlemen to your conversation."

She mumbled something about a book she wanted to read in the library and hurried from the room.

Aiden shot Duncan an apologetic look. "Sorry."

Duncan shook his head. "She's just anxious. It's a little tense this morning, and grateful as I am for your help, you'll understand it isn't helping any to be amidst a crowd."

Aiden grinned. "I remember throwing you off the property when I got married."

"You threw everyone off the property when you got married. It was really shamelessly rude of you."

"You're one to talk. I'm not the one who had my valet madly spreading feathers over my marriage bed during the ceremony."

Duncan shot him a wicked grin. "It was damned well worth it, too."

Aiden started to laugh. "I'll bet. You'll have to pay for that little comment about that feather in her hair, though."

Duncan linked his hands behind his head and leaned back in his chair. "You have to see the way her eyes shoot sparks when she's angry, to get the full effect. God, but I love to goad her temper."

Aiden laughed again. "I can tell your marriage is destined to be a veritable sea of tranquillity."

Duncan grinned. "Seas of tranquillity are deadly boring."

"That's one thing you'll never have to worry about."

He shook his head. "Not with Arren, I won't." He tipped his chair back down to the floor and spread his hands on the table, suddenly anxious to be done with the matter at hand. "When do you want to leave for London?"

Aiden put his pipe down on the table and raked a hand through his hair. "Early this afternoon, I think. My dispatch will have reached Fielding by then."

Duncan nodded. They had decided this morning to contact Jonathan Fielding, their source at the British War Department, and ask him to determine the Regent's availability. This time of year, it was uncertain whether or not the Regent would be staying at his London residence, but with the King's health deteriorating rapidly, His Highness was almost always in the city. "How long do you think it will take to gain an audience?"

Aiden shrugged. "As long as Prinney's in town, he should see you immediately."

Duncan grinned at the Regent's nickname. "Do people still call him that? He's a forty-year-old man now."

Aiden smiled. "With the heart of a twenty-year-old. Yes, the name has stuck, though his popularity is declining. If he doesn't become king soon, I'm afraid he'll do so under bad favor."

Duncan nodded. The Prince Regent had never been especially popular with a good number of the people, particularly the House of Commons, and Duncan knew that Aiden spent a good deal of time in the House of Lords trying to make some of the Royal initiatives a little more palatable. "Still oblivious to the need for social reform, is he?"

"Completely. I like to think he's coming around, though."

The door opened and Sarah reentered, Aiden looked at her and smiled. "How's my daughter?"

She smiled back. "Sleeping like the dead. I think all the excitement yesterday wore her out. I'll have to take her out for a walk later or she'll keep us up all night."

Aiden winked at Duncan. "I'll wager up all night is what our house guests had in mind."

Sarah shot him an exasperated look. "Aiden Brickston, I see your mind's in its usual gutter!" She looked around. "Where's Arren?"

"In the library," Duncan said. "Brick embarrassed her."

"Aiden!"

"I did not. Certainly not any more than Duncan's damn feather comment."

Sarah giggled. "That was really awful of you, Duncan. I know I'd have been mortified if I'd been in her place."

"Well considering she doesn't think either of you knows, she's going to be even more mortified if she finds out you do."

Aiden raised an eyebrow. "Does she think something like that remains a secret in a household this size."

Duncan shrugged. "I don't know what she thinks, but she may very well claw my eyes out when she finds out."

Sarah swatted his shoulder and took the seat between him and Aiden. "And you'll deserve it too."

"Now come on, Sarah. You've been known to pull a few stunts like that," Duncan teased.

"I have not."

Aiden picked up his coffee and studied her carefully. Duncan leaned down and said, "I remember hearing something about a carriage, and a purple and ivory gown."

Sarah shot Aiden a horrified look and delivered a quick kick to his shin. "You beast!"

"Ouch!"

"I can't believe you told him that."

Duncan was laughing outright and Aiden glared at him menacingly. "What did you expect us to talk about all that time I was away from you?"

She kicked him again for good measure. "Well not that! For heaven's sake."

Duncan leaned back in his chair and howled with laughter despite Sarah's disgruntled stare. Brick hadn't really told him anything other than the fact that shortly after he and Sarah were married, they'd gotten rather physical in his carriage on the way from London to Albrick Park. Based on her reaction, though, he suspected his friend had left out a few of the more graphic details.

Sarah pushed her chair back and glared at both of them. "I'm going to find Arren and commiserate over the two wretches we married."

Aiden stood up and caught her shoulders, smiling down at her. He knew she wasn't really angry, and he couldn't resist the urge to goad her a little more. "See if you can get some details on those feathers, will you?"

He neatly sidestepped another swift kick in the shin. He

could see the smile tugging at the corner of her lips and bent down to kiss her briefly.

She poked him in the chest. "You're such a cad."

"I know. That's what you love about me."

She shook her head and turned to leave, looking back when she reached the door. "Will you be traveling to London today?" she asked.

Aiden nodded. "Yes. We'll be back for dinner though. Is there anything you need?"

She shot him a slow suggestive wink. "You may want to pick up a few extra pillows." Sarah tugged the door shut after her, and smiled when she heard their combined laughter inside.

She found Arren in the library, curled up with a book. She looked up when Sarah entered the room and smiled. "I haven't thanked you yet for the clothes. It's wonderful of you to lend them to me."

Sarah smiled in return and settled herself on the long sofa. "It's really no problem at all. I order almost all my clothes from a dressmaker in London, and she's a wonderful seamstress with a horrid eye for color."

"What do you mean?"

"Sometimes when she sends my orders, she includes extra things she's made for me. It's usually nothing I can wear. Rather like that yellow gown I gave you yesterday."

Arren smiled at her. "I imagine it would make you look rather sallow."

Sarah wrinkled her nose. "Sallow isn't the word. Ill is more like it."

"Well thank heavens it worked out this way. I'd have been

running about in those filthy garments we arrived in if it hadn't."

Sarah nodded. "It's fortunate we're close to the same size. If you were staying in some ducal estates, we could wring three dresses out of each gown for you." Sarah held out her arms and puffed up her face in imitation of the often enormous women who presided among the *beau monde*.

Arren giggled. "I think you do that very well."

Sarah let the air out of her cheeks and laughed. "After you've seen as many of them as I have, it comes naturally."

"And one day, when you're old and gray, the younger duchesses will be making fun of you too."

"I'd be offended if they weren't." Sarah noticed Arren's dubious expression and laughed again. "Really, I would. If they didn't poke fun at me it would only be for two reasons."

"Which are?"

"They'd either be too scared, or too bored to bring up my name. Neither scenario is particularly desirable. I'd much rather be old and eccentric."

Arren smiled at her. "As opposed to young and eccentric."

"That's right." Sarah nodded her head, a warm smile on her lips. "It's terribly stuffy, you know. The *beau monde,* I mean."

Arren closed her book and set it on the table, turning to study Sarah more closely. "I always pictured it as gay and exciting."

"It is at first, I suppose. There are parties every night that go on until all hours of the morning. During the Season, most of the fops and dandies rarely retire before dawn."

"But how do they survive the next day with no sleep?"

Sarah laughed. "Oh they sleep until at least noon, sometimes later."

"Don't they do *anything* during the day?"

"Only if you count luncheons and teas as strenuous activity."

Arren tilted her head. "It all sounds extremely . . . frivolous."

Sarah nodded. "It is. And at first, especially to the debutantes, it's very exciting. All the lights and the gowns and the people are virtually overwhelming."

"When does the luster wear off?"

"For some I suppose it never does, and for some, it's never there to begin with. It became tedious for me after Aiden and I were married."

"I would think entertaining as the Duchess of Albrick would carry certain advantages."

"Oh it does. And I thoroughly enjoy the dinner parties and soirees we hold at Albrick House. It's entirely different when you are the hostess. You only have to invite who you want to come."

Arren laughed. "That sounds rather inhospitable of you."

Sarah grinned in response. "Terribly. I'm developing quite a reputation for being exclusionary."

"And it doesn't bother you in the least, does it?"

She shook her head. "Not one whit. We've had some of the most fascinating people in for dinner. Aiden knows nearly everyone, and I'd much rather listen to John Gibson pontificate about Michelangelo than hear some fop fawning over how wonderful he thinks I look in my gown."

"John Gibson the English Sculptor?"

"Yes. He's fascinating."

"But doesn't the upper crust of society consider artists beneath them."

"Only the part of the *ton* that's narrow-minded, which is most of it." Sarah paused and swept her hand in the direction of the enormous bookcases. "It's so fascinating to me.

Do you have any idea how much knowledge there is in the world? Things you and I have never even heard about?"

Arren nodded. "That's always bothered me. We were so isolated at Grayscar, I didn't have nearly the education I would have liked."

Sarah looked at her closely. "I wouldn't say that. You seem to know a good deal about a great many things."

Arren smiled slightly. "Books." When Sarah tilted her head curiously, Arren continued. "Grayscar is very near Inverness. As was Lawrence's estate. I was able to trade a good many books with travelers. So I have odd pieces of knowledge."

Sarah was fascinated. "Like what?"

"Well, once I traded a book on India to a gentleman who was on his way there as a British governor. He had this rather extensive tome on the history of horses and their role in different societies."

"But that's fascinating."

Arren nodded. "Yes. It discussed things like harnesses and shoes and bits in excruciating detail. It listed every kind ever made, and included diagrams. I read it from cover to cover."

"And now you're an expert."

"I know a good deal more than I need to, certainly."

"What did you do with the book?"

"I traded it to another gentleman for fifteen recent copies of *Vanity Fair!*"

Sarah laughed. "Well that certainly rounded things out for you a bit."

"Yes. It was really very interesting. I know all sorts of things no one has any use for."

Sarah grinned at her. "But you see, you're just the type of person I'd invite to one of my dinner parties."

Arren laughed and goaded Sarah into telling her stories about the last Season in London, and the two of them were nearly doubled over with laughter when Duncan and Aiden entered the room.

Aiden shot Duncan a wary look. "I'm not entirely certain I like this."

Sarah looked up and smiled at him brightly. "You needn't worry. We weren't really talking about you."

Duncan's eyes slid to Arren, and he smiled. The sparkle was back in her green eyes, and with the sun pouring in through the windows, her hair glistened a coppery red. She looked content. It pleased him. "Then what are you laughing about so uproariously?"

Sarah shot him a knowing look. "There are other things to talk about besides you, Duncan McCraig."

"But nothing could be half so interesting."

She rolled her eyes at him. "As it happens, we *were* talking about Aiden in a roundabout way."

Aiden had crossed to the beverage cart to pour himself a cup of coffee. He looked up when he heard his name. "How roundabout?"

Sarah smiled at him and extended her hand for the freshly poured cup. He handed it to her with a disgruntled glare and turned to pour himself another.

"I was telling Arren about the Season, and she was asking me about the gowns and the fashions and such."

Aiden started to walk to one of the large wing chairs, but Duncan took the cup of coffee from him and settled himself in the chair nearest him. Aiden glared at him, returning to the beverage cart once again. "And how did my name happen to come up during all this?"

Sarah took a sip of her coffee and grabbed the cup from Aiden's hand, passing it to Arren. He growled something deep in his chest. She ignored him. "Well, we were talking about the cut of gowns, and how low the neckline was this year."

"And?"

"And Arren asked if I'd ever seen a gown cut so low as to be nearly indecent. I told her I had a few that you severely disapproved of." He grunted his agreement and Sarah glared at him. "But that I'd only seen one that I thought was really improper."

Aiden walked to the other chair and sat down, jealously guarding his cup of coffee. "Whose might that be?"

Sarah shot him a mischievous look. "The one Camille Pickerton wore to the Broylstons' ball."

He rolled his eyes and groaned. "Oh God!"

Duncan started to laugh. "Good God, Brick! Is that woman still after you?"

Aiden sat his coffee cup down on the small table with a decisive *thud*. "I could have killed Sarah that night." Sarah started to giggle and he glared at her. "We went to Broylston's affair. I don't know what the hell possessed her to want to attend that thing."

Sarah interrupted him. "Now Aiden, you know very well why we went. It was Jace and Caroline's first event as husband and wife."

Duncan raised an eyebrow and looked at Sarah curiously. "Your brother has gotten married?"

Sarah nodded. "Oh yes. He married Caroline Ashton. She's an American. I didn't know we hadn't told you."

Duncan shook his head. "No. I hadn't heard. What is she like?"

"Oh she's wonderful. She was in London visiting an aunt when they met. Jace had been assigned the duty of delivering some papers to Caroline's uncle. They were quite the couple during the Season."

Duncan nodded. "I'm pleased to hear it. I'm sure your parents are happy with the arrangement."

Sarah nodded. "They really love her. She's so . . . free-spirited."

Duncan raised an eyebrow and looked at Aiden. Aiden explained. "What Sarah means is, Caroline wasn't raised by English standards. She grew up in America where things are a bit less staid. She doesn't much like convention."

Duncan smiled. "Well then, she should fit into this family just fine."

He nodded. "She does. There isn't a boring bone in her body. I think she's good for Jace."

"All right," Duncan said, "I want to hear about Camille Pickerton."

Aiden groaned again. "So we went to Broylston's ball. We weren't there ten minutes before Camille attached herself to my arm. Every time I broke free of her, I'd turn around and there she was again."

"There's not a vine in the world that clings tighter than Camille," Duncan said with a small laugh.

"And it wouldn't have been so bad if Sarah and Caroline hadn't stood in the corner laughing at me all night."

Sarah started to giggle again. "Well Aiden, you're normally so adept at taking care of yourself. It wasn't my fault you couldn't get rid of Camille."

"Didn't people start to talk?" Duncan asked.

Aiden nodded. "I told her that. She wanted people to talk. And she kept hanging on my arm. She wore this positively odious perfume, and I swear if she'd brushed her bosom against my arm another time, I'd have been forced to slap her."

Duncan started to laugh outright despite Aiden's glare. "It is a rather funny picture, Brick. I mean I've seen you dodge bullets, jump off bridges, and God knows what else, yet you fall victim to the likes of Camille Pickerton."

Aiden grinned at him. "Don't let Sarah fool you. She wouldn't have thought it was so funny had it been, say, Lady Emiline Thornton."

Sarah groaned with disgust and looked over at Arren. "Now's the part where they start to brag."

Arren giggled. "Who is she?"

"She's a tart, is who she is," Sarah answered, "and she's had her eye on my husband for years."

"Is she married?"

Sarah nodded. "Oh yes. Her husband is Lord Thornton. He owns several properties in Wales."

"But that's a good way away, isn't it?" Arren asked.

"That's the problem. He lets her run about London untethered." Sarah looked at Aiden and glared.

He grinned at her. "But she's awfully easy on the eyes."

Sarah mumbled something unladylike under her breath. "You give her another two or three years, and then tell me what you think. She may be voluptuous now, but if she keeps up that behavior of hers, she'll look like a ship in full sail after a few more Seasons."

Aiden and Duncan both started to laugh. Arren looked at Sarah curiously. She found it unfathomable that Sarah wasn't more possessive of Aiden. "Doesn't it bother you?"

"Doesn't what bother me?" Sarah asked.

"That she's like that."

Sarah looked at her curiously. "I suppose it would if I really considered her a threat to my marriage. I don't, though."

Arren tilted her head, studying Sarah carefully. She meant that. "That must be a wonderful feeling."

Sarah raised her eyebrows in surprise. "Yes. It is."

Aiden noticed the speculative look that settled on Duncan's features and coughed, breaking the slightly strained silence. "Sarah?"

She swung her head around, remembering his presence. "Yes?"

"What do you have planned for this afternoon while Duncan and I are in London?"

She shrugged. "I had planned to spend the afternoon keeping Arren company. Was there something special you needed me to do?"

Arren was studying Duncan intently. "You're going to London?"

He nodded. "Just for this afternoon. We'll be back tonight."

Aiden ignored Duncan's conversation with Arren and continued, "I think we'll probably be staying in London for the next few days. You and Arren will be with us."

Sarah nodded. "I'll see that the bags are packed."

Arren was completely oblivious to their conversation. She continued to study Duncan. "Why?"

Duncan deliberately misunderstood her. "Because I don't want to be away from you tonight."

She shook her head. "I mean why are you going to London?"

He knitted his brows in confusion. "I have to make an appointment with the Regent."

Aiden had taken another sip of his coffee while Sarah rattled off a list of questions about what they would need when they arrived. He smiled at her. "Well, you'll want to bring the baby, of course."

She shot him a disgruntled look. "Aiden, you know what I mean."

He grinned. "Just the usual things. I think we'll probably attend Aimsmond's affair tomorrow night, though, so make sure Arren has something to wear."

Sarah nodded. "I'm glad we're going to that."

Arren had fired off a list of questions to Duncan about how he intended to procure the appointment. He watched her curiously. "It shouldn't be too difficult," he said. "I think I can arrange it for the day after tomorrow, if not sooner."

She looked worried. "Duncan, what if . . ."

He interrupted her. "Nothing's going to happen. As soon as I put this bloody mess behind us, I'm going to haul you home to Strathcraig and make you promise to stop worrying about Alistar McDonan."

She smiled warily. "I hope you're right."

He sighed and placed his coffee cup on the table. Aiden had finished his conversation with Sarah and did the same. They stood up simultaneously.

"We'd better be leaving soon," Aiden said. "Sarah, come upstairs with me while I change."

She looked at him in surprise. "Aren't you going to wait to hear from Jonathan Fielding?"

He reached into his waistcoat pocket and removed a piece of folded vellum. "I received this just before Duncan and I joined you in the library."

She swung around and looked at the clock on the mantel. "Good heavens! It's after twelve o'clock. I had no idea it was so late."

He nodded. "We need to be on the road if we want to be back before dark."

She rose and took his hand, walking with him toward the door. "Will you want luncheon before you leave?"

He shook his head. "It's only an hour or so to ride. We'll eat when we get there." Aiden turned back and looked at Duncan. "Meet me in the foyer in fifteen minutes?"

Duncan nodded, watching the door shut behind them. He turned back to Arren. Her hands were clenched in her lap, and she was staring intently at one of the embroidered pillows. It had suddenly become the most fascinating object in the world. "Arren?"

She didn't look at him. "Have a good journey. Don't take any unnecessary risks just to get back by dark."

He smiled. "Arren, look at me please."

It wasn't a request. She nearly refused him, but thought better of it and raised her eyes. He smiled at her gently. "Arren, there's nothing to worry about."

She shook her head. "You don't understand."

He sighed in exasperation and sat down beside her, taking her cold hand into his. Her green eyes were wide with anxiety and he reached out, tucking a tendril of hair behind her ear. "I do understand. I understand very well, and I'm not going to let anything happen to you."

She sank her teeth into her lower lip to keep it from trembling. "I'm frightened."

"I know you are. But you needn't be. This will all be over in a few days. Alistar McDonan isn't going to hurt you."

"It isn't me I'm worried about."

"Then give me a little credit for knowing how to take care of myself. He isn't going to hurt me either."

She looked at him dubiously, and he kissed her gently. "Arren, have I ever made you a promise I didn't keep?"

She shook her head.

THE PROMISE . 357

"Then I promise. Everything will be fine. Just trust me a while longer."

She reached up and touched his face, her green eyes burning into his gold-flecked ones. She nodded. "Don't you dare betray me, Gypsy."

He smiled. "I won't."

He kissed her again before going to change his clothes, leaving Arren alone in the library. She sighed and sank back against the pillows on the sofa, fighting another wave of anxiety. All she had now was his promise.

Twenty-eight

Arren spent one of the most pleasant afternoons she ever remembered. She and Sarah spent a good deal of time with the baby, sitting in the library, telling each other stories. And once Cana had finally settled down for an afternoon nap, the two of them climbed the stairs to search through Sarah's extensive wardrobe.

"The Aimsmonds' ball," Sarah explained, "is always a wonderful event. They deliberately hold it after the peak of the Season."

"Why?"

"So they have an excuse not to invite people they don't want to."

Arren laughed. "How many people will be there?"

"It's hard to say. Usually there are at least five hundred."

"Five hundred?!"

Sarah nodded and pulled open the door to her room. "Yes. Their house is enormous."

Arren followed her into the room and watched as Sarah pulled open the doors of two large wardrobes. Sarah started to sort through the gowns, pulling out several as she went along. Arren watched in fascination. She was beginning to feel jittery about attending the affair. Seeing Sarah's practiced eye appraising the gowns wasn't helping.

With the exception of her own wedding reception, Arren

had never attended a formal occasion. As Lawrence's wife she had given only dinner parties. The guests were always men, and her joining in their conversation had never been welcomed. As a consequence, she'd never participated.

Now, she was faced with an immense social occasion where she would have to carry on appropriately frivolous conversation. She was the Duchess of Strathcraig. For that matter, she was the Duchess of Grayscar *and* the Duchess of Strathcraig. She would be expected to know certain social standards, and to act according to her station. The thought made a cold knot settle in the pit of her stomach.

"This one!" Sarah pulled a gown from the wardrobe and held it up triumphantly. "This is perfect."

Arren looked at her dubiously. The gown was deep emerald green. It was laced through with tiny gold threads that sparkled in the sunlight pouring through the windows. Its gold underskirt showed beneath the scalloped hemline, and Sarah held it up for closer inspection. "Do you like it?" she asked.

Arren looked at her warily. "It looks very . . . grand."

Sarah nodded. "It is. The silk was imported from the Orient. Do you not like it?"

Arren shook her head. "It isn't that. It's quite the loveliest gown I've ever seen. It's just, won't you mind if I wear it?"

Sarah smiled at her and laid the gown across the sofa, sinking down amidst the cushions. "You know, before Caroline, I never had any close lady friends."

Arren looked at her curiously and sat down. "You must have known dozens of people."

"Oh I did! But I wasn't really friends with any of them. I never had much patience for the interests of my peers."

"What do you mean?"

"I met Aiden when I was ten years old. He was quite

the most fascinating person I'd ever known. He would travel out of the country for months on end, and when he returned, I would pester him until he told me stories about the places he'd been. Naturally, by the time I was thirteen or fourteen years old, I fancied myself madly in love with him."

Arren smiled. "Weren't you?"

Sarah shook her head and laughed. "Not really. Not then, anyway. But I had the most horrific crush. And after he would tell me all those wonderful stories, I would rush off and try to learn everything there was to know about the places he'd been and the people he'd met."

"I imagine that was very interesting."

"It was! I loved it. I had a wonderful tutor who taught me languages and mathematics, and philosophy, and all other sorts of things young ladies of society aren't supposed to know."

"You don't regret it, do you?"

Sarah shook her head. "Not for a moment. But it made it terribly difficult to make friends. I couldn't bear to sit and discuss gowns, and marriage proposals, and society gossip for hours on end. I found the endless social chatter to be terribly boring, and on the few occasions when I did find someone interesting to talk to, they were usually entirely unsuitable."

Arren nodded. "It's very lonely not having anyone to confide in. I didn't even know any other women except for our house staff."

Sarah sighed and took Arren's hand. "So you see. You're my friend. Now I have you and I have Caroline. And I'm so glad I waited for the two of you."

Arren smiled. "I could, after all, tell you everything you want to know about horse bits."

Sarah started to laugh. "And I can tell you everything you want to know about society balls. So stop worrying so much. You'll chew a hole in your lip."

Arren laughed with her. "How did you know I was worried?"

"It's written all over your face. You haven't a thing to be concerned about. Aiden and I will be there, and unless their plans have changed, so will Jace and Caroline. My other brother, Tryon, will likely be there as well, and you and Caroline and I can giggle over the voluptuous woman he has attached to his arm."

"Is your other brother married?"

Sarah shook her head. "No. And with Duncan now attached, all the scheming mamas are running out of ducal coronets to pursue. Tryon's wealth has suddenly made him extremely popular—even though he isn't likely to inherit a title."

"It all sounds rather cutthroat."

"It's vicious. You needn't worry, though. Caroline and I can outsnipe anyone."

Arren laughed. "I think you're proud of that!"

Sarah grinned in response. "But I have a reputation to protect as a result. And that's why I want you to look devastatingly attractive tomorrow night." She paused and looked at Arren speculatively. "Besides, I think it will do Duncan a world of good to see men falling at your feet!"

Arren smiled and reached out to finger the green silk. "It's a beautiful gown."

Sarah grunted with satisfaction. "Then try it on and let's make sure it fits. And if you ask me again if I mind your wearing it, I'll take offense."

Arren stood up and started unbuttoning her rust-colored shirt. "I guess we can't have that."

* * *

It fit like a dream. Sarah had to tuck two pins in the waist where it needed to be taken in just a tad, but otherwise, the fit was perfect. The bodice was shockingly low. It dipped well below the swell of her breasts, and the soft flare of the skirt below the fitted bodice showed off her figure to perfection. Arren loved it. The color made her eyes sparkle, and she stood admiring herself in the mirror, while Sarah pinned the waist. Sarah looked up and smiled at her. "It looks wonderful on you. It never looked anywhere near that nice on me."

Arren looked at her curiously. "What are you going to wear?"

Sarah grinned and walked back to the wardrobe. She tugged out a gown still covered in its heavy silk drape. "It's brand new. I just got it last week. I was hoping Aiden would decide we could go to the Aimsmonds' ball, but I knew we wouldn't unless Duncan had turned up by now." She reached down and peeled back the silk.

Arren gasped. "Oh, Sarah! It's beautiful."

The gown was a masterpiece. It was made of deep purple silk, with tiny strips of black, edging the bodice and hem. The silk was woven with almost invisible iridescent threads, and when the light touched it, it sparkled like fairy dust. Sarah held it out and lovingly fingered the silk. "I saw the material last time I was in Madame Drussard's for a fitting. The Marchioness of Bedfordshire had ordered it, and I had to practically beg Madame to sell it to me. I actually think it was Aiden who twisted her arm."

"What do you mean?"

Sarah dropped the silk back over the dress and hung it in the closet. "When I left that afternoon, Madame Drussard still wouldn't give me an answer. I was even willing to order a second bolt for myself, but she insisted it was handmade, and that she couldn't use the same material in two gowns for two different customers."

Arren looked confused. "Why not?"

Sarah smiled. "Because unlike the Highlands, where everyone prides themselves on dressing alike, London is full of snobs. It's nearly unforgivable to arrive at a function wearing the same gown as another lady—even if it is your dressmaker's fault. With a material like that, it's so unique, it would be too obvious."

Sarah crossed the room to help Arren with the buttons of her gown. "So when you left, Madame Drussard wouldn't sell it to you?"

"Right. I got home and mentioned it to Aiden, telling him how much I'd admired the material. Two weeks later, the gown arrived."

"Did you know he'd arranged it?"

"No. He still won't admit to it either."

"Has he seen it yet?"

Sarah giggled and shook her head. "No. And when he sees the neckline, he'll likely choke at the thought of what he must have paid Madame Drussard to make it for me."

Arren laughed and dropped the green gown from her shoulders. "I think tomorrow should prove to be a fascinating day."

Sarah laughed with her and rehung the gown in the closet, waiting for Arren to slip back into her butter-colored breeches and rust shirt. Arren slipped the final button through its hole and smiled at Sarah. "All right, I'm ready. But you have to spend the rest of the day telling me what to expect tomorrow night."

Sarah nodded and, opening the door, she led the way

back to the library. The remainder of the day they spent curled up in front of the fire, talking about the Aimsmonds' party. They were, in fact, so comfortable, that Sarah had their dinner served in the library instead of in the dining room. Sarah pushed two of the large sofa cushions onto the floor, and they sat cross-legged at the low coffee table, laughing over their meal. Only after they'd eaten, and were leaning back against the sofa did their conversation change.

Sarah took a long swallow of her wine and sighed. "This has been the most enjoyable day."

Arren smiled. "I thought so too."

Sarah looked at the clock on the mantel and narrowed her eyes speculatively. "Aiden and Duncan should be home soon."

"How do you know?"

"Because Aiden doesn't like to be gone after dark when Cana and I are here alone."

Arren felt a shaft of fear trip up her spine. She had felt so cocooned here, she hadn't given a thought to their safety all day. "Doesn't he believe you're safe?"

Sarah laughed. "Oh we're completely safe. It would take a veritable army to get onto this estate when he isn't here. He doubles the protection the minute he sets foot outside the gates."

Arren's eyes widened. "Why?"

Sarah looked at her carefully. "Has Duncan told you anything about the days when Aiden and I were first married?"

Arren shook her head. "You must remember, he didn't know I was aware of who he was until after we came here. He never talked about you. It would have been too revealing."

Sarah nodded. "Duncan and Aiden were actively involved in an investigation for the War Department at the time. It was dreadfully intense. Even I don't know everything that transpired."

Arren nodded and Sarah continued the story. "I didn't see them, or hear from them for six weeks. It was awful. I had just learned I was pregnant with Cana after Aiden left, and I couldn't seem to stop crying. I was so frightened for him. When all that time passed and there was no sign of him, I was nearly out of my mind."

Arren nodded. "I can imagine you were."

Sarah took another sip of her wine. "Anyway, it's all a very long and complicated story, but when they finally returned, I was so relieved, I cried even more. I know Aiden thought I'd lost my mind."

Arren gasped. "It must have been horrible."

"It was. And ever since then, he's been terribly edgy about leaving me here alone. He seldom, if ever, goes into London for more than a day without taking Cana and me with him."

Arren nodded slowly. "I can certainly understand why he'd be that way." She paused and took a sip of her wine. "I can't imagine what it must have been like for you during those six weeks he was gone."

Sarah shook her head. "I was a complete wreck. All I did all day long was sit around and cry. It was awful."

"Did he simply turn up one day, or did he contact you first?"

Sarah started to laugh. "Actually, I surprised him."

Arren looked at her curiously. "What do you mean?"

"He and Duncan returned to London late in the afternoon. I was here, at Albrick Park. They met with the Regent early that evening, and His Highness insisted they stay for dinner at Carlton House. Aiden didn't know the Regent had already sent me an invitation to attend. I wouldn't have gone if Tryon hadn't told me Aiden was going to be there."

"You must have been terribly excited."

"Oh I was! I made, Aiden's friend, Frederick go with me. It took me all afternoon just to get dressed."

"What did he do when he saw you there?"

Sarah grinned and took another sip of her wine. "You mean besides nearly fainting on the spot?"

Arren laughed and nodded. "Besides that."

"He pulled me back in a corner and told me he wanted to tear my clothes off." Sarah laughed at Arren's stunned expression. "Well he said a good many other things, too. He made all kinds of apologies, and swore himself silly that it couldn't be avoided, but the gist was that he wanted to tear my clothes off."

Arren started to laugh. "What did you do?"

Sarah shrugged. "There wasn't much I could do. I really rather wanted him to tear my clothes off anyway."

Arren laughed harder. "Sarah, that's scandalous!"

"Oh that's not even the worst part."

Arren swallowed a sip of her wine and set the empty glass down on the table. Sarah reached over and filled it. "It gets worse?"

"Um-hmm." Sarah refilled her own glass. "I don't know how we made it through that dinner. I was between Duncan and Frederick, and Aiden was between two women. I can't remember who they were now, but I remember one of them was hanging all over him. I was furious."

"What did you do?"

"I sat there and simmered until dinner started to come to an end. As soon as it was over, the Regent made an excuse for Aiden and me to leave. He didn't waste a second.

He dragged me out to the carriage, threw me inside, and proceeded to do what I wanted him to do all evening."

Arren's mouth dropped open. "In the carriage!"

Sarah nodded and started to giggle. "It was a rather memorable evening."

"Sarah!" Arren started to laugh. "I can't believe you did that."

Sarah took another long swallow of her wine. "Well it's no worse than you and Duncan and those damn feathers."

Arren's head snapped around and she looked at Sarah, a deep crimson blush rising all the way to the roots of her hair. "You know!"

Sarah laughed again. "Well of course I know."

"That cad! He swore no one would know."

Sarah had to take several deep breaths before she could speak again. "He told Aiden's valet, for heaven's sake! Everyone knows."

Arren tried to look horrified but couldn't quite manage it. The wine was starting to have an effect on her, and she began to giggle. In a few minutes she was laughing outright, and the harder she laughed, the harder Sarah laughed in return.

Before long, they were clutching their sides, rolling about like two schoolgirls. Sarah sat up and gasped for breath, bracing herself back on her hands. "Wait. Wait. I have to tell you this."

Arren managed to stop laughing through an almost superhuman effort. "What?"

"I'll tell you, but you have to promise to tell me something about Duncan in return."

Arren stifled a giggle and nodded. "All right."

Sarah drew another deep breath and took a fortifying sip

of her wine. "Aiden does the most ridiculous thing some-times after we make love."

Arren choked on a laugh. "What?"

Sarah burst out laughing. "He hums to me."

Both of them convulsed in peals of laughter. Arren gasped for breath. "No! No he does not!"

Sarah was lying back on the floor, clutching her stomach. "Yes he does. I swear it!"

"Oh God, Sarah! How do you keep from laughing."

"Well it's kind of nice when he does it. It's only now, that it seems so funny." The world trailed off in another burst of hysteria.

Arren was laughing so hard the tears were pouring down her face. She collapsed back on the floor and pressed both her hands into her sides. "Oh I hurt!"

Sarah took a deep breath. "All right, you promised."

Arren gasped and thought for several minutes. "Oh God, he'd kill me if he knew I told you this."

"You promised."

Arren nodded, wiping her tears with the back of her hand. "He growls."

Sarah drew in her breath. "He what?"

"He growls. I mean not just low in his chest. You know." She paused and made the rumbling sound. "I mean he makes these noises." She clenched her teeth and growled, rolling the noise over her tongue. "Right in the middle of things."

Sarah's hand flew to her mouth to stifle a fresh surge of laughter. "How much in the middle of things?"

Arren barely stifled a giggle. "I mean *right* in the middle of things."

Sarah fell back and howled. Arren joined her.

Aiden and Duncan walked in on the scene. Duncan shot

Aiden a wary look. "I don't think I like the looks of this, Brick."

Aiden shook his head. "I have a strong suspicion we've been set up."

Sarah looked up and tried to stifle her laughter long enough to say hello. "Welcome home, My Lord . . ." the sentence trailed off and she fell back on the floor again, clutching her stomach.

Duncan groaned. "We've definitely been set up."

Aiden crossed the room and picked up the now-empty bottle of wine, holding it high for Duncan's inspection. "All right. You take care of your drunken wife, and I'll take care of mine."

Arren pushed herself up on one hand and looked at Duncan. "I am not drunk. I don't know why you would think sho . . . so." She corrected the slip of her tongue, eliciting another hysterical peal from Sarah. Arren fell back on the floor and doubled over again.

Duncan sighed heavily and walked across the room to stand directly in front of her. He extended his hand, waiting for Arren to slip hers into it. When she did, he pulled her to her feet and stooped, lifting her onto his shoulder in a single motion. He clamped his arm across the backs of her thighs, holding her steady, even while she slapped ineffectually at his back with her hands.

"Put me down!"

He swatted her behind. "No! I'm taking you to bed." He turned and looked at Aiden. Sarah was still laughing on the floor, and Arren had started giggling again. "For God's sake, Brick! Do something about that shameless woman you married."

Aiden laughed and watched Duncan stride toward the door of the library, with Arren securely over his shoulder.

Even after they left, Aiden could hear her protesting all the way up the long staircase. He reached down, helped Sarah to her feet, and wiped her tears of laughter away with his hand. "Sarah, are you drunk?"

She giggled and shook her head. "Not really. I'm just a little lightheaded."

She started to laugh again and he pinched her bottom. "Stop that."

She leaned against him, her shoulders shaking with suppressed laughter. "I can't. It was so funny." She ended in another peal of laughter and he rolled his eyes, waiting for her to stop.

She took several deep breaths and as she looked at him, a smile began tugging at the corner of her mouth. "I'm sorry."

He shook his head and kissed her briefly. "I'm not. I'm glad you two are enjoying each other. From what Duncan tells me, it isn't something Arren has done much in her life."

Sarah sobered suddenly and shook her head. "No. It's really very sad. I genuinely like her. I'm glad he's found someone he loves so deeply."

Aiden nodded. "He really does. He says she's scared to death of their relationship, but he's willing to go to hell and back if he has to."

Sarah sighed and leaned against him. "She loves him, too. I know she does. It will all work out."

"I hope you're right."

"It will," Sarah insisted.

Aiden smiled and stroked his hands up and down her back. She tilted her head back to look at him again. "Did everything go all right today?"

He nodded. "Yes. We'll meet with the Regent the day after tomorrow."

She smiled. "Good. I'm really looking forward to the Aimsmonds' ball."

"Did you find something for Arren to wear?"

"Did I find something for Arren to wear," she mocked. "Have you so little faith?"

"I have a lot of faith. I just want to make sure Duncan doesn't want to wring your neck when he sees her in it."

Sarah smiled. "She's going to look smashing, and he's simply going to have to get over it."

"Sarah."

His voice held a warning note and she smiled at him secretively, patting his chest. "Don't worry. She looks beautiful in it."

He sighed and tugged on her hair. "You're up to no good."

"I am not."

He clearly didn't believe her, and was about to say so when they heard a squeal from upstairs. Sarah looked at the ceiling speculatively. "He's probably ravishing her right now, you know?"

"Probably."

"Aren't you going to do anything?"

"Oh I'm going to do a lot of things."

She almost managed to glare at him, but lost her composure when they heard another squeal. She poked his chest. "Aiden Brickston, are you getting ideas?"

He nodded, his lips curling into a slow seductive grin. "Lots of them."

She leaned against him. "Then what on earth is taking you so long?"

He groaned and lifted her into his arms, striding toward

the door. They were halfway up the stairs when Sarah lifted her head from his shoulder and traced her finger over the curve of his mouth. "Aiden?"

He looked at her and continued to stride effortlessly up the long staircase. "Hmm?"

"Will you hum to me tonight?"

He grinned. "Anything you want, darling."

He turned down the hall, and only the echo of Sarah's giggle was left behind.

Twenty-nine

Arren sat on the wide bed admiring her husband. They had arrived at Albrick House in London early that afternoon, and Duncan was standing before the mirror, deftly tying his cravat. In two hours, they would leave for the Aimsmonds' ball. Arren watched him through slitted lashes, unwilling for him to know how entranced she was with his appearance.

He looked magnificent. He had stopped by his Saville Row tailor the day before, and his new evening clothes had been delivered to Albrick Park just twenty minutes ago. The black, stovepipe trousers fitted like a second skin, and the jacket set off the extraordinary breadth of his shoulders. He wore a gold brocade waistcoat over his fine, ivory lawn shirt. He gave the cravat a final tug, settling it in an intricate waterfall pattern, and reached to the dressing table for an emerald stickpin. He slipped it into his lapel with a slight smile and turned to look at his wife.

He was well aware that Arren had been watching him throughout the routine, and he had deliberately drawn it out for her benefit. "Did you learn anything?"

Arren yawned, pretending to wake up from her nap. "What do you mean?"

He grinned and crossed the room to sit down on the side

of the bed, facing her. "Watching me dress. Did you learn anything?"

Arren's face flushed. "I wasn't watching you dress. I was sleeping."

He nodded, and a smile flickered on his lips. "Of course you were. It must have been my imagination playing tricks on me when I looked in the mirror and saw your eyes open."

She looked at him a bit sheepishly and reached out to brush a piece of lint from his shoulder. "All right. Perhaps I was watching a bit, but you needn't look so smug over it."

"I'm not being smug. I was merely thinking that I rather enjoy watching *you* dress. I wondered if the experience is the same for you."

She rolled her eyes and poked him in the chest. "Well you aren't going to watch me this time. Sarah's sending a maid in to do my hair and help me into my gown."

He sighed dramatically. "I've always been warned that married life becomes frightfully dull."

"Well if you're bored already, you're in deep trouble."

"Perhaps you can find a way to rekindle the fires for me tonight."

Arren mumbled something unintelligible and he reached down and caught hold of her chin. "Arren, what did you say?"

She shook her head. "It wasn't important."

His grip on her chin tightened imperceptibly. "Wasn't it?"

Her eyes met his and he noticed the way her lip trembled. "No. It wasn't."

"Then why don't you tell me what you said and let me decide that."

She sighed heavily. "I said, 'There's no point in rekindling any fire.' "

Duncan made a small, exasperated sound in the back of

his throat and dropped his hand. "Dammit, Arren, how many more times will I have to endure this conversation."

"Please don't be angry."

"Why shouldn't I be? I've been running around this circle for weeks now. There's evidently nothing I can say to convince you everything will come right."

She leaned forward, laying her hand on his thigh. "I want so much to believe you, Duncan. Isn't that enough?"

He shook his head. "No, Arren. It isn't enough." He stood up suddenly and her hand fell back to the bed. "I'm tired of this."

He turned to go, and Arren threw back the covers. She scurried out of the bed, and caught up with him midway across the room. "Duncan, please don't be angry."

He pivoted on his heel and stared down at her. "What do you expect from me, Arren?"

She laid her hand on his arm and lifted her gaze to his, silently pleading with him. "We're going to this ball tonight as husband and wife. I don't want us to be angry when we arrive."

Duncan studied her for a long, tense moment before releasing his breath in a deep sigh. He took her hand and drew her over to one of the low sofas. He motioned for her to sit down, and waited for her to obey him before he settled himself next to her. "I don't want to fight with you any more than you want to fight with me. I'm just tired of this argument."

She nodded. "I know. I'm sorry."

He slid a sideways glance at her. "You're sorry, but you're no more convinced now than you were five minutes ago."

Arren spread her hands in front of her and looked at him. "Please try to understand."

He took another deep breath and absently rubbed the

back of his neck. "I think it would be best if we didn't discuss this right now. My temper's about to get the better of me."

Arren nodded, more than ready to change the tense subject. "Aren't you supposed to meet Aiden downstairs?"

"In a minute. I want to go over the arrangements with you one more time, though."

"What arrangements? The only arrangement is that I'm not to be out of sight of you or Aiden at any time during the evening. How difficult can that be?"

He studied her carefully. "I'm completely serious about this, Arren. There's going to be a throng of people at this thing, and I wouldn't go at all except I need to talk to several of the guests."

"You still haven't explained that to me yet."

"Many of the estates in Scotland are secondary holdings of English nobility. I'd like to persuade as many landholders as I can find to stand with me tomorrow when I talk to the Regent."

She looked at him curiously. "Do you think you'll be able to?"

"I'm certain of it. Social reform is high on the agenda of the English *Beau Monde*. They're still quaking in their Hessians over what happened in France."

"The revolution, you mean?"

He nodded. "It's been less than thirty years since the French people revolted against the ruling classes. With the rise and fall of Napoleon, the English are taking a much closer look at their own internal circumstances."

"If you can pull several English landholders on your side, do you think your chances of an alliance will be better at home."

"Immeasurably. As your husband, I now control the largest estates in Scotland times four. That's a lot of power to be tossing about."

Arren bristled noticeably, and he reached out and shook her shoulder. "Don't you think we'll have accomplished something worthwhile, Duchess, if we put all this land to use helping the people?"

She hesitated only briefly before she nodded. "At the risk of making you angry again, you know you may count Grayscar among your alliance should things not go the way you've planned."

He nodded. "I do."

She managed a slight smile and leaned over to kiss him briefly. "You'd better go downstairs now so I can get dressed."

"Are you sure I can't watch?"

"I'm sure."

Duncan sighed and rose to his feet, pulling Arren up with him. "All right. I'll let you have your way this time, but I'll not let you deprive me of watching you undress this evening."

Arren tried to keep the sadness out of her eyes. "I wouldn't dream of it."

He grinned at her and kissed her briefly, whispering something scandalous in her ear before he left her alone in the large room. Arren shut the door after him and looked at it sadly. Tonight would likely be their last night together as husband and wife. After tomorrow, everything would be different. Resolutely, she turned and looked at her reflection in the mirror. Tonight, she vowed, she would refuse to think about the bleak future that lay ahead. Instead, she would allow herself to fall into his fantasy, to believe that sometimes, impossible dreams do come true. Tonight, she would shine for him, and even if her world crashed down around her ears tomorrow, no one could ever steal tonight. She squared her shoulders and pulled the heavy cord by the door, waiting for her maid to help her dress.

She was ready in under an hour, and she stood anxiously inspecting her reflection in the mirror. A brief knock sounded and Sarah opened the door and entered. Arren drew in her breath when she saw her. The gown looked even more magnificent now than it had when she'd seen it yesterday. "Sarah, you look stunning."

Sarah smiled. "Do you think so? I'm especially pleased with the color."

Arren nodded. One of Sarah's most striking features was her wide purple eyes. The gown's deep color matched them almost perfectly. "It matches your eyes almost exactly."

Sarah laughed slightly. "When we were first courting, Aiden and I used to have this continuing argument over the color of my eyes. I desperately wanted them to be blue. He kept insisting they were purple."

"They *are* purple."

"Well I know, but I wanted them to be blue." Sarah paused and looked at Arren's appearance with a wide smile. "I suppose you've never had to debate the color of your eyes with anyone."

Arren laughed. "Not ever. They've always been most decidedly green."

"Well, you look magnificent in that gown."

Arren pulled at the skirt somewhat nervously and looked back at the mirror. "I hope my husband thinks so."

Sarah smiled knowingly. "Oh he'll think so, all right."

When they entered the salon together, they found Duncan and Aiden standing by the fireplace, discussing the evening that lay ahead. When Duncan saw her, he nearly dropped his glass. "Good God!"

Aiden mumbled something under his breath, and he stared at Sarah's dress.

Sarah giggled. "Well the two of you look positively bowled over by our obvious beauty."

Aiden strode forward to greet her, all the while eying the dangerous cut of her neckline. "Sarah, that gown is cut entirely too low."

She went up on her tiptoes and kissed him briefly. "And thank you for buying it for me, My Lord husband."

"I'm sending it back in the morning," he growled.

Sarah laughed at him and turned her attention to Arren. She was tugging nervously at the skirt of her gown, while Duncan stood, seemingly rooted to the spot by the mantel. Sarah looked at him in amusement. "Duncan, aren't you going to say hello to your wife?"

He looked at her in surprise, as if he'd forgotten Sarah and Aiden's presence altogether. "Of course," he muttered, stepping forward.

Arren smiled at him a bit anxiously and he took her hand, raising it to her lips. "You look stunning, Duchess."

She looked at him warily and drew her hand back. "Thank you. So do you."

He seemed to snap out of his reverie and he bent forward to whisper, "I'm sure I shall have to fight away your admirers all evening."

Arren relaxed with the return of their usual banter and poked his chest. "No more than I shall have to fight off yours, Gypsy."

He leaned back and smiled, pulling Arren's arm through his own. "Are you ready to go, My Lady?" She nodded and curled her fingers on his forearm, and Duncan looked at Aiden expectantly.

Aiden rolled his eyes. "Are you two finished mooning over each other?" he asked.

Duncan grinned and nodded. "You're one to talk, Brick. I was around a good bit when you and Sarah were first married. You defined the word 'mooning.' "

Aiden looked indignant. "I have never mooned over anyone." Sarah kicked his shin and he groaned loudly, looking down at her with a disgruntled glare. "Especially not bad-tempered ladies with flashing purple eyes."

She lifted her chin and shot Arren a slow wink. "My eyes are *not* purple. They're blue."

He smirked and dropped a quick kiss on her forehead. "Then perhaps I'd better sell all those purple jewels I've scanned the earth to find."

She shook her head. "That's all right. You may think they're purple if you want to."

Aiden laughed and drew her arm through his, walking with her toward the door. "I'm warning you now, My Lady, if I die tomorrow dueling some cad who's been looking down your dress all evening, I'm going to make you carve 'her eyes are purple' on my tombstone."

She smiled up at him and cast a glance back at Duncan and Arren. "As God is my witness, that's all he said he wants on the marker. Duncan, you'll help me order it, won't you?" She yelped when Aiden reached down and swatted her on the behind, as he pushed her out the door.

Thirty

The room shimmered with movement. Arren stood at the entrance of the enormous ballroom, her eyes wide with curiosity. The ballroom was packed with glittering people. Duncan held her hand firmly on his arm, and she looked about in amazement at the throng of strangers.

They had arrived in Aiden's carriage about twenty minutes before, and now they stood at the entrance of the ballroom, waiting for the butler to announce their arrival. Arren had been stunned at the long queue of carriages at the front of the massive house, and when they'd finally arrived inside, the sheer number of people proved to be overwhelming.

Aiden and Sarah seemed to know everyone. No one walked by them without stopping to say hello. Within ten minutes, Arren had met more people than she had almost in her entire lifetime. She looked around in fascination, clinging to Duncan's arm.

He studied her carefully. He knew she was unused to formal occasions, and while he wasn't particularly concerned with her ability to carry it off, he knew she was nervous. She seemed spellbound by the hum of activity that permeated the immense foyer, and he smiled at her as they neared the ballroom, and he saw her eyes widen.

Aiden and Sarah were announced first, and they entered the huge ballroom, moving slowly in the direction of the

Marquess and Marchioness of Aimsmond. Duncan closed his fingers over Arren's hand and stepped forward.

"The Duke and Duchess of Strathcraig, also Duchess of Grayscar."

She looked at him in surprise and he smiled at her, pulling her into the crowd. Arren pulled on his arm until he bent low enough to hear her.

"Why did you do that?"

"Do what?"

"Use both titles."

"Well they are both your titles, aren't they?"

They had advanced a good way into the room, and he paused to speak to someone, introducing Arren as his wife. They exchanged pleasantries, and he pulled Arren forward again, working his way steadily toward the Marquess.

Arren looked at him in exasperation. "Well of course they're both my titles. But why did you use them both?"

He shrugged and looked at her curiously. "Why not?"

She sighed and waited for him to greet another passerby. "Don't you think it diminishes your rank somewhat if I have two titles?"

Duncan stopped in the middle of the room and looked down at her in surprise. "That's ridiculous. Does it diminish you that I have four?"

"Well no, but that's different."

He rolled his eyes and pulled her forward again. "Arren, I'm not threatened by the fact that you are a Duchess in your own right. Where the hell did you get an idea like that?"

"It always bothered Lawrence that I stood to gain the title if something happened to Donald."

Duncan stopped again and glared at her. "Don't you ever compare me to that bastard again. Do you understand?"

Her eyes widened slightly at the cold tone in his voice and she nodded, unwilling to risk provoking him further. "I'm sorry."

He sighed and reached up to touch her face. "I'm sorry, too. Let's not argue tonight, all right?"

She smiled and nodded gratefully, relaxing against his side. Duncan led her across the room, introducing her to dozens of people before he reached the Marquess and Marchioness of Aimsmond.

"Your Grace!" the Marquess exclaimed. "What a pleasant surprise!"

Duncan smiled and shook the Marquess's hand. "I hope it didn't inconvenience you to add us to your guest list so late."

The Marchioness shook her head. "Of course not. We were so pleased to hear you were back in England."

Duncan pulled Arren forward and she extended her hand to the Marquess, dropping a small curtsy. "My Lord, may I present my wife, the Duchess of Strathcraig."

The Marquess bent forward and dropped a quick kiss on Arren's hand. "It's indeed a pleasure to meet you, Your Grace."

Arren smiled. "It was so kind of you to invite us on such short notice. I wouldn't wish to impose."

"You're both delightful additions to the evening."

Duncan briefly kissed the Marchioness's hand and thanked them both again. He pushed Arren forward, and they walked a few yards before she stopped him. "Did I do that all right?" she asked.

He looked down at her in surprise. "You were wonderful. Why are you so worried?"

"I wouldn't wish to embarrass you."

"You're not going to embarrass me."

She looked at him dubiously. "You seemed annoyed just now, though."

He sighed in exasperation and grabbed two glasses of champagne from a passing footman. "That's because I didn't like the way Aimsmond was looking down your dress."

Arren looked at him in surprise and accepted the glass he handed her. She decided perhaps Sarah was right. It would do him a world of good to see men falling at Arren's feet. For that matter, it wouldn't do her any harm either. She took a long fortifying sip of the champagne and turned to look at the crowd. She smiled when she saw Sarah approach.

Sarah reached for Arren's hand and started to tug her across the room again. "Come on. I've found Caroline and Jace. I want you to meet them."

Arren shot Duncan an anxious look and he nodded. "Go on. Just don't leave the ballroom, all right?"

She nodded and followed Sarah through the crowd.

Caroline Erridge turned out to be everything Arren had expected and more. They found her on the far side of the ballroom, surrounded by a throng of admirers. Her husband stood behind her, watching indulgently as his wife charmed her circle of friends. As soon as she saw Sarah, she grabbed Jace's hand and started forward, suddenly losing interest in the people around her. "Sarah! You found her!"

Sarah nodded and pulled Arren forward. "Jace, Caroline, this is Arren McCraig—Duncan's wife."

Caroline leaned over and kissed Arren on the cheek. "I'm so glad to meet you. Sarah was just telling me all about the fun you've been having together." She shot Arren a mischievous look, and Arren decided she liked Caroline immensely. Her odd accent seemed the perfect match for her pale gold hair and wide blue eyes. She wasn't really beautiful, not classically anyway, but she exuded a certain vivaciousness that made Arren understand why Sarah enjoyed her company so thoroughly.

"I'm pleased to meet you, too," she answered. "Sarah has the advantage it seems. She can talk about both of us."

Caroline smiled and nodded. "Don't worry, though. We'll pair off in a corner somewhere and exchange notes."

Sarah smiled conspiratorially at them both, and stepped forward to kiss her brother's cheek. "Jace, say hello and then go find Aiden. I think he wants to talk to you about the mine."

Jace groaned and raised Arren's hand to his lips. "It's delightful to meet you, Your Grace." He shot Sarah a disgruntled look. "And I see you're as bossy as ever, brat."

She smiled and patted his shoulder. "It's entirely your own fault. You spoiled me just as much as the rest of them."

"If only I'd known then what I was getting into."

She pushed him in the direction of the crowd. "Well you didn't, and now you're stuck with me. So go find Aiden and the two of you can commiserate."

Jace looked at Caroline and smiled. "Will you be all right by yourself for a while?"

She raised her eyebrows in surprise. "Jace Erridge, you know we want to be alone so we can gossip!"

He nodded. "That's what I'm afraid of."

Sarah and Caroline both gave him another push. "Go!" they said in unison.

He shot them a disgruntled glare and made his way across the crowded room in search of his brother-in-law. Caroline wasted no time taking Arren's and Sarah's hands and pulling them farther away from the crush. "Now, first thing we agree to do is drop all the titles. You both outrank me, and I'll never keep up with all the 'Graces.' "

Arren smiled and nodded. "Agreed. Your husband is a

Marquess anyway and I can barely pronounce whatever that makes you."

Caroline laughed. "In truth, neither can I. We don't have words like that in America."

Sarah grinned and stopped a passing footman to procure a glass of champagne for each of them. "What have you learned that's worth repeating, Caroline?" she asked when they were relatively alone again.

Caroline grinned at her. "Sarah, it's shameless of you to encourage me like that. You know how Jace dislikes it."

"And when has that ever stopped you before?"

A mischievous sparkle made its way into Caroline's eyes and she looked at Sarah and Arren while she took a sip of her champagne. "Well," she said meaningfully, "do you see that young gentleman over there in that horrid yellow jacket?"

Arren and Sarah both turned to look. Sarah smirked. "He looks like a canary."

Caroline nodded. "That's the one. He's Lord Roylston. I asked Jace why he was invited. You know Aimsmond can't stand him."

Sarah nodded. "He's never been here before."

"Do you know who he married three months ago?"

Sarah shook her head. "No. I hadn't heard."

Caroline looked about the room for a long minute, finally spotting the woman she sought. "Over there. By the arbor. In the blue gown."

Sarah and Arren turned to look in the other direction. "The young woman with the brown hair?" Sarah asked.

Caroline shook her head. "The *other* woman in the blue gown."

Sarah swung her head around and looked at Caroline in

shock. "My God! Aimsmond's sister. She's three times his age!"

Caroline nodded. "Not to mention ugly as sin."

Arren's eyes widened. "Why did he marry her?"

Sarah giggled. "Probably because Aimsmond paid him to. Is that right, Caroline?"

Caroline nodded again. "Reportedly thirty thousand pounds."

"Thirty thousand pounds!" Arren was shocked.

"Would you marry her for thirty thousand pounds?" Caroline asked pointedly.

Arren turned her head to look at the woman again. "No. I can't say that I would."

The three of them started to giggle, and before long, Caroline was telling them stories about nearly everyone in the room. Arren was amazed at her knowledge of the guests. She seemed to know everyone in the enormous ballroom. They were laughing uproariously at one of her stories when Arren finally gave in to her curiosity.

"Caroline, how on earth do you remember all these people?"

Sarah laughed. "Oh, Caroline's amazing. She knows the name and history of every person she's ever met."

Caroline shot her an exasperated look. "Now, Sarah, you know that's not true."

Sarah nodded. "Yes it is. I don't know why you deny it."

"I think that's amazing," Arren said. "How do you do it."

Caroline shrugged. "I don't know. I learned to do it because my father was a politician, I think. My sisters and I used to sit at his political functions and see who could name the most people. After we got older, we started keeping track of things we'd heard about them, too. It helped pass the time."

"So how many people in this room do you know?" Arren asked.

Caroline looked around, taking stock of the guests. "Nearly all of them, really. I've met them at one time or another."

Sarah grinned. "Show her, Caroline."

Caroline looked at her in surprise. "I don't know why you think this is so interesting."

Arren leaned forward and touched her arm. "I want to see you do this."

"All right." Caroline looked about the room for a good place to start. "Over there. By the door."

Sarah and Arren both turned to look at the large cluster of people near the entrance of the ballroom.

Caroline took a long sip of her champagne. "I'll start on the far right. The gentleman in the peacock blue jacket is the Count de Cremeaux. I met him last month at the French consulate when Jace and I went there for dinner. His estate is in the Burgundy region of France, and he's dreadfully dull. He slurps his soup, too."

Caroline ignored Sarah's and Arren's amused looks and continued. "Next to him is Madame Bouchard. She's his mistress, though neither of them admits it, obviously. The next person is Lady Margaret Benton. I first met Lady Benton at a tea the Duchess of Hawthorne held for me when Jace and I were married. Her husband, Lord Benton is very active in the House of Lords.

"Next, there's Devon Anesly, he's the Earl of Dane's youngest son, and quite the dandy around London. The man next to him is Marcus Brandton, the Marquess of Brandtwood. He is without a doubt, one of the meanest men in London." She paused and turned to Arren. "Stay out of his way, Arren, he's nasty."

Arren nodded and turned her attention back to the cluster.

"Then there's Lady Jeannette Willinham, Lady Alice Tippington, and Lady Katherine Gresham. They all debuted this Season, and they're only here because Aimsmond is friends with their fathers.

"In the next row is Lord George Dibbit, one of the primary leaders in the House of Lords. He's flanked by his wife, Lady Dibbit, and his colleague and sometimes adversary, the Earl of Dancross."

Arren looked at Sarah, her eyes wide. "This is incredible."

Sarah nodded. "Just watch."

Caroline had rattled off another half-dozen names before she came to the tiny crowd of people just inside the door. "Oh, and that's the Countess de Farée and her husband. Sir William Harrington and his mistress, Lady Grant," Caroline paused and strained her eyes to get a better look at the gentleman in the doorway.

Arren turned to Sarah once more and smiled in amusement. She was about to say something when Caroline snapped her fingers. "I've got it! That's Lord Alistar McDonan!"

Thirty-one

All the color drained from Arren's face. She didn't even need to turn her head to know Caroline was right: Alistair McDonan was standing in the doorway. Sarah snapped her head around and stared at her, her hand flying to her mouth.

Caroline watched their mutual reaction and her eyes widened in alarm. "Did I say something wrong?"

Sarah shook her head, drawing a deep breath. "No." She looked at Caroline. "It's a long story. We have to find Duncan and Aiden right now."

"What's wrong? Arren, are you all right?"

Arren was rooted to the spot. She was staring at Alistair McDonan, her eyes wide with horror. Sarah looked around frantically, nearly fainting with relief when she saw her brother Tryon standing in a small cluster of people just to their left. She grabbed Arren's hand and began dragging her in his direction.

Caroline followed in their wake, anxiously watching Arren. "Sarah," she said, "I think you'd better get Arren something to drink. She looks like she might faint."

Sarah looked over her shoulder at Caroline and continued to drag Arren in Tryon's direction. "She might." Sarah pushed her way through the throng of people, oblivious to the curious looks she was receiving, and thrust Arren up against Tryon's side.

He looked at her in surprise. "Hello, brat. What's got you so worked up?"

Sarah frowned at him. "I don't have time to explain right now. This is Duncan's wife. Don't let her out of your sight until I get back."

Tryon raised his eyebrows in surprise. "What's going on, Sarah? What do you mean 'this is Duncan's wife'?"

She sighed in exasperation. "Just do it, Tryon! Stop asking questions. Caroline and I are going to find Aiden and Duncan." She grabbed hold of Caroline's hand and started wending her way through the heavy crowd before he had a chance to answer.

Tryon watched them for a few moments, scanning the ballroom for signs of Aiden. When Sarah and Caroline disappeared into the crowd, he turned to look at the woman Sarah had unceremoniously thrust in his direction. His eyes widened and he snapped his head around again, this time in search of a red-haired woman in an emerald green gown. Arren had vanished.

Sarah tugged on Caroline's hand, fighting her way through the crowd.

"Sarah?" Caroline waited for her to look back. "What's going on?"

Sarah shook her head. "I can't explain it right now, Caroline." She turned to search the ballroom again. "Do you see them anywhere?"

Caroline stood on her tiptoes and looked about the room. She caught a glimpse of Duncan's red-gold hair in the far corner on their left. She pulled Sarah by the hand. "I see Duncan over there," she said pointing.

Sarah jerked Caroline's hand in that direction and started

off again. "I hope Aiden's with him!" Sarah brushed pas
half a dozen guests who would have stopped her, not spar
ing so much as a second glance in their direction. The crow
was so heavy, she and Caroline had to separate and pic
their way through the clusters of people. When they finall
emerged at the far side of the ballroom, Sarah sighed wit
relief. Duncan was leaning against the wall, with a glass o
champagne dangling between his fingers. Aiden stood be
hind him, embroiled in conversation with Jace. She pushe
forward intent on telling him she'd left Arren in Tryon'
care, and that Alistar McDonan had arrived.

Duncan's fingers were clamped so tightly around hi
glass, he'd nearly snapped off the fragile stem. He'd know
the instant Alistar McDonan had arrived. He and Aiden ha
spoken to Aimsmond yesterday and assured themselves tha
Alistar was indeed on the guest list. He had thought it bes
not to inform Arren, knowing she'd work herself into
frenzy over it. He had taken every precaution to ensure h
could keep the situation under control, but the instant Al
istar had stepped into the doorway, Duncan's eyes had begu
scanning the room for Arren. He was beginning to panic

Behind him, he could hear Aiden sketching in the essentia
details of the story for Jace, but the longer he searched for
glimpse of her auburn hair, the more agitated he became
Duncan felt the sweat trickling down his spine, and his hand
itched to find their way around Alistar McDonan's throat. H
was more concerned, though, about Arren's reaction.

He narrowed his eyes and scanned the room again, me
thodically checking each cluster of people for a glimpse o
her. His knees nearly buckled in relief when he saw Sara
coming toward him. He knew they were together. He mo

mentarily lost sight of her in the heavy crowd, and leaned forward, tilting his head for a better look. Sarah stepped from the crowd, and he waited expectantly, realizing only then, that Arren wasn't at her side. He did snap the stem off his glass then.

Aiden and Jace heard the glass shatter on the hard marble floor and looked up abruptly. Caroline stepped forward and took Jace's hand, looking at him in confusion. Sarah headed straight for Duncan. "She's with Tryon," she explained at the same instant he asked, "Where is she?"

Duncan drew a deep calming breath, waiting several seconds to release it. "Damn, Sarah, you scared me to death!"

She shook her head. "You know I wouldn't have left her alone."

Aiden stepped forward and wrapped his arm around her shoulders, studying Duncan intently. "All right, he's here. What do you want to do?"

Sarah raised wide eyes to his and stared at him in surprise. "You knew?"

Aiden nodded. "It's all right, Sarah. Duncan knew he'd have to confront Alistar before his meeting with the Regent tomorrow. We checked with Aimsmond to ensure the bastard would be here."

Sarah looked around, trying to identify Arren through the crowd. "Well I think you'd better find Arren before you do anything at all. She was terribly shaken when he arrived."

Duncan sighed and turned to scan the room again. "He was supposed to arrive later. I had intended to be with her when he showed up."

Sarah glared at him. "Well you weren't, and she's scared to death."

Jace reached out and tapped Duncan on the shoulder,

pointing to their left. "There's Tryon. He's making his way here."

Duncan's head swiveled around. He saw Tryon's dark head bobbing in and out of the throng. He narrowed his eyes, searching for Arren at his side. Tryon broke through the crowd and skidded to a stop before them.

"She's gone!"

Duncan stepped forward. "What the hell do you mean she's gone?"

Tryon looked at Sarah apologetically. "I watched Sarah and Caroline for the barest of seconds, hoping I'd see you so I could steer them in the right direction. When I turned around, she'd vanished. I can't find her anywhere."

"Dammit!" Duncan bit out the curse and raised his hand to rub the taut muscles at the back of his neck.

Aiden shoved Sarah in Tryon's direction. "All right. Sarah, stay here with Caroline." She looked like she might protest, but he cut her off. "I mean it. Don't move from this spot unless the damn house catches on fire." He looked at Jace and Tryon. "Keep an eye on them. If we're not back in fifteen minutes, start looking for us."

Jace nodded, taking Sarah's hand and pulling her to his side. "Try to keep him from doing anything rash."

Aiden looked at Duncan and narrowed his eyes. He was already stalking in the direction of the arched doorway. He nodded and hurried after him.

Arren looked at the note in her hand and made her way quickly up the large staircase. Almost the instant Sarah had left her side, someone had slipped the tiny piece of paper into her hand. When she'd read it, her eyes had glittered

with anger. Written in Alistar McDonan's own hand, the
note read:

*I have it within my power to destroy Strathcraig's
hope of building an alliance. I will have Grayscar tonight, or I will ruin him tomorrow. Meet me on the
third floor, second door on the left.*

Until that moment, she'd been afraid of him. Alistar had
always terrified her because of what he could do to her,
but now, he threatened Duncan. That was another matter
entirely. Arren had read the note and cast a wary glance at
Tryon Erridge. He was still watching Sarah and Caroline
make their way across the ballroom, and she narrowed her
eyes, turning her attention to the doorway. Alistar had disappeared from sight, and she felt her lip curl in distaste. It
was high time to put an end to his power over her.

She had clenched the note in her hand and slipped silently from Tryon's side, making her way as quickly as possible to the door. When she reached it, she stepped around
the corner, casting a furtive glance over her shoulder. Tryon
seemed to have noticed her absence, and was scanning the
room. She took advantage of his averted gaze and made
her way quickly to the long staircase.

She grew angrier with each step. The closer she drew to
her rendezvous with Alistar, the more she hated him, not
only for what he'd done to her, but for what she knew he
was capable of doing, as well. The man had all but sold
his soul to the devil for her damn land. She stalked up the
stairs, letting her anger grow inside her. She rounded the
corner and headed down the hall, searching for the staircase
to the third level.

She found it, and began climbing the narrow steps. She

kept her fist clenched around Alistar's note. The third floor of the enormous town house was deserted. When she stepped into the hallway, only the soft sound of her slippered feet on the marble floor disturbed the silence. She narrowed her eyes and stalked down the hall, intent on finding Alistar McDonan and telling him exactly what she thought of his evil mind.

Arren threw open the second door on the left, and stopped short when she confronted an empty room. She nearly jumped through her skin when the door slammed shut behind her. She whirled around in time to see Alistar turn the key in the lock and slip it into his pocket. She glared at him. "All right, Alistar, I'm here. Now what do you want?"

He leaned back against the door and watched her speculatively. "You know what I want, little Grayland."

"Don't call me that."

He raised his eyebrows at her proprietary tone. "And what would you have me call you? Her Grace, the wayward Duchess of Strathcraig?"

She glared at him and squared her shoulders, refusing not to back down under his evil stare. Alistar McDonan was a large man, though he was somewhat soft around the middle. An unbidden memory of his thick fingers on her flesh made a shiver race down her spine. She shoved it aside, determined not to cower in front of him. "You're despicable!"

He laughed that well-oiled laugh she'd always hated. He crossed his wide arms, as he leaned back against the door. "I'll have to compliment Strathcraig when I see him. He's put some of the fire back in those green eyes of yours. Tell me, Arren, does he excite you as much as Lawrence?"

She gasped, and drew back a little, wondering what he

knew. He laughed again. "Oh, yes, I know about Lawrence. In truth, I never knew why your brother was so committed to him. I used Lawrence several times myself, and found him wanting in that capacity."

Arren's eyes widened and she stared at him. "That's disgusting!"

Alistar shrugged and took a step forward. "I wanted the land and the money. To have it, I had to woo Lawrence."

"You obviously were no better at that than you were at wooing me." She managed a smug smile when she delivered the taunt.

Something dark flickered in his eyes and he took a step forward. "You've led me a merry chase, little Grayland. I never should have sent Euan after you. I should have gone myself."

"You would have failed as well."

"Ah yes! You were traveling under the protection of His Grace the Duke of Strathcraig." He took another step forward.

Arren refused to retreat. She forced herself to stand her ground. "This conversation is pointless. You want Grayscar. I'm not going to give it to you."

His lips curled in a smile filled with malice. "Then I suppose I shall have to convince you."

Before she had time to react, one of Alistar's thick arms shot out and curled around her waist, dragging her up against him. Arren pushed against his chest, trying to break free of him. "Let me go, Alistar! My husband will have your head for this!"

He laughed and pulled her tighter. "By the time I'm through with you, your husband will want no part of you."

Arren renewed her struggles and watched him warily. "What do you mean?"

He rubbed his pelvis meaningfully against her, and her

eyes widened in horror. He was becoming inflamed by her efforts to free herself and she froze, the bile catching in the back of her throat. Alistar leaned forward, letting his hot, whiskey-laden breath fan over her face. "I mean, little Grayland, that I'm going to ram my yard into you so many times that Duncan Strathcraig won't be able to stand the sight of you."

She shoved against his chest, her breath coming in painful gasps. "You can go to the devil, Alistar!"

He reached up and grabbed her bodice, tearing the fragile silk with his heavy hands. Arren twisted against him, but he curled his fingers painfully into one of her breasts. "I decided to go to the devil a long time ago." His thumb moved painfully against one of her nipples, and Arren turned her head away, fighting a wave of nausea. "Don't look so horrified, Arren. I've been told I'm quite good at this."

She pushed with all her strength against his chest, but he lowered his head and pressed his wet, thick lips against the top of her breasts, sinking his teeth into the sensitive skin. Arren swallowed hard and pushed her fingers into his hair, yanking on it until two clumps pulled free in her fingers.

He raised his head, and an evil smile settled on his lips. "Go ahead and fight me, little Grayland, it inflames me."

Arren opened her mouth to scream, but he clamped his hand over her lips, bearing down until she tasted the coppery flavor of blood on her tongue. "Don't scream. I'll snap your neck in two if you do. Do you understand?"

Her eyes widened and she nodded slightly. He slowly drew his hand back, and she opened her mouth again. He slapped his hand back against her lips and shoved her backwards, tumbling down on top of her on the bed. Alistar produced a long, sinister-looking knife out of nowhere and held it to her throat. "Scream now, little Grayland, and I'll slit your throat."

"Having my throat slit would be preferable to letting you touch me."

"Careful, Arren. When Strathcraig casts you aside, you'll need my protection. I don't think you want to anger me."

She tried to struggle with him, but she could feel his body straining against her, and she lay still lest she unwittingly excite him more. She was trapped beneath the weight of his body, and when he lowered his head to her breasts again, she closed her eyes and bit down on her lip to keep from crying out. His knife was pressed at the most sensitive place of her throat, and she feared her slightest movement would cause it to pierce her skin.

He ground his pelvis against her, and reached his free hand up to tear the fabric of her dress, exposing more of her to his lustful gaze. He stared at the rounded swell of her breasts, while his hot breath fell across her sensitive skin. Slowly, he lowered the knife, pricking the smooth skin along the top of her breast. She made a small sound in the back of her throat. Her eyes flew open to stare at him. His eyes had darkened ominously at the sight of the crimson drop of blood on her delicate skin. Arren lay perfectly still, lest he remember the knife was no longer pressed into her throat.

He mumbled something crude and slid his wet lips across the top of her breast, licking at the tiny drops of blood. She felt another wave of nausea make its way into her throat. She couldn't stifle the small cry of fear that slid unbidden between her lips. He raised his head, and his eyes glittered into hers. "I like it when you make those frightened noises, little Grayland. You sound like an animal caught in a hunter's snare."

As she glared at him, her fingers crept closer to the knife in his hand. "Let me go, Alistar! You have no right to do this to me."

He sneered at her. "Always arrogant, aren't you? You tried to make a fool out of me, Arren. No other woman would have turned down my generous proposal."

"Is that what this is? Revenge?"

He rubbed against her again. "It's a good deal more than revenge. It's time someone broke you. And I'm going to be the man that has that privilege."

She started to say something, but he ground his lips onto hers, silencing her. He drove his tongue into her mouth, stifling her cry of surprise. His hands tore at her gown, and she searched frantically for his discarded knife. When she sank her teeth into his tongue, he cursed something dark and venomous and tore his mouth away. "Damn you, Grayland! I've had enough of this. You will submit to me, or I'll kill you in the process."

His fingers had curled around the knife again. She eyed him warily, trying to prevent the fear from showing in her eyes. Alistar held the knife to her throat and reached down with his free hand to unbutton his trousers. He struggled with the task for a few minutes before swearing darkly and rolling to his feet. Arren drew a deep breath of relief when his weight was lifted off her. He looked at her ominously, holding the knife carefully in his hand. "Don't move, Arren. I swear I'll kill you if you do."

She watched him closely, frantically hoping his attention would be diverted long enough for her to seize the knife. She knew she couldn't flee him. The key to the door was still in his trousers pocket. Instead, she lay frozen upon the yellow satin coverlet, staring at him. He slowly raised the knife to his lips, clenching it between his teeth. With both hands free, he pulled at the buttons of his trousers.

Arren watched in horror as he freed his straining desire of its restraints. At the sheer size of him, she felt a river of fear course down her spine. He would surely rend her in two. She heard his cruel laugh and looked at him again. He reached down and fondled himself, stepping back toward the bed. "Strathcraig can't hope to compete with this, I'll wager. I've been told by half the whores in London and Edinburgh that there isn't a man alive with a bigger cock than mine. Once I use you to satisfy myself, Strathcraig will never touch you again."

Arren had to swallow against the bile in her throat when she felt him sink back down on top of her. She pushed ineffectually at his shoulders, shrinking in horror when his hot lips slid along the flesh of her exposed breasts. Only a miracle would save her now.

Duncan was becoming frantic. He and Aiden had searched every room on the second floor of Aimsmond's house, including a few where lovers had met for secret trysts. Then he strode up the third level staircase, taking the stairs three at a time. "You take the right side, Brick. I'll take the left." He crashed open the first door an instant before he heard voices in the next room down the hall. He growled something deep in his throat and strode to the next door. His fingers curled around the handle. Aiden had heard the voices, too, and turned to see Duncan push against the door.

It was locked, and Duncan stepped back, kicking it in without a second thought. It took him the barest of seconds to take in the sight before him. He saw Arren pushing fran-

tically at Alistar McDonan's shoulders. And he saw the glint
of the knife.

Alistar froze when he heard Duncan's angry roar from
the doorway. He turned his head in time to see Duncan's
hands closing on his shoulders and hauling him off the bed.
Arren's hand flew to her mouth in terror when she saw
Duncan hurl Alistar against the wall, and drive his fist into
his thick middle. She watched in horror as Duncan drove
his fists into Alistar again, and again, until blood began to
spew forth from his nose and his mouth. Duncan held him
pinned against the wall, his strong hand clamped around
Alistar's throat, and she barely noticed when Aiden strode
across the room and wrapped her in the coverlet. He tucked
it around her and turned around, reaching for Duncan.
"Enough, Dunc. Let him go."

"Damn if I will!" Duncan drove his fist into Alistar's groin,
wishing like hell it had been the knife instead. His fingers
tightened around his throat, and he hit him again, watching
in satisfaction when his eyes bulged in their sockets.

Aiden reached out and grabbed Duncan's shoulders to
pull him away from Alistar. Duncan landed another punch
between his ribs. "Let go of me, Brick. It's my right to kill
him!"

Aiden finally succeeded in pulling him away, and Alistar's
bloody, broken body sank to the floor in a crumpled heap
just as Jace and Tryon rushed in the room, Caroline and Sarah
in tow. Sarah gasped at the sight and rushed to the bed, pulling
Arren against her. "Oh dear God! Are you all right?"

Caroline raced across the room to join them. She brushed
Arren's hair from her flushed face. Aiden held Duncan's
arms firmly at his side, struggling to prevent him from re-
newing his attack on Alistar. Jace walked forward and bent

to check Alistar's pulse. He looked at Aiden and nodded. "He's still alive."

Duncan growled something vicious and renewed his struggles. Aiden turned him and gave him a hard shove in Arren's direction. "Dammit, Duncan, your wife needs you, more than you need to kill that bastard."

Duncan's eyes settled on Arren's pale face and he felt the rage drain out of his body. He strode across the room, nearly pushing Sarah and Caroline out of his way in his haste to reach her side. He went down on both knees in front of her and clasped her face in his large, bloodied hands. "Oh God, sweetheart, I'm so sorry he hurt you!"

She raised her eyes and met his gaze, reaching out gently to wipe a small splatter of Alistar's blood from his cheek. She stared at the crimson stain on her finger, unable to answer him. He groaned something unintelligible and crushed her against his chest. Arren leaned into him, and her whole body began to tremble almost uncontrollably.

Vaguely, she heard Aiden tell Duncan to take her home. Tryon, Caroline and Sarah would follow in Jace's carriage, and he and Jace would take care of Alistar. She didn't protest when Duncan tucked the yellow coverlet more closely around her and lifted her against his chest. Nor did she think to protest when he pushed her head down on his shoulder.

He carried her down the long darkened corridor, and Tryon rushed ahead to open the door to the secondary staircase. The stairs would exit at the back of the house, giving them the privacy they needed. Arren leaned her head against Duncan's shoulder, and tried to stop her teeth from rattling. She wanted to apologize for having disobeyed him by leaving the ballroom. She wanted to thank him for having saved her from Alistar. She wanted him to know how safe she felt with his corded arms holding her protectively against him. She desperately wanted to tell him that she'd decided she was horribly in love with him, but none of the words would form on her lips.

Duncan carried Arren down the long staircase, but his body was still seething with rage. He had never wanted anything as badly as he'd wanted to kill Alistar McDonan. The stricken look on Arren's face when he'd burst into that room had ripped his gut open. She had finally begun to lose the shadow of fear that lurked in the green depths of her eyes, and now, because of his own foolish pride, he'd allowed Alistar McDonan to put it back.

He had believed he could control the situation. He had believed he could trap Alistar into admitting what he'd done to Arren, so that Duncan could threaten him until he agreed to return home. But he'd failed. He had put Arren at risk, and but for a few seconds, he'd nearly allowed that bastard to . . . the thought trailed off when he felt Arren tremble almost violently against him, and he held her tighter, stepping out into the cool night air. He turned to Tryon, and waited for him to shut the door behind them. "Will you go and have the carriages sent around?"

Tryon nodded and headed for the front of the house. "They'll stop just outside the gate."

Duncan walked down the cobbled path, Sarah and Caroline at his side. Sarah looked up at him anxiously when Caroline stepped forward to swing open the gate. "Is she going to be all right?"

Duncan turned anguished eyes to hers. "God, Sarah, I hope so. This is all my fault."

Arren trembled against him, moving her lips slightly. No, it wasn't his fault at all. Surely he understood that. Try as she might, though, she couldn't make her eyes open or her voice cooperate. She heard the rumbling of the carriage in the distance, and she sagged against him. The coach pulled up beside them, and Duncan stepped inside, still holding Arren against his chest as he lowered himself on the padded seat.

The door snapped shut behind them and the carriage began to move. He held her close to him, whispering inaudible words of comfort in her ear. She wasn't sure, but she thought perhaps he started to cry. Then she realized the trembling in her shoulders was the force of her own sobs, and she wrapped her arms around his neck. Tears ran freely down her face. He wiped at the moisture on his face and held her tighter, as he rocked her against him with the gentle motion of the carriage.

Thirty-two

The carriage rolled to a stop in front of Albrick House and Duncan carried Arren up the stairs and through the foyer, without bothering to wait for Sarah, Caroline and Tryon. He walked up the wide staircase, down the hall to their room, and kicked open the door. He noticed with some relief that Arren's maid was not in the room. He paused to bellow down the hall for hot water before he kicked the door shut behind them, and crossed the thick Aubusson carpet to lay Arren gently on the bed.

She seemed unwilling to let go of his neck, so he held her, cradling her against his chest. She sobbed on his shoulder, her hot tears soaking his shirt. He rocked her tenderly as he pulled at the delicate pins that held her hair. One by one, her curls tumbled free. He tossed aside the rope of green emeralds and the handful of pins, then combed his hand soothingly through her hair.

He barked a command when a knock sounded on the door, and three footmen entered with buckets of steaming water. They quickly filled the tub, and left a pile of fresh towels on the long sofa.

He waited until the door shut behind them before he whispered, "It's all right, darling. Just let it out."

She cried harder, and clung to him. He clasped her to him, stretched out on the bed next to her, and ran his hand along her spine. Her anguished sobs tugged at his heart, and he remembered unbidden the day she told him she only cried one tear at a time. He felt his mind flood with self-recriminations and was suddenly filled with a need to absorb her into his soul.

Arren spent herself against his chest. Her tears flowed over him, soaking his elegant evening clothes. Her shoulders shook with long, hot sobs of relief and she clutched at his jacket, needing his strength. Finally, her tears stopped, and her breath came in ragged hiccups as she struggled for control.

Duncan sensed the change in her and shifted slightly so he could see her tear-streaked face. He reached up and gently wiped her cheeks with his hand, before staring down into her emerald green eyes.

Arren saw the anguish in his expression and raised her hand to cover his lips, shaking her head. "It's not your fault," she whispered.

A ragged groan tore from his chest. He cupped her face with his hands, and locked his gaze with hers. "I should have told you he would be there. I shouldn't have let you wander off by yourself."

Arren stroked the smooth skin of his cheek, rubbing at the tension around his eyes. "Duncan, stop. Please stop. It isn't your fault."

He pushed her head back against his chest and rocked her gently. "I'm so sorry. God, Arren, I'm so sorry."

She heard the desperation in his voice and clung to his jacket. Finally, he rolled to his side. Still holding her against his chest, he swung his legs to the floor. She looked up at him, and he smoothed her hair off her flushed face, so he could gently kiss her forehead. "I'm going to take care of you, sweetheart. Just relax."

She nodded, unwilling to argue with him. She sagge
against his chest, suddenly drained. He held her across hi
lap, gently removing the yellow satin coverlet still wrappe
around her body. He stifled something dark and ugly whe
he saw the tiny cut on her bare breast. He peeled back th
coverlet, holding her steady with one hand, while he slippe
her tattered gown down to her waist with the other.

Lifting her in his arms, he allowed the torn garment to fa
to the floor and he carried her to one of the long sofas. H
set her down and removed her torn undergarments befor
deftly untying her garters and sliding her silk stockings dow
the length of her legs. He slipped off her fragile green slip
pers, and dropped them to the carpet, followed by her stock
ings and garters. Carefully, he lifted her in his arms, carrie
her to the bathing closet, and lowered her into the tub.

He paused only long enough to shrug out of his jacke
and roll up his sleeves before he sank down on his knee
next to her. She looked at him, and reached out her finger
to touch his sleeve. "I'm making you wet. I'll ruin you
new clothes," she protested.

He shook his head and lifted the cake of soap. She wa
barely making any sense. He knew she was still sufferin
from shock. "It doesn't matter, sweetheart. Just close you
eyes and let me take care of you."

Arren shut her eyes and sank down into the hot wate
letting the warm strokes of his hands soothe away the hor
rible memory of Alistar's flesh pressed against hers. Sh
shuddered once, and a fresh wave of nausea swept over he
Suddenly, she could contain it no more. She choked on th
bile, her stricken eyes flying to his. He reached for one o
the empty buckets and held it for her, as he supported he
with his other arm.

She emptied the contents of her stomach in the bucke

and sagged back against his arm. He gently wiped her face with the wet washcloth and walked across the room to pour her a glass of water. He sank down beside her again, handed her the glass, and let her rinse the acid taste from her mouth. Arren looked at him gratefully, as she handed him the empty glass. He rinsed her fevered face, and gently wiped her tear-swollen eyes.

He bit off a curse when he saw the way her lips were starting to swell from Alistar's brutal assault. He ran the washcloth soothingly over her face, and waited for her to relax against him again. "Lean back against me, Arren. I just want to take care of you."

She looked at him. Her lips moved slightly before she gave up and closed her eyes. She was asleep before her head reached his chest.

Arren awoke in the middle of a nightmare. Alistar was on top of her, his hard, swollen flesh was pressing into her. She could feel the knife against her throat and she thrashed at him, struggling to break free of his grasp.

Arren sat up in bed, clutching the blankets to her breasts, and screamed. Duncan was right there with her. He reached out and clasped his strong, warm hands on her shoulders, pulling her to his chest. "Arren, it's all right. You're safe. I'm not going to let anything happen to you."

She struggled against him only briefly until she fully awoke and realized it was Duncan who held her now. He still wore his trousers and shirt. He had been seated in a large chair next to the bed, watching her. She wrapped her arms around his waist and clung to him. "Please don't leave me."

He shook his head. "I won't. Go back to sleep."

She trembled against him, as he ran his hand along her spine in slow, soothing strokes.

She tightened her grasp on him. "Hold me."

He sighed, shifted his weight, and stretched out beside her. Gently, he pulled her into his arms, and began rocking her against his chest until she fell asleep again.

He was alone. Duncan rolled to his back and waited a minute to orient himself before he realized he was in bed alone. He opened his eyes and found Arren by the window. She was wearing the white flannel nightgown he'd dressed her in after her bath, and she stood at the window, silhouetted by the moonlight

"Arren?" He waited for her to turn her head. "Are you all right?"

She nodded and turned back to the window. "I was just looking at the stars. Do you know they're the same stars that shine over Grayscar every night?" She looked at him again. "Isn't that strange?"

He narrowed his eyes and sat up, unsure what she was thinking. He swung his feet to the floor and padded across the room to where she stood. Wrapping his arms around her from behind, he pulled her back against him. They stared out the window at the stars.

She tilted her head back and smiled. "I never thought of that before. Grayscar was the only home I knew. I never thought that the same stars were everywhere."

Duncan wasn't sure what she wanted him to say, so he rocked her against him and waited for her to continue.

"If I look out the windows at Strathcraig, will I see the stars?"

He tensed slightly, going completely still. "Yes."

"I would like very much to do that with you, Gypsy."

Duncan sighed and turned her in his arms. "Arren, what are you saying?"

She looked up at him, while her fingers lingered against his chest. "I'm saying that no matter what happens tomorrow," she paused and looked at the clock on the mantel, "today," she corrected. "I want to go to Strathcraig with you."

Duncan swallowed hard and closed his eyes for a long moment. When he opened them, Arren was staring at his chest, tracing a lazy pattern on his shirt front. He reached down and tugged gently on her hair, waiting for her to meet his gaze. "Arren, there's nothing in the world I want more than to share Strathcraig with you."

She smiled. "There, you see. You were right, and I was wrong. Everything has come right after all." Her voice didn't quite ring true, and he shook his head.

"Arren, I have no idea what's going to happen when I meet with the Regent this afternoon." He paused, sighing heavily. "But I do know that Alistar McDonan is probably going to demand reparations for the fact that I beat him to a bloody pulp tonight."

She trembled against him slightly, dropping her head to his chest. "It doesn't matter. Give him whatever he wants. I don't want the land anymore."

"Arren, I'm not going to make you give up Grayscar, not after tonight."

She tilted her head back and looked at him. "You don't understand. I don't want it. I've never wanted it. If Alistar will leave us alone if he has it, then give it to him."

"It's not the land he wants, Arren. It's the power."

She trembled again. "I don't care."

"You *do* care. You wouldn't have gone through what you have if you didn't care."

"Duncan, I don't want to be afraid anymore."

He reached up and tunneled his fingers in her hair. "You don't have to be. I'll protect you."

Her eyes widened. "But what if the Regent places the lands under protectorate?"

"Then I'll leave Strathcraig and live at Grayscar with you."

She shook her head in disbelief. "You can't do that. Your people need you."

"My cousin Ian can tend Strathcraig. You need me more than they do."

"Duncan, I can't let you do that. I know how deeply you care about your family. I know what they mean to you. You'd hate me if I did that to you."

He smiled at her slightly. "I'd never hate you, Duchess. When I inherited that land and that title, I made those people a promise. I promised I'd protect them. But part of protecting them means putting their best interests ahead of my own."

Arren drew her brows together in confusion. "I don't understand."

"I can't be their laird, and care about their problems, and see to their needs if I'm consumed with my worry for you."

"But, Duncan, you can't just leave them without a leader."

"If I have to, I'll cede the title to my cousin Ian."

Arren's eyes widened in dismay. "No! Duncan, you can't. Don't you understand? I don't want to live at Grayscar."

"But you don't want Alistar to control it either. When I married you, Arren, your people became my people. The

Graylands need the protection my name will offer them more than the McCraigs."

Arren shook her head. "You aren't being reasonable."

He smiled at her. "Arren, are you ever going to stop arguing with me?" He didn't wait for her to answer, but ran his finger tenderly across her swollen lips instead. "Darling, nothing is more important to me than you are. I love you. And because of my own pride and arrogance, I let you get hurt. I betrayed you."

Arren shook her head. "No! Duncan, it wasn't your fault. You told me not to leave the ballroom. I should have trusted you."

"I should have told you he would be there," he continued, ignoring her protest. "I shouldn't have left you alone."

She raised her hand and placed it over his mouth. "Gypsy, listen to me! I only left the ballroom because of the note."

His brow furrowed. "What note?" he mumbled against her hand.

She dropped her hand and laid it against his chest. "Alistar sent me a note when he arrived tonight . . . last night. I don't remember it, exactly. He said he'd ruin you if I didn't give him the land."

Duncan groaned. "He would have ruined me if he'd done what he intended."

Her eyes darkened slightly and she turned her head away. "Duncan, if Alistar had . . . raped me, would you still . . ."

He cut her off. "The question doesn't bear asking. I love you. If he'd raped you, I'd still love you."

"But he said . . ."

"He lied, Arren. He's an evil man and he lied. He couldn't have made me stop loving you."

She sighed and leaned against him. "Duncan?"

"Yes?"

"I love you, too, you know?"

He closed his eyes, drew a deep breath and held it, unwilling to shatter the fragile moment. When he finally released it, he tipped her back and looked down at her, his fingers tenderly tracing the delicate arches of her eyebrows. "Have you any idea how I've longed to hear you say that?"

When she looked up at him, her green eyes were filled with all the love she had felt for so long. "I've wanted to tell you for the longest time. I've been so afraid, though."

He cupped her face in his large hands, his thumbs caressing her jaw. "You don't have to be afraid anymore, Arren. I swear I'll not let anyone hurt you again."

She shook her head. "No, you don't understand. I knew tonight when I saw the stars. I was so afraid for so long. Afraid of everything. I was afraid of my father. Afraid of Lawrence. Afraid of Alistar. But I was never afraid of you." She paused and smiled at him. "There were times when you irritated me nearly to death, but I was never afraid of you."

"I'm glad."

She nodded. "Tonight, when I saw the stars, I realized Grayscar had always been my universe. I was trapped in an entire universe of fear and pain. But the same stars shine here, at Albrick House. They're visible at Albrick Park. They canopied us every night when we slept under them on the way to Inverness. And they shine at Strathcraig, too."

She leaned forward and linked her hands behind his neck. "Don't you see, Duncan? All my life, I believed Grayscar was my whole world, the only place I was meant to be. It isn't true, though. I'm meant to be wherever you are."

He smiled and pulled her against him. It didn't really matter, he decided, that she wasn't making much sense. He didn't even care that all that nonsense about stars and worlds and universes didn't solve anything, and that he'd still have to face the Regent with some plausible solution. Arren believed it solved everything, and she knew her place was with him. If she wanted to, she could tell him the damn moon was square and he'd agree with her.

Arren sighed and rubbed her face against his chest. "Gypsy?"

"Hmmm?"

"What are you going to do this afternoon?"

"Whatever I have to, Arren."

"I don't want you to give up Strathcraig."

"I know you don't."

"I want to live there with you."

"I want that, too."

"But what if the Regent doesn't allow it?"

He leaned back and looked down at her again. "Arren, as a Royal subject, I'm bound by my honor to do what the Regent wants, but that doesn't mean I'd do it at any cost."

"What do you mean?"

"I mean if he told me I couldn't be married to you, I'd tell him to go to hell!"

Her eyes widened. "You can't do that."

"I damn well can! And I will if I have to." He shook his head, staring into her deep green eyes. "I promise you, Arren, I'm not going to let anyone hurt you."

"But what about you?"

He smiled at her. "The Regent can't do anything to me I don't let him do. I'll make whatever decisions I have to to keep you safe."

Her eyes were wide with anxiety and she chewed on her lip slightly. "I don't want anything to happen to you. I love you."

He reached up and clasped her face in his hands. "Tell me again, and I'll be invincible."

Thirty-three

Arren rolled over in bed and stretched her sore muscles—a reminder of the events of the previous evening. She groaned, and sat up in bed. Sunlight flooded the room, and she looked around, realizing she was alone. She squinted her eyes at the clock on the mantel. It was already half past eleven o'clock in the morning.

Arren threw back the covers and scrambled from the bed, trying to remember if Duncan had told her what time his appointment was today. She was sure he'd said afternoon. She breathed a heavy sigh of relief and walked to the dressing table to study her reflection.

She looked awful. Her eyes were swollen from her long hours of crying during the night. Bruises covered her arms and chest, and the tiny cut on her breast was inflamed. She leaned forward and looked closely at her mouth, satisfied that most of the swelling had gone down. She sighed and picked up the basin of cold water on the nightstand, carrying it back to the dressing table.

She splashed her face with the cool, soothing water, holding a clean, damp washcloth to her eyes until the swelling went down some. She picked up the brush on the table and brushed out her tangled hair, plaiting it when she was done. She looked at herself in the mirror again, and decided she'd probably look passable when she was dressed.

The door opened suddenly, and Sarah flew into the room, still wearing her dressing gown. Abby pulled the door shut behind her, leaving Arren and Sarah alone.

"Oh, Arren, are you all right?"

Arren nodded. "I look much worse than I am."

Sarah sat down beside her and took her hand. "We were so worried. Duncan told Aiden this morning you were feeling better, though."

"I am. I'm more shaken than anything."

Sarah looked at her, her purple eyes darkening with concern. "Is there anything I can do for you to make you more comfortable."

Arren nodded. "As it happens, there is. I made a decision last night, Sarah, and I need your help."

"You know I'll help you."

"Duncan is determined to give up Strathcraig if the Regent asks him to, and live at Grayscar with me."

Sarah's eyes widened. "Strathcraig is very important to him."

"I know. I can't let him do it."

"Arren, Duncan loves you. If he's already decided, I don't think you can change his mind."

"I don't want to change his mind. I just want to force his hand a little."

"I don't understand."

"I love Duncan. I really do, Sarah. And I'd rather stop breathing than be apart from him."

Sarah smiled. "I know. I've never doubted you felt that way."

"But I also know how deeply he cares about his family and his home. I'll not let him give that up for me."

"Then what do you plan to do?"

"As the Duchess of Grayscar, I have the right to petition

the Regent directly. It's why I came to England to begin with."

Sarah nodded. "But if he places the land under protectorate, won't you be back where you started?"

"Not if I give up the title, I won't. I never wanted the land, Sarah. I just didn't want Alistar to have it. There are over a thousand people that live at Grayscar. Alistar would strip them of their homes and their lands if he thought he could make money."

"But if you cede the title, who will tend the protectorate."

"The Regent can do any number of things. He can appoint a governor, he can hand it over to the alliance of landholders Duncan's been assembling, or he can bestow the title on someone else. It hasn't been common practice since the Norman Conquest, but King William used to dole out Scottish lands and titles all the time."

Sarah smiled. "And the Scots hated him for it, too."

"Nevertheless, it's his right as Regent to do so. Surely there's some landholder somewhere who'd like to control the largest estate in Scotland."

"I suppose. But why do you need my help?"

Arren sighed heavily. "Duncan is convinced I don't want to give up Grayscar. I've spent so long being afraid of my past, I've let it become a wall between us. I need him to know I want nothing more than to be his wife."

Sarah grinned at her. "You mean you're willing to settle for being the second largest landholder in Scotland?"

Arren laughed. "I'd settle for a lot less than that as long as I was with Duncan. I don't think he believes that, though, and the only choice I have is to force his hand." A smile tugged at the corner of Sarah's mouth and Arren looked at her speculatively. "What's so funny?"

"That's almost exactly what Duncan said to me yesterday.

He said the only choice you gave him was to force your hand. I think the two of you will have a marvelously peaceful marriage."

"Well it won't be boring anyway. In truth, though, Sarah, this scares me to death."

Sarah tilted her head. "What kind of woman flees her home in the middle of the night, sets off for London with the intention of petitioning the Prince Regent, travels alone across country, links up with a stranger, and survives the journey you two shared, and then says she's afraid of her own feelings."

"It does seem ridiculous, I know, but I can't seem to help it. There are so many things we don't even know about each other. What if we're sitting in front of a fire one day, with no dogs to outrun, and no ships to swim to, and we look at each other and realize we've nothing to talk about."

Sarah laughed. "Then you'll doubtless pick a fight with him over it."

Arren laughed in return. "That's really awful, you know. We fight all the time."

"No you don't. You disagree. It isn't nearly the same thing."

"I can't seem to help it. I love goading his temper."

"Just as much as he loves goading yours." Sarah sobered suddenly and took Arren's hand again. "Arren, Duncan loves you more than his very life. You've already told me you feel the same way."

Arren nodded. "Then why am I so afraid?"

"Loving someone like that makes you vulnerable, it's true, but it also sets you free. I'm not saying there won't be times when you'll disagree. Lord knows, Aiden and I fight like cats and dogs when the mood strikes us, but he's my closest friend in all the world. I'm so sure of him, I'm free to feel things deeply. To love, and to hurt, and to cry, and to laugh without worrying about the consequences. If you take a leap of faith, I think you'll find you won't fall at all before Duncan's there to catch you."

Arren nodded. "You're right. I know you are."

"So what are you going to do?"

"I'm not going to let Duncan give up Strathcraig for some ridiculous notion he has about Grayscar, but I know that's what he intends to put before the Regent this afternoon."

"How do you plan to prevent him from doing that?"

Arren drew a deep breath. "I'm going to interrupt the meeting."

Sarah looked at her cautiously. "I don't know if that's such a good idea."

"It's a bad idea, but I haven't got a choice. The Regent will be hearing testimony from the other landholders involved. There's no reason why I shouldn't be present in that capacity."

"But Arren, Caroline and I will be the only two women in the room. We're only going to be there because we were witnesses to what happened last night."

"I know. But you'll be there as English nobility. I'll be there as the largest landholder in the Highlands."

Sarah looked dubious. "How do you plan to manage that, when Duncan's already said he wants you to stay home?"

"I'm not going to tell him."

"I don't know, Arren. I don't think he'll be very happy about that."

"He'll be furious, but in the end, it's for his own good. Besides, Alistar McDonan is my adversary. I should be the one to confront him."

Sarah sighed. "There's no way I can talk you out of this?"

Arren shook her head. "None."

"All right, but I think you've no idea what you're getting yourself into."

Arren laughed. "If I knew what I was getting myself into, I wouldn't do it at all. I still need your help, though, Sarah."

"What do you need me to do?"

"If I remember correctly, Aiden is a McCraig. Is that right?"

Sarah nodded. "He and Duncan are actually sixth cousins."

"Does he have a McCraig plaid?"

"Yes. He has two, maybe three kilts, and several plaids. Why?"

"I don't need the kilt, just the largest plaid he has."

"What are you going to do with it?"

"I'm going to wear it." Arren saw Sarah's shocked expression and laughed. "I'm the Duchess of Strathcraig. When I appeal to His Highness, I intend to be dressed as such."

Sarah smiled. "I think I'm beginning to understand. Duncan wore his formal kilt when he left with Aiden this morning. It's rather ceremonial, isn't it."

Arren nodded. "A Scot's plaid is his mark. It's his family honor and his name all rolled into one."

"All right, I'll bring you the plaid. Do you need anything else?"

"I'd like to wear full formal dress, but I'll have to make do with what you have."

"I can probably find nearly all of it for you. You need a short black velvet jacket, right?"

Arren nodded. "Obviously one of Aiden's wouldn't fit."

Sarah laughed. "Not unless you wanted it to hang below

your thighs. I have one from one of my riding habits though. It's a woman's cut, but if you attach the plaid to the shoulder, I don't think it will make a difference."

Arren nodded. "I think you're right. I'll need the plaid and the jacket, then, a sporran if Aiden has one, plaid hose, a *skean dhu,* a jeweled pin for the shoulder, an ivory shirt, a bonnet, and black slippers."

Sarah pursed her lips and thought for a minute. "Yes, I think we can manage almost all of that. We may have to improvise a bit. But you can probably use most of Aiden's things with the exception of the jacket."

"And I need one more thing."

"What?"

"I need your help to get in."

Sarah's eyes widened. "I hadn't even thought of that. How do you hope to manage it?"

"You'll be interviewed by the Regent, won't you?"

Sarah nodded. "Yes. I'm supposed to tell him what we saw last night."

"Can't you recommend that he question me directly?"

Sarah shrugged. "I don't see why not. He wanted to talk to you anyway, but Duncan refused."

"There, you see. If you tell him I'm waiting for his summons, I think he'll agree to see me."

Sarah exhaled a long breath. "Duncan's going to be spitting mad at both of us."

"He'll get over it. He's going to get his way, after all, I just have to make him take advantage of it."

Sarah laughed. "All right, I'll do it. Aiden and Duncan have already left to see to some last minute details. I think Duncan had some interviews with a few more landholders this morning."

Arren nodded. "He told me he wanted as many as possible to stand in favor of the alliance today."

"You can ride over to Carlton House with me, then. We're supposed to meet Jace and Caroline there."

"How much time do we have before we have to leave?"

Sarah turned and looked at the clock on the mantel. "Less than two hours! We'd better get moving. I'll take Abby with me to round up the things you need."

Arren smiled at her. "Sarah, how can I ever thank you for this?"

Sarah reached out and hugged her close. "Make him happy, Arren. He's a very special friend."

Arren hugged her back, and Sarah finally broke the embrace, laughing a little at her tears. She wiped them with her hand and looked at Arren. "We'll have to wait until this afternoon to cry. I have less than two hours to help you pull this off."

Arren smiled at her gratefully and walked her to the door. "I promise we'll both sit down this afternoon and weep ourselves sick."

Sarah sniffed; a smile tugging at the corner of her mouth. "All right, but I'm going to hold you to that. I won't let you off the hook."

Thirty-four

"Arren, that's amazing." Sarah sat on the side of Arren's bed, watching her pleat the huge plaid into intricate folds. "How do you do that?"

Arren smiled at her and tucked the plaid into place at her waist. "I've been practicing for ten years, but you should have seen me the first time I tried it."

"You make it look so effortless."

Arren laughed. "The first time I tried to hand-pleat a kilt, it took me four and a half hours just to get the front properly tucked. It was a disaster." She picked up the furry sporran and looped it in front, wishing it weren't quite so large.

"It looks wonderful, though. Much nicer than the stitched type."

Arren nodded, tugging on the black velvet jacket. "I like the way it overlaps. I think it looks more intricate." She lifted the long, loose end of the plaid and slung it over her shoulder, securing it with the emerald and diamond brooch Sarah had lent her. She stepped into the black velvet slippers, and tucked the *skean dhu* into the top of her stocking before turning to check her reflection.

Sarah smiled and walked up behind her, handing her the McCraig bonnet. Arren dropped it on her head at the appropriate angle, and her eyes met Sarah's in the mirror. "Well, what do you think?"

Sarah looked at her reflection carefully. The McCraig formal plaid was predominantly dark green with a vivid yellow stripe running through it. The ivory collar of Arren's blouse showed above the black velvet jacket, and the furry sporran hung at her waist. Her cap of auburn hair was topped by the jauntily placed plaid bonnet, and her plaid stockings held the tiny jeweled-handled *skean dhu* in place. She looked for all the world like a Scottish warlord in miniature. "I think you look wonderful."

Arren smiled. "I think so too. Slightly unconventional, perhaps, but then it isn't every day one bursts in uninvited on a private counsel with the Prince Regent."

Sarah laughed. "No it isn't. And both our husbands are going to be terribly disgruntled about it, too."

"I think we can handle them all right."

Sarah smiled again and took Arren's hand, giving it a tight squeeze. "It's going to come right, Arren. I know it is."

Arren nodded. "I know it is, too."

Sarah took a deep breath, turned away from the mirror, and headed for the door. "I'll meet you downstairs in five minutes. I just want to check on Cana before we leave. She was giving Nanny fits this morning."

"All right, I'll wait for you in the foyer."

Sarah left the room and Arren watched the door swing shut behind her. Alone once again, she turned for a final look in the mirror. She reached up and gave the bonnet a tug, angling it slightly more atop her head. Satisfied, she drew a deep breath, squared her shoulders, and smiled resolutely at her reflection. The sun glinted off her emerald engagement ring, and she raised her hand to examine it. She still remembered how Duncan had tugged Lawrence's ring from her finger the first night they'd made love, and demanded she not wear it again.

The memory made something occur to her suddenly. She crossed the room, and tugged open the wardrobe. She delved inside and found the leather pouch where Duncan had kept his money. Pulling aside the cord, she reached inside, to search the bottom of the small leather bag. Her fingers closed over the object she sought, and she withdrew her hand, with Lawrence's ring tightly clasped.

She replaced the small pouch and looked at the ring carefully. It had been more like a shackle until Duncan had removed it, and she marveled at the difference between the ring she wore now, and the one she held in her hand. Sarah was right. Loving Duncan had set her free. Lawrence had clipped her wings, caging her like a trapped bird. Duncan had helped her fly. She grasped the ring tightly in her fist and walked resolutely across the room.

When she reached the large windows, she pushed open the casement and stepped back, looking at the ring a final time before she hurled it out the window. It disappeared with a soft whistling sound and she smiled in satisfaction, pulling the window shut once more. "Duncan McCraig," she whispered, throwing home the latch, "you've no choice but to keep me now."

Sarah joined Arren in the foyer of Albrick House a scant three minutes later, and together, they climbed into Aiden's carriage to travel to Carlton House. Arren's hands lay tightly clasped in her lap, but she didn't speak until they pulled into the drive. She shot Sarah an anxious look and Sarah reached over and squeezed her hand. "Wait for my signal in the hall, Arren. The Lord Chamberlain should come get you."

Arren nodded. "How long do you think it will take?"

"I don't know. It depends on when my turn is." Sarah
shot her a worried look. "I'm not nervous at all. Are you?"

Arren smiled at her and nodded again. "I'm scared too."

They waited for the footman to open the door and they
descended from the coach together, then walked up the
stairs to the enormous foyer of Carlton House. Sarah gave
the butler her name and looked at Arren reassuringly. The
butler motioned for her to follow him, at the same time he
cast Arren a suspicious look. Sarah turned back to her one
last time. "Wait here for me. I don't think I'll be long."
The butler seemed satisfied that Arren was a guest of the
Duchess of Albrick, and despite her odd attire, he should
leave her be. He nodded and led the way down a long hallway. Arren watched until Sarah disappeared. She sighed
heavily and sat in one of the hard chairs by the back wall,
wondering if Duncan was pleased with the way things were
going so far.

He was mad as a hornet. He and Aiden had arrived early.
Duncan had finished his appointments about a half hour
before his scheduled counsel with the Regent, and they'd
made the decision to go ahead to Carlton House so they
could be on hand when everyone else arrived.

All told, he'd managed to persuade seven landholders to
support his position. With the four proxies he carried from
Scotland, Grayscar and Strathcraig included in the lot, there
were thirteen estates in all. A good many of them were
exceedingly large holdings, and their owners held considerable sway at Court. It was an impressive show of strength.

The Lord Chamberlain had shown them directly into the
Regent's counsel room, and Duncan had proceeded to irritate Aiden nearly to death by pacing about like a caged

animal. "For God's sake, Duncan! Stand still. You're making me seasick."

He shot Aiden an apologetic look. "I'm sorry, Brick. I'm preoccupied."

Aiden rolled his eyes. "I haven't lost all my powers of observation in the last year. Give me a little credit."

Duncan reached up and rubbed the taut muscles in the back of his neck. He exhaled a deep sigh. "I want to get this over with."

"That makes two of us. What's got you so worked up? I would think you'd feel fairly confident after this morning."

Duncan nodded. "I would if it weren't for Arren. I don't want any scandal out of this."

"It's a closed meeting. I don't think you need to worry. Besides, McDonan's got more to worry about if there's a scandal than you do."

"I know, but I'd rather not drag her through it all the same." He looked at Aiden carefully. "I'd have killed the bastard last night if you'd let me, Brick."

Aiden nodded. "I'd have probably done the same thing if I'd been in your place."

Duncan slammed his fist into his hand. "Damn it all! This is exactly what I hoped to prevent by confronting him last night."

"I know you did, but try to see reason, Duncan. I think, in the long run, it will be better this way."

"What do you mean?"

"We could have scared Alistar McDonan nearly to death last night. There's no doubt about that. If he hadn't eluded us, we could have intimidated the bastard all the way back to Scotland. But nothing would have been solved."

"Arren wouldn't be afraid of him anymore."

"Wouldn't she? He'd still be out there, with only you to

stand between them. What if something should happen to you? Who would protect her?"

Duncan looked at him with surprise. "You would."

Aiden smiled. "All right, I would. But I couldn't necessarily be right at that moment. This way, you've got an entire alliance of some of the most powerful men in the country looking out for her interests. If things go the way we think they will today, Alistar won't be able to breathe without causing speculation."

Duncan nodded. "I hope you're right. I don't like not having control of this situation, though. It's damn frustrating."

Aiden agreed. "I wouldn't like it either. Let's just hope we can get this over with as quickly as possible."

They waited another ten minutes before the landholders began to arrive. Duncan began to feel more relaxed as each one entered the room. He smiled outright when young Lord Gresham arrived. He had spoken to Gresham last night, and the young man had been soft on his support. Duncan was surprised at his unexpected show of mettle. Gresham made his way across the room to Duncan's side, shaking his hand. "Hello, Your Grace. It's good to see you again."

"It's good to see you, too, Gresham. I admit I'm rather surprised, though."

Marcus Gresham smiled. "I know. I hadn't planned to come until I met with Aimsmond this morning. Is your wife all right?"

Duncan nodded. "She'll be fine. I'm glad you've decided to join us."

The young man shrugged. "My father never paid much mind to our northern holdings when he was alive. I suppose he left me with the impression they weren't very important. I have a conscience, though, and men like Alistar McDonan have no business running things up there."

Duncan smiled at him. "No they don't. Thank you for your support."

"It's the least I can do. Do you think, Your Grace, if I arrange to visit my northern estate, you could find the time to show me about? I'd like to understand it better than I do."

"I'd be delighted. I'll let you know after today where you can reach me."

Lord Gresham nodded and slipped back among the other landholders, leaving Duncan to talk with an older gentleman who had just arrived.

The room proceeded to fill, and when Alistar McDonan finally arrived, covered with bandages and bruises from the night before, he brought with him a scurrilous-looking group of men to stand at his side. Duncan recognized Euan among them, and barely resisted the urge to cross the room and sink his fist down Euan's throat. Jace arrived last, escorting Caroline and Sarah to their place in the room.

Aiden stepped forward and took Sarah's hand, as he decided he didn't like the looks she was receiving from Alistar's side of the room. Jace growled something unintelligible beneath his breath, and tucked Caroline against his side.

Typically, the Regent was late. The tension in the room started to mount as the minutes ticked by and the silence dragged on. A collective sigh of relief echoed in the room when a door at the back opened, and the entire assembly bowed, waiting for the Regent's arrival. George IV entered the room with his usual pomp and ceremony, sending a bevy of servants scuttling out after him. He settled himself in the heavy chair at the front of the room and motioned for the assembled occupants to rise.

He curled his fingers around the arm of his chair and looked at Duncan. "Now, My Lord Duke," he said, leaning back in the chair, "we do not have to tell you how much we dislike this type of unpleasantness."

Duncan stepped forward and bowed again before looking at the Regent. "No, Your Highness, I'm well aware that you find this type of counsel extremely trying."

The Regent sighed. "However, we are also aware that we owe a certain debt to our Lord Strathcraig for his loyalty to Our Crown. We have therefore decided to hear your case personally."

Duncan nodded. "I'm very grateful for that, Your Highness. I'm honored that you do not doubt my loyalty to your rule."

A rumbling whisper echoed from Alistar's side of the room, and the Regent turned his head, silencing them with his hand. "We will hear our Lord Strathcraig first. We do not wish to be interrupted."

Alistar shot Duncan a poisonous look, but fell silent. The Regent looked back at Duncan. "Very well, My Lord Duke. You have the Royal attention."

Duncan nodded. "Your Highness, I know your commitment to the Highlands is especially strong following your defeat of Napoleon's army."

The Regent nodded. "We are well aware of the contribution our northern territories made during the difficult campaign."

"That is why I know that you, especially as a Stuart yourself, would not wish to see the rich heritage and history of Scotland lost to greed and avarice."

"And you believe this to be the case?"

"Yes, Your Highness. In the years since the war, many Scottish landholders have found it more profitable to convert their land to pasture for flocks of sheep than to care for their tenants. As a result, thousands of Scotsmen have been driven from their land and forced to emigrate to London or elsewhere."

"We can hardly be in the business of telling our landholders what they can do with their own land, My Lord Duke."

"Yes, Your Highness, I realize that."

"Then what is it you ask?"

Duncan swept his hand over the crowd of noblemen behind him. "Assembled here are eight of your subjects who have estates in the Highlands. I carry with me the proxies of four more. When I add to that my own name, and that of my wife, the Duchess of Grayscar, that is fourteen landholders in alliance. I also have the blessings of a good many more."

The Regent nodded. "It is certainly an impressive number, but again, we are not sure what it is you ask of us?"

"Those of us who wish to maintain our land as it was, to work it and make it prosper, and to take care of our tenants, are finding it increasingly difficult to protect our borders. As Your Highness doubtless knows, a good number of the boundaries in the Highlands are unmarked. We have always relied on traditional lines instead of decreed ones."

The Regent nodded. "Yes, we know that to be true."

"And so, Your Highness, I would ask of you first that you establish our borders according to their traditional lines. Once our estates are clearly defined by Royal decree, it becomes a simpler task to protect what is ours."

The Regent seemed to consider the request a long moment before nodding. "It seems a reasonable request. Are there those that disagree?"

"Only those that wish to acquire land they have no title to. Such is the request with Laird McDonan, Your Highness."

The Regent turned his head and looked at Alistar. "Is this accurate?"

Alistar glared at Duncan and stepped forward. "I want only what's mine, Your Highness. His Grace is trying to simplify a far-reaching problem. Many estates have border disputes as old as the land itself. How does he propose to settle these disagreements?"

The Regent looked back at Duncan. "My Lord Duke?"

Duncan nodded. "Ever since King John signed the Magna Carta in 1215, we have owned our land. I consider it a divine privilege. Yet, there are indisputably times when the Crown must demand the land be at his disposal. Such was the case in the war against Napoleon. Entire estates were converted for the good of England. In the case of Scotland's disputed territories, I recommend that the land-holders have but two choices. They either settle the dispute to the Crown's satisfaction, or the lands fall under Royal protectorate, just as they would if a particular landholder left no heir to his title and his possessions."

The Regent nodded and turned back to Alistar. "It is a logical request. We see no reason why we cannot grant it."

Duncan drew a deep breath. They were halfway home. Alistar was beginning to look uncomfortable, and he said, "I do not mean to question Your Highness's wisdom, but I am here as a very result of the treachery of the Duke of Strathcraig in this matter."

The Regent raised his eyebrows. "We have known and trusted Our Lord Duke for some years, Laird McDonan. Your accusation is a strong one."

Alistar indicated the sling on his arm. "My own lands are the focus of one such dispute. Through her cunning, the Duchess of Grayscar stole over five hundred acres square of land that belongs to my family." He paused and indicated the group of men behind him. "We did our best to settle the dispute with her, but she left the country and traveled to London, intent on seeking the Royal ear for her case."

The Regent studied him carefully. "You say the Duchess stole this land from you?"

Alistar nodded. "The Duchess married my third cousin, Lawrence McDonan, and refused to provide him with an heir. When he was killed in a hunting accident, she insisted on keeping a parcel of land that lay between Donglass and Grayscar."

The Regent turned and looked at Duncan. His eyes were glittering dangerously. "Does your wife deny this story, My Lord Duke?"

Duncan nodded. "My wife was pledged in marriage to Lawrence McDonan by her father. The parcel of land Laird McDonan speaks of was her dowry. According to the laws of Scotland, the land reverted to her when her husband died."

Alistar cut in smoothly. "But they were not her father's lands to give, Your Highness. The lands were in dispute."

The Regent shook his head. "What is the meaning of this, My Lord Duke?"

Duncan gritted his teeth. "In his greed to acquire not only the disputed land, but Grayscar as well, Alistar McDonan threatened my wife on numerous occasions. Finally, in desperation, she fled to London to seek Royal protection. I intercepted her journey and she became my wife."

Alistar protested. "It's a trick, Your Highness. They are only married by mutual consent. The marriage can be undone at your command."

Duncan shook his head and reached into his pocket. "We were married by mutual consent in the Highlands, Your Highness, but I have here an English license as well." A footmen stepped forward to take the license from him and carry it to the Regent. The Prince looked at it carefully and handed it back to the footman.

"We accept this. Our Lord Duke is legally married by the laws of England to the Duchess of Grayscar."

Alistar stepped forward again, waving his injured arm. "Your Highness, he cannot be trusted. He assaulted me in his attempt to procure the estate. If Grayscar is added to Strathcraig, the sheer size of the combined estates will severely endanger the economic balance in the Highlands."

The Regent sighed and rubbed his temples. "You claim, Laird McDonan, that Our Lord Duke assaulted you." He looked at Duncan. "You are prepared to dispute this?"

Duncan shook his head. "No, Your Highness, I assaulted Laird McDonan last night. I am, however, prepared to present testimony that I assaulted him only after he physically attacked my wife."

The Regent's eyes widened slightly and he looked at Aiden. "You were witness to this, My Lord Duke?"

Aiden nodded. "Yes, Your Highness. It is true."

Sarah looked anxiously at Aiden and decided she'd better act now. It didn't look as though the Regent was going to address her directly, and she couldn't fail Arren at this late date. She stepped forward, ignoring Aiden's sharp tug on her hand. "Your Highness?"

The Regent looked at her, a slight smile on his lips. He'd always liked the Duchess of Albrick, and he found her pleasant voice a welcome diversion amid the angry babble in the room. "Do you wish to address the Royal ear, Lady Albrick?"

She nodded and dropped a deep curtsy. She saw Duncan shoot Aiden a wary look, but she ignored them both and walked forward. "Your Highness, I think perhaps you would be well served to interview the Duchess of Grayscar herself."

The Regent looked at her in surprise. She heard Duncan's startled exclamation and she didn't dare look at him. The Prince leaned forward in his chair and lowered his voice so only she could hear. "I was told the Duchess was indisposed."

Sarah noticed the way he'd dropped the more formal Royal "we" and smiled at him, shaking her head. In a conspiratorial whisper she said, "No, Your Highness. She waits outside these doors to address you. Wouldn't you much rather ask her directly instead of having to sort through all these conflicting stories?"

He nodded and leaned back in his chair again. Turning to one of the footmen he motioned him forward. "I am told the Duchess of Grayscar awaits an audience in the foyer. Please show her in."

The footman hurried off, and Sarah returned to Aiden's side, ignoring Duncan's angry glare when she slipped past him. An uncomfortable silence fell over the room. Long seconds stretched into minutes as they waited for Arren's entrance. Finally, the door at the far end of the room opened. The crowd parted expectantly, and Arren stepped into the room.

When Duncan saw her, he lost what remained of his anger and finally managed a smile. She stood in the doorway, covered from head to foot in McCraig plaid. He couldn't have been angry if he'd tried.

She was comforted by Duncan's smile. He evidently believed everything was fully under control. She realized suddenly that she trusted his judgment completely. He had promised her everything would come right, and it would. She smiled back at him and made her way to the front of the room.

Her attire had caused quite a stir among the other occupants of the Regent's counsel room, and a strange silence hung in the air. Arren had to fight an hysterical urge to giggle. She stopped directly in front of the Regent, dropping a deep curtsy. "I thank you for giving me audience, Your Highness."

The Prince settled himself back in his chair and studied the young Duchess carefully. "You are a Lord of this Realm in your own right, as we understand it. I could afford you no less."

Arren nodded. "Thank you, Your Highness."

The Regent pursed his lips and looked from Alistar to Duncan again before returning his gaze to Arren. "We would like to hear your side of this story, Lady Grayscar."

Arren raised her eyes to his and met his gaze steadily. "Grayscar was my father's land before me. As Your Highness doubtless knows, it is the largest estate in the Highlands."

The Regent nodded and Arren continued. "My father had two sons. My youngest brother, Donald, disgraced his family by taking his own life. It is believed, however, that Alistar McDonan's treachery caused the disappearance of my eldest brother, Mason, some five years ago. While it's never been proven, Laird McDonan stood to gain the most from Mason's disappearance."

She looked at Alistar briefly. He was glaring at her, but she realized with a slight smile that she was no longer afraid of him. She turned her attention back to the Regent. "In either case, when my father died, I inherited Grayscar and the title, according to the laws of Scotland."

The Regent nodded. "We understand as much."

"My husband had died two years previously, and I was alone, without protection. Laird McDonan began to pressure me to marry him in order to obtain the right to my land. When I refused, he began to threaten me as well."

"How did he threaten you?"

"On occasion, he used physical violence."

The room erupted in noise and the Regent held up his hand, looking carefully at Alistar. "Do you deny this, Laird McDonan?"

Alistar glared at Arren. "The Duchess is strong-willed, Your Highness. I do not deny that we argued bitterly. I believed she wanted to marry me in truth, though."

The Regent looked back at Arren. "You made it clear to Laird McDonan that you had no such intention?"

Arren smiled wryly. "Perfectly clear, Your Highness. On one occasion, I distinctly recall telling Laird McDonan I'd rather marry a viper than the spineless coward that he is."

Duncan barely suppressed a smile and continued to watch Arren carefully. He could picture her saying that, and he found the picture of her green eyes shooting sparks of fire at Alistar McDonan vastly endearing.

Arren waited for the room to quiet down again before she spoke. "The point is, Your Highness, I was prepared to do anything necessary to prevent Laird McDonan from seizing control of Grayscar. That's what prompted me to flee to London."

"And the Duke of Strathcraig intercepted you along the way."

She nodded. "Yes, Your Highness. We were married in Scotland by mutual consent, and according to the laws and the Church of England when we arrived here."

"We have seen the license and know this to be true. Please continue."

"My husband thought it best to seek an appointment with

you, and he traveled to London with the Duke of Albrick to arrange it."

The Regent nodded. "We granted him audience for this afternoon."

"Yes, Your Highness, and in the interim, he began to establish the alliance that stands before you today."

"Laird McDonan sought to prevent this alliance?"

"Laird McDonan followed me to London to force my hand on Grayscar. I doubt that he ever suspected my husband's plans. Instead, his intent was to seize Grayscar from me by giving my husband cause to petition you for an end to our marriage."

The Regent nodded thoughtfully. "It is true that Laird McDonan believed until today that your marriage was only binding under Scottish law."

Arren spread her hand in front of her. "That's why he confronted me last night at Lord Aimsmond's ball."

"We would like to know whatever details you feel are important, Lady Grayscar."

Arren nodded. "My husband warned me not to leave the room under any circumstances, but Laird McDonan sent me this note." She reached into her sporran and pulled out the crumpled piece of paper. Duncan's eyes widened. He had no idea she'd kept it. The same footman stepped forward and handed it to the Regent. Arren continued, "Laird McDonan cannot deny this is written in his own hand."

The Regent handed the note back to the footman. "And you went to meet Laird McDonan at the appointed rendezvous?"

Arren nodded. "Yes, Your Highness. I was afraid he would make good on his threat against my husband."

"And what happened when you arrived?"

"Laird McDonan locked us in the room and proceeded

to threaten me. When I refused to sign over Grayscar, he attacked me physically. Had my husband not intervened, Laird McDonan would have raped me."

The room erupted again in a hurricane of noise, and Alistar McDonan stepped forward. "It isn't true! She's lying about all of it!"

"No she isn't!" A voice sounded at the back of the long room and every head turned in the direction.

An older gentleman stood in the rear of the room. Aiden smiled to himself. While in London, he and Duncan had contacted Jonathan Fielding, their former War Department colleague, with Arren's suspicions about the disappearance of her brother Mason. The old card had come through at the very last minute.

The Regent leaned forward in his chair and hailed Jonathan Fielding forward. "Lord Fielding! I trust you are here to shed some light on this jumbled account."

Jonathan Fielding nodded and advanced into the room. "Yes, Your Highness. When the Duke of Strathcraig first arrived in England he asked me to check into the whereabouts of one Mason Grayland. It seems, Your Highness, that Mason Grayland, the rightful heir to Grayscar, was abducted by a press gang on his way to enlist in Your Highness's Scots Guards."

Arren's hand flew to her mouth. The Regent leaned forward in his chair again. "You mean there is a Duke of Grayscar after all."

Jonathan Fielding nodded. "I have located the young man on a ship in the Americas. I received confirmation just minutes ago at my office. I have taken the liberty of dispatching Your Highness's Navy to his liberation, and he will soon be en route to Grayscar to take his rightful place as chieftain."

"And do you have evidence to indicate who is behind this treachery?"

Jonathan Fielding nodded again. "Yes, Your Highness. It was Alistar McDonan."

The noise was deafening. Angry accusations sounded from both sides of the room, and Arren stood rooted to the spot, transfixed. Duncan had been watching her carefully throughout the exchange and he nearly stepped forward to her side, but the Regent turned his attention to her again. "Lady Grayscar, if this gentleman Our Lord Fielding has located turns out to be your brother, can we assume that you will surrender any claim you have to Grayscar on his behalf?"

Arren nodded and dropped her hand. "Your Highness, I have no wish for the title or the land. There is only one title I wish to hold."

The Regent raised his eyebrows. "And what would that be, Lady Grayscar?"

She looked at Duncan, her eyes wide with anxiety. "I wish only to be known as the Duchess of Strathcraig, Your Highness."

The Prince Regent smiled and leaned back, his fingers drumming happily on the arm of his chair. He looked carefully at Duncan. "We take it, My Lord Duke, that the title is still available."

Duncan grinned and shook his head, stepping forward to take Arren's hand. He didn't take his eyes off her when he answered the Regent. "No, Your Highness. The position has been occupied for some time."

The Regent nodded and turned to glare at Alistar. "I suggest, Laird McDonan, that you remove yourself from our presence. When His Grace the Duke of Grayscar reaches England, we will hear his request for justice."

Several footmen stepped forward and all but forced Alistar and his family from the room. He yelled something feral at Arren, but she didn't hear it. She was too busy trying not to faint with relief. The room erupted again in a cacophony of noise, and Arren leaned against Duncan exhaustedly, fighting a wave of fog that sought to overwhelm her. From the corner of her eye, she saw Jace step forward to speak with Jonathan Fielding. It occurred to her that she really should ask Duncan how he'd accomplished it. A movement to her left captured her attention and she turned her head in time to see Sarah lean against Aiden's shoulder, with the tears streaming unbidden down her face. Arren opened her mouth to remind Sarah of her promise to wait until they could both cry together, but before the words formed on her lips, the room swam around her, and she fainted into Duncan's arms.

He reached down, caught her to him and lifted her into his arms. The room had grown suddenly silent again, and he turned to smile at the Regent. "If you'll excuse me, Your Highness, I would like to take my wife home."

The Regent nodded. "Of course. We can finish whatever details need to be addressed with the gentlemen assembled here."

Duncan nodded and turned to go, but stopped again when he heard the Regent call his name. "My Lord Duke!"

He turned around. "Yes, Your Highness."

"When the Duchess awakens, I hope you will convey our deepest admiration for her."

Duncan nodded. "I will, Your Highness."

He strode from the room, Arren still held tightly against his chest. Only when he lifted her into Aiden's carriage and settled in next to her did she open her eyes and look at him anxiously. "Is everything all right, Gypsy?"

He reached up and touched her face gently. "Everything is wonderful, Arren. It has all come right."

She nodded sleepily and leaned her head against his shoulder. "I knew it would."

He grinned, thinking of how vehemently she'd argued with him to the contrary. "And just how did you know that, Duchess?"

She yawned, and turned her green eyes to his once more. "Because you promised."

Dear Reader,

The first time I met Duncan McCraig, I was sitting in a fifteen-mile traffic jam during 5:00 P.M. traffic. I was in the middle of brooding over how my life was moving about as fast as my car, when he lounged back in my passenger seat and said, "So snap out of it." Now if this kind of thing had never happened before, it might have concerned me, but ever since childhood, when twenty imaginary friends took up residence under my bed, I had grown accustomed to hearing strangers pop up at inopportune times.

Laird McCraig and I had a long talk about it. He didn't seem very concerned with my complaints, however. He seemed absolutely certain he deserved his own novel, and he simply could not understand why I was unwilling to write it. That's when Arren Grayland reminded me of our meeting just a few months before. I was in the library researching my family's Gordon heritage when she showed up between the paragraph on the family plaid and the coat of arms.

I knew right then that Duncan and Arren deserved an adventure of their own, and what an adventure it was! I stayed out of breath while I was writing this novel, and I hope you enjoy their tumultuous relationship as much as I did. The truth is, I would be tempted to linger here a little while, but Aiden Brickston is already rattling his saber at me. I should never have let those twenty friends of mine move in under the bed in the first place!

Sincerely,

Mandalyn Kaye

P.S. I enjoy hearing from my readers. You can reach me at 101 E. Holly Ave, Suite #2, Sterling, Virginia, 20164

FOR THE VERY BEST IN ROMANCE —
DENISE LITTLE PRESENTS!

AMBER, SING SOFTLY (0038, $4.99)
by Joan Elliott Pickart
Astonished to find a wounded gun-slinger on her doorstep, Amber Prescott can't decide whether to take him in or put him out of his misery. Since this lonely frontierswoman can't deny her longing to have a man of her own, she nurses him back to health, while savoring the glorious possibilities of the situation. But what Amber doesn't realize is that this strong, handsome man is full of surprises!

A DEEPER MAGIC (0039, $4.99)
by Jillian Hunter
From the moment wealthy Margaret Rose and struggling physician Ian MacNeill meet, they are swept away in an adventure that takes them from the haunted land of Aberdeen to a primitive, faraway island — and into a world of danger and irresistible desire. Amid the clash of ancient magic and new science Margaret and Ian find themselves falling helplessly in love.

SWEET AMY JANE (0050, $4.99)
by Anna Eberhardt
Her horoscope warned her she'd be dealing with the wrong sort of man. And private eye Amy Jane Chadwick was used to dealing with the wrong kind of man. But nothing prepared her for the gorgeous, stubborn Max, a former professional athlete who is being stalked by an obsessive fan. From the moment they meet, sparks fly and danger follows!

MORE THAN MAGIC (0049, $4.99)
by Olga Bicos
This classic romance is a thrilling tale of two adventurers who set out for the wilds of the Arizona territory in the year 1878. Seeking treasure, an archaeologist and an astronomer find the greatest prize of all — love.

Available wherever paperbacks are sold, or order direct from the Publisher. Send cover price plus 50¢ per copy for mailing and handling to Penguin USA, P.O. Box 999, c/o Dept. 17109, Bergenfield, NJ 07621. Residents of New York and Tennessee must include sales tax. DO NOT SEND CASH.

IF ROMANCE BE THE FRUIT OF LIFE—
READ ON—
BREATH-QUICKENING HISTORICALS FROM PINNACLE

WILDCAT (772, $4.99)
by Rochelle Wayne
No man alive could break Diana Preston's fiery spirit . . . until
seductive Vince Gannon galloped onto Diana's sprawling family
ranch. Vince, a man with dark secrets, would sweep her into his
world of danger and desire. And Diana couldn't deny the powerful
yearnings that branded her as his own, for all time!

THE HIGHWAY MAN (765, $4.50)
by Nadine Crenshaw
When a trumped-up murder charge forced beautiful Jane
Fitzpatrick to flee her home, she was found and sheltered by the
highwayman—a man as dark and dangerous as the secrets that
haunted him. As their hiding place became a place of shared
dreams—and soaring desires—Jane knew she'd found the love
she'd been yearning for!

SILKEN SPURS (756, $4.99)
by Jane Archer
Beautiful Harmony Harper, leader of a notorious outlaw gang,
rode the desert plains of New Mexico in search of justice and ven-
geance. Now she has captured powerful and privileged Thor
Clarke-Jargon, who is everything Harmony has ever hated—and
all she will ever want. And after Harmony has taken the handsome
adventurer hostage, she herself has become a captive—of her own
desires!

WYOMING ECSTASY (740, $4.50)
by Gina Robins
Feisty criminal investigator, July MacKenzie, solicits the partner-
ship of the legendary half-breed gunslinger-detective Nacona Blue.
After being turned down, July—never one to accept the meaning
of the word no—finds a way to convince Nacona to be her partner
. . . first in business—then in passion. Across the wilds of
Wyoming, and always one step ahead of trouble, July surrenders to
passion's searing demands!

*Available wherever paperbacks are sold, or order direct from the
Publisher. Send cover price plus 50¢ per copy for mailing and handling to Penguin USA, P.O. Box 999, c/o Dept. 17109, Bergenfield, NJ 07621. Residents of New York and Tennessee must
include sales tax. DO NOT SEND CASH.*